'One system yields to another that ends up looking mighty similar to the one that came before, and with each upheaval comes a steep price that citizens are forced to pay. Gorcheva-Newberry beautifully renders these historical trends using Chekhov as a blueprint in this moving, tragic, and distinctly Russian tale.'

'Full of heartbreak, beautifully written. I swallowed it up.'

'Charming and tragic, hopeful and disillusioned, profoundly intimate and sensitive to history, *Between Dog and Wolf* evokes Soviet perestroika in all its contradictions.'

'A timeless tale of memory, desire, dreams lost and altered, love changed and unchanged.'

'An intensely evocative and gorgeously written coming-of-age story.'

'Achingly sad.'

'A remarkable novel. Gorcheva-Newberry combines a timeless story of loss and longing with a viscerally personal account of Russia's recent past. Fizzing with life as much as it is suffused with unbearable sadness, the book perfectly captures the discombobulations of perestroika: the hope and the disappointment of the new — and a yearning for what might have been.'

'Every reader knows what it's like to lose a friend, but not everyone knows the loss of a nation. Kristina Gorcheva-Newberry knows both. Her novel immerses us in the tense, passionate, bloody best friendship of two unforgettable young women in the last years of the Soviet state.'

'[A] Stunning debut . . . Gorcheva-Newberry pulls off a tragic and nostalgic love letter to a much-tried generation. This is a winner.'

'At last, from Russia, the voice of a woman of my generation, writing in *Between Dog and Wolf* of dancing with other girls at school discos before Brezhnev died, of learning to love in a cold climate, and of navigating the choppy waters of the past. I so enjoyed this novel.'

© Ivan Morozov

KRISTINA GORCHEVA-NEWBERRY was born in Armenia and raised in Soviet Russia. She moved to the USA in 1995, after having witnessed perestroika and the fall of the Iron Curtain.

Writing in English, her second language, Kristina has published fifty stories and received ten Pushcart prize nominations. She is the winner of the Raz/Shumaker Prairie Schooner Book Prize in Fiction for her debut collection of stories, *What Isn't Remembered*, longlisted for the 2022 PEN/ Robert W. Bingham Prize and shortlisted for the 2022 William Saroyan International Prize.

Between Dog and Wolf, published to rapturous reviews in the USA as *The Orchard*, is her first novel.

BETWEEN DOG AND WOLF

KRISTINA GORCHEVA-NEWBERRY

THE
INDIGO
PRESS

THE INDIGO PRESS
50 Albemarle Street
London W1S 4BD
www.theindigopress.com

The Indigo Press Publishing Limited Reg. No. 10995574
Registered Office: Wellesley House, Duke of Wellington Avenue
Royal Arsenal, London SE18 6SS

First published in Great Britain in 2023 by The Indigo Press
This paperback edition published 2024

A CIP catalogue record for this book is available from the British Library

First published in the United States in 2022 by
Ballantine Books, an imprint of Random House, a division of
Penguin Random House LLC, New York, as *The Orchard*

This is a work of fiction. Names, characters, places, and incidents are
products of the author's imagination or are used fictionally and are not
to be construed as real. Any resemblance to actual events, locales,
organisations, or persons, living or dead, is entirely coincidental.

ISBN: 978-1-911648-86-4
eBook ISBN: 978-1-911648-64-2

Cover design © Luke Bird
Cover photograph 'Childhood in the country'
© M-Production via Adobe Stock
Art direction by House of Thought
Offset by Tetragon, London
Printed and bound in Great Britain by CPI Group (UK) Ltd, Croydon CR0 4YY

MIX
Paper | Supporting
responsible forestry
FSC
www.fsc.org
FSC® C171272

For my friends—Generation Perestroika—
the lost, undiscovered, unremembered

We shall see all the earth's evil, all our sufferings drown in the mercy that will fill the entire world, and our life will become quiet, tender, sweet, like a caress. I have faith, I have faith.

—A. P. CHEKHOV, *UNCLE VANYA*

PART ONE

1

Milka Putova and I had been friends since the first grade, which was pretty much for as long as I could remember. She was short and thin like a sprat, and every boy in our class called her exactly that—Sprat. She had small acorn-brown eyes, set too far apart and slanted—a result of one hundred and fifty years of the Tatar-Mongol yoke, as she often joked. Her face was broad and pale, her pulpy lips raspberry red, especially in winter, after we'd been sledding or building forts all afternoon, snow crusted on our knees and elbows, our fringes and eyelashes bleached with frost. We lived on the outskirts of Moscow and tramped to school together, across a vast virgin field sprawled around us like white satin. She'd walk first through knee-deep snow, wearing wool tights and felt boots, threading her legs in and out, and I'd trudge after her, stepping in her footprints. She'd halt and scribble our names in the snow with her gloved finger—*Milka + Anya*—and on the way back we'd rush to check whether the letters were still there.

Milka's hair was dark gold, straight and silky, cut in a neat bob around her jaw. She shampooed her hair every day, and I could smell it when we sat next to each other during classes, the delicate scent of apple blossoms resurrecting our summer months at my parents' dacha. How we'd sauntered through a corn maze, the stalks three times taller than we were, fingering green husks, separating soft, luscious silk to check on the size and ripeness of ears. Or how we roamed birch and aspen groves and gathered mushrooms for soup, their fragile trunks buried in grass, their red and orange caps burning under the trees like gems. Or how we swam in the river, racing to the other side and back and then climbing a muddy bank and drying off on towels, motionless like sunbaked frogs—bellies up.

At ten, we hadn't yet begun wearing bikini tops or shying behind bushes while changing swimsuits. We touched each other's faces, and shoulders, and nonexistent breasts, compared hands and feet, the length of our toes and fingers, noses, eyelashes, the colour and shape of our nipples. We counted moles and freckles, mosquito bites and scratches, searching for hidden birthmarks, grey hairs, some sign of indisputable distinction. We lazed in a hammock, suspended between the porch railing and a single pine tree, or threaded wild strawberries on long straws and sucked them off in one ravaging movement, our tongues, our mouths magenta foam. We carved our names into birch trunks so fat, so mighty, our arms wouldn't close when we hugged them. We trapped crickets in glass jars or matchboxes, which we placed under pillows for good luck, setting the bugs free in the morning; we made wishes while watching the full moon like an amber brooch pinned low in the sky. We longed for prettier dresses and Zolushka's crystal shoes and a fairy godmother to turn our dingy flats into splendid castles. At the dacha, we opened the bedroom window and stared into the darkness coalescing around us. The apple trees were bearing their first tiny sour fruit. The trees swayed their branches and threw trembling shadows on the ground, and we would sprawl halfway out of the window to touch their young tender leaves.

At eleven, we still played with dolls. Some were missing limbs; others had lost lashes and hair; all had patches of skin scraped and dulled by the years of dressing and undressing, incessant bathing. We owned no male dolls but a set of tin soldiers I begged my mother to buy. The soldiers were disproportionately small, which made perfect sense to us because most of the boys in our class were shorter than the girls. We protected the soldiers fiercely, and not because they were fewer in number and cost more, but because they seemed so delicate to us and somehow helpless, in need of nurturing and reassurance. We handled the soldiers with care and stowed them in their box every evening.

Sometimes we pretended that the soldiers had just returned from the war to their wives and girlfriends. Then we would strip them naked and lay their stiff cold bodies on top of the pink plastic ones and rub the figures together as hard as we could.

"Do you think she's pregnant by now?" Milka would ask.

"Maybe. How long does it usually take?"

"Don't know. Let's rub some more," she'd say, and slide her doll back and forth under my soldier.

Oddly, I was always in charge of the males, and Milka the females. My soldier would lean in to kiss Milka's girl doll, his lips so small, so hard against her curvy painted ones. Neither tin nor plastic participant had genitals, of course, but we pretended that they did, and Milka would even take a soldier's hand and touch it to the doll's belly and legs, the thick impenetrable place in between. Or she would press the soldier's face there. At that age, I still had no idea that oral sex existed, but Milka seemed sure in her gestures.

That year, Milka and I began studying our bodies in the mirror, anticipating all the womanly changes my mother cautioned us about when my dad wasn't in the room. Milka's father had died in a car wreck when she was a baby, and her mother remarried soon afterwards. Milka rarely talked about her family, except that both her mother and her stepfather worked in a fish-canning factory, and so their clothes and their hair smelled like dead seaweed. "Even their skin smells like it," she would say. "Rotten."

"Why do they never come to school?" I asked once.

"Because then the whole building would have to be sanitized," she said, and snuck her bony tickling fingers under my shirt. I yelped and smacked her hands and whirled on my toes. She laughed, that grainy, openmouthed laugh of hers, her teeth so straight and white as though brushed with snow.

Two years passed, and we had our first periods, grew breasts and pubic hair, started wearing bras and locking bathrooms when showering. I sprouted up and gained some weight and resembled my mother more and more—an ample soft-bosomed woman, who seemed stronger than my dad and all the other men in the world. But Milka remained a sprat—short and puny, with long, awkward limbs and a caved-in stomach.

When she stretched on her bed after school, I could count her ribs, outlined by her T-shirt. Her hair was still the same length, still redolent of summers and those apples my parents grew at our dacha.

Back then we paid no mind to scrapes or bruises or even pimples, which we often squeezed on each other's backs, and those summers seemed as endless as the lives ahead of us. We thought our parents were old and hopelessly outdated, wasting hours in lines for sugar or toilet paper. Generation Buckwheat, we called them. And my mother would turn and say, "Let's wait and see what they'll call you." By "they" she meant our future children, and we'd guffaw and chime in unison, "We won't have children. We'll elope to Paris or Rome and live happily ever after."

Like most Russians, we'd never been outside the Soviet Union, so any foreign city to us was just as far and impossible as the moon. We couldn't know that the Iron Curtain was about to fall, nor that the rest of the world was any different and not bound by the same brutal rules or years of stone-fisted dictatorship. We didn't even regard our present government as a dictatorship, but accepted the order of things as we did the ineluctable succession of seasons: poplar fluff and apple blossoms in the spring and a frigid ossifying blindness of snow in the winter. One had to live through it because one was powerless and, perhaps, resistant to change. And even if one wasn't, the change might not be for the best, for the good of the people. "This country is too old and too stubborn," my grandmother always said, and Milka and I would nod and shove her sauerkraut behind our cheeks. She really did make the most delicious, juicy sauerkraut, and we couldn't imagine our winter meals without it, just as we couldn't imagine not sharing a table or a school desk or our dreams, the future, as far away as it seemed. We knew we would marry one day, grow old, and resemble our mothers and then grandmothers, with saggy breasts and wrinkled faces and the grey hair most Russian women bleached or hennaed. But we also knew that we'd always be friends and nothing could change that.

There were not enough boys in our class, just as there weren't enough men in our country, which was what my grandmother often pointed out to us: "The war and Stalin wiped this land clean." So, at school discotheques, Milka and I danced together, like other girls. At thirteen, I was much taller and decidedly plump, but she was more agile, swift and pushy, guiding me on the dance floor. The school gymnasium was decorated with strings of flashing, coloured lights, and Milka's skin glowed pink, then blue, then green. Her hair swayed from cheek to cheek as she turned her head left and right, with a twist of her bony hip or her tiny stomping foot. The music was a medley of songs, fast-paced or lugubrious, by the popular Soviet singers: Valery Leontiev, Sofia Rotaru, and Alla Pugacheva, as well as by two famous rock bands, Mashina Vremeni and Akvarium. Also, the Beatles and ABBA, and the incomparable Italians, Al Bano and Romina Power, Adriano Celentano, and Toto Cutugno, who'd made every girl in our class aware of her burgeoning womanhood. He had such a seductive tremor in his voice, it seemed almost palpable. We could feel it touch our bodies somewhere deep inside. We cut his photos out of magazines and pasted them to the walls of our bedrooms and the backs of our textbooks, rubbing his image with our fingers.

For the school dances, we always wore our best clothes, sweaters or shirts we'd borrowed from our mothers' closets and put on in corridors or bathrooms right before entering the gymnasium. We'd roll up the sleeves and pad our bras with wads of cotton, open one too many buttons to reveal a hint of cleavage. Occasionally, we dressed in outdated blouses, trousers, or skirts discovered in family trunks or hunted down in *komissionkas*, those shabby secondhand shops. We would take the duds to my grandmother, who pedalled her stationary Singer sewing machine to alter our newly found treasures. Oh, how proud we were of those outfits our imaginations had designed and her crooked, arthritic hands had cut and stitched together. We would spot an actress in a Soviet magazine or in a movie, the few harmless foreign films, Italian or French comedies we rushed to see in theatres the first chance we had, and our minds would grow restless, cataloguing our existing wardrobes of dresses and skirts, altering their lengths to accommodate the rising fashion. Our shoes remained hopeless, however—thick leather in ugly brown or unpolished black, with square heels and blunt rounded toes, impossible for flirting. It was on the cusp of adolescence that Milka and I first began to realize the paucity of our choices, in clothes and in men.

One evening, after yet another discotheque, in an emptied school bathroom, we decided to have our first "practice" kiss, which we hated utterly and irreversibly. Too much flesh, too much wetness, and too much taste. Outside the window, the snow was turning into a fuzzy blanket. All was dark, and the only working lamppost in the schoolyard blinked and blinked, as though caught unaware by our touching lips.

"If we don't find boys, Raneva, I don't know what we'll do. I sure as hell don't want to be kissing you for the rest of my life," Milka said, wiping her mouth.

"Same here," I said. "Horrible. Your tongue is too long or something."

"No longer than yours."

I stuck mine out, and she did the same, and we turned to face the mirror. It was chipped and dull and not big enough for two people. We stepped back. Our tongues, pink and pale, had little white bumps and drops of saliva on the curling tips. They appeared unremarkably the same, slimy and disgusting. The rest of our faces didn't look alike, but from a distance, in our ridiculous strained grimaces we resembled twin dwarfs, all wrinkles and folds, dimpled chins and wide front teeth.

We both got strep that day and couldn't see each other for a week, which was the longest, quietest time in the history of humankind. It was also the time when Milka discovered science fiction books, and I discovered masturbation, but I wouldn't share that with her for many, many months.

2

We turned fourteen when Brezhnev died. Pert and insensitive like most teenagers, we had very little understanding of grief, of the weight it carried for the living. Back then we really thought Brezhnev to be eternal, like the earth itself or the sky. It was a gloomy November morning with a dusting of new snow on the ground and the wind sweeping the streets, knocking on windows, all alight, people gathered around their TVs, dumbfounded by the sight of Brezhnev's body in a nest of red carnations and white gladioli next to the blind hollow of the grave. It began to snow harder, and on the screen, we could see the flurries landing on the dead General Secretary's face, his tight lips and massive black eyebrows like twisted skeins of wool.

In our living room, which was also our dining room, as well as my grandmother's bedroom, we sat at the table, drinking hot tea. Milka came over to watch the funeral because we had a new colour TV, while her family still had a prehistoric black-and-white box with a jerking picture and no decent sound. "Not that there's anything important to hear," she said, scooping my grandmother's apple jam onto her plate. "A bunch of old, sad dudes putting another one away. It had to happen sometime. He was sick. They recorded his speeches before-hand and then dubbed him. So all he had to do was open his mouth. That's why the words sometimes didn't match up."

"They say he had a double. In the last few years he couldn't leave his room, he couldn't walk, but they hid it from us." I topped a piece of bread with cheese and began chewing.

"Don't repeat someone's stupid words, Anya. It won't do you any good," my father said, and dragged his chair closer to the TV while my mother poured tea into fragile porcelain cups and placed them back on the saucers. They made a gentle ring-ing sound, similar to the wall clock chimes. It was an old tea set, brought from Germany by my grandfather after the war. Even though my grandmother was opposed to drinking out of the enemy's china, my granddad insisted on keeping it. When he died, my grandmother passed the tea set to my mother. Not much was left of the original twelve-piece setting, which also included a sugar bowl, a tiny cream jug, and a teapot, all bro-ken or cracked. The teacups had sculptured edges like pleats of a skirt, the same as the edges of the saucers; the pattern of large yellow and pink roses over white porcelain had faded consid-erably, but still displayed the beauty I found almost too deli-cate to touch with fingers, only lips.

"They just dropped him," my father said, jumping from his chair. "Oh—that's terrible."

"Dropped who?" my grandmother asked while pouring tea into a saucer. She still drank her tea the old-fashioned way, slurping it bit by bit from the edges. She was a short buxom woman with long grey hair she hadn't cut since the end of the war.

"Brezhnev." My father spoke loudly, as though trying to compensate for my grandmother's deteriorating eyesight.

"That's bad. Very bad. It's a bad omen. All will go. It's the end." My grandmother pulled the shawl, which she never took off, even in the summer months, over her shoulders, and refastened her amber brooch. From where Milka and I sat, it looked like a giant bumblebee crawling up her breast.

"Maybe it's the beginning," my mother said. "Besides, he's dead. He can't feel a thing."

"But it's on national TV. They're probably showing it in America too." My father rubbed his balding head, the tufts of his light brown hair thicker on the sides. He sat back in his chair, and it moaned under his weight.

"Ah, they'll cut it out for Americans and the rest of the world," my mother said. "They always do. They'll also send the pallbearers to Siberia."

"I hate how you repeat every shitty thing every shitty person says."

"And I hate how you defend every Communist in this country, dead or alive."

"I do not."

My mother dipped a slice of lemon in sugar and sucked on it. "They've screwed up this country beyond salvation, and you're defending their greedy arses. They're like this cat." She pointed at Rasputin on the couch. "Fat, complacent, neutered animals who still piss everywhere. Arseholes."

My father slammed his fist on the table; the cups slid toward the edge of the saucers, and some of the tea spilled on the tablecloth. A large vein on the side of his neck became engorged, and I could almost see the blood pumping up and down. "Those arseholes," he said, "won the war. They saved the world from evil, from fascist hell. If it hadn't been for them, the world would've ceased to exist. All of it, all that is beautiful and righteous and worth living for—gone, extinguished. We would've either been fed to the ovens or become slaves polishing German boots and ploughing the land they stole from us. It's my land, and I'll die before I give it to any Nazi pig. What happened after the war? Well—it's a damned shame, but we survived. We raised this country from ruins, we made it proud once again, of its heritage and patriotism and fearlessness. We built an empire. Now that Brezhnev is dead, who's going to rule it? Who'll protect this place from the West?"

"Why do we need to be protected?" my mother asked, dropping the lemon in her empty cup.

"Because."

"Because what? It seems that we know so little, that everything is leaden with heavy, irrevocable truths."

"Light truth is no truth at all. Such is our history."

"We made that history, not vice versa."

"We made what we made, and neither you nor I, not even Anya or Milka, can change that. You dig a well, it fills with water, you drink from it."

"Wells dry out," my mother said.

"Then you dig them deeper. But you don't replace the well. It's crucial that you don't replace what your ancestors built."

"We do it all the time—in science and architecture. We replace old models with new ones. We improve, redesign, restructure. We want a better life."

"I don't. I have a great life. My country gave me every-thing. I have a well-paying job, free medical care and educa-tion, a city flat and a country house. I even have an apple orchard. How many Americans can boast about all that?"

"I don't know. I've never met any. But they own their lives. Unlike you. You can't even travel outside the Soviet Union. All of your possessions belong to the State. If the government wants to, it can take it all, including me or Anya."

"Don't be an idiot. Why would they want to?" he asked.

"Why not? Why do they do anything? Why did Stalin kill all those millions of innocent people? He didn't spare women or children either. Girls disappeared from the streets."

"Says who?"

"Everybody knows it. Khrushchev exposed him. Him and Beria."

"Khrushchev did many things he shouldn't have done." He paused to add more tea to his cup, plopping in three cubes of sugar and stirring vigorously. "Stability, Liuba, not change, is what every country desires. Changes are governed by im-pulses, no matter how noble but immanently crazy. Every time this country went through a change of government, our land was bathed in blood. Nobody wants that. This country is on its third empire, starting from the Romanoffs. Three is a magical number, let's hope it stays."

"If history teaches us anything, every empire is doomed to fall."

"Don't blabber." He spat three times over his right shoulder.

"The wrong shoulder, comrade. You jinxed it now." My mother produced a tight smile and began gathering cups from the table. My father inched forward and turned up the volume.

Tempted as we might have been to ask questions, Milka and I remained silent; we knew better than to interfere in my parents' arguments, to disrupt the fight that had started years ago and seemed to have continued with a steady beat. At times, it seemed that my parents would divorce before I graduated from high school; other times I was certain they would stay together always and age on the same pillow. Later, when I got older and the fights almost ceased, I found their absence disturbing and would seek any excuse to goad my parents into a war of opinions. There was heat in the room back then, and there was freedom, intimacy, and desire, and all of it mattered.

"Do your parents fight when they have sex too?" Milka asked when we went for a walk that afternoon. She wore a long grey coat and a matching hat in the shape of a dome, so from the side she resembled one of those Egyptian women—long neck, wide cheekbones, haughty nose.

"I don't think they have sex," I said, laughing.

"Lucky. That's all mine do—screw like rabbits."

"How do you know?"

"I can hear. My mum screams because my stepdad has a huge dick. It hurts."

I tripped, and Milka reached to grab my coat sleeve. She was biting her lips red like cherries against her pale face.

"Are you serious?" I asked.

"About what?"

"His, his . . . thing." I couldn't bring myself to say "dick"; somehow it sounded so unpleasant, like raw meat.

"Yeah. He likes to walk around naked afterwards."

"What about your mum? Doesn't she say anything?" I tried to imagine Milka's stepdad, that bear of a man, tall and hairy, with tattooed fingers, parading naked through her flat.

"She walks around naked too," Milka said, grinning. She ran to the swings and plopped her scrawny behind on a narrow metal seat.

The playground was empty, the sandbox piled with snow. I wedged onto the other seat, clutching the thick rusty chains. We swung in silence for a while; the chains groaned and creaked. The sky was grey, suppressed with clouds. Shreds of muslin-white air drifted through trees so stark, so solemn, against the bleak concrete buildings of flats. When the wind swept through the branches, they rattled like old bones. They made me think of the war, the Blockade, dead frozen bodies piled on the streets. Nearly forty years had passed, but my grandmother and my parents still talked about the war as though it'd just ended: there were all those demolished buildings to be restored, and all those deaths the country continued to mourn.

"I wish my parents fought more." Milka sucked in the cold air through her teeth.

"Why? What do you mean?"

"Nothing. It's just that yours will cuss and scream and don't think twice, and they both have university diplomas. Mine don't say a rude word, and they work in a cannery."

"All mine do is look for flaws in rocket drawings, when engineers are done designing them."

"What if there aren't any?"

"Then it's a pass. But if another person spots a mistake, my parents can lose their jobs."

"What if a flaw isn't in the drawing but in the design itself?" Milka pushed off hard, with her feet dressed in scuffed leather boots; she rose above me, and the wind muffled her words.

"What design?" I shouted.

But she didn't answer, swinging higher and higher until I became scared that she would flip over. I yelled, "Too high, too high. Stop."

She nodded and then jumped from her seat, flying like a goddamned bird, arms akimbo, the two sides of her unbuttoned coat stretched like wings. The sight of her body—so terrifying yet so graceful and free—made me leap from the swing too and drop straight down. I landed a few steps from my friend, who sat up, brushing snow from her face and her hands. There was blood on her palms as she reached in her coat pocket for a cigarette.

"You're crazy," I said. "You could've . . . could've hurt yourself. Died or something."

"Wouldn't that be cool to die on the same day as our Communist Leader?" She blew a stream of smoke in my face, and I waved it away.

"It's nuts," I said. "Death is nothingness." I pulled the cigarette from her hands and took a short drag, and another. "Shit, you scared me. Shit. Shit."

She stared at me, her face pale and fearless, a sweep of dark golden hair across her forehead. Her hat fell off, and she grabbed it and shook the snow from it before foisting it back on. She seemed perturbed, if only a little. "To die or not to die? Hmm, it's a damn good question. The high school is staging *Hamlet*. They do it every year. It'll be our turn soon." She snatched the cigarette back from me. "It's the last one. I have to steal more from my parents. While they have sex, I smoke."

"You smoke at home?"

"Yeah. They do too, so they can't tell."

"Mine don't smoke, but I think my dad hides it from my mum, because I can smell it on him when he comes back from work."

"Ugh, why marry if you can't even smoke in your own flat?" She offered me the last few drags from her cigarette. I declined just as she said, "I'll let you smoke all you want, and you can have your own bed and half of my kingdom." She threw the smouldering butt in the snow, and it fizzled out.

"Why half?" I asked.

"You want it all? You can have it—as much as you can carry, but don't you complain, Anya Raneva, and don't you stop, don't you ever fucking stop, not even after I die."

"Or what?"

"Or I'll come back and haunt you."

"You would, wouldn't you?"

I laughed, and Milka did too; we toppled into the snow and scooped handfuls and mashed it into each other's faces, blinking so hard, the snow crunchy and soft at the same time. It stuck to our lashes and our skin and then started to melt, droplets of water on our cold, flushed cheeks.

3

My grandmother always believed God had a design and that it took a lifetime to be able to appreciate it. My parents never openly disagreed with her, although my father used to ask my mother, "How could she say such a thing? After everything she's been through. The war? The Blockade? What kind of a design was that?"

My mother would shrug and say, "One has to believe in something. Life is unbearable without hope. Don't you think that's why she survived? Because she believed she was destined to?"

"No matter what design, people are the ones to implement it. We're responsible, not God. There's no divine prophecy in our actions."

"If there is no design, no prophecy, how come she and I survived?" my mother would say. "When the city lost close to a million in less than nine hundred days? How come we didn't freeze or starve to death? Weren't eaten by the neighbours?"

"Dumb luck," my father would say and kiss her. "Sheer, dumb, wonderful luck."

When Yuri Andropov took office in the autumn of 1982, there was much hope but perhaps less luck. Little was known

about him except that he'd led a group of partisans during the
war and that he'd been the Soviet ambassador to Hungary during the crisis in 1956 and then the head of the KGB. There were
rumours that to eliminate rivals for the job, he ordered the
KGB to stage automobile accidents, heart attacks, and apparent
suicides. Some also said he'd masterminded the construction
of the Berlin Wall. Others insisted that Andropov was involved
in the attempted assassination of the Pope in 1981, as well as
the death of Brezhnev. But there were also those who said that
he wasn't such an abominable monster at all, that in his heart
he admired Western culture and loved jazz, and that he was
just as ill and exhausted as the system.

During his short rule, however, Andropov made attempts
to reinvigorate our stagnant economy and to improve our
work discipline and ethic. My parents left for their jobs earlier
and returned later, slaving extra hours, attending office meetings, and conferring with their colleagues on new projects. My
parents' salaries didn't rise, but their days stretched into nights,
filled with worry about the shaky, unpredictable future. I could
see them brooding, hunched over evening meals, or scribbling
new proposals on the margins of old newspapers. They began
saving money, too, what little they could, adding five or ten
rubles to a stash inside a wool sock. When they accumulated a
hundred rubles, they would take the money to the bank, although some of their friends and neighbours advised against it.

My grandmother received a monthly pension, which she
gave to my mother, all except for a few rubles she hid in books.
My parents knew it, of course, but pretended otherwise. Occasionally, when Milka and I needed to buy cigarettes, we'd

prowl through the wall shelves, pulling out and flipping through heavy tomes until we harvested enough for a pack of Stolichnye or Kosmos. Years later, my mother would continue to find my grandmother's money, new slick bills tucked between the pages of Dostoevsky, Tolstoy, Turgenev, Chekhov.

It was an afternoon in early May, a smell of lilac and bird-cherry blossoms in the air. Spring had unfolded its arms; the trees rippled with leaves, and the poplars began to shed their fluff. Large puffy clusters wafted down in circles and landed on our faces and hands as Milka and I tried to brush them off, mesmerized by their remarkable softness. The sky was chaste blue, a thin tremor of clouds high above. In the mellow glow of the sun, everything appeared brighter, bathed in viscous, sensuous light: cracked pavement and dour buildings with shoe repair shops, pharmacies, bakeries, and hair salons.

The neighbourhood was filled with young women rushing along the pavements, sitting on benches, or chasing after toddlers in playgrounds. There was an ease, an airiness in their movements, how they swung their hips or lifted babies, or even in the way they carried mesh bags bloated with groceries— milk, kefir, *tvorog*, and live fish wrapped in brown paper. Sometimes the women would stop and, without setting the bags on the pavement, switch hands or shoulders, and then resume walking.

Most women wore black, brown, or grey, the only three colours available in Soviet shops, where the variety of clothes hadn't changed since the Revolution. Milka once said that we lived in a great incubator, only instead of chickens, the government bred people. Everyone looked and thought the same, so when someone died or disappeared, another citizen could easily fill the spot. "It all makes sense," she'd said. "When I die, you can replace me. We go to the same school, read the same books, write the same papers, and are taught by the same teachers. We watch the same movies, listen to the same music, and eat the same food. And we've been sleeping in the same bed forever. Even our voices sound alike. Everyone says so. Except that your hair is darker, and your boobs are bigger—but in that damn uniform, no one can tell. Insane, right?" I remember arguing that she and I were two vastly different people, but when she asked in what way, I couldn't answer her. We were indeed two Soviet teenage girls bred and raised by the same system, and whether I loved my parents while she hated hers didn't really make much difference in our upbringing, how we dressed or planned to live our lives, how we perceived the world, which looked just as drab and unsurprising from her window as it did from mine.

I saw two old, hunched, shaky women cross the road. With their drizzle of hair and frail pasty skin, they looked as though the winter had bleached all the colour out of them.

I suddenly felt great pity for Milka and myself. "One day it will be us," I said, pointing at the women, who moved no faster than turtles, resembling them too—wrinkled faces, coarse brown coats, small feet in ugly, scratched shoes.

"If we live that long," Milka said, eyeing the women.

"Why wouldn't we?"

"Do you want to be that old?"

"No."

"Exactly. We'll have to escape to Paris or Rome. Women there don't age." She laughed, took her keys out of her schoolbag, and climbed up the building steps.

My flat was more spacious; it had three rooms, while Milka's had only two. But she lived closer to school, so after classes we often went to her place and had fried sausages and boiled potatoes, ate sliced pickles her mother had canned, and drank plum wine her stepdad fermented year-round in a tall glass canister. After pouring ourselves some of the wine, we refilled the canister with a splash of water and set it back in its place, behind the kitchen curtains. Satiated and a bit tipsy, we would burrow in Milka's bedroom and feed the fish in her aquarium and listen to Freddie Mercury ululating *"we are the champions"* on a beatup cassette player. We loved that song, even though we couldn't understand all of the words. Still, we bleated along as loud as we could, imagining a skinny black-haired man in tight leather trousers and a wifebeater slide his hands all over our bodies.

Like all girls our age, we fantasized about being kissed, touched, coddled with attention. We dreamed about great love and strong, handsome boys who could rescue us from our parents, our crowded and ever-bustling households, our incessant chores. We dreamed about love that would take to our hearts like fire to a forest, burning everything in its wake. We dreamed about love as strong as an earthquake or a riptide, which would sweep us off the ground and hold us suspended in the air for one breathless moment, so that the world, though still ugly and unchanged, suddenly blossomed like a gorgeous flower, so when we glanced out the window one morning, we would see colour, bursts of turquoise and lemon yellow and mauve, instead of that hard, bleak uniformity of buildings that looked more like prisons than homes.

My parents never talked about love, only duty—to one's family and to one's country. I knew they'd been young once, but they couldn't remember being in love; that is, they couldn't remember what it meant. Before getting married, they'd only gone out on two dates, because they both worked and couldn't spend much time or money on movies or theatre or restaurants. Sixteen years later, the only thing my mother still remembered was that my father had been a terrible kisser and that his beard and moustache scratched her face, her neck, her breasts and belly. My father still remembered having to shave twice—morning and evening. And that he'd been always hungry. They got married not because they'd fallen in love, but because that was what people did back then to be able to have sex legally. My parents didn't have a honeymoon; they couldn't get away from work. They continued to spend most nights separately because neither had a room; both lived in communal apartments and shared space with neighbours and relatives. When they could afford to rent, my parents moved in together and started saving for a flat in a co-op building, which would be erected in the next decade. To their newly rented one-room place, my father brought a blanket and a kitchen stool; my mother, a saucepan and an old feather pillow. For a while, they slept on their coats and that one pillow. They ate boiled potatoes or eggs, sitting cross-legged on the floor.

"You know, back in the eighteenth century, rich women didn't even nurse their kids. They used serf women for that. I wish I'd been born then," Milka said, dropping a pinch of dry fish food into the aquarium, then climbing onto her bed. She lay down and folded her hands like a pillow under her head.

Milka was a dreamer, and, when we weren't together, she spent her time reading, seduced by worlds remote and beautiful and so different from the one we'd grown up in. She was like my other self, thinner and wiser, a more refined version, through whom I discovered my own desires and insecurities.

Stretching next to her, I said, "What if you were born a serf? You own nothing. Not even your tits. And do you know what they did to misbehaving serfs back then? They buried them alive up to their necks and let starved dogs finish them off."

"Then I would've married a prince and moved into his castle."

"A prince would never marry a poor serf. Why pay for something you can have for free?"

"What about Praskovia Zhemchugova and Count Sheremetev? She was his lover for seventeen years. And when she was no longer a serf, he married her." Milka rolled onto her stomach, her body limp and lazy, her eyes clouded with dreams. She smiled, parting her lips, her upper front teeth like two pearls inside a half-open shell.

"She was an actress in his theatre," I said. "She was gorgeous and could sing like a fucking nightingale. You have no such talents. Besides, she died giving birth to his son at thirty-four or something."

"That's old, especially back then. They started fucking at twelve or sooner."

"Which puts us years behind."

"Speak for yourself, Raneva," Milka said.

"You already had sex and didn't tell me?"

"Why? Was I supposed to call you right after and describe my torn hymen?"

"Ugh, I don't want to hear about that."

"That's why I didn't call you. But there was blood everywhere."

"How much blood?"

"I don't know."

"A spoonful? A cupful?"

"I didn't measure. A ladleful."

"Liar."

"Am not."

"Who's the guy? Anyone I know?"

Her face tightened and turned red. She shook her head. "A neighbour. Nothing remarkable. He had a birthday, and I didn't buy any gift, so I presented him with my virgin flower." Her lips folded in a grimace.

It occurred to me then that perhaps she was lying, that perhaps the person she'd slept with was someone I knew, but she couldn't reveal his name.

"Did it hurt? On a scale of one to ten?" I asked.

"Twenty-four!"

"That bad?"

"Even worse."

"Some girl from my swim team said it was nothing, like pricking your finger."

"Well, maybe she has a rubber pussy and can't feel a damn thing. Or maybe she'd been stretching it with candles for years so it wouldn't hurt later." Milka laughed, a short, abrupt chortle, then said, "Don't you fucking tell anyone."

"No," I said. "I'll post it on the school bulletin board."

She pinched my thigh and dragged a pillow over her face. "*'Cause we are the champions of the world,*" blared the tape, and just then I thought about the world as this enormous, wondrous place I might never get to see. I also imagined people everywhere listening to the same song and holding hands and making a continuous circle, like a variegated girdle or belt, all the way around the earth. And then I asked Milka, "What do you think it really means—*champions of the world?*"

She didn't reply, but curled on her side and became very still. The tape reached the end, and the cassette player kept spinning soundlessly and then stopped.

"You want to go for a walk?" she finally asked.

"We ought to study. We have a maths test tomorrow."

"Boring."

"The new teacher is strict. We won't pass just because we're cute."

"You think we're cute?"

"Yeah. But you need to gain weight. Guys like curves. Tits, arses."

"They like everything that spells 'pussy'."

"Still, you need to eat more."

"I eat when I can find food. When he leaves something in the fridge." By "he" she meant her stepfather, whose name Milka never used.

"Will you drive to the dacha with us?" I asked.

"Do I have a choice?"

"No," I said, grinning. "Not really."

She lifted her schoolbag from the floor and pulled out a few textbooks.

"Did you lie about having sex with your neighbour?" I asked.

"Only about the neighbour part." She pushed her cheeks up with her index fingers, faking a smile.

It was getting dark outside, and the room quivered with shadows. I could still see the aquarium on Milka's desk, but not the fish or even the rocks. Only the cloudy, mossy-green water.

4

Our dacha belonged to a small community of houses crowded together up on a hill, sixty kilometres away from Moscow. Each house was fenced off, and each piece of land that came with it was utilized, mapped out perfectly, establishing a sense of order in people's lives. There were virtually no yards, but narrow paved or trodden paths meandering among flower-beds, fruit trees, and compost piles. Most everyone in the community tended a vegetable garden and grew strawberries, raspberries, gooseberries, currants, and apples. That was how city people survived during the winter—eating what they cultivated and canned during the summer. My parents grew apples, and my mother also planted beds full of flowers: narcissi, gladioli, marigolds, daisies. She insisted the world could use more beauty, if only seasonally.

Our house was modest—two bedrooms and a kitchen, with a bulky antique cooking stove and a heavy scar-faced table, which had been in our family for three generations. The many stains, cuts, and burns contained histories, our family's loves and struggles. The kitchen always smelled of fruit because my grandmother made preserves; it also smelled of wild mushrooms, which she dried on long sewing threads tripled for sturdiness. She hung them like New Year's garlands across the room and above the windows steamed with whatever was cooking on the stove. Because we had no living room, our TV was wedged into a corner, next to the fridge. We could've added another room, but that would've meant cutting the trees, and my parents didn't want to do that.

Like our neighbours, my parents switched off the electricity and water in late autumn, just before the ground froze; they knew they wouldn't be back until next spring. For one thing, we had an old car and my father felt uncomfortable driving it in the snow; and for another, there really was nothing to do in the country unless one skied or skated. Back when we were little and the winters seemed longer, my parents, Milka, and I would take the train out to the dacha at the weekend and attempt to skate on the river, which was nothing but a thick slab of ice swept with snow my father had to scrape away. Some time ago, however, a seven-year-old boy had drowned in the midst of winter. We were told that the river must've developed a soft spot, closer to the middle, where the current could've been warmer; my mother compared it to a wound that refused to heal. Since then, we'd stopped skating or visiting the place in the cold months, and so did our neighbours, whose houses stood dark and lonely, like abandoned dens.

In the past couple of years, as the orchard matured and demanded more care, my parents started coming to the dacha for the weekend as early as March, to prune the trees and fertilize the soil. We grew several varieties of apples: Belyi Naliv, Slava Pobeditelyam, Bolshevik, and crisp, tart Antonovka. Belyi Naliv, small and pale, almost-transparent green, came into har-

vest first. The flesh was white and sharp; it bruised easily and
went soft soon after the apples were picked. Both Milka and I
relished them new and fresh, just plucked from the tree. There
weren't many and they didn't last, giving way to Slava and
Bolshevik. Both varieties were irregularly shaped and sometimes lopsided, round to conical and flattened at the base; the
fruit was blood-red with scaly russet patches and firm, fine-
grained yellow flesh. It was acidic and gave my mother heart-
burn, but otherwise didn't have much taste or smell. If we ate
these apples, we preferred them skinned and cooked, boiled
down to a thick gooey paste we added to oatmeal or millet por-
ridge. We had more Antonovka trees than any others, not only
because we harvested them last and the fruit could keep all
winter, but because it was a vigorous, well-anchored tree with
a single taproot, capable of withstanding Russian blizzards, as
well as a host of bacterial and fungal diseases, blight, scab, can-
ker, and even mould. "Someday, we'll all die," my grandmother would say. "But these trees will still be here, still full of
apples."

On occasion, when my parents visited the dacha in early
spring, Milka and I would tag along, helping them to unload
tools, shovel snow, or cook food: potatoes, fried sausages, and
pieces of cheese melted on black bread, which we then smothered in ketchup. We weren't trusted to tend to the trees, and we
refused to dig in the pile of frozen manure, so we served meals
and scraped plates with snow, heating up water in the kettle
and pouring it over the dishes. If they still appeared greasy, we
did it again and again until my mother ordered us to brew tea.
I would always remember those long, fragrant tea-drinking

ceremonies when we sat on benches outside, wrapped in a cloak of icy air, our breaths like miniature clouds sailing into the trees. We sipped steaming black concoctions, to which my mother added pinches of herbs, mint and marjoram and even dried hibiscus flowers or dog-rose berries. Dark maroon, they floated inside the old tin war mugs. Milka fished out her berries with her tongue and crunched them between her teeth, her face sour from the taste. I dipped shapeless lumps of raw brown sugar into my tea and sucked on them until they dissolved completely, filling my mouth with mushy sweetness.

Sometimes, when my parents didn't need us to cook or clean, Milka and I sauntered to the river. We would bring an old sled with us, taking turns dragging each other through the field and the birch forest. It would be mostly me pulling Milka, because she was always so much smaller; her petite body fitted perfectly on the wooden seat. We'd pack an old raggedy blanket with us too, since the seat was hard and missing a few boards, and Milka would bury herself in it, nestled in a cocoon of soft, faded wool. Only the red pompon of her hat was visible—a lonely poppy blossoming amidst the snowy fields. I would trudge along a narrow, barely visible path other *dachniki* had made before us, and she would pretend to be asleep, quiet as the trees crowding the river. When we reached its wide banks, we usually positioned the sled on the highest point and sat together, wrapped in the blanket. We would smoke and watch for cracks in the ice, where the water began to seep over the jagged edges. When the ice had melted somewhat and the river softened to livid-grey patches, we thought of the drowned boy, whose body had never been found and whose mother kept returning to the river every year. She left flowers and pieces of Easter bread and coloured egg, still in its maroon shell. We imagined the boy drifting under the ice, preserved and whole, in a foetal position, his knees drawn to his chest, his fists knotted under his chin, his eyes sealed with cold and fright.

In warmer weeks, when the river had partially thawed, we walked along the banks, following large broken floes that drifted leisurely downstream. They pushed and bumped at one another and occasionally careened to the side. They showed leaves and tree limbs and even pieces of clothing or plastic toys trapped between layers of ice and water. The river coughed and sneezed and farted, and made other bodily noises as it rose from its winter sleep. The world echoed with sounds; trees stirred limbs; birds fluttered through the clouds. The air was filled with the odour of resin and birch sap, and sometimes we would tear off the wet bark and cut into the tender wood with an old knife and wait for the sap to start dripping. We gathered the sap in a mayonnaise jar, or, if we'd forgotten to bring one, we would latch on with our bare mouths, sucking clear sweet elixir.

That year my parents decided to celebrate Victory Day at the dacha, as opposed to watching a parade in Red Square. The traffic promised to be mild and the weather sunny. As soon as we arrived, we began unloading the car while my father unlocked the house and the toolshed. My grandmother shuffled straight to the apple trees, studying the trunks we'd painted white in the autumn to protect them from rabbits and rodents.

The air was sharp, vigorous. It was early May, and the trees were already in bloom, covered in tiny white buds.

"Good year," my grandmother said. "We can make lots of preserves and have enough to last all winter."

"If the frost doesn't get them," my mother said.

"Might get the gooseberries, but the trees should manage."

"It's supposed to be even colder tonight," my mother said.

She went to the well and pumped water into the large enamel bucket she frequently used during apple harvest. My father carried the heavier shopping bags to the house, then went to the shed and brought out an axe and a pile of firewood. Earlier, they'd agreed with the neighbours to share a holiday meal, celebrating our country's victory over fascist Germany. Most of the food was already cooked, but my parents had offered to grill beef shashlik and also kielbasa links, which Milka and I pierced on long sticks and held over the coals until the fat started dripping and the sides blackened.

Bent over the kitchen table, my grandmother was slicing bread and arranging it on a plate; my mother scooped *olivie* into a salad bowl and patted the edges so they looked even. From a pink apple peel, she curled a flower, a semblance of a rose, and placed it in the middle, adding a few parsley sprigs to each side. Together with my grandmother, she piled freshly baked pierogi in shallow baskets, then cut raw onion into full perfect rings to decorate herring, which they also drizzled with sunflower oil. They were tireless in their preparation for the feast, disregarding age and pains and the chill of early May weather. Since my grandmother couldn't see very well, my mother assisted her up and down the porch steps and also urged her to use a smaller, duller knife. Soon she took that away, too, replacing the sliced cheeses and sausages with boiled eggs that needed peeling. By the time the neighbours arrived, Milka and I had the table laid, and the fire was raging toward the sky. At some point, my mother was concerned it would scald the side of the house, but my father took a spade and re-arranged the logs, then dipped a ladle full of water and sprin-kled it over the flames.

First the Semionovs ambled through the yard, carrying kholodets and plov. They were carnivorous and often pointed out the poor quality of Soviet beef and pork; the animals must've died from natural causes, they said. Boris was a large square-shouldered man who loved to dance and borrow money and who incessantly bragged about his health and pedigree, his old-Russian family. His wife had died a long time ago, and he lived with his daughter Dasha, who studied philosophy and quoted Nietzsche. She was thin and pallid, with glasses like window frames looming over her narrow, tight face. As a teen-ager, she was in love with our neighbour Garev, a bank worker fifty-one years old. Garev rarely attended dacha parties, but when he came, he usually brought Milka and me lollipops: roosters, monkeys, or bears on long cardboard sticks. He wasn't particularly handsome, of average height and paunchy, with thick auburn hair, but his passionate lofty speeches could sway a goat over, as my mother often joked.

Next the Khodovs appeared at our wicket gate with tort skazka—"fairy-tale cake"—and flowers for my grandmother. Panteley wore new leather boots, which creaked as he approached the fire, joining us. He'd been collecting guns all his life, illegally, and always lamented his poor fate, comparing himself to a small ship caught in a tempest. His wife, Aunt Charlotta, as Milka and I called her, was a gaunt woman who could tell fortunes and perform card tricks. She preferred to dress in all white, even at barbecues and when it was still cold and everyone wore old drab clothes. Aunt Charlotta never spoke of her age and often complained of not having a soul to talk to. Her daughter, Avdotya, was already eighteen and a head taller than me; she took evening classes and worked as a housekeeper for a Party official.

The shashlik was close to being done; my father kept turning the metal skewers while the meat dripped over the coals. They sparked and sputtered, the aroma drifting over the dachas. Khodov noted that it woke up all the neighbourhood dogs, because they growled and barked and refused to calm down.

"They almost tore me and Charlotta into pieces," he said.

"As always, you're exaggerating," Semionov responded.

"Not really. After all, I'm the unlucky one. I should carry a gun with me," Khodov said, tripping on a twisted tree root.

"Then you're liable to shoot Charlotta or one of us, accidentally," my father said.

"True." Khodov plucked a few strings of his guitar.

"I need to borrow money," Semionov said. "Couple of hundred rubles."

"What for?" my father asked.

"Someone said there's white clay here. I want to find it. Could be a gold mine."

"What are you going to do with it? Sell it to the government?" my father asked, laughing.

"They'll just come and take it," my mother said.

"Not a nice observation, Liuba," my father said.

"Not a nice government."

"What beautiful weather," Dasha said. "Nature is eternal, glowing and indifferent. Our mother, it births us and destroys us."

"She heard it from Garev," Avdotya said. "That's all he knows—words and more words."

"Someone said he received an inheritance from his aunt in Kharkov," my mother said.

"Not Kharkov, Yaroslavl," Dasha said.

"All the same," Khodov said. "He'll waste it on women."

"Not true," Dasha said. "He wants to travel abroad."

"Who'll let him?" my father asked.

"It'd be interesting, though, to see that moribund capitalist world. France, Italy, America," Semionov said.

"Mayakovsky loved America, especially the countryside," my mother said. "One-storied America."

"Then it's no different than here," my father said, and spread his arms. "Look around—one-storied America."

Everyone laughed, embracing the neighbourhood of shabby, squat houses surrounded by fruit trees and picket fences. The orchards were all white, so from a distance it looked as though the houses didn't stand but floated amidst clouds.

"I wouldn't mind finding a rich husband for Dasha," Khodov said.

"Rich doesn't mean good," Aunt Charlotta said.

"It doesn't mean bad either. No matter what our government tells us."

"Here's a deck of cards," Aunt Charlotta said, addressing Semionov. "Pick one, but don't tell me."

"Done."

"Now shuffle the cards. Don't cheat. Give it back. The card is in your coat pocket."

Milka and I watched Semionov retrieve the card, the three of spades.

"Amazing," he said.

"Now you," she spoke to my father. "Tell me what card is on top."

"Seven of spades," my father answered.

"Seven of spades it is," Aunt Charlotta said, and we blinked in total amazement as she flipped the card over.

"Ace of hearts," Semionov said.

"Got it." Aunt Charlotta smacked her palm, and the deck disappeared.

Both Milka and I applauded.

"If I weren't already married to you, I'd do it all over again," Khodov said.

"Not me," she said, laughing. "I'd never do it again. Ever."

"You said it." My mother nodded and offered everyone drinks.

"One more, Aunt Charlotta," I pleaded.

"Bring me a blanket," she said. "Any old throw."

I rushed inside the house and pulled a quilt from my bed.

When I gave it to Aunt Charlotta, she stretched and shook it, then said, "Marvellous piece. I'll sell it if anyone wants to buy it."

"It isn't yours to sell," Khodov said.

"One, two, three." She lifted the quilt, and we saw Milka squatting low on the ground. She stood up, bowed, and we all clapped, yelling, "Bravo! Bravo!"

"The meat is ready," my father said. "Pour the liquor."

The men all preferred vodka, but the women occasionally asked for wine, except for my grandmother, who always drank vodka and always out of her dented tin war mug. My father splashed some in it, and everyone waited for her to secure the mug in her hand. She sat on the bench, shivering slightly, and my mother wrapped the quilt around her shoulders. My grandmother was silent, staring into her mug, as though something had been hidden there.

The breeze swept through the trees, startling the birds. They clamoured and flapped their wings and shifted from limb to limb. A strange screeching sound reached us from the sky, and we raised our heads.

"What can it be?" my mother asked.

"An owl," Aunt Charlotta said. "Or a lark."

"At this hour?" Khodov asked.

"Eerie," my mother said.

"It happened before the war too," my grandmother said. "I was in the woods one day, gathering mushrooms for dinner, when I heard that sudden piercing sound I mistook for a bird's call. I looked up, into a tangle of branches, and saw no birds or nests, nothing but planes breaking through the clouds, descending low, lower, almost touching the tips of the trees with their wings."

"God forbid," my mother said.

"I have a toast," my father said. "Thirty-eight years ago, this country defeated the enemy, who wanted all of us gone, wiped out, along with Jews and Gypsies. Had the Nazis succeeded, our children wouldn't have been born. We would've stopped existing as a nation." He paused, but we all kept silent, trying to imagine the state of nonexistence.

"We're fierce people," my father continued. "We lost twenty-six million in that war, but managed to rise, rebuild the entire country in such a short time. We were given this mighty land. I feel like a giant, an unconquerable ogre."

"I don't," Semionov said. "I feel very small. Like a mouse."

"Papa, don't interrupt," Dasha said.

"Please, continue," Khodov said.

"All I want to say is that we must work, work harder than we ever did. Humankind is moving forward, and everything that seems foreign and inaccessible will one day become obvious, coherent. We must defend our country, our children, we must make sure they never endure what our parents, my mother-in-law, had to. Starvation. The fear of extinction."

He raised his drink, and so did the others. They touched their glasses with a loud clinking, and Milka and I poured Baikal fizzy pop into two spare teacups. The neighbours waited for us to join, and when we did, my grandmother stood up and straightened her shoulders; the quilt fell and bunched at her feet. She seemed very tall.

She took a moment to study each cold, silent face, then

pressed the mug to her thin bluish lips and drained it in one swallow. Everyone did the same, and Milka and I hugged and poured more Baikal into our cups. For us, Victory Day also meant that school was almost over. Soon there would be no homework, but long, lazy months of sunbathing, and swimming in the river, and gazing at the night sky.

5

Summer finally burst into our lives, with crickets and thunder and rainfall. The hissing of water against tree leaves. Nights were dark, humid, restless, while mornings were bright and crisp, filled with birdsong and wet grass, which tickled our feet as we walked to the bathroom. The main house had no indoor plumbing, and the toilet had been placed in a narrow casket-size building next to the toolshed. The building had nothing inside but a raised seat attached to a few boards, with a dark stinky hole beneath. Milka and I avoided going there at night and peed in a tin bucket on the porch steps. Every morning, we took turns dumping the pee under the trees, then washing the bucket and drying it in the sun.

During those summer storms, when it seemed as though the sky had split in two and the rain poured over the earth in one mad torrent, the electricity at the dacha would be cut off for days. We had a prehistoric gas stove, so we could still cook, although our meals were rather simple: eggs, sausages, hot dogs, frozen cutlets, served with pasta or potatoes, mashed or fried, sometimes with wild mushrooms we soaked in salty water to force out all the worms. We did most of the cooking by ourselves, my grandmother tasting things, then reaching for spices, which she shook and stirred into our boiling pots. She looked like a witch, hunched, in tattered sweaters and my father's old boots, with her long, grey hair hanging loose on each side of her wrinkled face and with her busy knotted fingers raising and lowering lids. Occasionally she mumbled something to herself, and we thought she must be casting spells, brewing magic potions. We wanted to believe she had supernatural powers that had allowed her to survive and not to starve during the Blockade. To the present day, she remained frugal with food, saving everything to the last crumb. We were prohibited from throwing away curdled milk, which she would turn into *tvorog*; or mouldy bread, which she scraped and soaked in milk and egg and then fried for breakfast. We never had enough meat for it to spoil, but if we did, she would've found a way to transmogrify it into something edible.

When we had no electricity, we kept milk and butter and cheese and even some of the meat in tall enamel buckets filled with icy cold water from the well. The buckets stayed in the toolshed because the sun never reached there. We also rubbed raw meat with salt and tried to cook it in the next few days. My grandmother noted that soon we wouldn't need her, that we were almost grown up and ready to have families of our own, with husbands and children. "But what if we don't want to?" we asked. "You must," she answered. "Women must give birth, because life must continue. Just like old people must die, to make room for the living."

In late evenings, if it didn't rain and after my grandmother had already gone to bed, Milka and I would sit on the porch steps and smoke, staring at the sky. There were stars to be discovered, and planets, their orbiting moons, but also black holes like opened mouths gaping down at the world. How big was it? How was it created? Who created it? How much of that world would we see? Were there other worlds? Other galaxies? How many? Was the universe as vast and limitless as we imagined? Was it expanding or rotating? Could we ever know? Some nights we lit candles and played cards and told ghost stories, or improvised a shadow theatre on a blank wall, using old dolls and tin soldiers. Most of our performances began as love stories, but ended with murders and broken hearts.

All great love stories Milka and I had ever heard or read about were doomed from the start. They mostly came from Greek mythology, novels, or operas, where someone always died in the most tragic way. Then there was the tale of Adam and Eve, which my grandmother had told us one summer at the dacha, revealing to us how the first man and woman had been thrown out of heaven for having sex. Unlike love, sex wasn't a beautiful thing we should be dreaming about. It spelled trouble, nasty diseases, and unwanted babies. We'd been told that for men, sex was a necessity; for women, an obligation. Only prostitutes coveted sex, while good virtuous women got married and fulfilled their duties. A wife should never withhold sex or food, leaving her husband at the mercy of lonely women, who would, no doubt, try to ensnare him. A woman must have children, three if she could: one for herself, one for her husband, one for those who'd perished in the war. It was a simple rule, yet we tried hard to understand it. Could a woman be happy without a man? Could she be respected if she had no children? Or didn't know how to dress herring or bake an Easter cake? Could she ever be as free as a man? Free to forget doctors' appointments, laundry and dirty dishes, free to get drunk, cuss like a butcher, piss in the trees, leave for work one morning and come back days, months, years later? Free to ram her fist or foot into her husband's face, gut, groin, free to watch him cry and plead before his children, swallowing tears, his own bloody snot?

"Why was it Eve who seduced Adam, and not vice versa?" I asked Milka once. "I mean, in real life, men seduce women more often, right?"

"It was incest," Milka said. "Eve was made from Adam's rib, so they were relatives."

"I've always thought that incest is when one forces the other to do shit," I said. "One is always older than the other, yes?"

Milka raised her eyes at me. She suddenly stopped smiling and bit her lip. Her hair was ruffled at the back where she'd been scratching her head. For a moment, she looked like a sparrow, just as small and helpless. "Yes," she said. "Adam was probably older. Who knows how long it took to grow a woman from a rib? Could've been years."

"Maybe it took nine months."

"Yeah. Maybe Adam was pregnant with Eve. Maybe Adam had a pussy. But after he went through the tortures of labour, he asked God to spare men from such horrors, make women suffer instead."

"Maybe that's why everything is so fucked-up," I said. "Women want to be like men. And men want to be like women."

"No man wants to be a woman. He'd die after the first

week. Cooking, cleaning, washing, working, on top of being pregnant with your third child. Fuck no. And can you imagine a man having a period?"

"No."

"Exactly."

My parents worked most of the summer months, so they only came to the dacha at the weekends. My father always painted and fixed things: the roof, doors, chairs, benches, or our lurching half-crumbled fence. He could never sit in one place, goaded into action by some hidden ubiquitous force. There was strength and determination in everything he did, as though he was trying to prove to my mother his worth, or that he was just as strong as when she'd married him sixteen years ago. His massive hands were always red and chafed, and when he touched my arms or cheeks, I could feel those hardened calluses on his palms. I couldn't imagine those hands doing anything tender: holding my mother's body in the dark, caressing her skin, which appeared too pale, too delicate and petal-soft, for his thick crude fingers.

At the dacha, my grandmother shared a room with my parents, who slept on a mattress on the floor. Milka and I occupied the twin metal beds in the other bedroom. The walls were eggshell thin, so I assumed my parents couldn't even attempt to have sex, even if my grandmother slept tight. But at home, sometimes I could hear them shuffle about their bedroom, my mother's stifled laughter, my father's whisper interrupted by his grainy cough. There would be silence, then gentle rocking, then sighing and soughing, which reminded me of leaves falling to the ground in late autumn. Unlike in the movies, where people often talked before, during, or after sex, my parents never uttered a word. Perhaps they were too tired or too old or too comfortable; perhaps they were afraid to wake up me or my grandmother; or perhaps that was true love—intimacy without words. Since my mother never talked about it, I'd always assumed sex for her was more of a duty. She didn't look happier afterwards, and if I ever happened to run into her in the bathroom, she seemed more embarrassed than satisfied. She didn't glow either, the way they'd described it in books. When I told Milka about it one afternoon, while we were lazing in a hammock, drinking fruit *kisel'* after dinner, she said, "But of course. Men wrote those books. That's what they think happens to women during sex. How would they know? Sex is pain, and then even more pain, if you get pregnant."

"But if it's always that painful, why would women ever want to have sex?" I whispered.

"If you want to keep your man, he must be fucked and fed, and preferably by you." Milka laughed, one of her loose scary laughs, which made me think of trees in winter, how they shook and bent and scraped the windows. And how they looked almost human, dark and lonely against the thick marrow-grey sky.

"That's stupid," I said. "My mother wouldn't do that. She's independent and tough."

"Maybe she is. But maybe she also doesn't want to lose her man."

I turned around and looked at my father, who was preoccupied with chopping wood. My mother stooped over a basin close to the house, washing dishes. She dried them with a stained linen towel that hung from her neck, then stacked them together on a bench. Milka and I got up and carried the plates and cups inside, arranging them on the shelves in proper order.

Since my grandmother was losing her eyesight, we'd been told to always put things in their designated spaces. Larger serving bowls had to be placed at the back of the shelves, while soup or salad bowls were stacked at the front, next to dessert plates. Cups filled a different shelf, and the cutlery remained in a table drawer. The pantry had also been organized in such a way so that all the canned vegetables in glass jars—pickles, tomatoes, squash, mushrooms—stayed on the top shelves, and all the preserves remained on the bottom. Bread was kept on the dinner table; tea and coffee were stored above the fridge. My mother was meticulous about rearranging both kitchens— at home and at the dacha—so my grandmother didn't feel helpless by mistaking salt for pepper, sugar for baking soda. She was the oldest person in our family, so we ought to think of ways in which we could meet her needs. That was what separated humans from animals, my mother had said—we didn't kill the weak and the old.

My parents brought most of our food from the city, packed in suitcases and canvas bags. The nearest supermarket was an hour's drive away, and it was a pitiful sight compared to Moscow supermarkets, although recently things had begun to disappear in the city too. Suddenly there seemed to be a shortage of toilet paper or matches or other small ridiculous items, and my mother once noted to my father that we lived in some perpetual absence, that ours wasn't just the country of monarchs and dictators, iron rules and iron fists, but that it was also the country of some ugly bottomless void that kept swallowing things and people, and in which one day we would all perish. But my father disregarded her worries. He believed in some unattainable ideal, some hidden mythic world, a refined version of our country that only a chosen few could see and understand. He also believed that all women, including my mother and grandmother, though possessing an incredible strength, capable of moving mountains under dire circumstances, were nonetheless softhearted and shortsighted. They could turn a dark mossy cave into a warm welcoming home, and yet they could do nothing to protect that home from being destroyed by a man or a child. They couldn't connect their lives to a larger context, to something that didn't involve family, kids, pets, flowers, cooking, or cleaning. Still, as much as he disagreed with my mother, he rarely argued with my grandmother, out of respect for her age and experience, the fact that she'd seen bombs fall from the sky and people turn into mounds of flesh. She'd lost her son but survived the war, as well as the merciless, famished, arctic winters of Leningrad; she told stories that made us turn silent and that stayed in the room long after she'd gone to bed. My father could never challenge her truth, the courage and sadness tucked into the folds of her old face.

In July, the apple trees groaned under the weight of fruit. We usually waited until apples started falling to the ground before picking them up, but that year was different. My father bought a stepladder for us to climb and harvest the fruit, which was large, succulent, and virtually undamaged. We had no idea what made the trees produce such bountiful crops, but our neighbours—the Khodovs and the Semionovs—confirmed the miracle. Their trees also thrived. My parents took bagfuls to Moscow and gave apples away to our city neighbours and friends, while my grandmother taught Milka and me how to make jam. We had to peel and core buckets of apples, then cut them into small pieces and boil them with sugar until they turned into a thick brown paste. It looked unappetizing, but tasted divine. My grandmother said that many things in life weren't what they looked, and Milka asked, "So how do you know the truth? You can't taste everything."

My grandmother rarely laughed, but she did at that. "When you grow up, you'll know what to taste and what not to," she said. "Trust your gut, always trust your gut."

"What if my gut is wrong?" Milka asked. "What if I'm too young to know? Can I be blamed for my mistakes?"

My grandmother puckered her forehead in thought, then rubbed her good eye. She was silent for a moment, her face broody, as though recalling an unpleasant dream. "During the Blockade, we were worried about one thing—not to starve or freeze to death. Nothing else mattered. We had to protect our children. That was the priority. Because they were our ties to the future, if we were to have any. There's no war now, of course, but life isn't that different. So protect yourself, in all circumstances. We'll die, and you'll live, and you'll tell our stories. Listen to your heart; that's where God lives. And remember—if something feels wrong, it most likely is wrong. Now, let's heat some water for your bath. I can smell those dirty feet for kilometres."

"Really?" we asked, sniffing the air. "No way. We washed in the river. We don't stink."

Taking a bath at the dacha could be an hour-long undertaking. We had to bring water from the well and heat it up; we had to pour the boiling water into a monstrous wooden vat and dilute it with cold water, then fill up two pails—one for Milka, the other for me. Naked, we stood in the yard, at the back of the house, behind a flimsy folding partition my father had built from old boards. We had the pails of water on the ground at our feet and two jugs, as well as a small stool with a hunk of soap and a bottle of shampoo and also two loofah sponges. While I washed my hair, whipping clouds of foam, Milka scooped some water inside her jug and dumped it on my head, again and again. After I finished with my hair, I would do the same to help her wash hers.

In the dusk, when she closed her eyes, her hands running circles over her head, I watched soapy rivulets crawl down her small fist-hard breasts, and between her legs, marvelling at how different her body was from mine. How it was undeveloped and boyish and puny, except for a healthy patch of brown curls between her legs. I had much less hair down there, but my hips, my breasts, were like Easter dough—ample, bouncy, yielding. We both had a honey tan, except for the triangles of luminous white outlining our privates. My breasts appeared even larger in the dark, two glowing orbs begging to be touched, which Milka did as soon as she rinsed the shampoo out of her hair and eyes.

I yelled at her and slapped her hands, but she only laughed, then lathered her hands with soap and drew them along my buttocks.

"Such arse," she said. "Someone will get lucky."

"Stop it," I said. "Get your hands off my arse. You act like such a whore sometimes."

"I feel like one. Sometimes."

She lifted a pail from the ground and dumped the leftover water on me, head to toe. I held my breath. I felt both exalted and aroused. Ashamed too. It was one of those moments when I was glad to be born a girl, not a boy. I picked up the other pail and poured the rest of the water over Milka's body. She shrieked, but didn't flinch, the water dripping from the tips of her hair, her nose, her protruding brown nipples.

"Can you nurse a baby with really small boobs?" she asked, looking down.

"Sure. They'll be swollen with milk, so they'll get bigger."

"What if I'm like your mum and don't have milk?"

"I don't know," I said. "What if we don't have children?"

"Then it won't matter."

6

Sometime after Andropov became our Communist ruler, a ten-year-old American girl, Samantha Smith, wrote him a letter, which was later published in our leading newspaper, *Pravda*. The letter was short, with a few comments afterwards, mostly to point out to the readers that the writer was just a little girl and thus had misconceptions and misunderstandings. Everyone who read the letter grew surprised that our government had allowed its publication. Milka and I cut out the letter and placed it under the protective glass on my desk, where I kept my most treasurable mementos: several pictures of famous Italian and Russian singers, snippets of poetry, dried flowers from my mother's garden, and a strand of Milka's hair from when she was seven.

We read the letter so many times that days later we knew it by heart. We discussed it with our teachers, classmates, parents, and neighbours. Samantha's words provoked different reactions among different people, but our Soviet citizens agreed that her letter was a harbinger of spring between the two countries, like a crocus poking its head through a sheet of snow. It also marked a turning point in our Soviet history. With Andropov as our newly appointed leader, we felt that we were no longer dumb blind miscreants forever immured behind the Iron Curtain. The world had finally begun to acknowledge our presence, if not our power.

The letter said the following, as quoted in *Pravda:*

> Dear Mr. Andropov,
>
> My name is Samantha Smith. I am ten years old. Congratulations on your new job. I have been worrying about Russia and the United States getting into a nuclear war. Are you going to vote to have a war or not? If you aren't please tell me how you are going to help to not have a war. This question you do not have to answer, but I would like to know why you want to conquer the world, or at least our country. God made the world for us to live together in peace and not to fight.
>
> Sincerely,
> Samantha Smith

We loved how honest and brave Samantha sounded and wondered if her honesty and bravery were typical American traits. What we also wondered about was the fact that she'd been able to send such a letter and that Andropov had actually received it. Try as we might, we couldn't explain why her correspondence hadn't been intercepted by the FBI or KGB. We also understood that such a bold move, such daring innocence, couldn't have taken place under Brezhnev's rule. Something indeed had changed in our country, although on the surface, things seemed exactly the same as they'd been since the Revolution: dour buildings, peasant clothes, sullen faces. We continued to study history, talk about the Cold War, and chew black bread and shop-bought dumplings filled with mystery meat, when, weeks later, another letter was published in the same newspaper—Andropov's response. That took us by surprise, but also made us suspicious about the entire nature of such correspondence. When we read the letter, we felt that we'd been inveigled into some new and dangerous game, the rules of which had been devised secretly by a few powerful individuals and then tested on us, like a nuclear bomb on Hiroshima. Andropov's letter was much longer than Samantha's, had an apologetic tone, but didn't contain any accusations or incriminating evidence:

> Dear Samantha,
>
> I received your letter, which is like many others that have reached me recently from your country and from other countries around the world.
>
> It seems to me—I can tell by your letter—that you are a courageous and honest girl, resembling Becky, the friend of Tom Sawyer in the famous book of your compatriot Mark Twain. This book is well known and loved in our country by all boys and girls.
>
> You write that you are anxious about whether there will be a nuclear war between our two countries. And you ask are we doing anything so that war will not break out.

Your question is the most important of those that every thinking man can pose. I will reply to you seriously and honestly.

Yes, Samantha, we in the Soviet Union are trying to do everything so that there will not be war on Earth. This is what every Soviet man wants. This is what the great founder of our state, Vladimir Lenin, taught us.

Soviet people well know what a terrible thing war is. Forty-two years ago, Nazi Germany, which strove for supremacy over the whole world, attacked our country, burned and destroyed many thousands of our towns and villages, killed millions of Soviet men, women and children.

In that war, which ended with our victory, we were in alliance with the United States: together we fought for the liberation of many people from the Nazi invaders. I hope that you know about this from your history lessons in school. And today we want very much to live in peace, to trade and cooperate with all our neighbours on this earth—with those far away and those nearby. And certainly with such a great country as the United States of America.

In America and in our country there are nuclear weapons—terrible weapons that can kill millions of people in an instant. But we do not want them to be ever used. That's precisely why the Soviet Union solemnly declared throughout the entire world that never—never—will it use nuclear weapons first against any country. In general, we propose to discontinue further production of them and to proceed to the abolition of all the stockpiles on earth.

It seems to me that this is a sufficient answer to your second question: "Why do you want to wage war against the whole world or at least the United States?" We want nothing of the kind. No one in our country—neither workers, peasants, writers nor doctors, neither grown-ups nor children, nor members of the government—want either a big or "little" war.

We want peace—there is something that we are occupied with: growing wheat, building and inventing, writing books and flying into space. We want peace for ourselves and for all peoples of the planet. For our children and for you, Samantha.

I invite you, if your parents will let you, to come to our country, the best time being this summer. You will find out about our country, meet with your contemporaries, visit an international children's camp—"Artek"—on the sea. And see for yourself: in the Soviet Union, everyone is for peace and friendship among peoples.

Thank you for your letter. I wish you all the best in your young life.

Y. Andropov

The letter puzzled us. Not only was it hard to believe that a grown-up man, who presided over our country and the rest of the socialist camp, could write a response to some unknown American girl from Manchester, Maine, and that our secret services would allow it to happen; it was equally hard to believe that *Pravda* would publish such a response. The third thing we couldn't believe was that Samantha Smith would be visiting our heroic motherland in the summer. The newspaper assured readers that it would provide a day-to-day itinerary of our American guest, as her trip approached in July. Below was a picture of a cute smiling girl, with a ponytail, a snub nose, and slightly large front teeth. She looked so clean and soft and petite we wanted to cuddle her, to smell her hair and rub her perfect unblemished skin. Her smile was frank, happy, and so trusting, hardly different from any other kid's, and yet somehow uniquely American. If we saw Samantha smiling on the street, we would've known she wasn't a Soviet girl, that she hadn't ever gone to a Pioneer camp, where she had to dress in a uniform, sing patriotic songs, and march under a red flag snapping in the wind like a bloody tongue. Choice lived in her face, the inescapability of a bright future, the right to decide her own fate, how to dress, which school to attend, where to travel on vacation, what to eat. It was a face we all dreamed of: kind, sincere, forthright. It was a face that made us aware of our own imperfections.

We spun a great fantasy around Samantha Smith. We pictured her among friends, all of whom wore blue Levi's jeans, red polo shirts, and white Nike tennis shoes. Convinced that Samantha excelled at school, praised by both her teachers and peers, we knew that she must love world history and geography and could find and name each country, each capital, on a map. We, on the other hand, didn't bother with such things, because we were never expected to travel outside the Soviet Union and thus didn't have to pay close attention to the locations of other countries, especially those that didn't border the USSR. But we could, of course, isolate Germany and the United States, as our country's enemies—past, present, and possibly future—which was what our government and our parents kept telling us.

As for Samantha's parents, we decided they never screamed, swore, or got drunk at the weekend. They never reeked of fish or fried meat. They had to be tall, fit, relaxed, and polite, living in a two-storey house of white stone, with carved oak doors and arched windows, where flowers bloomed year-round—purple violets and yellow marigolds and red geraniums. We imagined the Smiths owned three cats, a large shaggy dog, and a goldfish that possessed magic powers and fulfilled secret wishes, which was why Samantha's letter to Andropov had been answered and she was coming to see him. All the furniture in the house was white, and in Samantha's room, we imagined a tall bookshelf filled with novels, a desk cluttered with handwritten notes and newspaper clippings about our beast of a country. We didn't compare Samantha to Becky from the Tom Sawyer book, but to Alice in Wonderland, about to undertake a journey into some dark unknown treacherous world.

When Samantha set her girlish American foot on our hard Soviet soil that summer, Milka and I tracked her visit obsessively, waiting for my parents to come to the dacha and bring us newspapers. We had no TV at the dacha because our old one broke, and we couldn't afford to replace it. From the newspapers, we learned that Samantha and her parents had toured Moscow, brought flowers to the Tomb of the Unknown Soldier, and visited the Mausoleum, where the leader of the world proletariat rested inside a crystal sarcophagus. They went to the circus, the Durov Animal Theatre, the Obraztsov Puppet Theatre, and the Palace of Friendship, where they were shown a film about the horrors of WWII to remind Samantha and her family that neither the Soviet government nor the Soviet people wanted anything of that kind to happen again, including Hiroshima. One evening, Samantha received a call from Andropov himself, who asked if she liked his gift—a plush Russian bear—and whether she'd enjoyed her stay in the Soviet capital. He also told her that he was ill and couldn't meet. The next day, Samantha was flown to Crimea to spend a week in Artek, one of the most famous Pioneer camps on the Black Sea. When we were little, we all dreamed about attending that camp, but only a few fortunate children—those with special talents or special relatives—could go there.

On other pages of the same newspaper, we saw a picture of Samantha wearing the camp's uniform and a red silk Pioneer tie. Another showed her in a Russian national costume: a white shirt with puffed-out sleeves, a colourful hand-stitched sarafan, and a kokoshnik—a tall pointy headpiece with pearls, beads, and lace. But even dressed like a Russian maiden, Samantha still resembled a twentieth-century American girl from Manchester, Maine, with that unencumbered smile neither I nor Milka could ever imitate.

Samantha had been interviewed twice by the newspaper

and repeatedly said how amazed she was that the Soviets were so friendly, and how she couldn't believe the many gifts they'd brought her. She also said that the Russians were just like Americans, the kindest of people, and that the USSR was heaven. While in Moscow, Samantha stayed with her parents, but when she visited Artek, she preferred to live in a dormitory, sharing a room with nine other Soviet girls, most of whom went to special language schools and spoke fluent English. Samantha spent her time swimming, dancing, and learning Russian songs. She also wrote messages to other world leaders, sealed them in bottles, and tossed them into the Black Sea from a cliff.

"You think those girls are spies?" Milka asked. We lay in the grass by the river, chewing on pieces of straw.

"No. They're just like us, good with English because they attend a special school."

"They aren't like us. We don't hang out with an American girl who receives calls from our cosmonauts and the General Secretary."

"You're right, but we could've been. Maybe if we'd won that English Olympiad, we could've gone to Artek."

Milka turned on her back and tickled my neck with her straw. "Why didn't Andropov meet with Samantha if he invited her to be his guest? Think, Anya, think."

I rolled on my back too, raising my face at the sky shaded by clouds. They dragged lazily overhead, as though forgetting the destination or why they had to move at all. The day was peaceful, and you could hear the wind sweep through the grass. Insects whirred in the air, a swell of tiny creatures somewhere very close to our sweaty faces. I watched a ladybird crawl up my finger and counted the black dots on its back, then let it slip onto Milka's shoulder. She wore nothing but a long sleeveless dress my grandmother helped her sew from my mother's old skirt. It was tied at the waist with a scrawny belt we'd found in the woods. On her smooth, tan, bare shoulder, the ladybird looked like a drop of blood.

"Who knows, maybe he has no time," I finally said, reaching for the bug and placing it in the grass. "Or maybe they think Samantha could be a spy or an assassin. Maybe she carries a poisonous pen or some shit like that."

"Not a chance. Our guys have already checked every millimetre of their luggage and clothing before Samantha and her parents even entered the country."

"Are you serious?"

"Are you? Suggesting she could be a spy?"

"Well, think about it. How can an ordinary girl get permission to come to our country and talk to our Fierce Leader? To stay with other ordinary Soviet girls? To eat the same food? To sleep with them in the room? What if we wrote to Reagan? Do you think he'd answer our letter? Invite us to America?"

Milka sat up, her eyes zooming in on my face. "That's a great idea. Let's write Reagan a letter!"

"We won't be able to send it."

"Why not?"

"For one thing, we don't have his address. And for another, it will never make it there. Our secret services will snatch it as soon as it leaves the post office. In fact, it won't even leave the post office. The workers will call the KGB."

"I have an idea. We'll ask Yashka. He can take our letter to America when he visits his parents. They'll mail our letter."

Astonished by my friend's proposition, I lifted my head and stared at her grinning, audacious face. "Great thinking, Putova. Maybe Reagan will offer to pay for our visit to America, and they'll have to let us go because it would be only fair. Since they let an American girl come and witness our socialist heaven, they should let us travel to America and witness their capitalist hell."

Laughing, we jumped to our feet and ran to the dacha, where we got out an old notebook, found a blank page, and began composing a letter to the president of the United States. Two hours later, sweaty from the heat and effort, we took turns reading the letter out loud, correcting words or changing punctuation, but otherwise pleased with both the sincerity of the content and the ingenuity of our idea. We had little hope, of course, that our letter would make it to the president or that he would read it and respond. But miracles happened, as my mother often said, and in our Soviet universe, a life without an occasional miracle could be a bottomless pit. So we thought we could nudge our socialist fate a little and take a chance.

Before folding the letter and sealing it in an envelope, we skimmed the words one last time:

Dear Mr. Reagan,

　　Our names are Anya Raneva and Milka Putova. We are almost fifteen years old. Born in the Soviet Union, we have never travelled anywhere, except once to Leningrad and once to Sochi, for a summer vacation. Recently, an American girl

*Samantha Smith visited our country, and we are wondering if
we can visit yours too. We attend a special English school #55,
where we started learning the language at the age of eight.
We speak English well and won't need an interpreter. We read
many books by American writers: Mark Twain, O. Henry,
Graham Greene, F. Scott Fitzgerald, Ernest Hemingway, and
Theodore Dreiser. Some of them were funny, others a little
disturbing, but we still enjoyed them. However, we heard many
bad things about America (just as Samantha heard about the
Soviet Union). Somehow, we don't believe that things can be
so bad, and that your country is in great decline, that people
are starving, and that there's no free education or medical care
for all citizens. We also heard that some families have servants
or slaves, that black people aren't allowed to eat with white
people at the same table or ride in the same bus or drink from
the same cups. We're also told that your subway looks like a
bomb shelter and that there're lots of homeless people in New
York, and that sometimes they die from cold and lack of food,
under piles of rubbish on the streets. It seems impossible that
such terrible things can happen in such a great country.*

*We don't have a variety of foods in our country, and re-
cently it's difficult to find toilet paper and salt, but still, it's
hard to believe that people can freeze or starve to death when
there's no war, and no Blockade, like there was in Leningrad
in 1942. Also, we really want to try real American food—
hamburgers, Coke, and fries. But most of all, we want to try
your famous apple pie. We know it's delicious. We grow apples
here too, different varieties (which varieties do you grow in
America?), and bake pies, and this year we had lots of apples*

and learned how to make jam. We can bring you a jar when we come to visit. We don't have to come with our parents or stay long, maybe a week. But we hope that you can help us with visas and plane tickets. We really want to see your country, where they say all dreams come true.

Sincerely,
Anya Raneva and Milka Putova

7

Soon it was my birthday, at the very end of August. When I woke up and opened my eyes, shielding my face from the sun, Milka stood by the bed in her panties and an oversized T-shirt, quiet like a ghost. In her hands, she held a large parcel or rather a plastic tube for transporting paintings or architectural drawings. My parents used similar tubes at work. I also spotted a slim blue bag on the floor.

"Happy birthday!" she said. "Pick one gift to open now. One at the party."

I pointed at the tube, and she shook it and pulled out a tightly rolled paper. Kneeling, she spread it on the floor, using our slippers to hold down each of the four corners. Before me, Freddie Mercury posed spread-legged in his tight black leather trousers with chains. I held my breath in awe, sliding off the bed. I squatted and touched the poster. I drew my fingers along Freddie's arms, naked and etched with veins; his bumpy hairy chest crossed by a gem-studded strap of his guitar; a massive eagle-headed buckle of the belt, his tight bulging crotch.

"Wow," I said. "Where did you get it?"

"I know places."

"Black market?"

"No. Ruchnik. His parents sent it from New York."

"I envy him. His parents are diplomats."

"He says they want to stay in America permanently. Everyone is happy there. Everyone is free."

"But if everyone is free, then there are no prisons?" I asked.

"Of course there are prisons. Some people don't deserve to be free, so they put them behind bars, but generally speaking."

I leaned over the poster and wrapped my arms around my friend, squeezing her body as hard as I could.

"It probably cost a bunch."

"Oh, yes! But I saved my birthday money from last year."

"Are you kidding?"

"I had to get you something special."

"Thank you."

"Are you trying to break me in half?" Milka asked, her lips against my ear.

"I'm trying to be as close to you as I possibly can."

"That's nasty."

"You like nasty."

"True. But you're too good to be nasty. I want you to stay the way you are. Someone has to stay good."

We both fell on the floor giggling, tickling, and pinching each other, but then my mother walked in and told us to stop messing around and start getting ready for the party. There was much to be done, and she needed our help.

For the next two hours, we whirled around like electric brooms. We swept the house, the porch, the steps. We tidied the backyard. We cut fresh flowers from my mother's garden and arranged them in a primitive clay vase—large magenta asters and yellow and white gladioli. Milka kept fidgeting with their length, cutting them shorter and shorter until they resembled odd chubby arms. We blew up balloons and tied them to the apple trees. We set the table and skewered marinated chicken while my father started the fire, letting it burn down to coals before we would place the kebabs on the grate. Finally, it was time to change clothes. Milka slipped into a long loose skirt; it reached below her knees and made her look like a housewife out of a nineteenth-century novel. I wore a red velvet dress, which my mother had bought and my grandmother had altered. It wrapped around my figure in soft voluptuous folds, accentuating my breasts and "royal arse", as Milka put it. The colour was that of ripe pomegranates; it complemented my tanned skin and brown curls. Milka kept saying that I looked like a queen. "The only thing missing is a diamond tiara." So she wove a wreath from bluebells and delicate white flowers and placed it on my head. It smelled like withered grass, like the end of summer.

My parents, together with my grandmother, had bought me a new tape player, and a few recent albums by Mashina Vremeni and Akvarium, and one by Viktor Tsoi. I knew very little about the singer, except that he was a saboteur of Soviet music tastes. He took risks and composed his own songs, music and lyrics, which often reflected a rebellious anti-Soviet streak. Someone recommended him to my parents when they were buying the other two albums on the black market, and they paid double for the tape, hoping that I would enjoy Tsoi's music as much as I enjoyed Freddie Mercury's. My parents didn't know enough English to understand Queen songs, and neither Milka nor I wanted to translate for them, fearing that they would confiscate and destroy our only tape. We explained that all Queen songs were about anything broken: homes, hearts, lives, friendships, people. And my mother asked, "What remains if everything is broken?" And Milka said, "Hope. Hope that someday all will be fine." My mother sighed, as she often did after listening to us talk. "We need that," she said. "In this country, we need a lot of hope." We followed her gaze to the clouds, concentrating, as if there were some important truth to be found there. But seeing nothing special, we returned to our chores and the business of being teenage girls: dreamy, awkward, lustful, longing for young men with hairy chests and tight bulging crotches and music that sprouted desire. Or so we felt as we listened to the band play and sing, the heat spreading through us like sun through the orchard in early spring, giving life to everything it touched, every seed, every bud, every blossom.

The guests arrived at three, and the party was soon underway. Semionov presented me with a song he'd written, and I turned off the tape player so he could sing it. The song was heartbreakingly sad, about a young girl who'd lost her youth chasing a ghost of her beloved. His voice was liquid, with dark, deep notes that reminded me of mossy river stones.

The Khodovs came without their daughter, who'd stayed in the city for the weekend. She had a date, I heard Panteley whisper into my mother's ear. He hugged me and gave me an old pair of German binoculars his father had kept from the war. He said he wanted to give me a small gun, but Aunt Charlotta had objected, and I assured him that I didn't need a gun, raising the binoculars to my eyes. Through the lenses, his face was a blur. Aunt Charlotta passed me a white fuzzy scarf and a deck of cards, which depicted planets. When I wrapped the scarf around my neck, Milka said that I definitely resembled a queen—chic and imperious.

Aunt Charlotta took the cards from my hands and flipped them a few times.

"Make a wish," she said. "But it can't be anything material. No clothes or furniture."

"What does she need furniture for?" my father asked, sprinkling beer over the kebabs, then turning the metal skewers.

"You never know. Maybe she wants a new bed," Aunt Charlotta said. "But I can only conjure new lovers, not beds."

Everyone laughed, and I tried to think of something important. I wanted to graduate, to enter a prestigious university, to get a job, to become someone important. But most of all I wanted to travel, to see other countries. I also hoped to find something unpleasant or despicable in those countries, something that would make me love and appreciate Russia more.

"If I could ask for one thing, it would be world peace," my father said.

"That's so banal," Khodov said. "I would've asked for a wife who's thirty years younger."

"Oh, and that's definitely original," Semionov said and chuckled.

"You know the anecdote about a goldfish and a married

couple?" my mother asked, preening her hair. She'd forgotten to curl it that morning, and it hung limp around her face. With her hair down, she looked prettier but sadder. A wrinkle formed between her brows, and I had an urge to rub it away with my finger.

"Pushkin's tale?" Khodov asked.

"A modern interpretation," my mother said. "A fifty-year-old man catches a goldfish, and in exchange for letting it go, the fish promises to fulfil three of his or his wife's wishes. The man comes home and describes the magical encounter to his wife, who exclaims: 'I want to go on a world cruise.' 'Done,' says the voice. 'And I want a wife who's thirty years younger,' says the man. 'Done,' says the voice. And in the next moment both are on a cruise ship, and the man is no longer fifty but eighty."

Silence hovered about the yard, and then I burst out laughing; the others did too.

"Wait," Khodov said. "Didn't the man have one more wish?"

"Yes," my mother said. "But guess what he wished for?"

"For everything to go back to the way it was before?"

"Exactly."

"I wish for Anya and me to remain friends forever," Milka said. Her voice was high-pitched all of a sudden. It rang like a snapped guitar string.

Everyone switched their eyes to her face while she reached inside the blue bag I'd seen earlier in the bedroom. There was nervousness to her movements, but only I could detect it. I thought of the privilege of knowing someone so long, so intimately, that even a subtle shift of her head or a slight pull of her fingers could be a sign of worry or love or care. How much life we'd shared in those years of growing up, how many laughs or tears—over a scratched knee or an aching tooth or a bad grade—how much was yet to come. Our friendship was like those apple trees that surrounded us. It would grow and mature and give sweet fruit. At that moment, I felt extremely proud, as if I'd just won some important prize, and all those people had gathered at our dacha to celebrate.

"Happy birthday to my best friend in the whole world," Milka said, and presented me with a book of Chekhov's plays. "We're reading them next year. He's the best!"

"Thank you," I said, running my finger along the cover. It had a picture of a blossoming orchard that resembled ours, except that the trees were shorter and the flowers much smaller.

My mother took the book from me with that same authority she did things around the house—cooked, cleaned, ironed—and continued reading silently for a few minutes before passing the book back to me.

"*If you want to be happy, the chief thing is not to want anything*?" She frowned but only for an instant, adding, "Great writer. Awful fate."

"All great writers have awful fates. At least in this country," Semionov said.

That time, nobody contradicted him, and nobody laughed, staring silently at the coals. The kebabs hissed and dripped juices, which caught fire in a brief roar of flames, then died down again. My grandmother appeared on the porch steps and suggested we all move inside, where it was cooler and there were no bugs. Shaded by the trees, the house remained pleasant even on the hottest of days.

Milka and I didn't want to sit at the table with the adults, listening to them speculate about politics and the future, the staggering fate of our socialist world, so we begged to stay outside and eat our cake. My mother agreed to pour us some wine, but only enough to taste. She lit the candles, and I blew them out in one fierce movement, forgetting to make a wish. She pulled out the candles and cut a few thick slices, and everyone patted me on the back and climbed the steps, disappearing inside the house. I could hear the women complain about the stuffiness, and I saw my father's large hands pushing out the side windows of the house, and then the front windows.

We finished our cake while the adults clamoured and made generous toasts to my health and the health of my parents and my grandmother. The sky was a deep turquoise blue, the sun a splendid golden orb. When I looked straight at it, trying not to squint, it seemed time had been suspended, and the air was melting, along with the trees and the house and everything else. There was a buzz of insects somewhere close to my ear, and then one of the balloons popped, and Milka said, "Let's walk to the river."

"Now?" I asked.

"Yeah."

We went to the shed and changed clothes, putting on shorts and T-shirts and flip-flops.

We heard my father arguing with Khodov, whom he accused of being a "piss-arse capitalist" who'd never seen shit other than his own "goddamned face in the goddamned mir-

ror". And then he shouted something about the war and people eating their pets and dead babies. "Hunger will turn you
shit-crazy," he added. My mother and grandmother started
chanting their favourite song, *"What you were, you remained—
a jaunty Cossack, a steppe eagle"*, and we knew that if we left
now, we wouldn't be missed for hours.

Outside the dachas, we sauntered along the unpaved, grass-
patched road, kicking dust and dry dog turds. Behind the
fences, apple trees sagged under the weight of fruit. Men hosed
off their cars or spread manure under the trees while women
tended their gardens, squatting or kneeling, scarves tied
around their heads, their faces flushed and glistening. Some
dachniki swung in hammocks, some cooked on open fires,
some played cards in flimsy gazebos burrowed under grape-
vines and bindweed. The air smelled of burning wood and
fried meat and rich, tilled soil.

We crossed the valley, the grass up to our knees, dotted
with buttercups, cornflowers, and bluebells nodding in the
breeze. Dragonflies darted by. The willows shivered, their
branches like old spindly fingers dabbling in the water. Here
and there, the banks were pencilled with reeds, a mob of furry
cattails. We climbed down to the water's edge, slipped off our
flip-flops, and stretched on our backs, feet in the river, which
rippled through our toes. Not a soul was around. In the distance, a narrow plank bridge swayed lightly. I remembered
how one early morning, when the grass was still wet with dew,
my father, Milka, and I had fished sitting on that bridge, while
far on the other side a band of Gypsies camped out, coiled on
blankets around the fire pit. They often came in the summer

and stayed for weeks, sleeping in tents or just in the grass, under an open sky. Milka and I weren't allowed to talk to Gypsies when we were alone because, as my grandmother had warned us, Gypsies stole everything they saw. And what they didn't steal people gave them, hypnotized by their mellifluous voices and dark, doleful eyes.

"What if we didn't have anything to steal?" Milka had asked.

"Then they would take your innocent soul and store it in a locket, hooking it on a bracelet. Did you see how many bracelets the Gypsies had?" At that point, my mother had walked into the room and told my grandmother to stop scaring us with such nonsense. We were supposed to grow up strong and independent women, free from prejudice. My mother always had a way of cutting off conversations, as she did heads off live fish we caught.

The sun had slipped down a notch, but it was still hot and humid. The earth felt liquid, passing under me, my body weightless. I touched Milka's hand, and she responded with a light squeeze. We hadn't seen any Gypsies all summer, but in the field, on the other side of the river, we spotted a small tent fashioned out of blankets.

"Let's check it out," I said.

Milka turned her dreamy face and blinked. "What if someone is in there?" she asked.

"We'll be quiet."

"It's your birthday. You rule."

We put our flip-flops back on, climbed the bridge, and crept along the rotten boards, hopping over the few that were missing. The river gurgled, lapped against the banks. Once on the other side, we squatted and crawled on our hands and knees, inching along like caterpillars through tall grass. Every now and then, we paused to make sure we were still together. As we got closer, we saw wraparound skirts, not blankets, that had been draped over the tent, perhaps to dry, perhaps to shelter it from smoke or rain. It was still quiet, but the tent seemed to be shaking from the inside. I put my finger to my lips and Milka nodded. I scooted toward the opening and pressed my face to the slit, my hands already pulling the sides apart. I held my breath and for a moment didn't know what I was looking at.

It was fairly dark inside the tent; the floor covered in sheepskins, on top of which lay a naked woman, her legs wide open and bloody. She arched her back and let out a growling sound and raised her feet up high. Blood poured out of her, and the air filled with the smell of rain and mushrooms, but also rusty pipes. At that moment, Milka wedged her face next to mine. She found my hand and clutched it, her hot fingers pinching my skin. We swallowed, both frightened and mesmerized, watching the woman jerk and writhe and low and claw at the blankets. Her belly heaved, her breasts like two balloons tied at the end with brown knots.

"I lost my shoe," Milka said, her hand groping in the grass.

The woman dropped her legs down and rose on her elbows, glaring at us, her tan face wet from tears or sweat. Her hair was black and messy, coils of snakes. I stared at her, spellbound, unable to avert my eyes from hers, their strange orange glow. For a moment, I thought she was about to smile, but she parted her lips and spat at us, and then her body was crippled with pain again, and she collapsed on the sheepskins. We could no longer see her face, but the wound between her legs grew wider and wider, with a baby's head, like an angry fist, forcing its way out.

We took off running, through the grass, toward the river, entering it with loud splashes and screams. We shook from the cold of the water, but also from fear and shame and excitement, having witnessed something private and forbidden. Milka was the first one to crouch and slide into the river all the way, her head going under. I was wading after her, trying to catch her T-shirt like a fish tail wavering back and forth. She bent over and filled her mouth with water. She stood up and made a tight hole of her mouth and resembled a gluttonous beast. Her eyes glinted with mischief as she shot a fat stream in my face. I flinched and brought my hands forward, slapping the river as hard as I could, and kept on slapping and pushing my way closer to her. She didn't try to escape or protect herself. The two of us grappled and laughed, ducking in and out of the river, our nostrils and ears flooded.

Minutes later, we climbed up the bank, wringing water from our clothes. I slipped out of my shorts and Milka took off hers, and we spread both on the grass to dry. With her back to the river, Milka lifted and pulled off her T-shirt, the slim curves of her figure etched against the blue of the sky. Her hair dripped all over her body. Water flowed between her legs, her nipples pointing straight at me. In the full dazzle of the sun, she looked almost transparent, like some mythic creature forged from air and light.

—

As expected, neither my parents nor my grandmother believed our story, and when we returned to the river the next morning, the tent was gone. Still, the grass where it had stood appeared flattened, and someone had been burning a fire all night. The coals were warm when we touched them with our toes. Not too far from the fire pit, Milka found her flip-flop, torn in the middle. We picked it up and laid birch leaves on each half and set the remains of the shoe afloat, our eyes following the worn orange rubber until it disappeared downstream.

8

And then it was autumn again, the beginning of classes. Almost fifteen, Milka still remained thin as a willow tree, her long arms drooping at the sides of her body like branches. She had a good appetite, though, and at the dacha my grandmother always added an extra cutlet or a piece of cabbage pie to her plate. Milka would eat all of it, sweeping the juices with a heel of black bread, but an hour later she'd be starved again. "It's as if they don't feed her at home," I heard my grandmother tell my mother. And my mother said, "Something is wrong with that family. They never come to school or attend any parental meetings. And Milka doesn't seem to miss them either, staying with us for nearly three months. I don't mind, but you'd think her mother would at least offer to send some sweets." "You'd think," my grandmother said, and sighed, sucking on a lump of raw brown sugar while sipping her tea.

Milka never had birthday parties; she never invited anyone except for me to her flat. She said she was embarrassed by her ugly furniture, but I found it hard to believe. For one thing, there were very few things that embarrassed Milka—if she had to pee, she could squat on the side of the road, flashing the pale moon of her arse before the rest of the world. And for another, most Soviet flats had the same primitive sets of brown tables and chairs, beds and dressers, devoid of grace or character. No one thought them ugly. They were what they were—ordinary pieces used by ordinary people and intended to last a lifetime.

I knew that Milka didn't want anyone to meet her parents, even though she would never say so. In all the years that we'd been friends, I'd barely spoken to her mother and stepdad on the phone or after school, if I stayed at Milka's flat later than usual, finishing a project. They always seemed either tired or in a hurry, or both. Occasionally, Milka's stepfather would peep into her room while I was still there and ask, "Got cigarettes? I know you two smoke. I can smell it." Milka would jump off the bed and slam the door shut, without saying a word.

Milka had been seven months old when her dad died in a car crash, so she had no memories of him. Later, after her mother had remarried, she threw away all of Milka's father's possessions, except for an old wooden chess set he'd carved out of an oak tree. As children, we played with the pieces, not knowing the game rules, and as a result, half of the pieces were broken or lost; the others were stored in a box under Milka's bed. Sadly, despite my parents' wishes, we never learned how to play chess, but every once in a while, she'd take out the box, wipe the dust off with her hand or the sleeve of her dark-navy school blazer, and place the box on the bed. She'd open it and fish out the wooden figures one by one—two queens, a black king, a white rook, two bishops, and a handful of pawns—polishing them against the blanket. She'd set them up on the chessboard and study their hard shapes, drawing her finger along the familiar angles and curves. She seemed so focussed, concentrated on what she was doing, that I felt awkward, like an intruder or a thief who'd invaded someone's home, intruded upon the sanctuary of one's life.

Milka had only one photo of her dad, a large, framed portrait that hung above her desk. Once her mother had tried to dispose of it, but Milka rescued it from a pile of old newspapers and torn shoeboxes next to the building's entrance. She brought the portrait back to her room and threatened to burn her mother's favourite blouse if she ever again threw away any of her personal belongings. During those moments of explosive anger—which were propelled by the riot of hormones, as my mother would later explain to me—I felt dwarfed next to my best friend. Physically I'd always been stronger, bigger. In gym class, Milka couldn't even climb a few centimetres up the rope or muster more than a couple of push-ups. She had no muscles, no womanly flesh, no stamina. And yet, when she fought with her mother, she became a giant, stomping about her flat, crushing furniture and people with her mighty feet. She said things, too, things I could've never articulated to any adult, much less my parents. I would've been embarrassed, and I would've been grounded, denied movies or ice cream, trips to the dacha. But Milka tossed words at her mother the way she tossed cigarettes in the bin. She told her mother to shut up; to drop dead; to scrape her nasty pubic hairs from the soap bar; to stop soaking her bloody underwear in the bathroom sink. "I wish I'd died in that car too," I heard her say once to her mother. "Then you would've been free. Free to screw or get drunk or fry fish all your life."

Later, I also found out that Milka's neighbour, who used to babysit her, had told Milka that her mother had been drunk for weeks after the funeral and thus couldn't breastfeed. So Milka had to be bottle-fed with some other woman's milk.

"Maybe I'm not even her daughter," Milka said. "Maybe that's why she didn't feed me."

"My mother didn't breastfeed me either. She had no milk. And then her breasts got hard. She was miserable."

"That's why I don't want to have children. I don't want my pussy or my boobs to suffer like that. And then that arsehole, the husband, wants to have sex all the time. Fuck that shit."

One afternoon, right before Milka's birthday, her mother returned from work early and caught us drinking their home-made plum wine diluted with water. She sniffed at Milka's glass, then set it back on the kitchen table and smacked her daughter's head. "This one is for drinking. And this one is for stealing." She raised her hand and was about to slap Milka a second time, but Milka turned around and caught her mother's hand.

"If you touch me again, I'll go to the cops and tell them how you and your beloved husband have been abusing me for years. Since I was a baby."

"What are you talking about? That's not true," her mother said. She was a short mousy woman, with ashy skin and blond hair a shade or two darker at the roots.

"It *is* true," Milka said. "Don't make me tell Anya what a horrible monster you are."

"I give you everything I can. You might not think that, but I love you."

Milka shrugged, looking out the window, where the leaves had begun to change colours.

"You think it was easy after your father died?" her mother asked. "To be left like that? With a baby and no job? No money? Nothing but one egg and three beetroot in the fridge?"

The woman's eyes filled with tears. Fingering the hem of her stretched brown sweater—the colour matching the floor—she went to the sink and started washing dishes. As her hands moved in circles over a greasy frying pan, her shoulders stooped even lower. Her narrow, hunched back, her drooping head, gave the impression of a wounded animal. There was something so pitiful in the way she stood, but vulnerable too. I watched her shoulders jerk as she made a sniffling sound, and I knew she was crying. I switched my eyes to Milka's face. Winter lived there, with its ferocious winds and dead ossified earth and hard frozen snow. Her eyes glinted like ice chips, and in her dark pupils, I could see my own face, baffled. I was afraid to say a word, afraid of what Milka might say back. The silence grew, billowed like a storm cloud, grey, menacing, unapologetic, threatening to swallow everything in the room—me, Milka, her mother, the mound of dirty dishes she kept rinsing over and over again—but then I remembered that I had to pick up sheets from the laundrette, so I packed my bag as fast as I could, excused myself, and scurried out the door.

Once outside, I stood in the yard, lighting a cigarette, still thinking about Milka and her parents, who were so different from mine. Her mother had said that she loved her, and yet, it was not the kind of love I experienced at home. There was no sentiment in it, no longing, and no tenderness. In a way, it reminded me of a piece of stale bread, which was still food, but not nourishment. I thought of love then, of how it was supposed to be beautiful and free, and how my mother had always said that it wasn't a nuclear bomb that would destroy us but lovelessness. How one day we'd wake up and not recognize our country or one another—children would become strangers to their parents, husbands to wives, friends to friends. My mother was convinced that it was love that allowed us to know people and tell them apart, or form a connection. For her, love was a true feeling; hatred, an emotion. Living without love was like living in a cave: you were always cold and always in the dark. If my grandmother thought that God was the reason she'd survived the war, my mother thought that it was my grandmother's love for her children that made her live. I thought of Milka, and how thin she was despite all the food she gobbled at all hours, and realized that perhaps it was indeed lovelessness that kept my best friend famished.

To celebrate her birthday, I took Milka to her favourite ice cream café, Kosmos, on Barrikadnaya, where she ordered chocolate scoops one after another, until her lips turned blue and I ran out of money. Afterwards she seemed somewhat satiated, lolling against the back of her chair, smacking her sticky lips. I presented her with two tickets to an American movie, *Tootsie*. It was showing in only one cinema in Moscow, and I had had to pay double to some tout, who'd been selling extra tickets outside the box office. The sum equalled my monthly lunch money, but I knew I could borrow from my classmates and pay them back later, in January, because my parents and my grandmother always stuffed rubles in my slippers on New Year's Eve.

Back in 1983, no mortal in our country, except maybe our classmate Yashka Ruchnik, had a VCR, and very seldom were any American movies shown on TV or in Soviet cinemas. Once every few years, foreign film festivals took place in Moscow, but the tickets were impossible to procure, and most films weren't suitable for anyone younger than sixteen. I looked more mature and could maybe pass, but Milka resembled a twelve-year-old, with her puffy lips and her fringe cut short, barely reaching her eyebrows. She couldn't fool a fly. So, if we ever saw a foreign film, it was usually a harmless sentimental melodrama or a comedy. Most popular were French and Italian comedies, as well as Indian family sagas with music and dancing. American cinema was a rare, delicious treat. We also suspected that because of the heavy censorship, they couldn't show many American films; by the time they cut out all the sex and politics, nothing was left to show.

To say that we loved *Tootsie* was a vast understatement. The story fascinated us—a desperate actor, a man, dressed up like a woman to get a role in a soap opera, continues to pretend to be a woman so he can become friends with a young gorgeous actress he's fallen in love with. That was more than we could bear! Milka laughed so hard she almost threw up all the ice cream she'd ingested. I had to pass her my handkerchief, and then an empty candy bag. When we left the cinema, she squeezed my hand and kissed my cheek. She said it was the best gift anyone had ever given her, and if she were a man, she'd try and dress up like a woman, just so she could be friends with me, without any kind of implied weirdness. She said it was the best feeling in the world—to know that someone loved you enough to sacrifice a month's worth of food for two hours of pleasure.

Lazily, we dragged back home. The streets had been swept clean; lights popped up in the buildings like many spying eyes. The sky was blank, not a star visible, the moon asleep behind clouds. It had rained earlier, and the air smelled of dirt and trees soughing all around us. Milka kept gathering leaves from the ground, so when we finally reached her building of flats, she hugged an entire bouquet against her chest. They were mostly orange or red maple leaves, and a few others, poplar or ash, unremarkable in colour but distinct in shape. Milka passed the bouquet to me with a pompous, theatrical gesture, getting on one knee and extending her hand forward, her other hand at her chest.

"Will you marry me, Anya Raneva?" she asked.

"Will you stop being a fool and get up? Ridiculous."

"Will you stop being so seriously boring and accept my proposition? At least pretend to?"

A few older women shuffled by. They carried enormous tote bags in both hands, their backs and arms sagging under the weight. Every once in a while, they would pause, set the bags on the ground, rub their hands together and squeeze them tight a few times, then pick up the bags and resume walking.

"All right. I accept," I finally said, and took the bouquet. "Please get up. It's embarrassing."

"I'm declaring my eternal love to you. And love could never be embarrassing." She rose from the ground, brushed her knee, and straightened her sweater.

"What if I suddenly died?" I asked. "What would you do?"

Milka gave me a long, hard stare; her face grew serious. "Then I'll die too," she said. "I'll stop breathing."

"You can't just stop breathing," I said.

"No. But I'll swallow shit, my mother's sleeping pills. Or I'll slit my wrists."

"You wouldn't," I said. "You wouldn't kill yourself. My grandmother says that if you commit suicide, you don't really die. I mean your body will die, but your soul will be lost, wandering from place to place."

"Great. I could see the world. Maybe go to Paris or Rome. Maybe even America. This socialist shit is so fucking boring. You're born in a hole, you live in a hole, and you die in a hole. If it wasn't for books and movies, we wouldn't have known anything else existed."

The wind suddenly picked up and ruffled our hair. I tried to hold it in place by pressing my free hand to the sides of my head. But Milka raised her chin, straight at the wind, so when it blew, it pushed all her hair back, exposing her face, pale and vulnerable. I thought how anything could hurt it—a stick, a pebble, a blade of grass.

"But don't you think that any existence is better than non-existence?" I asked. "That's what my mum says."

"No. Because if your life is hell and others' is great, then it makes yours an even worse hell. You keep comparing, and you keep thinking: Why was I born? Why should I live? What's the purpose of this hell?"

"What if life has *no* purpose? No special meaning?"

"Then why are we here?"

"I don't know. But when we grow up, we might find out."

"I don't want to grow up."

"You don't?" I arched my eyebrows. "Why?"

"Because then you can't blame anyone else for the shit that's happening. It's your own responsibility."

While we continued to stand in Milka's backyard, the evening grew thick with shadows. Trees rustled and locked limbs, more leaves dropped to the ground, and for a moment it felt as though we were the only two people left in the world. I reached out and hugged Milka as tight as I could, my heart beating against hers.

"I don't want to die," I whispered in her ear. "I don't want you to die. I want us to grow old, fat, with stretched skin and no hair or teeth, but I want us to be together."

"All right," Milka whispered back. "You can be fat and old, with huge tits. And I'll be thin and glamorous, with fake teeth and a wig." Laughing, she ran up the building steps and disappeared, leaving me alone, in the dark, with a bunch of leaves I kept scrunching against my chest.

9

Autumn winds swept us off the streets. We shivered for hours and had to drink cups and cups of hot chicken soup to be brought back to life. We rubbed our chests and feet with menthol or eucalyptus ointments and snuggled under blankets in wool sweaters and socks. We took long baths, soaking in hot water with dried chamomile or lavender my grandmother had gathered in the summer, keeping the herbs in pillowcases hidden under the beds. We stuffed old rags and strips of foam rubber between our windows to keep the cold air from pouring in through the cracks. We stocked up on Zvezdochka balm and gorchichniki, flat rectangles of paper covered in dry mustard to be applied to our backs and chests if we caught colds and developed a cough. We were prepared to survive anything: illnesses, hurricanes, earthquakes, blizzards, permafrost.

When the winds had finally ceased, rains came crushing the earth, like God's wrath. My grandmother talked about the Great Flood, and how we would all wash away eventually. Rain whipped trees and buildings, hammering against roofs and windows for hours, and nothing else could be heard or seen. The electricity blinked on and off, but we had candles and a gas stove, so things continued to be chopped, boiled, fried, or baked.

On those dark wet nights, bewildered by the petulant fits of nature, we remained quiet at the dinner table. One Saturday, however, my father got up and turned on the TV in hopes of watching the news, but there was nothing but a scramble of blue and green lines, like an eerie void, or a hole into another world. Once or twice, he slammed the TV with his fist, but the screen didn't change, and he pounded and pounded until my mother grabbed him by his shirt and pulled him away.

"The TV tower is probably flooded by now," she said. "It's a weekend. No one's working."

"Don't be ridiculous," my father said. "They can't keep us in the dark for two days. What if there's a nuclear attack and we don't know about it?"

"First of all, we've been in the dark for sixty-five years, since the Revolution. And second of all, if there's a nuclear attack, no one will be able to do a damn thing about it. The government will hide in the bunker while we'll all be choked by the mushroom cloud. Like everything else in this country, our deaths will be long and painful."

"You and your theories. Stop saying that shit and scaring Anya," my father said. He stood by the window, his face drawing in all the darkness. "There'll be no attack and no cloud. No one is going to die anytime soon."

I was pulling the bones from my grandmother's fish and piling them on the side of my plate, so she wouldn't swallow them accidentally. They were hair-thin and hard to dispose of, so by the time I'd finished cleaning her fish, both our plates were a dishevelled mess, with stinking carcasses and heaps of skin. My grandmother hunched over the table, her fingers separating fried potatoes from cauliflower. She could still see shapes and colours, but not textures, and we tried not to mash her foods, so she could continue to feel independent, at least while eating. For my grandmother, dependency equalled death because life always ended the way it started—in total darkness, relying on others to exist.

"Did you hear anything about a Korean plane that our pilots hit somewhere near Sakhalin?" my mother asked, scraping her plate with a knife. "Over two hundred people died. Where are their bodies? Why wouldn't our government respond? Allow the authorities to investigate? Is Andropov really ill? Or is he playing games with the rest of the world?"

I stopped chewing and looked at my father, who'd returned to the table but didn't sit down. His eyebrows rose and his eyes trembled, pupils darkening to resemble those of the dead fish on the table. His expression became first discontented, then sombre, then furious. A storm was brewing in his heart, with rain and hail and mad winds. I cowered and pretended to be invisible. My grandmother, silent, leaned against her chair, pulling at the sides of her shawl, wrapping them around her large breasts.

"What are you talking about, Liuba?" My father tried hard not to yell, but his voice was like a brass plate that was being hit with a hammer. It echoed through the silence of the room. "Are you out of your fucking mind? Look at you. A lunatic, who thinks the whole world is out to get her."

"Not the whole world," my mother said. "But one country, which sometimes feels like the whole world, with its ridiculous taboos, and conspiracies, and propaganda."

"Shut up. Please shut up. Before I do something we'll both regret."

"What are a few impotent threats compared to the prosperity of our blessed glorious State?"

"What's gotten into you? I thought you liked Andropov? The man fights corruption, tries to sober up the country, even negotiates some sort of an agreement with the Americans, with that Hollywood clown Reagan. Why won't you admit it?"

"Admit what? That all those people died on that plane and our government won't even investigate? Won't allow the relatives to know what happened to their loved ones? They should be able to recover something."

"Maybe there's nothing," my father said. "No remains. The plane went into the ocean. They smashed against the water."

"So you knew about it? And you didn't say anything?"

"Say what? Why is it important to you?"

"Everything is important to me, while nothing is important to you! You won't even admit that Andropov was responsible for the invasion of Hungary in 1956. They executed people, including Imre Nagy, the prime minister."

"But it has nothing to do with us, with our family."

"What about Sakharov, Solzhenitsyn? Nothing to do with us?"

"They were dissidents. They got what they deserved."

"What if Anya and Milka become dissidents? Will you let

them be executed, or sent to gulags, or forced out of the country without the right to return?"

My father flipped his plate, scattering the remains of the fish across the table. I lowered my head and tried to disappear.

A lot of my parents' arguments started like that. My father made a political comment, and my mother reciprocated by attacking it, or coming back at him with a shocking statement. Sometimes it seemed as though my father said things on purpose, testing his ideas, and he needed my mother to argue against them. As aerospace engineers working for the government, their jobs implied a certain level of secrecy. They weren't at liberty to discuss their projects with others or talk politics with their colleagues and neighbours. Perhaps the rule, which became a habit, had stemmed from the Stalinist era, when anyone could've been spied on, accused, and sent to prison. People were afraid to talk to their neighbours because the next day they could disappear, their possessions, their flats assigned to strangers. My parents often told me that what I heard at home, during meals, behind closed doors, stayed there, sealed off by those doors. It was our home, our life, our secrets, our well-being. By protecting my parents' arguments from exposure, I was really protecting myself and my future.

More than once, my mother wondered whether our flat had been bugged. My father would smirk, saying that neither of them knew anything so important that it could sabotage our country's safety, and it would be a colossal waste of money to listen to us piss and argue. While he spoke, he would move from room to room, lifting chairs and picture frames, looking under beds and dressers, knocking on walls, performing a mock investigation. Like many Soviet men, he could be crude, prideful, and dramatic, though he was also smart and stoic. To argue with him meant to endure hours of history lessons and interrogations into politics. At the end of most arguments, I often felt that if he said another careless spiteful word, either my mother would leave him or their argument would escalate into a bloody fistfight.

Yet, their disagreements, though loud and explosive, weren't violent, never transgressing the boundaries of human decency or common sense. They fought with pride, but their pride wasn't hateful or hurtful, their personal feelings sacrificed at the altar of truth. They could turn and raise a curiously indifferent, polite eye at the world, could sugarcoat their opinions in front of their colleagues or shrug off a vulgarity, a disturbing comment, but between them, they preferred no ruse and no disguise, but truth and vehemence, mean righteous sparring. There had been threats of divorce in the past, and there had been tears, but in the end my father always apologized, and my mother always forgave him.

My grandmother usually abstained from commenting, despite my mother's efforts to draw her in. "Am I right, Mum?" she would ask. "Don't you think the truth is on my side?" My grandmother would either remain silent or shake her head and say, "I'll tell you in ten years, if I live that long."

But that Saturday evening, after my mother had voiced her speculations, which darkened not only my father's face and mood, but everything else in the room—the walls, the curtains, the air, which was suddenly thick and bitter, sticking to our lips—my grandmother raised her hand, asking permission to speak. Oddly, she looked like a schoolgirl, with her thick braided hair lying across her shoulders. Milka once said that my grandmother's hair was a testament to her will and character—both remained strong and unyielding.

"A strange thing happened," my grandmother finally said. "I hadn't dreamed for a very long time. It used to bother me, but then I thought that I had simply run out of dreams. When you get older, you run out of things: hair, teeth, years. Why not dreams? So I decided it didn't matter. Every night I closed my eyes and fell into darkness. But last night, I dreamed about my son. He was alive and healthy, occupying a large empty house, sleeping on the floor. It was Easter, and he asked me to bake him a *kulich*. With raisins and candied orange peel. I kept telling him that it'd been a while since we'd had any oranges, but he kept insisting. When I finally opened the fridge, the oranges fell out, jumping off shelves and hitting the floor like rubber balls. I tried to catch them, but they slipped through my fingers and rolled in all directions."

"So?" my father asked, his voice hushed, softened by curiosity.

"So," my grandmother said. "Not only did I dream, I dreamed in colour. Only crazy people dream in colour. You ought to start looking for a clinic or a home, where you'll have to place me. I don't want you to have to feed me or wipe my behind. Let the government do it. That's why we live under socialism, so they can smell our shit and pay for it."

Trying hard not to laugh, I turned to face my mother, who narrowed her left eye, the other remaining wide open, staring at my grandmother in disbelief. Not only had she managed to dispel my parents' argument, she'd also made us aware of her presence, of what it meant for us to have her in our home, at our dining table. My father walked over and touched my grandmother's shoulder, and my mother reached for her hand while my grandmother stretched her other hand toward me. I was afraid to touch it, though, because it crawled with veins like earthworms. Gently as I might, with the tips of my fingers, I patted her knuckles and felt their hard ridges. I remembered how Milka once said that touching an old person was like touching an old tree, with her twisted knotted limbs and skin like dry, scaly bark. But then she also said that hugging my grandmother was like hugging an old beloved novel, breathing secrets and wisdom from its pages.

At school that autumn, everyone talked about a new, cheaper, low-alcohol vodka, named Andropovka, after our General Secretary and his attempt to fight the ever-rising drinking problem among Soviet people. The second thing we talked about was *The Cherry Orchard* and why Chekhov's play still continued to be relevant eighty years later, what the orchard really represented and why it had to be cut down. Our class even went to see the play at MXAT, Moscow Art Theatre, where it had been originally staged in 1904 by Konstantin Stanislavski, less than a year before Chekhov's death. It was the last of his masterpieces, written to celebrate life while the writer was dying from tuberculosis. Intended to be a comedy, the play derided the Russian aristocracy, its laziness and vanity, its inability to cope with grief and financial burdens. However, we found it hard to laugh at the characters and especially Madame

Ranevskaya, the main heroine, who, having returned home from abroad, was about to lose her estate and the cherry orchard. Neither did we connect with the middle-class businessman Lopakhin, the son of a former serf yet an obsessive, greedy merchant, the future owner of Ranevskaya's property.

The third thing that everyone discussed that autumn was the disappearance of our classmate Yashka Ruchnik. Most students avoided asking the teachers about what they knew might have happened to Yashka. They didn't talk about such things over the phone either, because most still feared the KGB.

Yashka had joined our class in fifth grade. His parents first worked in England and then in America, and Yashka lived with his grandmother. He was a brisk, mischievous boy with a harsh mouth and a lack of manners we took for the excessive bravery and freedom of expression he'd picked up abroad during his summer trips. The teachers blamed Yashka's petulant behaviour on that capitalist world of moribund ethics and loose morals. He was often late to school, sleepy, lazy, lolling back in his chair, chewing gum, blowing large pink bubbles that burst with loud hollow sounds like gunshots. It startled teachers and distracted pupils, all of whom asked him for a piece to try. He shared reluctantly and sometimes pulled a wad from his mouth, separated it in two, and let some needy boy have the smaller half.

Though shorter than most girls, Yashka loomed large and unattainable, full of mystery and danger and something else we couldn't quite articulate. He wasn't handsome, with red hair and freckles, fat lips, but he was savvy and independent, swaggering in his new white Nike or Adidas tennis shoes. Most of us had never owned tennis shoes, much less white ones. Yashka was aware of his superior status and often bargained American pens, stamps, or erasers—fruity and soft like skin— for lunch snacks or sweets or even raisin buns sold at the school cafeteria. Then he began making a profit from more significant transactions, swapping issues of *Playboy* for writing assignments or physics tests; Marlboros, makeup, and lacy lingerie for tongue kisses. A few girls let him finger them in exchange for clothes, foreign T-shirts, or a pair of secondhand jeans.

When Yashka didn't show up for school five days in a row, we first thought that he'd gone to visit his parents in America. But when he didn't return the next week, or the week after, we grew concerned. A few boys tried to call him, but no one picked up the phone. Others went to his flat, all in vain; no one answered the door. We began to suspect that Yashka's insolent, lascivious behaviour had been exposed to our principal, Galina Ivanovna, a shark of a woman who knew no love, only duty. She had a burden to her step and a wilful sonorous voice that echoed through the hallways, the cafeteria, and the gym. Everyone feared her, and everyone envied her. We thought that perhaps she'd found out about *Playboy* and all the inappropriate touching, which, most of the time, took place in the dressing rooms or behind the school building, but there was no proof to our speculations. And it would be impossible for her to know for sure unless she'd caught Yashka with his hand up a girl's skirt. So we continued to discuss the matter and call his flat, until one day, during an urgent Komsomol assembly, the truth finally came out: Yashka's parents had officially defected, and he could no longer attend our school, or any Soviet school, for that matter.

"As future Communist leaders," Galina Ivanovna said, leaning over a tall wooden podium in the middle of the stage, "you must always choose community over self. Responsibility over desire. Sacrifice over gain. What the Ruchnik family did is shameful and irresponsible. They robbed their son of his future. You must always remember that your decisions don't just impact you, but generations. This country has given you everything. Free medical care, free education, free housing, free vacations. So it's an indispensable duty of every Soviet citizen to make her country proud, not ashamed. We're all parts of the same system, the same body. Only together can we overcome personal difficulties and capitalist aggression and not be turned into slaves. That's what they do to people in America, turn them into slaves. That's what Hitler tried to do when he tried to conquer us. Be fierce, be proud, be strong. Do not succumb to shallow materialistic ideology and self-indulgence. Think of our country, our nation, as well as others who have decided to follow our righteous path toward the Communist ideal. We must lead, and we must prevail."

In Founders' Hall, we stood silent, mulling over the news, which continued to thunder through our heads. I also thought of our letter to Ronald Reagan; we'd given it to Yashka at the very beginning of the school year, and he'd promised to send it. What if Yashka was arrested and they searched his apartment for any evidence of anti-Soviet propaganda? What if they found the letter? It'd been written by Milka's hand because her penmanship was so much better than mine, but we had both signed the letter—there would be no denying our guilt, the fact that we were willing to betray our motherland. I shivered, armpits wet with cold sweat. My heart began to hammer under my blouse. I whispered about the letter in Milka's ear, but she only shrugged, her face just as dark as everyone else's.

None of us, including our teachers or Galina Ivanovna, could possibly know that in less than two years, Gorbachev would come to power and perestroika would start and the Iron Curtain would fall, sweeping away our fears, our adolescent insecurities, allowing us to travel abroad, marry foreigners, become American, French, Italian, Swiss, to trade motherlands, without losing our homes or relatives, pride or heritage, the right to attend any school or college. But at that moment, when Galina Ivanovna had finished her diatribe, when we heard that Yashka's parents had dared to defect, causing him to be expelled, once again we acknowledged our government's ubiquitous autocratic power, as well as our own vulnerability and powerlessness. That realization made us tremble. It made us pick up our bags and leave the hall without a word, fleeing to our classrooms like ghosts: quiet, pale, languid, doomed to hover about the world without the right to see it or experience all its mysteries, its beauty and promise and opportunities. There were only two ways to escape such a life—to die or to defect, which was also to die, only slowly and without dignity, rejected by your motherland, your friends and family, everyone whom you loved and who loved you.

——

When my father first found out about Yashka, he screamed that Yashka's parents were selfish arseholes who'd pissed away their life, but my mother said that it was their life and they could do whatever they damn pleased.

"Yes. Except coming back to their country or seeing their kid."

To which my mother replied, "Maybe they don't want to come back to the country that punishes children for their parents' decisions, no matter how faulty."

"You don't choose where you're born, Liuba. Just as you don't choose your parents."

"But at least one can try and choose where to live. Good for them."

"Good for those traitors? Maybe you want to leave this place too?"

"Maybe I do, but I can't," my mother said, rubbing her hands with lotion, so that our entire flat started to smell like lavender. "To want something and to be able to do it are two different things. Perhaps only a few fortunates get to experience both. Perhaps that's what happiness is all about—to be able to reconcile your desires with your abilities. But often, it isn't up to us."

By the time winter arrived, no one at school discussed Yashka's fate, and after New Year's break, his name had been erased from the class roster, his seat taken. Occasionally, during a Komsomol assembly, one of the teachers would mention a missing pupil, counting and recounting heads, until another teacher would point out that our class was down a number.

From several of our classmates who dared to keep in touch with Yashka, we learned that he was still in the country, waiting for his American visa. But how he spent his days and whether he was allowed to leave his flat or call his parents, we did not know. Milka and I decided that if we were ever questioned about the letter to President Reagan, we would pretend that it was a joke, and that the letter had been composed as an English assignment but never turned in.

10

It was a frigid day on 9 February 1984, the fortieth day of the year. The snow had fallen for hours during the previous night, so the city had lost all colour but grown new augmented forms. The air was sharp, crisp, hard to swallow. It needled our throats, our breaths coming out in small white puffs, our scarves and collars beaded with icicles. Before school that morning, Milka and I shook the trees and stood under them, in a dazzle of flurries that spun and spun, gently, like tiny flowers: baby's breath or bird-cherry blossoms. When the flurries turned to water and rolled down our cheeks, we both looked like melting Snow Maidens.

Because there was no sun and wouldn't be for days, the city seemed lulled to sleep, frozen in a cradle of time. The streets were nearly empty, the shops dark, people late for work. But government offices never closed; neither did schools. During hurricanes, blizzards, or ice storms, classes had never been cancelled, except maybe when the temperature outside was arctic, minus thirty Celsius or below. We'd always been told that our winters, our harsh climate, was one of the reasons Napoleon and Hitler had lost the wars—foreign soldiers couldn't

withstand the merciless marrow-numbing cold, while our soldiers could piss or fuck behind stiffened, frozen trees.

"Even if their dicks turned to icicles and broke off, they
could still fight to the death and defeat the enemy," Milka said.
"That's the spirit of a Russian soldier." She lifted her fists in
the air and shook them. Her mittens were crusted with ice.
"Let's skip the last classes and invite over a few boys. My parents have a late meeting. But we need an excuse, so let's just
pretend it's your birthday."

"Why?"

"So it doesn't look too obvious. Besides, your birthday is in
summer, you don't get to celebrate it."

"We celebrated at the dacha."

"Not with our classmates."

"But they'll want to bring gifts."

"Good for us." She gave me one of her full-mouth grins,
disconcerting in its sincerity.

The two boys Milka suggested inviting were Aleksey Lopatin and Petya Trifonov, who were as different as sky and earth.
Lopatin was already sixteen, the oldest in our class, and had the
looks of a warrior—tall, thick-skinned, with full-grown feet
and arms that could engulf a girl completely. He had square
shoulders and a wide billowing chest, and we imagined him
having the heart of a whale to fill in the immense space. His
hair was brown mud and curly. He had an ample mouth and a
shrewd smile, although somewhat crooked teeth, which didn't
spoil his face but added distinction, a playful boisterousness.
But perhaps his eyes—deep, unsettled, opaque green—drew

the most attention. We could feel their fervour and pulse. Catching his stare inadvertently, during breaks or lunches, we succumbed to fantasies, eager to follow Lopatin through forests and coppices, rivers and mountains, waist-deep in snow, by horse or on foot, all the way to Siberia, as the Decembrists' wives did after their husbands' revolt in 1825. That would never happen, of course, because Lopatin had no ambitions to match those of the Decembrists; neither was he that brave or intelligent. But to naïve adolescent girls in our class, he seemed worthy of dreamy glances and wistful sighs.

It was no secret that Lopatin's ancestors were from a small town in the Urals, close to Ekaterinburg, and that his grandparents and great-grandparents on both sides were peasants who'd aided in the overthrow of the czarist regime in 1917. Now Lopatin's parents, members of the Communist Party, occupied warm cushy seats in warm cushy offices, working for the government, although someone in our class speculated that after Andropov came to power, they fell out of favour. Yet, Lopatin's arrogant attitude toward his peers remained unchanged. Lopatin wasn't a model student; he frequently cheated on tests or forgot his homework. But he was never late to classes, arriving dressed in an ironed school uniform and starched white shirt, the collar crisp like new snow. His black shoes must have been polished every morning, because, we swore, we could see our reflection in their glossy surface.

Petya Trifonov, on the other hand, was nothing like his classmate. He was a bookworm, nosing through the dirt of history, seeking forbidden texts, the key to a better existence.

"What are you going to do when you find that key?" Milka asked once.

"Start looking for the door it opens," he answered.

We knew that he read Herzen, Belinsky, Chernyshevsky, and other great Russian thinkers. It wasn't rare among high schoolers to be drawn to superior minds, especially those who'd advocated freedom based on spirit, humanism, and education. The odd thing, however, was that someone had spotted the Bible in Trifonov's book bag. We were aware that most great thinkers defied God. The Soviet system did too; it forbade religious education at school.

There was nothing mighty or attractive in Trifonov's appearance. He was tall, lanky, with a long blonde fringe brushed to one side of his pale, anaemic face. He had blue eyes with brown specks like grains of sand. When he blinked or teared at the wind, it seemed as though the specks floated around, stirred by the motion. It gave us an eerie, unsettled feeling but also made him illusive somehow, a ghost in a short, weathered coat and dull shoes, the hem of his trousers barely reaching his ankles.

At fourteen, Trifonov developed asthma and was excused from playing sports; we would see him hovering on the outskirts of the soccer field, a book in one hand, an inhaler in the other. The girls pitied him in a kind of motherly way, brought him sweets and fruit. One girl knitted a blue-and-red scarf for him during "labour" classes, when boys and girls were separated to learn their respective duties as future husbands and wives: cooking and sewing for the girls, designing and building for the boys. However, even during those classes, the boys avoided Trifonov or snarled and pecked at him, like animals who perceived sickness in their own species as something that must be eradicated. But perhaps a few boys acted that way out of jealousy, because Trifonov's ailment gave him a "white card," meaning that he would never be enlisted. A two-year obligatory service in the Soviet army could be a brutal, dehumanizing experience that entailed beatings, loss of limbs, rape, and even death, especially during the war in Afghanistan.

Despite his illness, it'd been reiterated over and over that Trifonov was of noble blood. The Trifonov name, which was spelled Trifonoff before the Revolution, had belonged to an old clan of aristocrats, most of whom had either emigrated between 1915 and 1917 or been executed soon after workers and peasants stormed the Winter Palace and seized power. There was also a rumour that Trifonov's great-uncle knew Chekhov, and that the family owned a few original pages from *The Cherry Orchard*.

Milka and Trifonov often exchanged books and engaged in heated discussions about plots, themes, and the plausibility of characters, especially females. Contrary to Trifonov, however, Milka disregarded interminable historical novels and, while reading *War and Peace*, ended up skipping Tolstoy's battle descriptions and ruminations about Masons and religion. It also bothered her that extensive parts of that novel had been written in French, the translations provided as footnotes in tiny script.

"Tolstoy's wife rewrote that novel twelve fucking times," Milka once told me. "She could've cut something out. I doubt he would've noticed."

"Maybe she did," I said. "Maybe it was two thousand pages originally."

"Or maybe she should've just told him to rewrite the damn thing himself. He hated women."

"He did not."

"Did too. Just think how he describes them—all helpless sluts. Oh, and then Prince Bolkonsky confirms it to Bezukhov, warns him against marriage. So that's where our men get that attitude. It isn't the war, it's Tolstoy." Milka laughed her wet, gritty laugh, and I did too, once again amused by her defiant mind and scoffing honesty.

That day, we got back from school early and started preparing for the boys' visit. At Milka's flat, we soaked in the tub together, our naked breasts floating amidst the suds. We sipped Milka's stepdad's wine and smoked his cigarettes while listening to the Queen tape playing over and over again, "Bohemian Rhapsody" and "Somebody to Love", our heads in dreams and smoke. I felt Milka's foot crawling up mine, wedging between my legs. A playful tickle of her toes. Her pink nails resembled seashells gleaming underwater. I didn't flinch but continued to float, offering my body to her explorations. Prickly sensations like tiny bubbles rose through the water. Ever so gently, she probed with her big toe until it touched my pubic hair. Her foot burrowed in, and I swallowed smoke, then let out a puny cloud of breath. We both became quiet while Freddie Mercury sang, *"Mama mia, mama mia, let me go . . ."* Milka's eyes were locked on mine, full of dare and lust, and curiosity. I felt aroused, not so much from Milka's subtle movements, but her intentions, her non-embarrassment, her raunchy assessing gaze. The more she touched me, the more I imagined a man with pale skin and loam-dark hair, a thin moustache, dressed in chains and a T-shirt with cutoff sleeves, and jeans tight as skin, emphasizing his large fist of an erection. I didn't bring my legs closer together, and I didn't part them any farther. Milka's big toe ran up and down my split. My face sweated, my eyes lost focus, a veil of tiny sudsy beads separating Milka from me. Her toe slipped deeper, and I jerked and dropped my cigarette in the water.

"Just as I thought. Still a virgin."

I didn't answer, spellbound by the moment, the promise of lost pleasure.

"Girl, we got to do something about that. It just isn't right." She gave out a chuckle, loose like a wave of water.

I scooped an armful of foam, lurched forward, and bathed her smug face.

An hour later, we were dressed and preened, the food cooked, the table served. We didn't have money to concoct an elaborate meal, so we fried potatoes with onion and made open-faced sandwiches from sausages and cheese and slices of fresh cucumber, a delicacy in winter. From under her parents' bed, Milka also procured a jar of pickled squash and chopped a salad from cooked beetroot we found in the fridge. We dressed the beetroot with garlic and mayonnaise. Just before Trifonov and Lopatin arrived, Milka discovered a can of sprats and boiled a few eggs. Arranging the oily fish on slices of egg, she wiggled one sprat in the air.

"What does it look like?" She replicated a sly smile.

"Like you," I said, also smiling.

"Wrong. It looks like a baby penis."

"Is everything sex with you?"

"Yep."

When Milka had invited Trifonov and Lopatin to her flat that afternoon, she'd asked Trifonov to bring her something to read, and he was eager to oblige. It was Mikhail Bulgakov's *Heart of a Dog*. Milka held the book in her hand, as though trying to gauge its significance by its weight.

"Good, eh?" she asked, and Trifonov nodded, waiting for permission to shed his coat.

"It's for Anya, though," he said. "But you both can read it."

"Thank you," I said.

"Almost forgot." He produced from his breast pocket a doll-size bouquet of yellow mimosas. It had cute fuzzy blossoms no bigger than peas and a sweet, stifling smell.

"For me?" Milka asked, a melting grin on her face.

"No. For her. That's all I could find, Anya," he said.

"It was short notice." I gave Milka a rebuking stare.

"True," she said.

"Oh, and this." His hand delved into his other pocket and extracted a small oblong box of sugared cranberries.

"Where did you get them?" I asked, charmed by the gesture.

"In my mother's cupboard. She'll be mad when she finds out." A smile stretched across his face. "But who cares, right?"

And then the bell rang, and Lopatin entered, dragging in snow and cold air. His long tweed coat was unbuttoned, a red scarf looped around his neck. He wore no hat, and we could see flurries trapped in his brown curls like premature grey. He seemed taller and wider in the chest, but also softer than usual, a warrior without armour. In his hand, he had five white carnations wrapped in newspaper.

"I didn't want to get red," he said. "They remind me of funerals."

"Usually it's the other way around," Trifonov noted.

"Really? I wouldn't know." He peeled the newspaper and discarded it on the floor. He passed me the flowers, saying "Madame," then bent to kiss my hand.

"Miss. She isn't married yet," Trifonov said.

"Such intricacies escape me. I'm the son of a peasant after all." Lopatin straightened his posture and pulled a bottle of Armenian cognac from his hidden coat pocket. "Girls, I couldn't procure French. Yashka is all out."

"Are you two communicating? How's he doing?" I asked.

"Fine, homeschooling himself."

"Self-discipline! Who could've thought," Milka said, taking the bottle from Lopatin and slipping the book under her arm.

"One can't afford to stay ignorant," Lopatin said. "Our Eternal Student here will tell you as much." He gestured at Trifonov, who summoned a weak, unconvincing smile, lips sealed and stretched.

"Hungry?" Milka asked, and their chins tapped at their chests in confirmation. "Then follow me."

She strutted toward the kitchen in her black tights and a flowing silky tunic my grandmother had sewn from some old leftover fabric. I wore a black skirt and Milka's mother's pink blouse, tart from her citrusy perfume. The shirt gaped between the buttons, offering a glimpse of my bra and generous cleavage. My face tingled from the foundation and blusher, and my mascaraed eyelashes stuck together each time I blinked. Milka had used a curling iron on my already curled hair to give it shape and texture before spraying it heavily. She'd said I looked seductive.

Before the boys arrived, Milka and I had discussed our options. We both, of course, pined for Lopatin, longed for his ample, protective arms. But Trifonov seemed smart and kind, and also shy. His asthma scared us a bit as we kept envisioning him reaching for his inhaler in the midst of kisses. "What if you push your tongue too far, he might suffocate," Milka had said. "Imagine the school paper: 'Trifonov found dead in the arms of his lover.'"

"Let's just see how it goes. Perhaps it won't go that far," I'd said.

"Speak for yourself. It'll go as far as you let it. Someone needs to pluck that precious flower of yours." Again she'd laughed, and again her laughter was grained with cruelty, though maybe it only seemed that way because I felt my own inexperience.

While Lopatin and Trifonov took their seats at the kitchen table, I placed the flowers in two vases, leaving both on the counter for the lack of room on the table. Lopatin poured the cognac into four silver thimbles. Milka claimed that they dated back to Tatars, passed through her family from generation to generation. It was her only inheritance and dowry. The amber liquor shivered, catching glints of the ceiling light.

"The first toast is to Raneva," Lopatin said, and raised one of the thimbles. He wore a blue shirt and a pair of new dark Levi's jeans. His shirtsleeves were rolled up above his elbows; long, golden-brown hairs covered his arms. "You're now as old as I am. Sixteen. According to the Soviet law, we can even get married," Lopatin said.

"I don't want to get married," I said. "Not anytime soon."

"Neither do I," said Lopatin. "Ever."

"Works for me," Milka said.

"That's terrible," Trifonov said, sniffing the liquor, then dipping his tongue in it. He was dressed in brown trousers and a tartan flannel shirt. His sleeves were buttoned, which made his hands appear thin and pale, the skin almost translucent. We could see a meandering of blue veins.

"It's the best cognac after French," Lopatin noted.

"It's terrible you two never want to have a family," Trifonov said.

"I agree," I said. "Family is important."

"It depends on the family," Milka said.

"Exactly. Mine is full of drunken arseholes," Lopatin said.

"Mine are maniacs," Milka said.

"Well, you two can go ahead and enjoy your careless existence while Anya and I share some quality conversations."

"Trifonov, what are you, stupid or just pretending?" Lopatin asked. "Who wants to have some quality conversations when you're sixteen? Sex, my friend, sex is all the pleasure we can afford in this country. Unless you do drugs."

"I don't do drugs," Trifonov said.

"I didn't think so." Lopatin stood up and raised his thimble.

"To you, Raneva." He dumped the cognac down his throat, reaching for the sprats. He pulled several spikes of green onion from the top and folded them between his lips.

Milka and I took minute sips, cringing. The liquor tasted bitter and spicy, a hint of cedar and cardamom. Inspired by Lopatin, Trifonov swallowed the cognac in one courageous gulp. He turned red, his spindly fingers clawing at his throat as he tried to breathe deeper. He began coughing; his eyes bulged.

"Fuck," Lopatin said. "Fuck. Why did you have to drink the whole damn thing?"

Trifonov shook his head and continued coughing.

"Water," I said. "Give him some water. Hurry."

Milka jumped from her seat and filled a cup in the sink.

"Trousers," he wheezed.

"What?" Lopatin asked. "Trousers?"

"Inhaler." With a trembling hand, Trifonov fumbled for his pocket.

"He needs his inhaler," I said, and patted both sides of his trousers, along the seams. I felt something hard and round and almost jerked back. Finally, I managed to finger out a small plastic tube, rather light, that looked like a miniature can of hair spray. Trifonov reached to grab it. At first, we watched him draw anxious, thirsty gulps, and then we turned away. We stared out of the window, at the city that lay buried under snow, all that soft whiteness. It felt as though we were inside a yurt or an ice cave.

Milka shivered, picking up cigarettes, but I shook my head, and she placed them back on the table. Lopatin rubbed and squeezed our shoulders, then glanced at Trifonov.

"I'm better now," Trifonov said, his voice weak and apologetic.

"Shit, you fucking scared us," Lopatin said.

"I don't know what happened," he said. "I was fine, and then I couldn't breathe. It never happened like that before."

"Fuck," Lopatin said. "I kind of assumed you bullshitted everybody about your asthma. To dodge the army."

"I didn't mean to scare anyone. I'm good. Let's eat."

"The potatoes are cold," I said. "Want me to reheat them?"

"Thanks," Trifonov said. "That'd be great."

"I need a cigarette," Milka said. "But obviously not here. If I crack the window in my bedroom and close the door, will the smoke bother you?"

"No. I don't think so," Trifonov said.

"I'll smoke with you," Lopatin said.

Milka nodded and scooped the pack from the table. She pointed at the ashtray next to the stove, and Lopatin grabbed it.

Silent, Trifonov and I remained at the table. We didn't drink any more, and we didn't eat, even though I reheated the potatoes and spooned some onto his plate. He forked them, but neglected to take a single bite. Minutes wavered, half an hour maybe, but Milka and Lopatin didn't return. The longer they stayed there, the quieter we became, our faces and bodies strained with concentration. There was a slight shuffle, like the raking of leaves, and I imagined hungry, anxious fingers, clothes being stripped off and tossed on the floor, Milka's silky tunic pooling at the foot of the bed, Lopatin's shirt, like a guard dog, lying beside it. And then there was a cadence, gentle yet prominent, a rhythmic pulsing. I imagined Milka's scrawny, lissome body, her arms and legs wrapped around Lopatin, her faint wet smell mingling with his strong musty one. A trickle of his sweat between her breasts. I imagined his long hard penis reaching inside her, inside all that darkness, the ripe mellow flesh, somewhere so far she moaned, and then again.

I exchanged glances with Trifonov, aware of my own awkward longing. I wanted to experience what Milka just had, but I lacked desire for Trifonov. Sensing my reservations, he rose and walked to the window, began fidgeting with a portable radio on the sill. It grew dark outside, the glass frosted around the edges, gusts of wind rattling the frame. The radio was on, but Trifonov kept switching the channels, shaking the plastic box, fumbling with the knob, bending the antenna, until amidst scrambled noise and rags of phrases, we could hear a broadcast in English.

"The enemy?" I asked, chewing on a slice of cucumber.

"Voice of America," Trifonov answered. "Do you ever listen to it?"

"No. What for? It's all lies anyway."

"Maybe," he said, and planted himself in Lopatin's chair. "Maybe not." He became quiet, the radio at his ear.

"I mean, not that it's going to change anything. So why—"

"Shhhh." Trifonov touched his finger to my lips. It wasn't an erotic gesture, but it made me warm inside. A sudden delicious prickling that climbed up my spine.

I chewed with as little noise as possible, plucking cucumbers from all the sandwiches, then potatoes from Trifonov's plate. They crunched between my teeth, and I covered my mouth with my hand, slow on my jaw movements. We sat like that for a while, Trifonov staring into the darkness pressing against the window and me stealing glances at his tense, burdened face. He wasn't unattractive, despite the long nose. He had a sadness to him and a tenderness most boys his age lacked. And a kind of bookish, outdated sense of honour. It wasn't an empty, vulgar façade as it was with Lopatin, but a sincere belief that one's life depended on one's honour, which had to be kept intact from early childhood. And even though I couldn't imagine Trifonov winning a street fight over a girl, I couldn't imagine him running away either.

"No, it can't be," Trifonov said, his mouth wide open.

"What?" I asked, startled by the sharpness in his voice. It felt like an icicle pressed to bare skin.

He waved me off.

"What is it?"

He set the radio down and muted it, his face pained with the news.

"You look as though you just buried your entire family," I said.

"Maybe worse."

"What could be worse?"

"Andropov died."

"No. Are you kidding?"

"What kind of a joke would that be?"

"A sad one."

"Yes, very." Trifonov rubbed his forehead, pushing his shaggy fringe up and to the other side. His hair refused to obey and stood up on his forehead in one defiant wave. "Shchelokov's wife did it, shot him in the back when he'd fired her husband and appointed a new Minister of Internal Affairs."

"But that happened, like, eight months ago or more! It could be a rumour," I said.

"It's true. They just confirmed it. Our press is going to claim that he was sick, I'm sure."

"Maybe she didn't do it. I mean, why would she be so stupid? Maybe someone set her up. Someone who wanted him gone."

"Could be. Ugh, it's hopeless, all of it. *Forever you, the unwashed Russia! / The land of slaves, the land of lords / And you, blue-uniformed ushers / And people who worship them as gods.*"

"Nice. Your love for Lermontov is profound," I said, standing up. "Let's inform Putova and Lopatin. While the country is mourning, they're happily screwing."

"Only the officials know, and us. It's a secret buried in snow." Trifonov faked a smile.

"Snow melts, Trifonov. There's hope," I said on my way out of the kitchen.

Before entering Milka's bedroom, I knocked and then turned the knob and pushed the door open, letting a finger of light crawl across the floor. In the whispery darkness of the room, my eyes isolated the bed and a tangle of bodies, still warm with sex. The air smelled of smoke and flesh, sweet musky tanginess.

"Wake up," I said. "Andropov just died."

11

When Konstantin Chernenko was appointed to rule our Socialist State, the feelings of fear and anxiety continued to rise among adults. My parents stopped arguing but gazed out of the windows, at the interminable rueful sky like a slab of grey ice frozen over the city. My father avoided speaking and chainsmoked on the balcony. For weeks, our flat was steeped in silence, except for the rhythmic muttering of my grandmother's sewing machine, the thudding of the foot pedal against the floor. She stitched and vamped pillowcases, sheets, and duvet covers, large pieces that didn't strain her eyes and demanded no attention to detail. Because she could barely see but refused to give up sewing, my parents made her promise that she would only do it when someone was home, to avoid accidents. My mother would help her replace threads or arrange the fabric, keeping her fingers away from the needle. She also started helping my grandmother take baths, trim her nails, and identify foods on her plate. Not that there was a startling variety, but it seemed that she forgot what they were. Midway through meals, she would ask for peculiar things, like candied sour *alycha,* hand-braided honeyed *kalachi,* or whole stuffed pike. She would recall their taste from the time when she was a young woman, dating my grandfather. She rejected red meat. Every now and then, she would reminisce about the old days, but it would always start with the foods she ate as a child and end with the war. If my mother served canned peas, for example, my grandmother would talk about her firstborn and how he loved to pick individual peas from a bowl and balance them on the tip of his tongue. Or how, when little, my mother would leave a teaspoon of food for him on her plate, long after he died.

When my grandmother talked, I couldn't help staring at her hands—brown, crooked, furrowed with veins, the skin as dry as corn husks. When she rubbed her hands together, they made a rustling sound, and I imagined flakes of skin shedding from her hands like dust. Inconspicuously, I would switch my eyes to my mother's hands—pink, wide, with protruding knuckles and chafed spots from doing all the cooking and laundry. And then I would look at mine, still silken, the texture of a tree without bark. At night, I would slather glycerin on my hands, slip them into old gloves, then lie in the darkness, hoping for the ointment to prevent my hands from ageing.

My father's suddenly sullen behaviour made my mother think that perhaps he was having an affair. When he barked back, calling her a dumb bitch, it disconcerted her because he'd never before called her such names. All their married life, he cursed heartily but never directed it at my mother. He never hit her either, but when she lectured him about tobacco and cancer and how she wouldn't be the one to spoon-feed him after treatments or wipe his weak, suffocating, post-surgery arse, he grew furious and just about kicked her. I was doing homework in the kitchen that afternoon, eating *salo* on a slice of black bread, and he was standing next to the balcony, and she was towering in front of him, hands on hips.

"You keep your feet and hands in check, Comrade Ranev," my mother said. "See this frying pan, it'll knock the living hell out of you." She secured her hand on the handle as she flipped the fish cakes.

My father lit a cigarette. He ingested a cloud of smoke, then took another drag and blew out. "For the first time in my life, I'm scared," he said, his voice hoarse, threadbare. "Scared for you, Liuba; scared for Anya. It really is the end of the era, of the world as we know it. What will come to replace that world is hard to tell, but many will perish in the process. Anya, Milka—poor girls. It's their generation, their boyfriends, who'll suffer most while trying to survive." And then he began to cry, which I'd never seen him do, except maybe while watching his favourite war movies, *Seventeen Moments of Spring* and *The Cranes Are Flying*.

My mother dropped the spatula in the sink and rushed to comfort him. My hand scribbled against the paper, but the letters formed into monstrous spiky clusters, like booby traps about to explode.

In the spring of our junior year, everyone had to take a military training course, called NVP, for Nachal'naya Voennaya Podgotovka. We were taught to use gas masks while performing simple tasks. We ran with heavy backpacks from one point to another and crawled on our bellies under a barbed-wire ceiling stretched low across the soccer field. We learned to provide medical aid, to treat burns and puncture wounds, bandage mangled body parts. Boys often pinched girls or nuzzled their cleavages while sitting on benches or kneeling on the ground, having their heads dressed in cotton and gauze. At some point, we were expected to clean and assemble a Kalashnikov, but no girl in our class, except for Milka, could master the meticulous routine. No other girl could hold a training gun in the right position either or hit a paper target—the silhouette of a man's head with a bull's-eye in place of a face. When I asked Milka how she could do it so well, hit the target from such a distance, she said, "Easy. I pretend it's my arsehole stepfather."

"That's horrible," I said.

"Tell it to my mother."

Most boys could shoot well, however, including Lopatin, who swaggered about the field, gun across shoulder. Trifonov, of course, was excused, so he either didn't come to school on those days or volunteered to help nurse the wounded or re- place the torn paper heads. He also argued with Lopatin about his attitude toward the training. "Put the gun down or hold it right," he'd say. "You could hurt someone."

"Fuck off, Trifonov. Learn to hold your dick first."

One day, after the training, Trifonov said, "If the Iron Cur- tain collapses, we'll be blinded by all the light."

"So, if we're blinded, all will become dark and hopeless again?" Milka joked.

"Or bright and glorious," Lopatin said.

"Nothing will ever be that way," Trifonov said. "Just think about it. You're a cripple, you have no legs. But only you and your relatives know it because you don't go outside. But if you

did, if you did let others see your disability, would your feelings change? Or would you feel even worse, being exposed to
the rest of the world? And it isn't like the world can grow you
new legs. All it can do is pity your crippled existence. Sometimes I think we're like Gogol's dead souls—we don't live,
only exist on paper. So, when we do die, no one will ever notice. No one will remember."

"That's terrible to think that way," Milka said. "And what if
the opposite is also true, if we discover that the world is a cripple and all that time we've been mistaken? That whoever is
there, behind the Iron Curtain, has no superpower, no special
purpose or destiny?"

"I personally think that if the Curtain falls and Americans
decide to conquer us, we'd surrender without so much as a
cry," Lopatin said.

"Speak for yourself, traitor," I said.

"You have no feelings of patriotism, Lopatin. How come?
Your folks are the Party people; they've been kowtowing their
way in and out of government offices since long before you
were born," Trifonov said. "You'd think they'd have taught
you to be the same."

"Fuck off, man. I'm my own person. I kowtow to no one.
I'm telling you—all will change. Not tomorrow, of course, not
even in a year. But soon. Were one of us to emigrate and return
in twenty years, he or she wouldn't recognize this country. It
would feel more foreign than the other one."

"I disagree," Milka said. "This could never feel foreign to
me, no matter how much it changes. I'd never feel the same

about any other country. It's in the fucking air, these birches and the road dirt. Everything. Sure, it may not be the best place, but it's the only country we'll love and hate at the same time. It's like loving and hating your mother; she may be a bitch, a filthy cunt who makes you do things, but she's also the one who fed you and bathed you and put dry mustard in your socks when you got sick. That's why we won the war, with our bare hands against Nazi tanks, wall on wall—'For Motherland! For Stalin!' the mantra was."

"He killed more people than he saved," I said. "Don't repeat that."

"No. We plan to announce it at the annual school ball," Lopatin said, guffawing, spurts of smoke shooting from his nostrils.

"Go ahead. Milka won't ever sleep with you again," I said.

"You won't, baby?" he asked, and scooped Milka under his wing. He rubbed his face in her hair, then gave her a quick peck before taking a drag.

"No." She took the cigarette from him and puffed lightly, then returned it. "Raneva is my best friend. I do what she says." Milka grinned, and I could see smoke curl under her tongue.

"I envy your friendship," Trifonov said. "I wish someone cared about me that way."

"It's love," I said.

"True love," Milka said.

"What I sense here is maybe group sex?" Lopatin asked.

"Fuck off, Lopatin," the three of us chimed. "Nasty."

"Suit yourselves," he said. "I thought I'd offer." He laughed his warrior laugh—loud, fierce, cracks of thunder in the afternoon sky.

Another important change took place that year: I lost my virginity to Trifonov. Milka had offered her flat while her parents were at work and she and Lopatin at Yashka's. He was waiting for his American visa to be approved, but everyone at school seemed to have forgotten him.

"Does he still have our letter to Reagan?" I asked Milka.

"Says he does. Says he'll mail it as soon as he leaves this hell."

"Maybe he should tear it up or burn it," I said. "It might get him—and *us*—into trouble if they search his suitcase."

"I don't think so. At this point they can't do shit to him other than delay his visa. His parents are no longer Russians but Americans, and sooner or later he'll be reunited with them."

"If someone doesn't die first," I said.

"Always a possibility."

It was the end of April, the air redolent of spring and hormones. Birds looped through clouds; trees stood swollen with buds. As children, Milka and I loved to touch them, to run our hands up and down their soft knobby limbs. Every year, we waited for trees to do that, to weave new life out of the dull, naked wood, and every year we seemed to miss it, the very moment when the buds burst open, exposing their tender green bellies.

"I want proof when I come back," Milka said before giving

me the keys to her flat. "Bloody sheets and all, like during the old times when mothers-in-law hung them in their yards for all the neighbours to see."

"I'm bringing my own sheets, and you aren't allowed to touch them. What about his asthma?"

"He seems all right. Although spring can be hard. Keep his inhaler under the pillow, next to the condom. Here." She passed me a shiny golden packet. "Compliments of Yashka."

"You told him?"

"No. Of course not. Lopatin buys them from him. So I took one for you."

"Thanks. I thought of getting one in a pharmacy."

"Ugh, the Soviet rubber is as fat as dough. Like sticking a pierog up your pussy." She laughed, then patted me on the shoulder. "It'll be fine. Don't think about it too much."

"I don't know. I really feel like I should wait."

"How long? Until college or until you marry? Are you saving it for your future mother-in-law?"

"No. But Trifonov and I aren't in love. He says we're better than that. And shouldn't it be about love the first time?"

Milka's face dulled for a moment; her upper lip twitched. "It's no big deal. Your first time. You need to get over the pain, heal, and enjoy the real thing when it comes. Besides, think about Trifonov. Who else will fuck him if not you?" She lit a cigarette and passed it to me, then fingered another one out of the pack.

"That doesn't really make me feel any better," I said, channelling smoke through my nostrils.

"It should. It's charity, and charity always feels good. It's selfish as much as it's unselfish. If you don't give it to him, chances are he'll die a virgin. And what if you don't meet that one-and-only for ten more years? Your pussy will rot from grief." She attempted to laugh but choked on smoke, coughing.

"See? You're being punished for saying such terrible things."

Milka continued to cough and gag, and I hit her on the back several times. When she finally stopped, she flicked her cigarette into the trees, then rubbed her hand against the nearest trunk of a maple, thick and grooved, pressing her face into the bark.

"Smells like books," she said. "All the books I haven't read."

When Trifonov arrived at Milka's flat that afternoon, he did his awkward best not to sound or look nervous. I asked if he was hungry and suggested sharing a roast chicken leg—the last of Milka's supper she'd so graciously offered to us. But Trifonov declined. He hung his coat on the rack, took off his shoes, and aligned them next to mine facing the wall. He swept away his fringe and tried to press out the wrinkles on his clothes. He wore his navy school trousers and a denim shirt I hadn't seen before. His fine just-washed hair spilled again over his face, adding guilt or shame to his expression.

From his coat pocket, he produced a small jar of cherry jam.

"I picked the pits out myself," he said.

When I twisted off the lid, the hallway filled with summer, the smell of ripe sweet fruit.

"Thanks," I said, and swirled my finger into the thick dark-red preserve. I brought it out for Trifonov to try, and he licked it off with pleasure.

"Now you," he said, and scooped a bit of jam on his finger. I hesitated but closed my eyes and sucked the fruit off as quickly as I could. It was delicious. Fitting the lid back on the jar, I asked Trifonov to wait in the hallway while I undressed in Milka's bedroom, and he obeyed without a sound, all the time staring at my shoulder.

The curtains had already been drawn; I tossed my clothes on the floor and slipped under the blanket, shivering. I'd forgotten to bring my sheets, and Milka's smelled of her apple-scented shampoo and cigarettes. I thought about her hiding somewhere under the bed and whispering instructions to me as she did during tests. My body tensed; my cheeks flushed, not from shame or heat but the proximity of sex. There was a shy knock on the door, and when Trifonov entered the room, he was already naked, his body as white as a birch trunk, arms wrapped around a pile of clothes.

"May I?" he asked, before dropping the clothes on the floor and getting under the covers.

I nodded, but couldn't say anything. My throat tightened, my heart—a wild beating thing.

I forgot about his inhaler when he began to kiss me, suddenly, daringly. His hands were cool and unexpectedly strong, like those of a pianist toughened by hours and hours of practice. A current of pleasure rolled through my body, from my mouth to the soles of my feet, a delicious warmth low in my stomach and between my legs. He caressed me with such knowledge and abandon, my skin seemed to mellow away under his stroking fingers. I passed him the condom and closed my eyes, lost in the fog of desire so pure, so strong, I couldn't feel Trifonov but a sea of molecules, infinitesimal atoms, shifting and merging, building new patterns. He was thin, with his ribs fanning out on each side of his body, but in my imagination, he was muscular and square in the chest, a trunk of a man. I reached to touch his penis, which seemed disproportionately large, a healthy curving tree limb, but he gently moved my hand to his hip, his lips grazing my nipple. When he pushed through me, he caught my moan, my pain, with his mouth and continued to kiss me, one hand underneath my head, the other supporting my raised buttocks. He held tight for a moment, a tremor of muscles, a shape of one body enfolded within the other, and then let go.

Afterwards, we lay in silence, watching the fish in Milka's aquarium. A few hid under the rocks; others feasted on the tiny growth on the walls—you could see their slimy lips pecking at the glass. It was still daylight outside, and the waning sun slipped through the narrow opening between the curtains and made its lazy farewell arch across the bed.

Trifonov touched my arm. "Are you hurting?" he asked, a shy tenderness in his voice.

"Not bad. More unpleasant than painful."

"I'm sorry. I tried to be gentle, as gentle as I could."

"You were," I said, pausing. "I'm not your first, am I?"

"Does it matter?"

"No. I was just surprised. All the fancy moves."

"Oh, that . . . I recently procured a book—*Modern Sex Techniques* by Robert Street. Lots of useful information there."

"Can I read it too?"

"Sure. We can even read it together and try things the next

time we meet. Maybe my place, when my mother works late shifts."

"Has she always worked late shifts?"

"No. Not when my dad was alive. We had more money."

"How did he die?"

"Appendicitis. They couldn't save him. I was seven." His voice trembled, however slightly.

I nuzzled his shoulder, and he lifted his arm for me to scoot under, my cheek on his chest. I trailed it with my finger, all the imaginary muscles Trifonov didn't have. I blew at the few golden curly hairs around his pale nipples.

Trifonov took my hand in his and studied it for a long minute.

"What do you see?" I asked.

"That we'll live happily ever after and age on the same pillow." He placed my hand on his eyes.

"Really?"

"No. Your life will be filled with adventure, and you'll outlive me by fifty years. It'll be lonely too," he added, gurgling with laughter.

"You're such a bullshitter, Trifonov," I said, and jerked my hand away.

"I am indeed. But only half as bad as Lopatin. What Milka finds in him, I'll never know."

"He's strong and handsome. Every girl wants to sleep with him."

"He's dumb. And she's smart, although uninhibited. Fragile too."

"Milka isn't fragile. She's as tough as they come."

He turned to look at me, then cupped my face, kissed me on the nose. "You're the one who's tough," he said. "Capable of enduring great pain."

"I don't like pain."

"Those who don't suffer don't rejoice." He was kissing me again, covering my face with soft, warm smooches. His hands were running through my hair, and it reminded me of the wind brushing through apple branches, through new silky leaves.

12

Soon it was May, and our class was scheduled to take an eight-day trip to the Black Sea. It was an educational tour of the Crimea region, and, needless to say, we embraced the opportunity to escape the city, as well as expand our knowledge of the country's historic past. On the train, the four of us occupied an entire *kupe,* with two bunk beds on top and two on the bottom, separated by a tiny square table in front of the window.

"I personally want to see the Swallow's Nest," Milka said. "It's right on the edge of a cliff overlooking the Black Sea. How did they build something like that back then?"

"The original structure was called the Castle of Love," I said. "It was built by some general as a gift to his beloved, whom he captured at war—the Russian–Turkish, I think. He married her too."

"What a nice way to start a family," Lopatin said.

"Didn't the woman disappear soon after?" Trifonov asked.

"Yes, but it's a legend—no proof of anything," I said.

"Did she run away or kill herself? Jump from the window straight into the sea? Would've been easy." Lopatin grimaced; he pinched his cheeks and stretched them to the sides, folded his lips.

"You're such a clown, Lopatin," Trifonov said.

"And you're such a bore, Trifonov. All you want to see is Chekhov's dacha. Where are those pages that your great-uncle stole from Chekhov?"

"My great-uncle stole nothing. Chekhov treated his daughter, who later died from consumption. Chekhov himself died a year after."

"Liar."

"Am not."

"Then show us the pages?" Lopatin asked.

"No."

"You don't have them."

"Shut up."

"Hey, did you know that they brought Chekhov's body back from Germany on a train, and to preserve it better—it was July—they put him in one of the cars used to transport oysters? He stank like crazy," Milka said.

Our faces wrinkled in disgust and also in disbelief that such a foul fate could have befallen our great writer.

For a while, we didn't speak but stared out of the window, embracing the familiar Soviet countryside, birch and pine forests, farmers' fields, creeks and rivers flowing somewhere far, as far as Siberia. The sky resembled a watercolour drawn by an amateur hand: shy, uneven pinks in a pool of dusky blue. Birds swept through the air, dogs chasing after them. Here and there, huts squatted behind crippled fences, pillars of smoke rose from chimneys. Trapped behind tall skinny trees, the sun flashed its gilded face as though on sped-up film. It seemed that we were travelling back in time, to czarist Russia, to dirt roads

and horse-drawn ploughs, pitchforks and scythes, squeaking
wooden drays covered with hay, unwashed bearded peasants,
and the misery of serfdom. All looked peaceful, ungroomed
for centuries, somehow nostalgic and dear. I wondered how a
country so big, so mighty and rich, could be so humble and
poor. And why, despite all that suffering and deprivation, we
felt so proud, protective of our motherland, and not just of its
history, the grandiosity of its art and culture, but of those
scrawny birches, those forlorn, weed-choked fields and harrowed farms. Like kids who loved and pitied their ill, disabled
parents, so did we love and pity our country; we worried for it,
and we revered it, and we wished desperately for it to get well.

The train chugged along the tracks, the sway and rattle of
cars, and we began to excavate the meagre supplies of food our
parents had packed. We found half a roast chicken, four hard-
boiled eggs, a heel of black bread, a tuft of green onions, pickles, sliced sausages, a square of Yantar processed cheese, and a
bag of boiled potatoes still warm and unpeeled. Lopatin had
also brought beer and a can of sprats. He passed them to Milka,
saying, "That's all I could buy you. Some give castles, others
fish."

She chuckled and kissed him on the lips, and then Trifonov
produced a whole Slava chocolate and held it on his palm before laying it on my lap.

"My favourite. It's spongy inside," Milka said. "Nearly ex-
tinct now."

"I know," he said. "I love it too."

"We'll share," I said.

"Indeed," Lopatin confirmed, and began pouring beer into

tea glasses ensconced in ornate tin sleeves. "Drink quickly before the teachers find out."

"Nothing for me." Trifonov held his hand over his glass.

"Agreed. We don't want to have to stop the train to resuscitate your suffocating arse."

Both Milka and Lopatin laughed, but Trifonov shrugged and turned to face the window.

The sun had almost set, the sky thickened except for a finger of red still lingering, like a warning. I rubbed Trifonov's shoulders, nuzzled his warm neck. Despite his feeble, pale looks, there was courage in his expression and a kind of eternal destitution Lopatin sarcastically compared to that of crucified Jesus. But the truth was, we often felt insecure next to Trifonov, our posture, our thoughts insignificant, diminished by the wisdom he soaked up from all those books, including the Bible. As teenagers, we didn't believe in God, nor did we disbelieve. We allowed for the existence of a mysterious light shining into the darkness of our socialist universe, but it was up to man to stifle or sustain it. We didn't believe in reincarnation, and we didn't care about life after life, because we assumed it would be the same unfortunate circumstances. All things began sometime somewhere, and all things ended, although many of those things had been ended for us. We were aware of that. We knew we had a fate, a destiny, designated by the Communist Party, and it was as irrevocable as the stars or the moon, as life itself.

In Crimea, we were fortunate to stay at Artek, the same Pioneer camp where Samantha Smith had spent a week the summer before. An avenue of trees had been planted in her honour, and there was a plaque with her name on one of the dormitories, but we didn't sleep in that building, because it had been renovated just for her and was reserved for more important guests. Soon the camp would open for the summer season, but until then, the administration used the place as a hostel for schools that visited the region.

The following days were filled with sun, wind, and salty humid air—pre-summer balm. When we left Moscow, we wore light jackets and thick-soled shoes, but in Gurzuf and Yalta people had already undressed down to their flip-flops and shorts and put on straw hats as large and yellow as sunflowers. Our skin glowed; we felt weightless, transparent, far away from the concrete vaults of our flats and the steel drum of the city. Here, amidst the mountains and tall narrow cypress trees, life seemed to slow down, pause, and thicken as though in a dream. We rode tour buses and tramped after our teachers in a kind of melting delirium. Our eyelids fluttered, our speech slurred, and our faces tingled from the breeze. The light was dense with gold, as if flowing from some hidden well, dazzling us into weary oblivion. Clouds like diaphanous scarves floated across the blue sky, brushing the mountains: Ai-Petri, with its brilliant-white limestone peak and jagged teeth, and also Ayu-Dag; it resembled a bear sprawled on its belly and drinking from the sea. The water had deepened its colour, luminous where the sun brushed against its surface. It looked like a slab of malachite from which the wind carved out seahorses, octopuses, dolphins, and other creatures.

We had a private tour of the Livadia Palace, the summer residence of the last Russian czar. After the Revolution, the palace had served as a tuberculosis sanatorium for peasants, and later it became a dacha for state officials. It was also here that the Yalta Conference took place in 1945, where Roosevelt, Churchill, and Stalin determined the fate of Nazi Germany and postwar Europe. As we moved from one gaudy room to another, surrounded by the original décor—Carrara marble columns, handwoven oriental rugs, and mahogany-panelled walls—Lopatin kept saying, "This is where the great leaders slept, ate, and shat while cutting the world in pieces. What power! Can you fucking believe that?" He wore new sunglasses he'd traded with Yashka for a small can of red caviar, but Milka pulled them off and slid them on her face as soon as we arrived at the Swallow's Nest.

The place had been completely rebuilt in 1912 by an oil magnate, Baron von Steingel, and bore no resemblance to its original wooden structure. Perched on top of the high Aurora Cliff and overlooking the Cape of Ai-Todor, the grey stone neo-Gothic construction indeed resembled a swallow's nest tipping over the abyss. It was a miniature two-storey castle, only twelve metres high, with the main foyer and three bedrooms and a stairway climbing to the top of the tower. An architectural marvel, it appeared delicate and airy, but at the same time sturdy and solid. However, as we'd approached it by boat, we did notice a large cleft in the rock, where a significant part of the cliff had separated and threatened to collapse into the sea and where they had reinforced the walls with steel trusses and grappling hooks. It was a frightening sight and many refused to climb the castle steps or even walk up to the front.

On the last day of our trip, we visited Chekhov's dacha, a two-storey grey rock house, overgrown with vines. As tall and impressive as it appeared on the outside, it was rather small and modest on the inside. After the writer's death in 1904, his sister, Maria, had ensured that the interior of the house and the beautiful garden, including a few cherry trees, were preserved exactly as they were during Chekhov's lifetime. She opened the White Dacha as a museum after the Revolution, defending it during the Civil War and later from Nazi occupiers. It was there that Chekhov wrote *Three Sisters* and *The Cherry Orchard*, as well as "The Lady with a Dog". Most of us considered his writing somewhat dull and outdated. Try as we might, we couldn't compare the fragile buckram world of Chekhov to the hit-and-run of ours. The misery was there, the poverty and gloom, but the characters spoke and moved about the world in a manner so stiff and distant we felt disconnected from our cultural heritage, our imperial roots of monarchs or peasants, dirty, starved, uneducated.

"But they're immortal, don't you see?" Trifonov asked.

"To me, they never lived," I answered.

"All the rich did was eat and party. And all the poor did was drink and shovel," Lopatin said, nodding.

"But isn't it how things are today?" Milka asked.

"No. Today we're all the same, all educated and poor," I said.

"But we aren't," Trifonov said. "Lopatin eats caviar, while I eat black bread."

"I eat black bread too," Lopatin said. "I love it."

"The peasant in you," Milka said.

"At least I don't whine like Trifonov. Or like Chekhov's characters. What would be the point? Can't change it." Lopatin shrugged and walked away, slouching, hands in pockets.

The house tour was rather monotonous and unimpressive, even further diminishing our interest in the writer's work. Only Trifonov seemed riveted while navigating the rooms that still held the original nineteenth-century furnishings. He swerved between three-legged claw-footed corner chairs and narrow velour daybeds, heavy bookshelves and petite coffee tables, a gleaming mahogany cupboard and a round dinner table draped with a white tablecloth and set with dusty crystal goblets.

For a long moment, Trifonov stood in front of a dark wooden coatrack in the corner of the foyer, eyeing the writer's black cape and hat. At the foot of the rack sat a valise of weathered leather, a display of primitive medical tools on the side table: a thermometer, a stethoscope, a tongue depressor, an otoscope, an ophthalmoscope, and a percussion hammer. In a shallow metal dish, we spotted finger-long glass tubes like a growth of icicles.

"He used those to suck out phlegm from a sick boy's throat," Trifonov mumbled in my ear. "Remember the story? That's how he got tuberculosis."

"I haven't read it," I confessed. "Sounds awful."

We both studied the pictures on the wall that showed Chekhov's evolution from a chubby little boy, to a bored gymnasium pupil, to a young, wistful doctor in country clothes with a bale of dark hair and a thick soft beard. In one picture, the writer appeared thinner, with deep wrinkles and snowy patches in his hair. He squinted at the camera, looking haggard and distrustful. One would never guess him to be only forty-four, half a year before his death. Neither could you guess that the man was a lascivious egocentric, a regular Russian Don Juan.

As we stepped into Chekhov's office, Trifonov grew excited approaching a rather small cluttered desk. There, among books and envelopes, we discovered the writer's pince-nez and magnifying glass, a tarnished silver letter opener with an engraved handle, a matching quill and a silver-lipped glass inkwell, the last three given to Chekhov by his long-term lover, Lika Mizinova. Letters were stacked in a glass case against the wall. Ninety-seven from her and sixty-seven from him. Above the case hung a photograph of Mizinova and Chekhov, taken in 1897, at the end of their relationship, right before Lika moved permanently to Paris. In the photograph, she leans toward him, but Chekhov appears canted away from her, almost recoiling, his eyes elsewhere, legs crossed with his hands clasped tightly over his knees. His face is hard and unyielding.

"She wanted him to marry her," Trifonov said. "But he didn't want to commit."

"Not much has changed since Chekhov's times," Milka said; she and Lopatin had caught up with us and now loitered in front of the glass case.

"He married Olga Knipper," I said.

"Almost at the end of his life," Trifonov said. "He also wrote to his brother that things should never change for him. That his wife should be like the moon in the night sky— sometimes there, sometimes not."

"A typical male," Milka said. "What's hard to believe,

though, is that he wrote Mizinova all those fancy love letters. *It seems that I overlooked you, dear Lika, as I did my bacillus.*"

"He was a writer. That's how he got a hard-on—using fancy words. Someone mentioned he had visited brothels since he was a teenager. His parents left him in Taganrog to look after their stuff and his younger brother," Lopatin said, a curl of a smirk at the corners of his mouth. "What I want to know is where the brother was when Chekhov screwed prostitutes. Did he take him along, telling him to close his eyes?"

"All you can think about is sex in its dirtiest forms. That's what you live for," Trifonov said.

"At least I live," Lopatin said. "Unlike some people, who need a whole lot of petting and sucking." He was now scowling, and Milka put a hand across his mouth.

"Shut up," she said. "You're ruining everything. We all have our wicked sides. And even if Chekhov visited brothels, he's still Chekhov. He's allowed to be horny and free. Perhaps that's why he could write so well."

"Speaking of which," Trifonov said, his face blushing with excitement. The lower lip folded under his upper one as he dug in his jacket. "I have something to show you." He searched his pockets, his hands trembling, diving in and out. "Where the hell is it?"

"What?" I asked.

"The pages. From *The Cherry Orchard*. I brought them. I put the envelope in my jacket before we left Moscow."

"Maybe you put it in a different jacket," I said.

"No. I only have one jacket. They should be right here."

His hand thudded at his chest. "I haven't taken the jacket off unless to sleep."

"We noticed," Lopatin said. "When most people are wearing T-shirts, you're still bundled inside a winter jacket."

"I feel cold, I can't help it."

"Maybe they fell out when you dressed this morning. Maybe they're still in the room," Milka said, her hand on Trifonov's back, rubbing gently.

His shoulders jerked. "No. I would've noticed."

"Maybe they're on the bus," I said. "I remember you took your jacket off for a short while. Don't get upset yet."

"My mother will kill me if I don't bring them back."

"You sure you had them?" Lopatin asked.

"What do you mean?" Trifonov stared at him with the kind of helpless look of a puppy who'd been caught chasing its tail.

"I mean maybe you're lying. Maybe you just want to impress the girls by pretending that you had an important historical document."

"Shut up, Lopatin. I hate your stupid jokes and ugly peasant manners." Trifonov turned around and began walking away, shoulders limp, arms swaying like broken tree limbs. I could also see that he was reaching inside his trousers for an inhaler.

"You can be such a fucking jerk, Lopatin," Milka said. "Why do you have to hurt people?"

He stood tall, brazen-faced, chest out, his expression a blend of absolute permissiveness and cocky assuredness.

"Fuck you," I finally said. "Arsehole. Don't talk to me again. Ever."

"Sorry," he said. "Sorry, it was a joke. Why is everyone so serious all of a sudden?"

"Some things aren't funny," I said. "And if you don't know the difference, chances are you won't learn. Get a dog, Lopatin, and abuse the shit out of it. Maybe it'll let you. And maybe it'll still love you."

13

We were just falling asleep on our last night in Crimea when we heard a puny scratch on the window, next to our heads. Milka sat up in bed, rubbing sleep out of her eyes, while I squinted, trying to make out the source of the noise. There were four more girls with us in the room, but they didn't wake up, still snoring, with blankets pulled over their heads. Milka fussed with her hair that stuck to her cheeks and forehead. Mine was still in a ponytail I had forgotten to pull loose before going to bed. We wore wrinkled terry shorts and old, stained, oversized T-shirts that slid off our shoulders to one side.

The noise became louder, and when I touched the dark window, I could almost feel someone's fingers beating a rhythm on the outside. I gave the window a few soft knocks, and a moment later they came back, followed by a rapid drumming.

"If it's Lopatin, I'm going to be pissed off," Milka said, dragging her feet off the bed.

"I'll walk with you." I stepped into my shoes and draped a flimsy blanket over my shoulders, following Milka into the hallway.

When we poked our heads through the building's front

door, we saw Lopatin and Trifonov, who jumped back, startled, and Lopatin dropped a plastic bag on the ground. It made a ringing noise when it first hit his foot and then a rock. Both boys wore sweatpants stretched at the knees and shirts that had been washed to death. Trifonov also had his jacket on, which hung loose and floppy and made him look like a beggar.

"Fuck," Lopatin said. "Probably broke." He bent to pick up the bag but was delighted to discover its contents intact.

"What are you doing?" I asked. "I told you we didn't want to speak to you again."

"Don't be mad. I apologized, and Trifonov here forgave me. Right, buddy?" He turned his pleading eyes to Trifonov, who nodded, clutching the sides of his jacket.

"Well, I don't forgive you. I hate the way you talk to us, boss us around," I said. "Milka too."

"True," she said.

"It's our last night. Let's be romantic. I procured wine and cherries from the janitor. Fresh cherries. Cool, right? Let's go to the beach. Party a bit. Fuck a bit. Look at the stars. Can't pass up such an opportunity. How many more trips before we graduate and split? None. Zero." He made an O with his thumb and forefinger, bringing it to his right eye like a monocle. He closed his other eye and studied us through the hole.

Milka and I exchanged glances. We had to admit that Lopatin was making sense and that we were both surprised and charmed by his spontaneous behaviour, his dishevelled, apologetic looks. We decided not to go back inside for swimsuits so as not to wake up the other girls. Still wrapped in our blankets, we trudged after the boys, who took us behind the cafeteria and down a set of countless cracked steps, all the way to the sea. We had no torches, so Lopatin kept clicking on his lighter to lead the way, and Trifonov offered his hands to me and Milka.

The night was warm, quiet, the stars as fat as marshmallows. The moon cast ripples of silver light on the water. Shadows of mountains in the distance. The deserted beach was rocky, with two stone piers like arms reaching into the water, toward the heart of the sea. Tufts of algae lay scattered underfoot, wet and slimy. The smell of fish rose in the air. We found broken shells swept between pebbles, pieces of bottle glass smooth as skin.

Waves rolled ashore, lapping at rocks and our feet. We sat on one of the blankets and passed the wine bottle around, and even Trifonov ventured to take a few sips. Milka and I scooped cherries out of the bag, popping them into our mouths, then spitting the pits into the water, which was like oil—black, slippery, pungent. The sea itself was a live body that responded to our touch and presence. It sensed our proximity and our warmth, our desires, the urge of young flesh impatient against its wet lip. When we spoke in whispers, it too turned to murmur, but when we raised our voices, the waves lumbered up and nose-dived into the pebbles.

"Solaris," Milka said. "It studies us, our subconscious, then regurgitates it all back."

"I love that book," Trifonov noted.

"What's it about?" I asked.

"A scientist is sent to a space station orbiting a distant planet in order to discover what's caused other astronauts on board to go crazy. They all claim that Solaris's ocean is a living thing, that it reads their minds and knows their desires and gives back what they lost, including people."

"How can it do that?" Lopatin asked.

"It's sci-fi, anything is possible," Milka answered.

"So, does the guy help them?" I asked.

"No," Milka said. "Because his girlfriend killed herself, and he blames himself for it, and the ocean knows it and gives her back to him. I mean a version of her. He tries to fight it, to dispose of her, but she just keeps coming back, the ocean keeps re-creating her. But then she sort of starts remembering things, becoming more and more alive. It's very weird."

"How can you like such books?" Lopatin asked.

"How can you not? When you're stuck in a crappy flat, eating sausages all day long?"

"Look at this sky," Trifonov said. "See how bright that one star is? Right above us? That's where we're going. Ahead, toward the stars."

"Right," Lopatin said. "When I'm dead."

"Hey, did you find those pages?" I asked Trifonov.

"No. We looked everywhere."

"We did," Lopatin confirmed. "On hands and knees. The damn thing evaporated."

"It probably fell out on the train," Milka said. "Sorry. I know you're upset. We can try and make a copy. I'm good at forging handwriting." She forced out a helpless smile.

"No. We can't age paper and ink by eighty years."

"I know. I was just trying to make you feel better."

"Let's go swimming," Trifonov said.

"None for you, my boy," Lopatin answered. "We wouldn't be able to help you there. Besides, someone should watch our stuff."

"We have no stuff. And nobody is here. I'll be fine. I swim every week."

"It's true," I said. "At AZLK. They have a new pool. Huge."

"Pools are safe, wilderness isn't," Lopatin said.

"I haven't had an episode in months. My mother took me to some old woman, a manual healer, and I'm feeling much, much better."

"You went to a witch doctor?" Lopatin asked. "What did she do? Put you to sleep and then touch your body with her gnarly little hands? Did she touch your balls? Did you get aroused?"

"Shut up," Trifonov said.

"Woooo, you're feeling better, much better now." Lopatin circled his hands in the air in front of Trifonov's face. "When you wake up, your asthma will disappear. You'll be cured, cured, cured."

"Shut up, Lopatin. It was nothing like that. She brewed some herbs, which were bitter as hell. She also showed me a few points on my body I should apply pressure to."

"Medieval," Lopatin said.

"Perhaps. But it works. I don't get short of breath as much as I used to. I can do many more things now, maybe even play sports next year."

"Still, you aren't swimming, not where it's deeper than

your chin." Lopatin took a long swig from the bottle, then finished it. "I don't want to be responsible for no—"

"Careful," Milka warned.

"For no one," he continued. "That's all I'm saying." He rolled the bottle away with his foot, and it gritted against the pebbles. Lighting a cigarette, he leaned toward Milka, tugged at her ear with his lips. "Right, girl? You want to go on that pier?" She pulled the cigarette from his mouth and took a puff, and several more.

They were gone for some time, and all we could see of them was a hump of pale naked flesh that quivered and changed shapes on the rocks. When Trifonov placed his hands between my legs, I didn't stop him either, nor did I stop him when he pulled my terry shorts gently to the side and slipped his fingers in and out of me. He eased me on the blanket and heaped his clothes under my head. I was wet and soft, dissolving, as he advanced with his lips, his tongue, his penis. I wrapped my legs around him, the soles of my feet tracing his behind. The sky swayed above, the moon full, lazy, lolling among the stars. He lifted and held me with force and tenderness against his chest. His arms were strong, enveloping, shutting off the darkness and the cold. We lay like that for a while, rocking slightly, until we heard someone's feet crunch the pebbles next to our heads.

"We're swimming," Milka whispered, and tapped my shoulder with her finger.

"Wait for me," I said, still shielded by Trifonov.

"Hurry," she said, then ran into the waves.

Lopatin was already there, splashing her in the face. We

rose on our elbows and watched her straddle him, her back to us, his hands at her waist.

"They're naked," I said.

"Yep," Trifonov said. "So are we." He stood up, his penis soft, swinging between his legs in the nest of light brown hair. His hand thrust at me and I grabbed it, and he pulled me up.

The salty water prickled our flesh. Waves slapped us in the face, grains of sand and fine-ground shells coating our bodies. We could still feel the bottom paved with large slippery rocks. Milka was shorter, so she stood on her toes and Lopatin had to lift her every now and then on his hip like a child. She giggled and looked up at the carpet of stars suspended so low you could touch them. She screamed at the top of her lungs, "Hey!" The echo of her voice carried over the water—"Hey! Hey! Hey!"

We all took turns yelling into the universe. We held hands in a circle, jumped up and down, splashing, unashamed of our nakedness, the differences in our bodies, or the funny gurgle of sounds they produced. Our hair gathered in clumps on our lips and cheeks and made us look like mad people. We whirled in one direction, and then in the other, along the current and against it. Guffawing, Lopatin and Trifonov jumped up and touched chests, and so did Milka and I.

"What was that game we played as children?" Milka asked. "Something about the sea rolling."

"The sea rolls once, the sea rolls twice, the sea rolls thrice," I said.

"On the third time, we all must halt and impersonate a sea creature, real or mythic."

"Let's do it," Lopatin said. "The sea rolls once, the sea rolls twice, the sea rolls yet again. Freeze, everyone." He assumed the pose of a giant, arms lifted and strained, the outline of his tough muscles covered in droplets. His head was tipped high, signalling his superiority, while he tried hard not to laugh.

Bent in two, Trifonov had his arms swaying about the water like many tentacles. We could see the curve of his spine and his protruding ears. The rest of his body seemed motionless. I was submerged underwater, all but my head that darted back and forth, back and forth. Milka, on the other hand, was halfway out, her breasts like two cold birds perched on her chest. The long, dark nipples pointed at us. Her belly button was visible, but nothing below that. Her skinny arms dribbled in the water and gave the impression of hair.

"You're a mermaid," I said to her.

"Lopatin is Neptune," Milka answered.

"Trifonov is an octopus," Lopatin said.

They kept looking at me while I continued to jerk my head and tread underwater.

"We give up," Trifonov said.

"A tadpole. A fucking tadpole."

"There're no tadpoles in the sea, only in the river," Lopatin said.

"Sure there are," I said.

"Nope, don't think so."

"Doesn't matter. I won," I said.

"To that rock," Trifonov said, and pointed ahead, where a chunk of a cliff towered in the distance. It had a flat top, eaten away over time or perhaps lopped off during a storm. Before anyone could protest, Trifonov was rising above the water and diving back in, his thin nimble body arched, his arms rotating like the sails of a windmill.

We all followed, of course, and he waited, floating on his back, resting, the sea colder and shinier. The cliff wasn't too far away, and we made it there without much effort; we climbed on it, slipping a few times, scraping our legs on barnacles and shells, but otherwise the surface of the rock was soft and mossy; it tickled our feet when we stood up.

The waves heaved and smashed against the sides, spitting foam, an occasional pebble. Naked, the four of us faced the darkness, the terrifying infinity of water and night sky.

"It's like the end of the world," Trifonov said, exhaling. "Isn't it?"

We didn't comment, but continued to stand, shivering, our tongues, our hearts, numb with cold and fear. Far in the distance lay the countries we might never visit. Back behind us was the land we could never leave.

14

As a protest against the Soviet invasion of Afghanistan, America had boycotted the 1980 Moscow Summer Olympics. In response to that, the USSR and fourteen European countries refused to participate in the 1984 Summer Olympics, held in Los Angeles. Many Soviet citizens, including my mother, voiced an open dissatisfaction with our government's decision. She said that everything our government had done in the past forty years, it had done to outsmart or punish Americans, but in reality, it was punishing us. We were the ones who suffered most from turning our backs on the world.

At first my father listened to her without any enthusiasm, used to her expostulations on all themes political, but when she mentioned Afghanistan again and how many soldiers had died there, fighting for other people's land—the casualties had been enormous—he bent over and squeezed her shoulder. She remained very still, and all I could hear was her heavy breathing. I knew that it caused her a great effort not to slap him or jerk his hand off her shoulder. Her face seemed to have aged in just minutes. Fear lived in it, years of struggle and hunger, not the kind of hunger that she'd experienced during the Blockade— she couldn't remember that—but hunger for the discovery of new things, new places, new desires; hunger for freedom to choose, to go, to be. I'd begun to develop it too. But my hunger was a life younger; it was brave, defiant, prompting, while hers was tired and irritable. Hers told her: If you forget about eating, you won't be needing any food. Mine: You must fight for every morsel, every damn piece of food that comes or doesn't come your way.

Both my parents continued to work hard, harder than they ever had, and things continued to disappear, and prices continued to rise. There were rumours that the country didn't have any money left to pay pensions and salaries, which was impossible to comprehend. I tried to imagine empty vaults, where they used to keep gold bricks stacked in neat pyramids, or hollow safes that once overflowed with royal jewels and ancient coins, or vacant windowless rooms where new money was printed and that still smelled of ink and paper. My parents took what little savings they had from the bank and kept everything at home, under shaky detached parquet boards. They would lose it all in the early nineties, due to a money exchange reform. But back in the summer of 1984, my father placed a rug over the floorboards and then an armchair, in which he sat and watched TV, although he often hesitated to turn on the volume, fearing the news: each day another government official was fired, another policy implemented. He sagged in the chair after work and didn't get up until my mother called him for dinner. In the darkness, his tired shapeless silhouette was barely visible, like a shadow.

It was sad to see him like that, taking no interest in my mother or grandmother or even me. He began to drink more too, stopping at beer stalls after work and slipping vodka into his mug, and at some point, my mother had to threaten him with divorce if he didn't sober up and take charge of his life.

"What life?" he asked. "What are you talking about, Liuba? It's gone. All is gone. They ruined it. They killed the spirit. The dream. The next generation will grow up without knowing what it means to be Russian."

"Can you change that?" my mother asked. "No. So stop feeling sorry for something you can't control. Anya needs her father. She doesn't talk to us. Hangs out with those two boys, Trifonov and Lopatin. I fear early pregnancy."

"Fear none," I yelled from my room. "Milka and I won't have children but will elope to Paris or Rome."

"Hear that? No children. Paris. Rome. That *is* something to worry about."

In the following weeks, my father couldn't sleep, and I would hear him shuffle about the flat all night long, stepping out on the balcony to smoke. We lived on the fifth floor, but it never occurred to me that he might have been contemplating suicide until my mother slapped him in the face one evening after he'd admitted it. I'd always remember that—her angry, cold eyes confronting his helpless, weary ones; the sound of her hand coming in brief contact with his cheek. The surprise on his face, the sudden agony, as though being dipped in a tub of ice. After that, they didn't speak for a while, but his sleepless wandering had ceased too. At meals, he would listen to her talk about the lines in supermarkets, or how she might have to start selling what she'd canned last summer, to be able to afford meat, assuming the rest of Moscow's population didn't have the same idea, or how we might quit eating meat and become vegetarians, which was supposed to be healthier anyway. My father wouldn't comment, but would cut his food into tiny pieces, just as he did for my grandmother, feeling no need to participate in the conversation, his expression absent, his thoughts as far away as planets. He also began cleaning up after meals, washing and drying dishes and even wiping the table and the stove, which was as disconcerting to my mother as my grandmother talking in her sleep, calling after her dead son.

By then my grandmother was nearly blind, her eyes roaming about the sockets, under her thin trembling eyelids, as though trying to break free from the darkness. Her face resembled a shrivelled frostbitten yesteryear apple, collapsing in on itself.

On top of the conversations about wars, hunger, and our survival as a nation and a species, neither Milka nor I got to celebrate our sixteenth birthdays—I was sick and stayed in bed for a week at the dacha, and Milka returned home. When school started and her birthday arrived, it rained for three maddening days, the sky an ashy swollen body, inseparable from the earth. Milka had her period a week late, which gave her an abominable headache and a foul mood she blamed on hormones, her parents, and our dick of a country. I suspected she blamed me too, but didn't say it. I avoided talking to her on such days because everything I said provoked an unwanted reaction, like drinking milk after eating herring. I gave her a short call that morning, but otherwise remained in my room, completing

homework. It was only mid-September, but assignments kept
piling on like fallen leaves. Each day added a new burdensome
layer.

The next few months were unremarkable in their sameness
and the amount of homework we had to accomplish in our
preparation for the final exams and college entrance exams.
The four of us hadn't gathered but once for milkshakes. Milka
and I hardly saw each other outside of school, and, for whatever reason, she grew sullen and irritated. She still loved a
dirty joke and a good book, and she and Trifonov discussed
literature obsessively, but she hadn't been inviting me to her
flat, and when I offered to come to her place one afternoon, to
finish a history presentation about WWII, she suggested that
we use my flat instead. I tried to guess what the matter was or
whether I was to blame for her moodiness, but she shook her
head and said that she was on the rag, and that I shouldn't turn
a fly into an elephant.

Winter approached, slowly but surely. Trees shed all their
leaves, a swirl of them on the streets. It was getting colder and
colder, until one morning I woke up to a sheet of snow on the
ground. My bedroom window had frosted, tiny ice crystals
gathering at the edges, and I ran my finger from one corner to
the other. Since I was a child, I loved the early hours of a new
day, in which hundreds of little dreams lay folded like petals
within a flower. I grew happy from knowing they were there,
waiting for me at the brink of every day. I felt strong too, en-
dowed with purpose, even though all of my purpose was to
finish school, matriculate into a decent university, graduate,
find a job and a spouse, reproduce. Fill our socialist heaven

with more wombs and labouring hands, who would continue
to grow and build a brighter Communist future.

Unlike Milka and Lopatin, Trifonov and I could never manage to secure an empty flat to have sex. My grandmother didn't
leave home anymore, and Trifonov's mother was sick a lot in
the autumn months, so she stayed inside too. On occasion, we
used Milka's flat, but only when she and Lopatin weren't there,
because otherwise Trifonov couldn't relax or sustain an erection, self-conscious that Lopatin would bust through the door
and act despicably crazy, as usual. I didn't find Lopatin all that
crazy as much as unabashed and thoughtless to some degree.
He did things on a whim, which was unacceptable for Trifonov, who weighed not only his decisions but also his words,
adding them together with great care and precision. He was
afraid of hurting anyone, including flies or cockroaches, whom
he deemed an important link in our food chain. He said they
were the oldest and the most resilient of all species. They could
hold their breath for forty minutes, survive a month without
food and a week without a head. To which Lopatin replied,
"Damn. A cockroach is more powerful than a man!"

"Maybe our Communist leaders have a cockroach gene,"
Trifonov said. "Maybe they've undergone some genetic muta-
tion and become virtually indestructible. You have to freeze
them for a hundred years to be able to kill them. Oh, and the
pest also loves alcohol."

"Cockroaches drink?" I asked. We all stood in a supermarket, eyeing the half-empty shelves, searching for food.

"Do they fuck too?" Milka asked, unbuttoning her long,
oversized coat.

"Those facts aren't known," Trifonov said. He pulled off his mittens and rubbed his hands together, trying to get warm. His long, spindly fingers and sharp red knuckles made me think of soup bones with bits of meat clinging to them. "But there are four thousand species of cockroaches worldwide," he continued. "A baby cockroach becomes an adult in just thirty-six days. But even as a baby, it can run as fast as its parents."

"Fuck that shit," Lopatin said. He'd grown a beard and wore one of those tall mink-fur hats with earflaps.

"Indeed," Milka said. "I hate them. Our flat is crawling with the damn things. Can't go to the kitchen at night. They make that horrible crunching sound if you step on them."

"And yet, we need them," Trifonov said.

"Why?" I asked.

"We just do. They're our ancestors."

"Yours, maybe," Lopatin said.

"Where do you think you came from?" Trifonov asked.

"A monkey?" Lopatin asked, pulling off his hat and stuffing it inside his book bag.

"But before that? Before monkeys?"

"Cockroaches existed before monkeys?" Lopatin asked, his face a tableau of agony.

"Da-a-a."

"Fuck. Did you two know about that?" He looked at Milka and me, scratching the back of his head.

"Of course," we said in unison. "Where have you been?"

"Reading *War and Peace*. Fucking endless. I can't think of no cockroaches when I'm being gorged with Tolstoy. He takes up all the damn space. This isn't made of rubber, can't stretch, you know?" He prodded his head with his thick finger, which was twice the size of mine or Milka's.

"Not of rubber?" Trifonov asked. "Who would've thought."

Lopatin scowled and then grinned; he scooped Milka in his arms, pressing his lips to her head. "She'd still love me even if I had a rubber head. Wouldn't you, baby?"

"Yes. But I'd love you even more if you had a chocolate head," she said.

"Really?"

He looked around the supermarket, which was empty, save for a few people fingering the meagre produce. Quickly he skimmed through the aisles until he found a box of cacao powder, ripped it open, and dumped the powder on his head. A saleswoman saw him do that, but before she could yell at us or call for help, we backed toward the exit and ran out, a puff of snow in our laughing startled faces.

15

Soon it was New Year's Eve, and we decided to celebrate it at my place, then sleep over at Trifonov's, since his mother worked the night shift as a hospital nurse. In our home, New Year's Eve was a family affair, and I had to be with my parents, but my mother usually cooked a feast, so she suggested inviting my friends. I suspected that she wanted to get to know the boys better. Milka had volunteered to help stuff the duck and chop the *olivie*. My father was in charge of the holiday tree, which he always bought at the last minute, so as not to waste money on a dead pine. When he finally dragged one in, it looked scrawny and lopsided, leaving a trail of needles on the floor. My grandmother kept sweeping them into a dustpan, missing at least half. Milka squatted to help her, gathered what she could with her hands, stood up, and dumped the needles in the commode.

"Don't flush them. Let the bathroom smell like a forest," my mother said.

She'd been dressing herring, and her hands were stained red with beetroot.

"Looks like you murdered someone," my father said.

"Not yet," she said. "But if you don't get that tree decorated in time, it could be you."

She laughed, a gurgle of happy sounds echoing through the
flat, and for a moment, things seemed as they'd been when I
was little and they joked more than fought. With her bent finger, my mother adjusted her hair, which had been washed and
styled that morning. She avoided touching her face with her
beetroot hands, and yet she managed to leave a ruby imprint
on her forehead. My father reached across the table and wiped
it with his thumb. In his gesture, there was a tenderness I'd
forgotten he had. It made me uncomfortable somehow, and I
looked away, at the space beside the sink, where Milka had the
duck washed inside and out, ready to stuff.

I halved the apples and scooped out the seeds. Milka rubbed
every inch of the bird's skin with salt and pepper, then poured
some sunflower oil on her hands and groped inside the cavity.

"Pass me the apples," she said. "And hold the duck's legs
apart while I push them in."

By the time the first guest arrived, we had the table set, the
potato salad chopped, and the duck in the oven, baking. Both
Milka and I took showers and changed clothes. Each Soviet
household brimmed with habits and superstitions peculiar to
that particular family, but most of us shared the same celebrating traditions: you had to cook for days and you had to dress
up. It was believed that if you greeted a new year in your pyjamas, then you'd be sick and in bed the remaining 364 days. So
that night, the last night of 1984, I wore my mother's eggshell
blouse that had shrunk after just one wash and a dark maroon

skirt she allowed me to borrow, and Milka wore my red velvet dress, which fit her much better than me because it had become too tight in the bust. My grandmother was able to adjust the waistline by taking in a few centimetres from each side. Also, because Milka was shorter than me, the dress reached below her calves and could pass for a fancy gown. We used a curling iron on our hair, but an hour later Milka's hair seemed just as straight as it'd always been.

When Lopatin stepped into our flat and closed the door, there was no room left for anyone to stand in the hallway, so Milka and I inched backward, in the direction of the kitchen. He was shaved, reeking of expensive cologne, and wore a white shirt and a grey suit, somewhat loose around his chest, which made me think that perhaps he'd borrowed it from his father. His shoes were of new sleek black leather, and he asked to keep them on, wiping his feet on the doormat three times. On his shoulder he carried a red sack, which he passed to me. "Gifts," he said.

"What gifts? No one said anything about gifts," I said, flummoxed. I'd prepared something for Milka and Trifonov, wrapped and stashed under the tree, but I'd completely forgotten about Lopatin.

"No worries. It's food."

"Hello, Aleksey," my mother said, peeping from the kitchen.

"What's your mother's name?" Lopatin whispered in my ear. "I forgot."

"Liubov Andreevna," I whispered back.

"Hello, Liubov Andreevna," he said loudly and with distinction, like the title of a poem he was about to recite. He gave Milka a peck on the cheek, grabbed the bag from my hands, and strutted into the kitchen. He set the bag on the table and began pulling things out: a box of chocolates, mandarins, a can of crabmeat, a can of black caviar, and a bottle of Sovetskoye Shampanskoye—the so-called Soviet Champagne. "From our table to yours," he said. "Happy New Year!"

My mother folded her hands on her chest, smiling absent-mindedly, as though she'd discovered a chest of jewels hidden in her kitchen wall. "Such riches," she said, picking up the caviar. "I didn't know you could still buy it."

"My parents can."

"They shop at a special supermarket, yes?" my father asked, stepping into the kitchen. "For the government workers?"

"Yes. I believe so."

"Well, we can't starve the government, can we now?" my father said, a barely visible smirk curling at the corners of his lips.

"I don't think we've ever met. You're Anya's father?" Lopatin offered his hand; my dad shook it and squeezed it hard, but Lopatin didn't seem to notice. His hand was a lion's paw compared to my father's. "I'm Aleksey. I'm in the same grade as your daughter."

"I know who you are. And I've met your parents a while back, at some school assembly when we discussed how to raise money for a new gym."

"Exercise is important," Lopatin said. "In a man, everything should be beautiful—his face, his clothes, his soul, and his body. Who said that?"

"Chekhov," I said.

"Not his body, but his thoughts," Milka said, laughing, pinching a piece of cheese from the plate on the counter.

"Let's go to the table," I said. "Petya is late, but we can start without him."

"He's probably reading some important book. Or writing a dissertation on cockroaches," Lopatin said.

"Cockroaches?" my father asked. "It's about damn time someone addressed the matter. The beast is indestructible."

"My parents buy this magic mix that kills everything it touches," Lopatin said. "I'd be happy to ask."

"It doesn't have radiation, does it?" my father asked. "Because a hundred years from now, those things could grow as large as dinosaurs and colonize the planet."

"Are you serious?" Lopatin asked.

"Of course I'm serious."

"We can't let that happen."

"Some things aren't up to us, you know," my father said.

"You were a boxer in your other life, yes?" Lopatin asked.

"Yes. In my other life. One where we fought inside boxing rings and not inside supermarkets, for sugar or toilet paper."

"He had impressive footwork," my mother said. She'd sliced some white bread and was spreading butter on it, then caviar. "But he was too kind. Couldn't watch others suffer."

"I am still kind," my father said. He picked up a black morsel of caviar with his finger and licked it. "But kindness isn't in demand. Nowadays, it's who can push harder and faster."

"Where are we pushing?" Lopatin asked.

"Good question. Ask your father."

"My father is never home, and when he's home, he's drunk."

"That's a shame," my mother said.

"Shame or not, I need a drink too," my father said.

"Good idea," Lopatin said, then snapped his mouth shut. "I mean *some* drink. Lemonade or Baikal."

"Right. I can just see you drinking lemonade." My father shook his head, laughing, and we followed him into the living room.

In the corner, the holiday tree had been propped up on top of an old suitcase, where my mother kept trinkets they'd bought on their vacations, when they could still afford to go places. Every once in a while, she'd drag out the suitcase from under the bed and sort through its contents, memories unfolding like tree leaves under the touch of her fingers. She and my father would sit on the floor and pass those souvenirs back and forth, trying to recall where each one had come from: a print with the view of a cliff jutting from the sea, a photo of my parents feeding squirrels in some park, a broken-in-half conch, a straw hat with a wide ragged brim, a clay whistle in the shape of a bird. Postcards, letters, used theatre tickets, beads, bookmarks, scraps of old fabric, buttons—my mother kept it all. She said the old suitcase stored her life; all she needed to do was to open it to remember how things looked or smelled and to know that she too had been young once. Even our tree ornaments were stories in disguise. My mother started collecting them when she and my dad had married. My dad had carved the first few toys from tree bark or thick fallen branches; others were bought in shops or at vernissages, dates of purchase scratched on the bottom of the ornaments. Each time we hung one on a holiday tree, my mother would tell us what important event had happened that year: my birth, the death of my grandfather, first trip to the dacha, first car, my first day of school, first apples, my parents' tenth wedding anniversary.

The pine tree, where my father had attached it to the suitcase, was draped with a white sheet, to cover the rope, but also to imitate snow. Surrounding the tree lay small and large parcels wrapped in newspaper or colourful fabric, cut out from old shirts. The gifts were mostly for me and Milka, a few from her to my family, whom she considered her family too. My parents' gifts often surprised us in their meaningfulness. That year, my mother and I had purchased for Milka an edition of the complete works of Ray Bradbury. She'd stumbled on the series in one of the secondhand bookshops, where she often went after work. And from Milka, my parents would get a set of garden tools I helped pick out. They weren't expensive but were hard to find, so Milka had been stopping by the same shop nearly every day until they brought out the tools for sale. I'd offered to pay half, but she refused. She said that my parents always gave her the best of gifts; most books that she owned were those we'd bought for her. And what we didn't buy, she borrowed, also from us.

For as long as I could remember, our living room felt

crowded because of all the books lined on the shelves against the walls. My father joked that if our government switched off the heat some winter, we would never be cold, we'd start burning books. But my mother didn't think it was funny; she said she'd rather freeze to death. Because what good was life without books? Books were our gateway to eternity, our bridges from past to future, from pain to joy.

Now, since we'd extended our dining table from the window to my grandmother's bed, the living room felt even smaller. Above the bed hung an old wall clock my grandparents had bought before the war, one of the few things that hadn't been chopped and burned for heat during the Blockade. It was a mechanical clock, and my mother wound it every night. It was very important to my grandmother that the clock never stopped, because she was afraid that if it did, time would stop too, her life, her memories.

When we entered the living room, we found my grandmother sitting at the table in front of the blank TV, obedient like a schoolgirl, her back straight, hands on knees. For a moment, it seemed as though she was asleep, but I noticed that her eyelids trembled as we approached. They were thin, colourless, like withered petals. Her hair was braided halfway and lay across her shoulder, a shiny silver mass. She wore one of her old dresses, which my mother had washed and ironed. It was dark green with a spray of white and yellow flowers, so from a distance it looked like a meadow. It made me think of summer, and how she taught us to weave wreaths from young dandelions and bluebells and forget-me-nots, and how she would never again see any of those flowers.

"She's almost blind," I whispered to Lopatin, who leaned over to introduce himself.

Without turning, my grandmother touched his hand, her fingers crawling up his arm, until she reached his elbow, then she brought her hand down, satisfied. "Strong man," she said.

"A giant," my father said. "But that doesn't really matter, does it? As long as here"—he pointed at Lopatin's head—"you have something to say, the rest will fall into place."

"Oh, I have plenty to say," Lopatin said.

"Of course you do," my mother said. "You're probably one of the smartest students in the class."

"Not me. But Anya and Milka. They're our stars, shining through the darkness."

"Right," I said, prodding his back. "Let's turn on the TV and eat. Milka and I have been slaving all day."

"I wish I could marry you both," Lopatin said.

"Not a chance," I said. "Bigamy is against the law."

"Too bad. But look at all this food," Lopatin said. "And they say people are starving."

"Some people," my father said.

"Yes, like in Africa."

"No, like in our country."

"Really?" Lopatin asked, genuinely surprised.

"Really," my father said.

"But I thought that was the purpose of socialism—everyone was fed, educated, and taken care of. Free medicine, free housing."

"Nothing is ever free. Neither trees nor the apples that grow on them. You first had to buy seedlings, graft a limb onto the root, cultivate the soil, add manure, fence off the trunks from rodents, spray mint oil for bugs and diseases, tie the limbs, prune. All of it involves money and labour. Lots of labour."

"Wow," Lopatin said, rubbing his shaved chin. "When you put it like that, everything is so complicated. And everything is so expensive. Even taking a crap—sorry—still costs money, because we're using water and toilet paper."

"If you're lucky. Some people—and not that far from Moscow—don't even have toilets. And they sure as hell don't have toilet paper."

"What do they use? Newspaper?"

"Where would they get newspaper?" I asked. "Think, Lopatin."

"What then?" he asked.

"Leaves," Milka said. "And old rags, if they have any."

"What on earth prompted such a conversation?" my mother asked. "It's hardly the time or the place."

"It's exactly the time and the place," my father said. "Food turns to shit, pardon my Russian, so it's inevitable that we started talking about the latter."

Milka and I exchanged glances, the unfolding scenario all too familiar to us. A seemingly casual conversation about toilet paper could spark an eternal argument about socioeconomic injustices and the ineptitude of our Communist leaders, turning the dinner table into a war zone. If we were lucky, the sparring between my parents might cease at midnight, with the sound of the Kremlin chimes, when we would all get up and raise our champagne flutes.

My grandmother waved her hand in the air. "May I say something?"

"Of course, Mum," my mother said. "You don't need our permission."

"Thank God for that," she said. "Now please, let us all pray."

"But I thought we killed God in 1917," Lopatin said. He leaned forward, so that his face was directly in front of mine, burning with questions: *Is she serious? Do you do that at every meal? How come she still believes in God when the rest of the country doesn't? Do I have to pray too?*

But then my grandmother, who couldn't of course see Lopatin's face, asked, "You remember a joke about two men who argued about the existence of God?"

"No," Lopatin said. "Never heard it."

"So listen. One man asked the other: 'You know why a goat poops tiny round pebbles, and why a cow poops fat hot muffins, and why a horse's crap is in the shape of an egg?' And the other man replied: 'No.' So the first one said: 'Exactly! First you should try to answer all the shit questions, and then deal with the God issue.'"

My mother was the first to laugh, then Milka, Lopatin, and me. My father held a champagne bottle in his hands, trying to open it, and, as he started laughing, the cork tore out of his hands and hit the ceiling; the champagne flowed down the sides of the bottle and onto the tablecloth. A stain spread faster than we could cover it with the napkins. I ran to the kitchen and grabbed a towel and another from a drawer and tossed them to Lopatin and Milka, who raised the dishes and moved them around, sliding the towels under the tablecloth. My mother held an empty plate under the bottle still in my father's hands. When the champagne stopped oozing, he began pouring it. We only had five flutes, and he dribbled some champagne into a shot glass.

"That's mine," he said. "I'll need vodka. Champagne is for the bourgeoisie."

"It's a bit too soon to toast to the new year," my mother said.

"Let's toast to the old one. To all the shit we had to crawl through. Of various shapes and sizes."

Still laughing, Lopatin, Milka, and I got up and raised our flutes while my mother passed one to my grandmother, who remained seated. But she too was smiling. I wished I had a Polaroid camera to capture the scene, so simple, so pleasant, so brief. It seemed as though time had slowed down and paused, a moment stretching into infinity. I would always remember our faces: my parents' warm encompassing expressions, my grandmother's blind disoriented gaze, Milka's familiar impish grin, and Lopatin's benevolent yet boisterous self-important stare. We all grew quiet at once and began drinking, and I could hear the wall clock count off the last hour of the year.

The phone rang, and I went to the kitchen to pick it up. It was Trifonov, whose cough had gotten worse over the evening, so his mother forbade him to leave the flat, fearing pneumonia. And she didn't think we should visit, so as not to spread germs. He would be spending New Year's alone. He did have food, though, thanks to Lopatin, who'd delivered a bag of produce last night—his contribution to the party.

"Now there'll be no party," I said, sitting back down. "That's so sad."

"I feel sorry for him," Milka said. "Alone on New Year's. There's nothing worse."

"Oh, I can name plenty of things that are worse," Lopatin said in a low voice.

"Like what?" I asked, also in a low voice.

"Like being stuck at your parents' flat," he said in my ear. "I think we should still go to Trifonov's. The sooner the better."

"My parents wouldn't like your idea."

"Let me handle that," Lopatin said, getting up. "I want to propose a toast. To friendship, which has been the most important thing in my life." He straightened his shoulders and adjusted his jacket. His long curly hair was pushed to the side, making him look old-fashioned and even chivalrous. A dash of coy humility appeared in his eyes. "I think I'm a better person," he continued, "because of Anya, Milka, and Petya, especially Petya, who's like this universal intelligence, trying to heal the world."

"Wow," I said. "I'm so impressed right now. Trifonov should hear what you really think of him."

"What I really think of him I'd like to deliver in person, which brings me to my next point—would you, Liubov Andreevna, allow your daughter to leave right now and visit her sick friend, who can't come to our party? I believe it's our indispensable duty to help him meet the new year in style. And not alone, lying in bed."

"What about me?" my father asked. "You aren't asking my permission?"

"Oh, of course. But I was taught to ask the Queen first." He touched his flute to my mother's and bowed ever so slightly, before emptying it.

"I can see that your parents also taught you how to drink," my father said.

"No. All my doing. All the good stuff comes from them, all the bad stuff I picked up on my own."

"You're a clown, Lopatin," my father said. "But I like you. I like your old man too, despite the politics."

"Yes. Let's not talk about that," my mother said. "You may go, of course, can't leave your friend in need. But what about the duck? It should be ready any minute."

Lopatin hesitated. He was a man, after all, for whom food came before love or friendship.

"Duck," he said. "My favourite."

"We'll just have to try it the next time," Milka said. "Instead, could we maybe take some *olivie*? You make the best potato salad."

"Yes. Take all of it," my mother said. "I have more in the fridge."

"Tell Petya 'Happy New Year!'" my father said.

"And also, that joke," my grandmother echoed. "Humour is the best medicine."

16

Snow sifted from the sky, fine like powdered sugar. It padded the streets, adding layers as we walked, filling in our footprints. Milka and I opened our mouths and caught shoals of flurries while Lopatin trudged ahead, carrying bags of food. All the buildings glowed with festivities; TVs blinked in windows, holiday trees did too, wrapped in tinsel and strings of coloured lights. The roads were empty, with just a few cars here and there braving the snow. While Lopatin tried to find a cab, Milka and I stepped under the awning of a bus stop and placed our bags of gifts on one of the wooden seats dusted with snow. The Bradbury edition was heavy, and I had added a scarf for Trifonov and *Heart of a Dog* for Lopatin, hoping that Trifonov wouldn't mind, since it had been his gift to me. Milka had brought the chess set for Lopatin. Just recently, he'd learned how to play, and she thought that it would hold a sentimental value for Lopatin to own her father's chess set. She'd replaced the missing or broken pieces with new ones, also wooden, and now the set was complete.

Lopatin gave up on a cab and ended up persuading some guy in a scratched, dented Zhiguli to give us a ride. Trifonov had no idea we were coming; we wanted it to be a surprise, hoping to cheer him up and aid his convalescence. Trifonov usually caught colds as soon as the weather started to change. When winds picked up and the first morning frost glazed the windows, Trifonov would pull on a hat and cover his mouth with a scarf, plodding to school and back, hunched and folded in half like an old man. Often, what seemed like harmless head congestion that others could fight off without much effort, for Trifonov would turn into weeks of bed rest, his runny nose transmogrified into a vicious sinus infection, his cough into bronchitis. When his mother allowed, we visited him after school, brought him *rombabas* and other sweets from the cafeteria. Other times, we had to stay away so as not to introduce new germs to his fragile recovering body.

Trifonov's mother was a tired, quiet woman who devoted all of her efforts and free time to her son. Worry lived in her face and cold dreamless nights. Her voice was low and her manners tender. She never screamed or seemed angry, and all her actions, her behaviour, exuded care for Trifonov: his food, his health, his studies, his growth, his future. After Trifonov's dad died, she worked as a school nurse, later finding a job at the hospital. The money was better, but the hours were worse. Her vacation time had been shortened from three summer months to one, and during winter holidays, she stayed the busiest because that was when Soviet people ate and drank the most. There were lots of cases of food poisoning and liver failure, not to mention loss of fingers, ears, noses, and entire limbs from frostbite. The number of alcohol-related deaths escalated

KRISTINA GORCHEVA-NEWBERRY

in the months of December and January; some drunks disappeared and weren't found until the following spring, when the snow melted.

Faithful to her deceased husband, Trifonov's mother hadn't dated a man in a decade. In our country, there had been a shortage of men, and all the good ones had been long taken. For a Soviet woman, a good man was one who worked, didn't drink, and brought all of his salary home. Whether that man was violent, stupid, unfaithful, or made less money than she did mattered little to most women. They could scrape a nest from mud and twigs if they had to. And they would place a man in the centre of that nest and drop food in his mouth as long as he stayed. Trifonov's mother, however, was different. She chose to be single, despite the fact that she was surrounded by men at work.

"She still loves my dad," Trifonov had told us once.

"Lucky you," Milka had said. "Mine brought in that dick the first chance she got."

"Some women can't be alone," I'd said.

Unlike Milka, however, Trifonov knew and remembered his dad well. He often spoke about him with a kind of veneration reserved for the dead, especially those who'd departed early. Trifonov had a theory about that too. He said that when one's life ended abruptly, it created a certain rift in time, a loose end. From that moment on, our lives were severed from that of the deceased. But because we continued to exist, we continued to project memories, which continued to grow with us. Premature death forced us to romanticize, to supplement images, to fill in the absence. At some point, we started to lament or miss things that never happened, because we'd projected them into being and made a memory of them.

All that seemed too convoluted for Lopatin, who insisted that we forgot everything and everyone, dead or alive, that we only remembered those moments that made us feel insanely good or insanely shitty, and the rest was tossed away, swept or stored under the bed, like dirty socks or old photos. He hated both; socks stank, and old photos evoked pity and panic. Pity because you couldn't control life any more than you could control those frozen expressions. Panic because one day, someone would say the same thing about us, and you couldn't do shit to change that. We had to admit, Lopatin's words rang true, but so did Trifonov's. Milka thought that photos trapped pieces of our souls, that was why old people looked so sad—all happiness had been snapped out of them. And I thought that photos, especially old photos, were a gateway into another world. They were nuggets of imagination, stories to be told, reckoned with. If I were a writer, I would've turned those people into characters and made them talk. But I had no such talents, and if anyone could become a writer, it would be Trifonov. He had a keen eye for beauty—in nature and in literature— and a kind of gentle righteous soul; he worried for cockroaches and the planet as one enormous ecosphere he must save.

The flat Trifonov shared with his mother was no different from Milka's: two poorly lit rooms, one bathroom, a coffin-size kitchen. All the windows had been sealed shut with strips of paper to prevent drafts; heavy velour drapes sagged low, touching the floor. The fabric was the colour of the Black Sea when the sun skimmed its surface—deep seaweed green. I imagined my grandmother transforming the drapes into a beautiful jacket and maybe a skirt, so Trifonov promised me the drapes if his mother decided to redecorate. This seemed unlikely, though, since the average Soviet interior of an average Soviet flat was bound to outlive its tenants. The furniture was built to last centuries. My mother often said that we had to take better care of things than people because people could take care of themselves, but also because my children would sit at the same table, eat from the same plates, and sleep on the same bed as I did, with the exception of perhaps a new mattress, pillow, or blanket.

When Trifonov opened the door, on the fifth ring, he stood tall and pale before us, wearing grey flannels and a ragged wool scarf wrapped around his throat. His feet were stuffed into a pair of thick oversized socks. His emaciated looks and his domestic outfit awoke a maternal instinct in me, and I tried to make him go to bed as soon as we stepped inside. I also suggested rubbing his feet with Zvezdochka balm and maybe putting mustard sheets on his chest. He shook his head, smiling, feeling energized from the sight of us, laden with bags, and our faithful faces, cold and red. Lopatin took our coats, brushed the snow from them, and hung them on the wall rack. Milka and I pulled off our boots and carried the food into the living room, unpacking everything onto a long coffee table covered with medicine. The table sat in front of a massive brown couch, where Trifonov had been sleeping before we arrived.

"So glad you came," he said, sitting down, rubbing his face. "You didn't have to."

"Of course we had to," Lopatin said. "Raneva's parents are too fucking serious. I had to get out of there." He bent down and massaged his feet. "Damn, those new shoes are killing me."

"Where is your tree?" Milka asked Trifonov. "Where should I put the gifts?"

"No tree. I decided against wasting wood."

"Meaning that you didn't have money to get one?" Lopatin asked. "You could've told me, and I would've paid."

"You can't pay for everything," Trifonov said.

"Why the hell not?"

"Really, why the hell not?" Trifonov said in a low, sonorous voice, imitating Lopatin, then coughed, leaning against the pillows.

"What we need is to heat you up some milk," I said, slipping the gifts under the coffee table. "You have cocoa?"

"I think so."

"The best thing for chest colds," Milka said.

"Vodka is the best," Lopatin said.

"That's why you couldn't wait to leave my parents', so you could get drunk," I said.

"I meant rubbing Trifonov's chest with vodka. But I want a shot too." From inside his jacket, Lopatin produced a small bottle of Stolichnaya. "Undress. We shall rub," he told Trifonov.

"The only way you're rubbing my chest is when I'm dead, lying in a morgue," Trifonov said.

"No one would let me near your corpse," Lopatin said.

"Exactly my point—you're never rubbing my chest. You aren't touching me. Period."

"We shall see about that." Lopatin hunched over Trifonov, so the only thing visible was the top of his head, his hair like a tuft of straw, spiked out.

"Help," he pleaded, in a fading exasperated voice, choking with laughter and cough, fighting off Lopatin. "You're hurting me, you idiot."

Lopatin's hands snuck under Trifonov's pyjama top.

"Stop it," Trifonov said, his voice thin, trickling. "I'm too weak to argue."

Milka and I tried to tear Lopatin away from Trifonov, but he wouldn't budge. Milka ran to the kitchen and grabbed a kettle and poured the water over Lopatin's thick nest of hair. He jumped from the couch and shook his head.

"What the fuck," he said. "What am I, a palm tree?"

"Worse," Trifonov said. "A baobab. You leave no room for anyone else."

"Baobab is called the tree of life," Milka said. She spooned the potato salad into a crystal bowl. "The oldest tree is like six thousand years."

"Let's not compare people to trees," Lopatin said. "Although if I could live six thousand years, I'd feel pretty mighty."

"What would you do if you lived that long?" I asked.

"The same thing I do now. Eat, drink, sleep, fuck. What else is there to do?"

"Figures."

"Honestly. I can't pretend to care about shit if I don't."

He walked to the TV and turned it on, waiting for the picture to appear, but nothing happened, the screen remained black. He slammed his fist against the box. "It's like five minutes to midnight. I want to hear Chernenko speak."

"Why?" Trifonov asked. "You don't give a shit. And it's the same speech every year, no matter who's at the wheel."

"I want to hear it too," I said. "They say he's been sick, maybe poisoned."

"Soon they'll reopen gulags," Milka said.

"Don't say that," Trifonov said. "It isn't a joke."

Lopatin turned the TV around and stared at its back, fingering and shaking some wires. He yanked one out, rubbed it, then plugged it back in. "Can we please stop talking about tales from the Soviet crypt and start thinking about champagne? Can someone find the flutes?"

"In the cabinet," Trifonov said. "Champagne is in the fridge, where you left it yesterday. My mother wasn't happy, by the way."

"Is she ever happy?"

Trifonov shrugged, scratching his head, pushing the hair away from his forehead. "Maybe on her birthday."

"My mother hates her birthdays," I said. "She always tries to forget about them or go away."

"Lucky she can," Trifonov said. "Mine puts on some music and dances."

"Alone?" Milka asked, licking the spoon. "That's crazy."

"I dance with her," Trifonov said.

"That's even crazier," Lopatin said.

I brought in the champagne, plates, and forks, and Milka found the flutes and set them on the coffee table, moving Trifonov's medicine to the windowsill, except for the inhaler. He slipped it under his pillow on the couch. Trifonov rubbed each flute with the hem of his pyjama top. "They haven't been used since last year."

"We've always known that you're weird. Now we know just how weird. You don't drink, you don't smoke, no sports, no TV. That's why you read all the time," Lopatin said. "It's a shitty life."

"Shut up," Trifonov said, getting up from the couch. "Your life is just as shitty. Or worse—you haven't discovered the pleasure of learning. That's the worst."

"Fuck off, Trifonov. You learn, I live. You read, I play. We'll talk in twenty years, see whose life is shittier."

"Deal. Let's meet again in twenty years. In 2004. New Year's Eve."

"Great. But can I have a fucking drink now?" Lopatin asked and switched the TV around, back in its place, flipping it on and off a few more times before abandoning the idea. "Fuck. Let's just pretend we heard the speech and get on with the celebration." He picked up the champagne bottle, peeled off the foil, twisted and loosened the wire, and began to slowly tug at the cork. "I need to hear the Kremlin clock or something," he said. "I can't get into the mood."

"Bong, bong, bong," Milka said.

"Bong, bong, bong," Trifonov and I echoed.

"And now our socialist hymn," Milka said. *"Soiuz nerushimyi, respublik svobodnykh, splotila naveki Velikaya Rus'—"*

"Fuck that shit," Lopatin said. "I have a new Tsoi tape with me. Let's listen to that. Or we can listen to your favourite, that weirdo Freddie."

The cork made a popping sound, but remained in his hands. A puff of whitish air escaped from the bottle, some foam oozed, and we brought out the flutes to catch the champagne. It was clear and golden in colour, hissing with tiny bubbles that rose to the surface of our glasses as we raised and touched them together.

"I wish for us to graduate, to matriculate into top colleges, to remain friends," I said.

"I wish for Trifonov to become a fat academic and write many important books, so I can read them," Milka said, laughing.

"I wish for Milka to never leave me," Lopatin said, grinning the silliest of grins, then turning serious, mouth shut, cheeks puffed out.

"I wish for this moment to last. To retain its truth and its meaning twenty years from now," Trifonov said.

"Happy fucking New Year!" Lopatin screamed, and kissed Milka, then me, and then tried to kiss Trifonov, who escaped his fate by retreating back onto the couch. He took a sip of champagne, his face puckering, then lowered the glass onto the coffee table as soon as he swallowed. We joined him. I plopped on the couch, and Milka and Lopatin sagged onto the floor in front of us. He scooped a spoonful of the *olivie* and dumped it in his mouth, chewing vigorously.

"So good," he said. "In another life, I want to marry your mother, so she could cook that shit for me."

We laughed, reaching for the potato salad.

"Let's open gifts," I said, plucking a piece of salami from the plate.

"Yeah," Lopatin said. "As soon as I drink some vodka. Champagne is for you, girls."

He poured himself a shot, dumped it in his mouth, then reached for a pickle. "My mother's. Fuck, but they too are the best."

"Indeed," Milka said, and bit off a piece from Lopatin's pickle.

I dragged the bags from under the coffee table, and Trifonov pulled his and Lopatin's from under the couch. He started coughing again, and we told him to stop talking and lie down, which he did, the pillows propped behind his back.

We passed around the gifts and, on the count of three, started ripping the newspaper and plastic bags. When we were done, each had two or three things. I got a dark burgundy mohair scarf from Milka and a bottle of French perfume, Fidji, from Lopatin. He, in turn, held Milka's gift—her father's chess set—to his mountainous chest, wearing a childish sentimental grin. From me, Lopatin received *Heart of a Dog*, which he promised to read during the holidays. Trifonov didn't seem to notice that I regifted his book, or he was too polite to mention it. Milka's scarf almost matched the one I gave Trifonov, except for the colour; she'd probably bought it at GUM, just like I did, standing in line for hours. He pulled the old scarf off and looped the new one around his neck. The dull blue colour complemented his skin, but also made him look sadder, frail, like my grandmother's porcelain vase, which turned greyish blue as it aged, its surface paved with tiny cracks.

Lopatin and Milka's gift for Trifonov caused more admiration: Nabokov's *Lolita*, some foreign edition they'd procured with the help of Ruchnik. Milka had already read the novel before wrapping it. But even more superior was my gift to Milka, the Ray Bradbury books, most of which neither Trifonov nor I had read. Lopatin hadn't even heard of the author, which, of course, didn't surprise us. He was more prosaic in his gift-giving and bought for Milka a bottle of a different French perfume, Climat. She peeled the plastic from the box and flipped the lid, raising the bottle to her face. When she smelled it, she closed her eyes, her face mellowing from the scent. Lopatin massaged her shoulder, toying with the tiny pearly buttons, then bent down and pretended to tear them off with his teeth.

We still hadn't opened Trifonov's presents, and we each weighed in our hands a clear plastic case with an audiotape inside. The label read "The Cherry Orchard, 1983."

Lopatin raised the tape to the light. "What the hell is it?" he asked.

"Remember last year we did a reading of the play in class?" Trifonov asked.

"Of course we remember," Milka said. "You were Trofimov, the Eternal Student, and Lopatin was the merchant who was buying the estate from Anya, I mean Ranevskaya. And I was Varya."

"I also read for Gaev," Lopatin said.

"Right. Well, I recorded it, then made copies. I divided the play into four parts. One for each of us. Only when we're together can we listen to the whole thing."

"Let's start then," I said. "Where's your tape player?"

Trifonov rummaged under the couch until he produced a primitive beaten-up silver box. We lifted it onto the coffee table, sliding the food around—the potato salad, sprats, black bread, a plate of cold meats—and Lopatin inserted his tape first, snapped the lid, and pressed Play. The tape dragged for a few moments, and then we heard Lopatin's voice reaching us from the darkness.

LOPAKHIN Our Eternal Student is never far from the young ladies.

TROFIMOV None of your business.

LOPAKHIN He's almost fifty, and he's still a student.

TROFIMOV We can do without your inane jokes.

LOPAKHIN What's the matter, you funny chap—are you getting cross?

TROFIMOV Just stop badgering me.

LOPAKHIN (*laughs*) Well, let me ask you then. What do you think about me?

TROFIMOV I, Yermolai Alekseevich, think that you're a rich man and soon will be a millionaire. And, as with the conversion of matter, there needs to be a carnivore, who eats whatever comes his way. So you're necessary.

VARYA You, Petya, better tell us about the planets.

RANEVSKAYA No, let's go on where we left off yesterday.

TROFIMOV What was that?

GAEV Human pride.

TROFIMOV We talked for ages yesterday, but we didn't get anywhere. Human pride, in your sense, there's something mystical about it. And maybe you're right in your own way, but if we're going to talk about it simply, without fancy trimmings, then what sort of pride can there be? Does it even make sense if man is physiologically ill-constructed, if in the vast majority of cases he is crude, ignorant, and profoundly unhappy? We have to stop admiring ourselves. We ought to work.

GAEV You will die all the same.

Mesmerized by our own voices, which seemed so different on tape, so theatrical and loud, stoic even, we continued to listen to Chekhov's play. The lines stood out precise and clear, woven together and connected to one another by logic and the writer's deep understanding of Russian culture, as well as humanity, all its vanity and paradoxes, and those small petty moments, which filled our existence from birth to death. We kept drinking the champagne and vodka and feasting on my mother's *olivie* and Lopatin's pickles, and the snow kept falling, spooling lacy shawls around us.

The new year had arrived—1985. And with it a new president, a new regime, a new country. But that night, we knew nothing about it. We listened to Chekhov and then Freddie Mercury and then Tsoi, with his deep throaty voice of someone who smoked and drank and never slept. His songs exploded with caustic questions, addressed not so much to us as to those in charge of us. He loved the words "sun" and "fight", and there was an edge to his voice, a sharp point, like a needle, about to break off. His music wrapped around our hearts like a serpent, filling us with excitement, daring, anxiety, fear, and power. It was crude, unapologetic, beastly even, but it told us that a change was underway, that if it was possible for someone to challenge our Soviet institutions by singing such violent verses, the rest was possible as well: to travel abroad, to live in America, to buy jeans and burgers, to be free from gulags and dictators, the Communist Party, our teachers, our parents, who always reminded us of duty to our country, our land, our history, to everything we called home.

So we danced, and we smoked, and we made jokes, feeling so infinitely happy. We also felt free, free from having to grow up, to lie or worry or make fate-altering decisions, from any responsibility other than being teenagers in love with life and all it had to offer at the moment: music, liquor, food, cigarettes, sex, and friendship—the greatest gift we would know.

17

We were midway through our senior year when Chernenko
became seriously ill and then died. By the time Gorbachev,
or Mikhail the Marked, stepped into office in March of 1985,
our country was rutted with doubt and grief. We'd buried
our Communist leaders one after another and didn't really expect Gorbachev to last long. Some began quoting Nostrada-
mus and the Bible, claiming that both mentioned Mikhail the
Marked as the last ruler of Russia. Others called him the Dev-
il's messenger—with that liver-shaped spot glistening on his
forehead—destined to stomp and smash our country under his
stone hooves.

My parents grew more sombre with each day. For one thing,
they worried whether they would have jobs a year from now,
and for another, they weren't sure whether they would fit into
that new world Gorbachev was determined to scrape from the
debris of the old one. They said it would be like learning to
walk again after being in a coma for nearly seventy years. My
mother was more open to change than my father; she explained
that it came from being a woman whose body had been in the
throes of hormonal shifts since the age of twelve. "You learn to
adapt," she said. "To manipulate, to fool your mind. It must

function just the same even if your body feels as alien to you as those clouds—puffy, swollen, barely dragging." She stood by the window, sweeping the sky with her troubled eyes, then pressing her hands to her face and rubbing it furiously as though wishing to erase the image.

That spring, we weren't yet seventeen, and our vocabulary had been extended by two words, *perestroika* and *glasnost,* and our history exam was about to be cancelled. As it turned out, we no longer had a history; our country's past demanded drastic revisions if not complete rewrites. We teetered on the cusp of happiness and importance, mostly because we didn't have to study for the exam, but also because we felt that we were privileged to witness the country's transformation from an impoverished, terrorized state into a free, prosperous, democratic world. We didn't understand and couldn't care about the time or mountainous effort it would require to rebuild our mother ship. My parents kept saying, "A jug only holds so much. You need to pour out before you're able to add." But we spurned their words, eager as we were to defy anyone who didn't believe in the future of our emerging democracy.

Spring breathed in our chests: cold, gusty, fretful. The weather was moody, and the sun was in no rush to warm the numb, crusted earth. One morning we would wake up to a sheet of snow, and the next, all would be washed away by a torrent of rain. Clouds hung over the city like large puffy hats; each day they grew bigger and greyer, until the entire sky was engulfed by them. Occasionally, it would seem to us that we were inside a dinosaur egg, stuck in membranes and mucilage, and that the egg would never hatch and we would never see the world, or that we would die as soon as we came out. It was our spring, nonetheless, and what we also thought about was graduation, a life without school or teachers or textbooks. In the summer, we would be applying to universities, and, if we matriculated, we would drag out another five woeful years of exams and papers. But we didn't want to think that far ahead, because that was how most Russians existed—tomorrow could be a life away; today, on the other hand, was all one owned.

"Love the moment because it never repeats," my mother told us when we got back from school one day.

And Milka replied, "What if I hate it? What if I don't want it to repeat?" As much as my mother pitied Milka for her father's premature death, she also occasionally disliked her for her spontaneous honesty, her bursts of "smart anger", which my mother interpreted as involuntary self-defence, an instinct not only to survive but to assure others that loss and suffering, after all, were noble Russian traits.

"Do you and your mother ever talk about your father?" my mother asked.

"What for? No one remembers. I don't remember, my mother doesn't remember, and as far as my stepfather is concerned—the man never lived."

"That's not right," my mother said.

"Why? What would be the point in resurrecting him? He isn't Jesus."

"That doesn't mean he didn't love you or that he didn't suffer."

"My mother said he died instantaneously."

"Doesn't she miss him at all?"

"I don't think so. It's been sixteen years. All the missing is gone by now."

"Are you sure?" my mother asked.

"She remarried six months after the funeral."

"It's hard to be by yourself, especially with a small child."

"But did anyone consult that child? Maybe I didn't want a new father."

"Is he that bad?" my mother asked, and placed in front of us a plate of old bread fried in egg and sprinkled with sugar.

I took a piece and folded it in my mouth. Milka tucked her lower lip, then crossed her mouth with her finger, looking concerned or puzzled. "He's a man," she finally said. "He eats a lot. She gives him all the food so he can stay strong and satisfy her. Not that he can, because she's always horny."

I glanced at my mother, who blushed, if only for a pitiful instant, but long enough for me to notice. "Does she say that to you?" she asked.

"No. But one doesn't always have to say things for others to understand them."

I reached for another slice of the sweet sticky bread, but Milka intercepted my hand and grabbed one herself. She ate it with gusto, smacking her lips and licking her fingers, as though suddenly awakened from a yearlong sleep. A nervous tremor ran down her throat and disappeared between her breasts, which had finally begun to fill into shape.

After Milka had left that evening, my mother kept saying that there was something wrong with her, that she seemed too mature for her age, but also too angry, too resolute. She even wanted to call Milka's mother and share her concerns, but I persuaded her not to, that it would be betraying my best friend.

Soon it was the Easter holiday, and our homes smelled of *kuliches*, sunny-yellow dome-shaped cakes the women spent hours preparing. The dough had to rise three times before you could add nuts or raisins and transfer it into a tall form. It was then left to rise yet again, at which point all the windows had to be shut to avoid draughts. I wasn't allowed to enter the kitchen, to open or close doors, so the cake wouldn't collapse or develop a hole in the middle. My grandmother compared *kuliches* to people's lives: some were sweet and buttery; others crumbled at the touch. Before starting on the Easter cake, my grandmother always crossed herself three times in front of the icon. She also stood silent for a long minute before mixing all the ingredients together, forming dough she spared no effort punching and folding and flipping. According to her, a woman could be a sublime cook, but baking a fine *kulich* was the pinnacle of one's culinary mastery, the art of the divine. A perfect *kulich* took a dozen eggs, a hunk of butter and three fists of sugar, a pinch of yeast, a dash of salt, and as much flour as you could knead into it. Even when she could still see, my grandmother measured pretty much everything that way, not in grams but hunks and fists and pinches. The rest was left to the cook's skill and imagination. That year, however, because of the shortage of groceries, some families joined their meagre supplies to bake a perfect cake, while others made a simpler "war" version: margarine, cheap unbleached wheat flour, occasionally mixed with other grains, and one or two eggs. Such cakes didn't rise well and weren't as tall, and instead of having a sweet vanilla glaze, they were barely dusted with powdered sugar. They looked shrunken and sad next to the few coloured eggs, which, boiled in onion peel, resembled blood-red rocks.

More people, even the nonbelievers, went to church that week and stood in lines to consecrate their cakes and eggs. My grandmother always put on her lilac dress that had a cream collar and matching buttons on the sleeves, and even though it was always cold on Easter, she refused to wear anything else, except maybe for her favourite shawl pinned with the amber brooch. She lit a candle under the icon in the kitchen and kept it lit until the following Monday. As usual, she'd fasted for forty days prior to the holiday, subsisting only on water, bread, and root vegetables, and appeared even weaker and more fragile, her skin the colour of March snow.

When my parents tried to convince her to eat some fish or cheese, she shook her head and said, "The Lord didn't suffer from hunger, only thirst." My father gave up on the second try, but my mother continued to tempt her with various foods she'd been saving or had managed to procure right before Easter. She'd been so lucky as to purchase a tiny can of red caviar and spooned it thinly on slices of white bread, scooping up the last of the salted roe with her fingers and placing it on her tongue. At that moment, she looked like a little girl who'd just discovered something delicious. When we all sat down at the table in the living room, my grandmother listened to us eating the caviar without a modicum of interest, her good eye, the one that could still distinguish shapes, now focussed on the cluster of trees outside the window.

"She's thinking about the Blockade," my mother said to me as soon as we moved to the kitchen to start on supper.

"How do you know?"

"I just do. My brother died in January of 1942, but she kept his body frozen on the balcony until she could bury it in the spring, closer to Easter."

"That's awful. I don't want to hear that."

"It's true. Some people hid their dead in their homes, so they could continue to use their ration cards. Remember when we went to Leningrad? The war ended how many years ago? But the city remains doleful, despite all the beautiful buildings and art. The people are sad too."

"Why don't they leave? I mean, they can move to Moscow or other cities."

"Why would they? That city holds all their memories—good, bad—they can't betray it, they'd be betraying themselves. If your grandfather wasn't offered that job after the war, your grandmother would've never left Leningrad."

"Still, doesn't everyone want to be happy?"

My mother didn't answer but studied my face for a long minute. She tucked my curly hair behind my ears. "Happiness means different things for different people," she said. "I hope that you'll find it—what makes you happy—and that you stick to it, and that your life and the life of your friends makes more sense than ours. That your dreams don't get crushed under all the snow."

My mother began cleaning the chicken, slipping her hand

inside the cavity and pulling out the liver and the heart, like slimy pebbles nestling in the palm of her hand. She washed them, then cut them up and called for Rasputin. Lazily, the cat jumped off the chair and wove between her legs, waiting for my mother's generous hand to fill his bowl with raw, bloody viscera.

Milka, Trifonov, Lopatin, and I arranged to meet the night before Easter at the old church in Taganka, where both Milka and I had been secretly christened as babies. We suspected that most of our classmates had undergone the same ritual, but would never admit to it. Lopatin hadn't been christened, since in his family all the men were faithful Communists. Trifonov, on the other hand, had chosen to become a Christian when he was thirteen years old. He'd suffered through the entire ceremony: stood naked in front of the Pakhra River, waded into the cold spring current, and had been submerged underwater three consecutive times.

The churchyard was tracked yellow; earlier it'd been shovelled and sprinkled with sand that gritted underfoot. Built in the past century, the church had lost its original lustre; the walls showed scuffed brown patches. The tarnished, dented brass domes resembled old samovars. The stained-glass windows were dark, and it was difficult to see their design, all seams and grooves, like fragments of valuable pottery someone had tried to reassemble and that now, in the poor light of a declining day, looked mismatched and even malicious, a warning to the world that had gone awry.

The weather was cold but clear; dirty snow lay heaped

against buildings and the road. It was close to eight in the eve-ning, and more and more people had gathered for the Krestnyi Khod, a sunrise liturgy. Among them were little children and even babies huddled against their mothers' breasts. A few of the women carried icons and bright fake flowers; a few brought *kuliches* and coloured eggs; but others held candles with tiny wiggling flames they protected from the wind with their hands. If I stood on my toes, I could glimpse hundreds of lit candles as thin as twigs burning in tall flat dishes inside the church. Two clergymen, with fat lips tucked in the nests of grey beards, wore white-and-gold floor-length vestments and cylindrical bejewelled hats. They swung reeky *kadilos* on long thick chains, and when they approached the doors, the air began to smell like myrtle or other incense used at funerals. In their deep sonorous voices, the men chanted prayers, aided by a choir we couldn't see.

"I don't feel well," Milka said in my ear. She was still dressed in her winter coat, a heavy brown *drap* with a white-rabbit shawl collar. Her head was covered with a kerchief, the thick-fringed ends tied at the back and sticking out like a pair of hands.

"What's wrong? Are you sick?" I asked, and slid the hood of my coat toward the front of my face, pulling the scarf higher to warm my lips.

"I don't know. Kind of nauseous."

"I wonder how much those crosses on their necks are worth," Lopatin said, curtailing our whisper. "Do you think they're fucking real?" He wore his father's lambskin fur coat, glossy at the elbows and on the pockets, no hat but gloves and a fuzzy tartan scarf.

"Can you not swear on such a night?" Trifonov asked.

"Fine. But I'm getting cold and hungry. I say when they start walking in circles around the church, we split."

"I don't want to go home," Milka said.

"Me neither," I agreed.

"What about a dacha? Raneva? Yours is really close, no?" Lopatin asked.

"How do you suppose we get there and back? The trains will stop running by midnight."

"I'll find some loser with a car," Lopatin said. "I have money."

"Losers don't have cars," Trifonov said.

"That's right, Trifonov. That's why you'll never have one." He laughed at the top of his lungs, and a few people reproached us with stern glances. Some pressed their fingers to their lips, forcing us to step away, closer to the road, which was empty except for a caravan of cars parked along the curb. On the other side, young trees, maples or poplars, rose under the open sky. The wind blew, and the trees grappled like bodies.

"Let's not fight," Milka said. "I have a headache."

"I feel your period coming," Lopatin said. "We need to hurry, or I won't get to enjoy that pussy for another week."

She smacked him on the face lightly, but he only smiled, then folded his lips and pretended being hurt, pouting.

"You deserved it," she said.

"Agreed," he said. "Look at this building, will you? What kind of important individuals live there?"

We all turned to view a tall, wide formidable construction, called Stalin's *vysotka*. Unlike faceless *khrushchevki*, or anthills,

BETWEEN DOG AND WOLF 201

where most of us lived, it had columns and arched windows and even some type of sculptures. It was hard to tell what they were in the dark.

"The Party people live there," Trifonov said. "High ranked."

"And maybe scientists. Anyone important," I said.

"I'm important, aren't I?" Lopatin asked. "I'll live there one day."

"No, you won't." Trifonov said. "You'll never be that important."

"Fuck off. In this new country, I'll do whatever I damn please. Hire you as a doorman."

"I don't want to go to the dacha. I want to stay here," Trifonov said.

"No, you don't," Lopatin said. "Not if Raneva is going, which she is because we can't go to her dacha without her. It'd be like breaking and entering."

"Wouldn't be a first for you, I'm sure," Trifonov said.

"I wonder what Yashka is doing now," I said. "I mean, they should allow him to graduate, assuming he passes all the tests."

"Didn't Milka tell you?" Lopatin asked. "Yashka is in the States, sucking Coke on Brighton Beach. They finally approved his visa. I have an idea, though. Let's go to my place first. My parents will be asleep soon. I can pack some food, get my father's car keys. We'll drive to Raneva's dacha and spend the night. Come back early in the morning, no one will even notice. They think we're at this sunrise bullshit anyway." He paused. "You know how to get to your dacha, right Raneva?"

I nodded. "It's off Kashirka. Thirty minutes tops."

"I'll find the road, and you can point out the turnoff. There's still a lot of snow out there probably."

"Probably," I said. "My parents won't go for another week or two."

"You don't drive," Milka said to Lopatin.

"Of course I do. Practised all autumn. I'll get my licence as soon as I turn eighteen."

"I'm not getting in a car with you," Trifonov said. "You're dangerous, Lopatin."

"I'll be careful, I promise." He chuckled, then said, "Let's have some perestroika fun, yes? The whole country is changing. We can do whatever. We're free."

"One can't live in a society and be free from it," Trifonov said.

"If you cite Lenin or Marx or any of those arseholes one more time, I'll personally choke you to death," Lopatin said.

"Your folks revered those arseholes all their lives and you want to choke *me* to death? Ha!" Trifonov raised the short collar of his eternal-brown coat and rubbed his ears.

Lopatin lit a cigarette. "So? What's the verdict?"

Milka's face was paler than usual, but her lips were just as bright and juicy, perhaps because she'd been licking them incessantly. "I'll drive with you," she finally said.

"Raneva?" Lopatin asked.

I glanced at Trifonov; his face softened under my pleading stare.

"Fine. I suppose I'll feel better if I go too," he said. "I mean I won't worry to death."

18

As much as we hated to admit it, Lopatin drove with confidence, sprawled languidly in his seat, one hand nudging the wheel, the other resting on his knee. Every now and then, he grabbed the wheel with both hands when I pointed to ruts and holes in the road. I sat next to him, nervous at first but finally relaxing as we approached the familiar grounds. Lopatin entertained us with stories, grand epics in which he always appeared as a proud hero, fighting the khans of the Golden Horde, always on a white horse, with a sword or a lance no one else could lift.

"Strong and mighty is a Russian warrior," he said. "He's taller than a forest, and when he straightens his shoulders, he can reach the sky. The earth shakes under his feet, and if he walks ashore, the sea heaves and spills."

"Don't flatter yourself, Lopatin," Trifonov said. "You can't lift mountains on your shoulders. You aren't a Russian warrior but a Soviet man, meaning you're this small." He made a gesture with his fingers, shrinking Lopatin to the size of a pinkie.

"Fuck that," he said. "If we lived back then, Raneva and Milka would've been my whores. I'd be fucking them both."

"I'd rather kill myself," I said.

"And I don't like to share, Lopatin," Milka echoed. "One night, when you'd be drunk, sleeping heavily after sex with Raneva, I'd creep in the dark with a knife and plunge it straight into your heart." She leaned forward as much as she could and hit Lopatin in the chest. His face contorted in exaggerated pain. He pressed his hand to the imaginary wound, secured his fingers around the imaginary hilt, and yanked the knife out.

"Listen. I've been reading *Slovo o Polku Igoreve*," Trifonov said. "Feudal wars between ancient Rus' principalities in 1185. Knyaz' Igor loses to Polovtsy. What does it tell you?"

"That it happened exactly eight hundred years ago?" Milka said.

"Well, yes. But also that it's bound to happen again because history repeats itself."

"So, you're saying that Russia will become feudal?"

"More or less. But its people will separate and fight with one another."

"That's what my father thinks," I said. "But my mother thinks that there's no more chance for that to happen than World War III."

"Both are strong possibilities," Trifonov said.

"Bullshit," Lopatin said. "You need to stop reading all those books. It's all a lie. The old ones anyway. Soon they'll rewrite them, and there'll be a new history, a new truth."

"If left up to your people, there'll be no history at all."

"How much longer do I have to put up with his bullshit?" Lopatin asked.

"Until we graduate," I said. "Then you can follow your Communist stars."

Milka laughed, and so did Trifonov, but Lopatin kept quiet, eyes focussed on the road. We all turned silent, contemplating the snowy fields rolling and weaving behind the windows. Scrawny naked trees. The landscape was dark and desolate, like our country's past and also future, although we didn't know it at the moment. Neither did we know that it was indeed the last time we would be together, riding in Lopatin's car— our lives, our fates, still undiscovered, unimaginable.

"Soon will end the era of Lopatins," Trifonov finally said. "We're all moving toward the higher truth, the higher happiness, and I'll be walking in the first rows."

"You think you'll make it?" Lopatin asked.

"If I don't, others will," Trifonov said.

"You'll die like a mangy dog," Lopatin said.

"Perhaps," Trifonov said. "But what does it really mean—to die? Bodies rot, feelings don't. Like our souls, they float somewhere in the universe."

"I'm sick," Milka said.

"Oh, shit," Lopatin said. "You need me to pull over? We can't mess up the car."

"Just open the window," Trifonov said. "Here, take my hat." He took it off and passed it to Milka. "You can vomit in it, no big deal." The back window rolled down and a blade of cold air sheared through the car. Milka stuck her face out and was drawing long breaths.

No one said a thing for a while, our eyes drawn to the blackness stretching out into nowhere. As we got closer to the dachas, Lopatin became more and more focussed on the road, afraid to miss our turn. The traffic was light, but it'd gotten colder, and the road glistened with icy patches. It had also begun to snow, a spray of fine flakes like dust mites. They knitted lacy webs on the windshield but then dissolved.

Finally, Milka broke the spell. "Hey, did you finish *Lolita*?" she asked Trifonov. "Such a sad book."

"Hard," Trifonov said. "It took me longer than usual to read it, but in the end, I came to the conclusion that Humbert Humbert's feelings for Lolita were really Nabokov's feelings for Russia, which he first loved, then lost and missed, but which later disappointed him."

"Humbert fucked Lolita," Milka said.

"She'd seduced him," Trifonov said. "Sometimes a girl has all the power."

"Not when she's twelve. He was a life older."

At the dacha, snow lumped under the trees and on the roofs, but a lot had already melted. Bare scraps of land lay exposed underfoot. The apple trees hadn't budded yet, their branches shivering against the toolshed. As we emerged from the car, Milka drew lungfuls of frosty country air and spread her arms out as far as her coat would allow.

"I love this place," she said. Stooping, she pulled two wooden pickets apart and revealed a hidden entrance in the fence.

My parents kept spare keys in the outhouse, inside a red plastic jug on the wall. I groped in the dark until I found it. Unlocking the main house, I moved toward the toolshed, from which I fetched a few short logs and an axe. There, I also spotted a torch and turned it on. It made a moon face on the snow.

Trifonov dragged the bags of food and drink from the boot while Lopatin found a tall enamel bucket and pumped water from the well located on the other side of the fence. The pump had a long, rusty arm, which Lopatin kept jerking down hard until the water sloshed on the ground.

"Let it run for a bit," I yelled. "It'll taste like blood otherwise."

"It looks like blood." He scratched his lighter on and off, a cigarette pinched in the corner of his mouth.

To build a fire, Milka and I scraped snow and leaves from the pit in the yard, which was nothing but a stack of old bricks arranged in a circle. I picked through a box of wooden chips my father kept under the porch steps while Milka wadded newspapers she'd discovered in the toolshed. I put a small log on a tree stump and hit it with the axe. I missed; the log tumbled on the ground; the axe wedged deep into the wood.

"Whoa, whoa," Lopatin said. "Drop that shit, Raneva. I can do that." He carried the bucket to the porch steps, spilling some of the water.

"Or I can," Trifonov added.

"You—stay back," Lopatin said. "You can't lift that axe without injuring somebody."

"Not true."

"Why don't you help fix food? I gathered what I could from my home. Should be plenty." Lopatin fitted on his gloves and secured his hands around the handle. "Stay back, stay the fuck back." He wrested the axe out and lifted it high above his head.

"Doesn't he look awesome?" Milka asked.

"He looks mean, like he's about to destroy a village," I said.

"What kind of trees are these?" Trifonov asked. "Apple?"

"Yes," I said.

"The orchard must be beautiful in late spring, when all the trees are blooming."

"It's gorgeous," Milka said. "Like you're walking in a dream—all white and ghostly."

"It smells nice too," I said.

"Why have we never been invited?" Lopatin asked.

"You're here now," I replied.

"True," Trifonov said. "But summers are warmer." He rubbed his hands together, then brought them to his mouth, blowing air.

"Someday, all this will belong to Raneva," Lopatin said, and cleaved the log in two. He bent to pick up the larger piece, put it on the stump, and hit it again. It didn't budge this time; the axe stuck midway. "You need to hurry up and marry her, Trifonov, and then it'll all be yours—this dacha and the orchard, and Raneva too. You can sell the place or rent it out. You can also contribute to society by reproducing little Trifonovs, who can lecture the shit out of the world." He smashed the log against the stump, the crack deepened, but still the wood didn't break. He waved it above his head, making a few tentative swings, then brought it down as hard as he could. The log busted open, and a few chips sank in the snow under the apple trees; a few landed at our feet. Milka squatted to gather them.

Flurries shed from the sky; they dappled our skin, turning into tiny beads of water. When I moved the torch closer to my friends' faces, they looked wet and shiny.

"You have very little imagination, Lopatin," Trifonov said. "But I still like you. A word of advice, though: stop waving your arms. Lose the habit. To make such plans—marry, sell, rent out—that too is waving."

"Fuck off, Trifonov. We'll talk in twenty years. My people were peasants; yours, pharmacists. And who knows what our children will be." He scooped the split wood and piled it inside the pit, then flipped his lighter, but nothing happened: the newspapers ignited for a brief moment and shrivelled into a black fist.

"Damp," Milka said. "The wood too. No fire tonight."

"We'll make fire," I said. "Let's pour some vodka over it."

"I didn't bring any," Lopatin said. "Only beer."

"What about some gasoline?"

"Dangerous," Trifonov said.

"For once, I agree," Lopatin added. "It'll stink like a chicken's arse too."

"We just need to get it started," I said, shivering.

Milka blew on her hands, then massaged her cheeks. "I'm cold, and I'm hungry."

Lopatin untied his scarf and looped it around Milka's neck, raising it all the way up to her ears. "Start making sandwiches," he said, and trudged toward the fence. "There's lots of good shit in that bag," he shouted, squeezing between the wooden posts and popping open the car boot.

In the kitchen, we lit a candle, and Milka and I cut salami and cheese into thick uneven slices, and Trifonov arranged them on bread. He peeled hard-boiled eggs and placed them on a plastic bag.

"Look how the onion peel ate into the egg when they coloured it," he said. "It must've had tiny cracks."

"Just like marble," Milka said, and cradled the egg in the cup of her hand. "Too beautiful to eat." She rolled it back on the table. "Still—it's a dead baby."

We opened two cans of sprats drowned in oil and a jar of pickled cucumbers and tomatoes Lopatin had pinched from his mother's pantry. He'd also brought oranges, a box of chocolates, and a half of a *kulich* that was wrapped in a linen towel and whose vanilla smell clashed with that of smoked fish.

"Maybe put the cake away for now," Milka said.

"Yeah," I said. "We'll have it later, with tea. If Lopatin gets the fire going."

"Can't we use the stove?" Trifonov asked.

"No. The gas tank is disconnected."

"Ah, but these sour tomatoes are the best," Milka said, sucking on one. "Delicious. Here." She brought a meaty, dark maroon vegetable to my mouth. I opened wide, and the tomato disappeared.

"How can you eat those things?" Trifonov asked. "Too much vinegar upsets my stomach."

"You're too gentle a creature," Milka said. "And we're tough." She laughed; red bits of tomato skin flashed between her teeth.

"Yes, we are," I said. "We can survive anything, like these trees. They fought droughts and diseases; blizzards only made them stronger."

"And yet, a man can destroy them with a simple axe," Trifonov said. "Just like anything else around him."

"Sometimes you sound too pessimistic," I said. "You allow no joy or even love."

"I'm above love. It encourages pettiness and illusion, which is the impediment to freedom and happiness—which are the purposes of life anyway."

"How Chekhov of you," Milka said, her nimble hand fishing out another tomato. "One has to live a life in order to discover its purpose."

"True," I said. "And sometimes it changes too. Like this orchard—it looks dead now, but in just two months it'll be alive, swelling with leaves and blossoms. And then, there's no place in the world more beautiful."

"The whole country is like your apple orchard. But how did you come to own this land, Anya? Think about it. Your grandparents and great-grandparents were probably dutiful revolutionaries. They sang Communist hymns and spied on their neighbours and friends, to survive, to get ahead. And who can blame them? Those were the times, right? But they betrayed and buried many, walked on corpses. The dead are looking at you, whispering at you from every apple tree, from every branch. We owe our lives to the dead, and yet we haven't come to terms with our past: we don't know it. All we do is talk and get drunk. But to own our present, we must own our past."

"Stop your highfalutin bullshit, Trifonov, before I stuff a rag in your mouth and burn you at the stake," Lopatin shouted from the doorway. "Your folks are just as guilty as mine or Raneva's. Everyone spied, and everyone killed, and everyone pissed blood when arrested. Now come out and look at this hot, raging beauty, people, and bring beer and food."

The fire kindled in the pit; Lopatin kept feeding it slivers of wood and paper we assumed he'd found in the boot of the car. The flames climbed higher and higher, and he squatted, warming his ungloved hands over the burning logs. He fetched a stick from the split pile and poked at the wood, releasing a host of sparks. Lopatin's face glowed with a swanky smile that also seemed malicious. His cheeks were grubby from not shaving, and his mussed hair stood up in clumps. His shadow hunched on the ground, and when he rose, it rose too, projected against the toolshed. He leaned over and picked something from the stump, tearing and scrunching the paper before feeding it to the fire.

"Nice and dry," he said.

Milka passed him a sandwich while I handed him a beer. He poured half of the bottle down his throat, then took a ravenous bite, and another. I popped a whole egg into my mouth. Trifonov was peeling an orange and tossing the peel in the fire, his long, delicate fingers separating the fruit into perfect fleshy sickles. Even with the smell of burning wood, the air tingled with a sharp scent of citrus.

"Could you bring those tomatoes?" Milka asked, and Trifonov rushed to finish his orange before ambling into the house. He emerged a moment later, with a sandwich clamped between his lips and a jar of pickled vegetables under his arm. His coat hung open, and we could see his light brown sweater, threadbare and too short.

Lopatin threw some wood into the pit and reached for more paper. But Trifonov, who'd already placed the jar on one of the benches, caught his hand.

"Are you out of your mind?" he asked, spitting the sandwich and lifting a book high above Lopatin's head. "Are you burning Bulgakov?"

"I tore a few pages, so what? You all read it, and Raneva gave the book to me on New Year's. I tried to read it, but couldn't understand shit. *Heart of a Dog*—you can't turn a dog into a man, that's insane."

"That's all you got from it?" Trifonov asked.

"I got plenty. But I don't need you to rub my nose in it."

"You're an ignorant peasant swine, Lopatin."

Lopatin sucked the rest of his beer, then waved the empty bottle in the air, finally setting it on the stump. "I am a pig. I don't deny it. But if you think my peasant grandparents are to blame for everything that happened to this country, think again. They didn't start it, weren't smart enough. It's your people who started the shit, and now it stinks all over. Fucking *intelligentsia*. Shall I remind you who the Decembrists were? Counts, princes, the royalty, the elite. They worried about dumb paupers, sweaty plebs, drunkards, wishing to turn them into something noble. Why? What if the mob didn't want to be educated or transformed? Did they think of that? Did they think that maybe it's as impossible to change a peasant into a prince as it is a monkey into a *Homo sapiens,* even though the functional portion of human DNA is 98.4 percent identical to that of chimpanzees? See, I've done my research, Trifonov, and you've done shit. So, whose fault is it? Your people pretty much fucked up this country and then tried to blame mine, but it's over now. We'll build a new country, a new empire. Plant a new fucking orchard. Give me that book." Lopatin brought his hand out, but Trifonov stepped back and held it even higher than before. Lopatin tried to jump and snatch the book from Trifonov's hands, but missed, slipped, and fell in the snow.

"Fucking stop it," Milka said. "I hate it. You always ruin shit. Fuck you, Lopatin. How can you burn books? It's like burning these trees. They're alive. They have souls. If you don't understand it, that doesn't mean you should destroy it."

"You have a dog's heart, Lopatin," Trifonov said. "You'll never be anything but a dog. This new country you're talking about, it won't happen until the last Communist dog, the last KGB pig, dies."

Lopatin spat through his teeth and rose first to his knees and then to his feet. With a slow, deliberate gesture full of overt contempt, he brushed snow off his trousers, wiped his hands on his coat, unbuttoned it, and shook it loose off his shoulders. His face was calm and bitter, dark thickening in his eyes. I could see a germ of loathing in them; his eyes were devoid of their usual non-malicious fun-poking, but instead burned with mockery. It seemed as though he'd always limped under the weight of his masks but was now free from that weight and from the need to hide or counterbalance his hatred for Trifonov.

"I'm leaving," I said. "I'm locking everything up. Milka and I will go to the station and hitchhike toward the city. You both can kill each other. I don't give a fuck."

Neither heard what I said; my words were dulled by the sound of Lopatin's fist hitting Trifonov's face, first his cheek, then his chin, and then his forehead. Milka and I screamed as they rolled under the trees, pounding and clutching and clawing at each other. Trifonov flung the book, and it barely missed the fire; I darted to pick it up while Milka summoned all her strength, endeavouring to pull Lopatin away from Trifonov, who'd begun to wheeze. I saw a trickle of blood on his neck.

"Stop it!" I yelled. "Fucking stop it!"

Trifonov no longer swung his arms or legs, but lay buried under Lopatin's weight, his head deep in the snow. His eyes were bulging, his face whitewashed. He gulped air like a dying fish, without sound but with much effort.

"You fucking killed him!" Milka yelled. "You fuck, fuck!" She grabbed Lopatin by the collar and tried to drag him away.

He finally crawled under the tree and sat against the trunk, panting, the hatred on his face replaced with fear. His lips were bruised, and his left eye began to swell. His jeans and sweater were smeared with dirt and blood. He massaged his hand too, which was scraped and swollen.

"Where's his inhaler?" I screamed, kneeling down, cradling Trifonov's head. Blood poured out of his nose. Broken, it resembled a flattened lump. "It isn't in his coat or trousers."

"The car?" Lopatin asked, and Milka ran to the fence, slipping between the pickets. "Not here!" she shouted after a short while.

"Fuck," I said. "Maybe it's fallen out of the pocket. Look, Lopatin. Please. Don't just sit there."

Minutes stalled while Milka and Lopatin searched the ground on hands and knees. The fire had almost burned down, so nothing could be seen unless illuminated by the torch, which only covered a pitiful patch of land, the size of an apple.

Trifonov continued to wheeze and lose strength, and I continued to stroke his head on my knees. Tears dripped down my chin, a few plopped on his face, and he opened his eyes and blinked, weary and confused. "Please don't die," I said, and bent to kiss him on the mouth, ever so gently, tasting my tears and his blood, salt and iron and grains of dirt. "Please, please don't die." I pulled off my scarf and wiped his face.

"Get up, Raneva. Let me have him."

Lopatin moved like a large injured animal, lifting Trifonov from the ground and limping toward the car, knocking down the wicket gate with his feet. Trifonov's body was a pitiful sight; it sagged in Lopatin's arms like an uprooted sapling, withering. Milka had left one of the car doors open, and Lopatin placed Trifonov in the back seat, then climbed behind the wheel.

"Get the fuck in the car!" he said before shutting the door.

I rushed inside the house, tossing all the food into the bags, and Milka stomped out the flames and plucked up the jars and bottles. With shaking hands, I snapped the lock on the door when she yelled, "I found it! I found it!"

Trifonov's nose finally stopped bleeding, but even with the inhaler, he wasn't able to draw much air and panted all the way to the hospital. His hair was dirty pink, clammy, sticking to his forehead. Before getting into the car, I pinched some snow into Milka's handkerchief and applied it to his nose and bruised cheek. His eyes were open, but the pupils didn't move, dark and glassy. Only now did we realize that we had forgotten Lopatin's coat, but Lopatin said he'd return for it later. We didn't say anything else, but stared grimly at the road uncoiling before us like a black ribbon.

I first suggested driving into the city, but it meant losing more time, not to mention that Lopatin worried about being pulled over and arrested, as late as it was. He resembled a mean highwayman: bedraggled clothes, dishevelled hair, scraped face, one eye swollen shut completely, the other blood red. He kept sucking on his lips, touching his finger to the wound.

I remembered a small country hospital fairly close, in Belye Stolby. My parents had taken my grandmother there one summer. The hospital building was long and narrow and could be mistaken for a prison, metal bars on the windows and doors. As soon as we arrived, Lopatin helped us out of the car and even waited for someone to turn on the porch lights after we rang the bell. The three of us, Milka, Trifonov, and I, stood against the wall, Trifonov's weak, swaying body buttressed by ours. His whole face was purplish red, swollen to the size of a pumpkin.

Lopatin lit a cigarette and shuffled to his car.

"Where are you going?" I asked.

"To the dacha and then home. I can't risk it. If my father finds out, I'm grilled meat, a fucking kebab."

"How will we get home? How will we explain this?" Milka asked. "Don't leave."

"Call Trifonov's mother. Say you were attacked by some drunken arseholes, and Trifonov tried to protect you. Make him a hero."

"You're such a fucking shit, Lopatin," Milka said.

He shrugged. "I don't deny it. I really don't."

It must've been midnight. The hospital door finally opened, and we saw a tall pale man with a groomed pointy beard and intent eyes. He wore a doctor's robe and small rimless glasses; around his neck hung a stethoscope. His dark thinning hair was pushed back.

"Can I help you?" the man asked, his voice calm yet urgent. "Is anyone sick?"

We didn't answer but viewed him in silence, trembling, inundated with fear and uncertainty and the impending punishment, all that we were about to endure. I reached up and touched Milka with one hand and Trifonov with the other just as the man drew in a sharp breath and said, "Come in. Come in quickly."

19

My parents forgave us for sneaking to the dacha at night without permission. They also believed our story about being attacked by some drunks as we walked down the country road, trying to catch a ride. Neither Lopatin nor Trifonov returned to school, though. Trifonov was too sick, and Lopatin had been arrested on his way back to the city for driving without a licence, so we assumed that he either was in jail or got expelled or both. Milka said she couldn't care less what happened to him, because he'd betrayed us. But we felt terrible about Trifonov and blamed ourselves for letting Lopatin beat him up. We stopped by Trifonov's flat each day after classes, but his mother wouldn't let us see him. It was decided that he would be homeschooled for the remaining month and would only come back during exam week. We saved our lunch money and bought him his favourite rombabas or ponchiki, fat powdered-sugar doughnuts, from a local bakery that would soon close, like many old Soviet shops. Trifonov's mother opened the door only as far as the safety chain would allow and accepted the sweets, still warm, wrapped in grease-blotched paper. She did it without a word or a smile, her face haggard, disapproving. She looked twice her age, with drab cheeks and pasty sunless skin, the residual sorrow in her eyes. Her hands trembled as she pulled the packages through the opening. She never accused us of anything, and yet her expression told us that we were guilty. Just as we'd been that time in Yalta, when Trifonov had lost the *Cherry Orchard* pages.

All around us, a desire for political and economic changes only bred more despair and confusion. Teachers stalled during classes, not sure what to teach next or what homework to assign. During recess, they conferred at the cafeteria, or the gym, or the principal's office; they moped through the hallways, eyes on the ground, as though searching for some right thing that could be found there and bestowed on us. We grew quiet and wary and at times felt like machines, robots with rusty parts and defective wiring. We shuffled from one classroom to another, knowing that we had to unlearn everything we'd learned. We gossiped, too, and seethed with questions, to which no one could provide answers: Are we free now? Can we go anywhere we wish? Can we listen to Tsoi and Queen openly? Can we buy Levi's jeans? And if Lenin and Stalin were despicable tyrants who'd cheated millions of people out of their beliefs and murdered all those innocent but insubordinate Russians, who is left to lead this country into the future? What is the future? Can we tour the gulags?

The weather began to warm up, and spring showed its new, softer face, the sky washed with colour, blue and lively. Trees stirred in the gentle breezes, grazing windows and buildings. It was really the death of winter, and we celebrated it, as we always did, by trading our fur coats for trench coats and jackets, wool tights for nylon hosiery. We continued to study for final exams and rehearse *Hamlet*. The play was our farewell project, and most senior students were expected to participate. I wasn't eager to act, but Milka looked passionate onstage, heady, and I felt compromised by not so much her talent, but her stubborn desire to understand things. I also felt jealous. Not of my friend's ability to memorize and perform, unabashed, flaunting her knowledge and her acting skills; I was jealous of her as a human being who wasn't afraid of looking ridiculous in front of our classmates, or the whole world. It wasn't that she didn't feel insecure pronouncing old-fashioned words in a foreign language or that she thought herself to be unquestionably gifted; the truth was, she seemed unaware of all those things when she was onstage; she seemed to have become engaged with the text on a different, intimate level that demanded a certain kind of understanding and refinement that I didn't possess.

I played Queen Gertrude because everyone had decided I was mature enough and had a womanly figure. And Milka agreed to be Prince Hamlet because no boy wanted the part— since our classroom discussions of Shakespeare's play revealed that Hamlet might have lusted after the queen. All the boys in our class said they wouldn't fuck their own mothers even if someone paid them a million dollars. We'd spent hours memorizing our lines and rehearsing. We'd even watched *Гамлет*, a 1964 film adaptation, directed by Grigori Kozintsev and with an original score by Dmitri Shostakovich. My mother had sewn costumes for me and Milka, and we were able to borrow a foil from a fencing club. With her jaw-length hair, dressed in my father's old white shirt to which my mother had attached a pleated-lace jabot and cuffs, a short red velvet cape and matching pantaloons, white pantyhose, and with the foil on her hip, Milka indeed resembled a prince. She strutted around our living room, her gait full of the unhurried dignity bequeathed to royal heirs at birth. On her feet, she wore a pair of men's black leather slippers she had to stuff with wadded newspaper because they kept falling off.

A few days before the performance, we walked back from school to Milka's place. The air was sweet, redolent of fresh growth. Everywhere trees swelled and budded; leaves were beginning to unfurl like baby tongues. The sun was high in the sky, melting the last ashen patches of snow crusted on the curbs. I burst with energy and gabbed about us becoming a revived nation, a new people, who would bewilder the world—Generation Perestroika—and about both of us getting into the Institute of Foreign Languages and maybe studying abroad. Milka didn't say much, but nodded every now and then, her mind as far away as the crowns of poplars bowing in the distance. When we reached her building, she said she had vodka and cigarettes upstairs and that we should celebrate.

We burrowed in her flat, as we had for years, frying potatoes and blaring Queen from the tape player. We poured vodka out of her stepdad's bottle and added some water to it. Milka was unusually quiet, shuffling around like an old woman, her slippers flattened at the back. She'd changed into a cotton housedress, and I noticed that she'd filled out in places. I even joked that she no longer resembled a sprat but a full-grown herring. She forged a tart smile, and I pinched her arse, hoping to make her laugh. I felt tipsy after just a few shots; my heart pounded under my shirt.

In Milka's bedroom, we opened the window and lit cigarettes, hanging halfway out, blowing a quivering tail of rings in the air. I stuck my finger out and put it through one of Milka's rings, so it resembled a wedding band, but then it dissipated right in front of our eyes.

"I need a favour," Milka said, her voice hoarse, raspy.

"What?"

"You're my best friend, right?"

"Wrong. I'm your *only* friend," I said, flipping the cigarette out, chuckling.

"I need you to hit me in the stomach."

I turned to look at her, but she continued to smoke, her eyes on the lilac tree in front of the window, its slim crooked branches covered with new leaves.

"What the fuck?" I said. "Are you drunk?"

"Pregnant."

"No!"

"Yes. And you don't know the worst part," she said, and stubbed the cigarette on the windowsill blotted with pigeon shit.

"What can be worse?"

"It's my stepdad's."

I blinked and cupped my mouth, dragged my hand all the way down my chin and neck. "You're kidding, right?"

"No."

"You're fucking your stepdad? What about Lopatin?"

"What about him? He's a dick, like any other. He betrayed us."

"Are you sure the baby isn't his?"

"Yes."

"That's terrible. I can't believe you'd do that."

"Shut the fuck up. It's fucking complicated. You don't know shit."

"What do you mean I don't know shit? You're screwing your mother's man. What else is there to know? You don't do that. Are you fucking crazy?"

"My mother used to put me naked between them in bed when I was little. As soon as he'd get a hard-on, she'd throw me out the door, so he could hurry up and screw her."

"Are you shitting me? Ugh, this is fucked up. We need to tell somebody."

"Like who? Who gives a fuck if your own mother doesn't? Anyway, it's too late for the abortion. Almost five months. I had my period the first two. It was light, but I didn't pay much attention, so I had no idea I was pregnant. My boobs were sore, but I thought—growing pains, you know. When I told my mother, she started crying and pleaded with me not to do this to her, not to steal this fucking man of hers. He's all she's got. She can't be alone. I'll get married and leave, and who will she have? She said we could sell the baby to some rich people, but I'd have to go away for a while, until the baby is born, to live with my grandparents in Norilsk. Do you know how far that is? It's fucking Kolyma. Gulags. Permafrost. I have to get rid of this baby. I don't want it, and I don't want to sell it to some sterile fucks who can abuse the shit out of it."

I was silent. I couldn't breathe out a word, my tongue in my throat. I stared at a small rectangular aquarium on her desk, the walls overgrown with algae. Through the greenish, murky water, I noticed a few small fish not really swimming but stalling in place as though waiting out a storm.

"I've thought this through. I even bought some herbs to induce labour. Women used to do it all the time—drank shit, then hit themselves in the stomach with stones or irons. And then, boom—a miscarriage," she said.

"I'm not going to hit you. I won't be a part of it. No fucking way."

"Then you aren't my friend."

"I *am* your friend. But this is fucking crazy. And what are you going to do with the baby?"

"We'll bury it somewhere."

"And what if it's alive?"

"We'll take it to the hospital and tell them we found it in a rubbish bin in the yard—happens all the time."

"No, it doesn't. What the fuck is wrong with you?"

"I'm pregnant, and I hate it. I hate everyone. You too."

"Me? Why? What did *I* do? I'm the one who should be mad. I told you everything, and you told me shit. You could've slept with *my* dad and cared less."

"He's on my list. I'm already wearing his shirt." Milka laughed a short, sharp laugh.

"You're such a bitch. A dumb fucking bitch. We used to be best friends, like sisters. When I was little, I begged my mother to adopt you. And you're just like Lopatin—you betrayed us."

"There's nothing good or bad, but thinking makes it so." She gave me a prickly smile, her eyes cold and distant, like those of the fish in her aquarium.

"Stop mocking me. This isn't some dumb play," I said.

"Life is a stage; all men are actors. Who said that?" She reached to touch my shoulder. "I'm sorry. Let's just have sex and make it all go away. Hamlet forgave his mother for sleeping with Claudius because he too wanted to fuck her."

Gasping, I took a step back and then jumped at her and began to pound on her face and chest and everything I could reach. She didn't defend herself, but retreated deeper into the room and cowered next to her bed as I rammed my feet in her crotch and higher, between her ribs. The more I hit her, the more I wanted to continue, the less she protected herself. I knew I should stop before it was too late, before we would both collapse: she, from pain; I, from fear and remorse. Suddenly she rose and started flailing her arms like a wild person, and I caught several blows. I managed to seize her, using all my strength, to pull her to me and hold her tight as she pummelled my back, tears streaming down her cheeks, and mine.

That night I couldn't sleep, my heart thrashing about my chest. In my bedroom, I lay surrounded by shadows that writhed on the walls. It seemed as though everything bright and happy in the world was gone, fought away, that I would never see or feel the sun again, its brilliance and its warmth. All was dark, dirty, irrevocable. I wanted to tell my mother, but I couldn't bring myself to do that; I feared that she would never let me be friends with Milka again. So I continued to lie in my bed, breathing heavily, chewing on my nails.

Milka called the next morning. It was early, the sky shy with dawn. I'd finally managed to doze off, but when the phone rang, I jumped and ran to the kitchen and grabbed the receiver.

"I'm having it," she whispered. "Can you come? I'll tell my mother I'm sick, and they'll be gone for work in an hour. I'll leave the door open."

Back in my room, I dressed in my school uniform and packed my bag, my knees weak, hands trembling. In the wardrobe mirror, I discovered a reddish bruise on my cheek and concealed it under a thick layer of makeup and powder. I waited until six forty-five to wake up my parents and inform them I had play rehearsal before classes. They nodded, rubbing their faces. "Did you fix yourself a sandwich for lunch?" my mother asked, and I said I'd be eating at school.

Milka lived a fifteen-minute walk away, but I made it in ten, running, taking shortcuts through muddy yards and playgrounds, climbing up a kindergarten fence and exiting on the other side. When I arrived at her building, I was panting like a dog, tongue out, eyes bulging.

Milka's flat was quiet, the air still and eerie. I saw two sets of slippers under the coatrack and a newspaper tossed on the chair. Milka's bedroom was closed. Without taking off my jacket, I tiptoed down the hallway and listened by her door, the book bag on my shoulder. I thought I heard someone whimper, so I pushed the door open, just with the tips of my fingers.

Milka half sat, half lay on the bed, her face puffy and smeared with blood and tears. The blanket was drawn up to her neck, shielding her scrawny body, her knees bent, legs somewhat apart. There was also blood in her unkempt hair as though she'd been running her hands through it.

"It's over," she said.

"Over?" I repeated.

"Yes."

"Where is it?"

"Here." She nodded at her knees, then exhumed one arm from under the blanket. She began to peel the covers away, slowly, as though afraid that whatever hid underneath might escape.

I couldn't force myself to look at it, so I shut my eyes and, jerking the beret off my head, pressed the wool to my face.

"Can you bury it?" Milka asked. "I'm too tired, and I have to wash the fucking sheets."

"Where should I take it?" I mumbled.

"I don't know. Just don't bury it where dogs can get to it."

From the headboard, she dragged an old T-shirt with a faded rose print, wrapped the baby in it, and passed me the bundle. I placed it in my schoolbag, taking a few books out and leaving them on her desk, next to the aquarium.

As I stepped out the door, I said, "You all right? Will you be all right? I'll come back after."

"Don't." She closed her eyes, then curled into a foetal position and pulled the blanket over her head.

On the wall, above the desk, hung the picture of her father. It was a black-and-white portrait, large and square, the wooden frame chipped at the corners. The man in the picture had a smooth shaved face. He smiled—lips curving in a pulpy half-moon—but his eyes held deep sadness as though he'd already known what would happen to him and to his daughter and to his grandchild.

—

Outside, I stood on the empty street, watching a stray dog nose a pile of rubbish near a newly painted dumpster. I thought of sneaking the baby in there, but then I remembered my mother preaching to my father that the dead had to be buried, laid to rest—otherwise they'd come back to haunt you—that if the government had bothered to give Lenin a proper burial, as opposed to preserving and displaying his wretched body, our country wouldn't have been in such pitiful shape sixty-odd years later.

I walked to the bus stop and considered going to a park and burying the baby there, under a tree. But I had no tools, and the ground was too hard to paw with my hands, and I was scared that someone might see me and call the cops. Finally, I decided I had no choice but to ride to the dacha. My parents hadn't yet gone there to prune or fertilize the trees, so the keys would still be where I'd left them.

There were mostly women on the bus and a few older men, who carried mesh totes with newspaper-wrapped packages and fruit saplings sticking out like brooms—naked branches tied together at the lower end. I had the odd feeling that everyone on that bus was watching me and that they somehow could guess what was in my bloated bag. The bus shook and rumbled, and I held tighter to my bundle, pressing it against my belly.

It was a brisk ten-minute walk from the bus stop to the village, which seemed abandoned like during the war. I couldn't see or hear any dogs or livestock, and no smoke rose from the chimneys. The squat dark-brown log houses stood silent, the windows draped with cheesecloth or nailed shut with boards.

The road was uneven with ruts and puddles, exposed rocks and fallen branches. For years, my parents and their neighbours had tried to persuade the authorities to pave it, at least the part that connected the village to the dachas, but no one had ever paid any attention to their requests.

When I arrived at the dachas, I walked by Garev's house and the Khodovs', keeping my head low, avoiding anyone who might recognize me, although I was pretty sure our neighbours never visited the dachas on weekdays this early in the spring. When I reached our place, I stepped through the hole in the fence that Lopatin had torn while carrying Trifonov to the car. There remained no traces of our visit three weeks ago, except maybe for a few slivers of wood on the ground and the axe that lay abandoned behind the stump.

From the jug in the outhouse I extracted the keys, and from the toolshed my father's shovel. I debated whether to bury the baby in the field, the birch grove, or on the bank of the river. But what if Milka wished to visit the grave sometime and I wouldn't be able to point out where it was? And what if someone happened to see me walking around, carrying a shovel? They would most certainly call my parents. So, as I stood there, next to my mother's flowerbeds buried under leaves and twigs and palm-size patches of snow, I raised the shovel and began to dig under one of the apple trees, its limbs already covered in tight pearl-white buds. I rammed the shovel into the ground and hacked away at the hard dirt, breaking it up and chipping a piece at a time, trying to carve out a wide enough space.

When I finished, I retrieved the bundle from the bag. The

blood had soaked through the T-shirt. I went back to the shed and searched for some kind of burial box and found nothing but building supplies, paints and brushes, a trunk of old toys and a jar of nails, and a rusty basin filled with my father's tattered shirts torn for rags. There was not much I could do but put the baby into the hollow of the still-frozen earth. Before covering the bundle with dirt, I brought it back up and slowly unwrapped it, parting the layers of fabric like cabbage leaves.

In there, curled on its side, was a miniature person—a boy. He was scarlet and tiny, with an elongated, egg-shaped head; knees bent, fists clamped against the button mouth as though in defence. He just lay there, like a skinned animal—a squirrel or a rabbit—a hump of bare flesh on a strip of snow. His eyes were shut, body pleated with wrinkles. When I drew my finger along his shoulder, it felt cold and hard and slick. There was a tiny hose protruding from his belly, ragged at the end, as though chewed off. I pulled the beret from my head and gently tucked the baby inside, as Milka and I had tucked dolls inside paper boats before setting them afloat in puddles of rain. I lowered him into the ground, folding the T-shirt on top.

Tears washed down my cheeks; my skin tingled and burned. I gathered an armful of clumpy dirt, shoved and patted it back in place, and then scooped some leaves. I watched them fall through my mud-caked fingers, landing under the tree.

20

That evening, I kept calling Milka, but no one picked up, and the next morning she wasn't in class. In the school bathroom, where years ago we'd experienced our first kiss, I stood smoking one cigarette after another, leaning out the window, hoping to spot her slim figure emerging from behind the trees. On the wall hung the same cracked, square mirror that had once reflected our silly, grimacing faces. How happy we'd been, how innocent; our friendship as pure and whole as our dreams. The bell rang, and I shivered, taking one last drag before tossing the cigarette in the commode. I stepped closer to the mirror, so close that my breath fogged the glass. I reached out and drew a face with two slanted eyes set far apart and thick heart-shaped lips. I watched the face disappear, fade into nothingness behind the dull silver surface.

Back in the classroom, time stalled. An hour dragged by—sixty minutes—three thousand six hundred seconds—all of which I spent biting my nails until my fingers were raw. Then, during biology, our class was interrupted with an announcement: the play had been cancelled because Hamlet was dead.

Everyone stared at me, and I began to shake. Milka's vacant seat echoed with a terrifying silence. The teacher stroked my back and shoulders, offering a glass of water, which I couldn't swallow. She hugged me and said that time healed the deepest of wounds, bridged the widest of gaps, and that one day I would wake up and realize how wonderful life was, despite all the grief and heartache. I tried to answer her, but couldn't form any words, my vision blurred, my throat choked with tears.

My mother arrived at the school to pick me up. She told me that Milka had died from mushroom poisoning, that by the time her parents returned from work and found her, it was too late. She barraged me with questions: "Do you know anything that I don't? Was she upset, angry, hurt? Did you see her yesterday? Did you miss school because you were together? Did you two have a fight? Is that a bruise on your cheek? Are you telling the truth?"

I didn't know. I didn't know the truth.

In the days that followed, I became desperate to talk to Milka's parents, but they wouldn't answer my phone calls. A few times I went to their flat, but they refused to open the door. They became the gatekeepers of their daughter's death. I would return home and stay in my room for hours, replaying all the details of that afternoon when Milka and I had gotten into a fight, as well as the next morning, when she'd asked me to bury her baby. I refused to believe that she'd died from mushroom poisoning. I kept wondering: had her parents found out about the miscarriage? Or had she been able to clean up? Had they seen any bruises on her body? And what if her stepfather had killed Milka and her mother had done nothing to stop him?

But then—for sure—the police would have been involved, and the school wouldn't have been able to hide the truth.

Not knowing what had really happened to my best friend made me obsess even more. I imagined Milka jumping out the window, or slicing her wrists, or swallowing a bottle of pills, chasing it with her stepfather's vodka. I imagined her dangling from the ceiling light or stabbing herself in the gut. But nothing would satisfy me. I felt guilty and bereft. I would stare out the window, at the sky and the emptiness it harboured, and mutter, "I'm sorry, I'm sorry, I'm sorry," first biting my knuckles and then hitting myself in the chest and lower.

I didn't want to go to the funeral because I couldn't bring myself to watch the casket being lowered inside the darkness of the earth. But my mother insisted. She told me that our friendship must be honoured, that saying one last goodbye to my beloved friend was not only about respect, but also a promise to carry on—through years and loneliness, heartache and silence. We were responsible for the dead as much as for the living; we carried them with us always, no matter how heavy the burden. In the end, our burdens defined us, made us who we were.

At the cemetery, the same one where Milka's father had been buried, grass sprouted on graves, along with errant patches of flowers—irises and lilies of the valley—poking their shy heads through old leaves. The air smelled of loam and new foliage, the raw energy spring breathed into the world stirred awake after many dark, frozen months. I remembered how Milka used to say that we lived in a perfect world filled with imperfect people. But it was also an ugly, cruel, merciless world that she and I no longer shared, one robbed of her jokes and love of books, her jubilant daring and the passion with which she dissected life and fiction, the characters' fates she imagined as her own. Never again would I see how Milka's face was transformed by a smile or her raucous laughter; how doubt wedged upon her childish features, or scorn or anger. How her voice escalated with jealousy, or broke into thunder, or mellowed with desire.

I pressed my head against a mighty birch, its branches thrust toward the sky like pleading arms. The rough, knotted bark grazed my cheek, and I leaned in even harder, the grain cutting into my skin. Right above, clouds fretted, pulling together, gathering rain or tears, which was what my grandmother always said, that one must cry in order to feel better, to endure and surpass grief. I drew in a mouthful of air, but tears wouldn't come as I tried to swallow—again and again.

There were so many flowers you couldn't see the casket, which remained sealed. I stood behind my mother, who stood next to Trifonov's mother and Lopatin's parents. Milka's family remained on the opposite side of the grave, among the crowd of classmates, teachers, neighbours, and others I didn't even know. Dressed in all black, her mother seemed pale and shaky, with a wadded handkerchief pressed against her wet, puffy face. Milka's stepfather kept rubbing her shoulders, rearranging her shawl. He wore a brown suit and a white shirt, and his face was freshly shaved. He appeared more baffled than upset, as though he'd just learned about his stepdaughter's death. His eyes avoided mine, but when, inadvertently, he caught my silent stare, he looked away. At one moment, I almost walked up to him, but my mother, guessing my intentions, caught my hand.

The principal from our school had encouraged everyone to contribute a word, one fond memory, and Trifonov, still weak, with a partially bruised face, pronounced a short soulful sermon, which he ended with Lermontov's poem, *"A far sail shimmers, white and lonely . . ."*, reciting it from memory and almost until the very end before having to reach for his inhaler.

Lopatin was there too; he towered at the foot of the casket, looking at no one. He didn't talk, and he didn't cry, but somehow appeared humble. When the principal touched Lopatin's shoulder, he trembled, blinking hard. Folded, his lips disappeared from his face, eyes red and dry, feverish. I noticed a raw place on one of his cheeks, closer to the temple, a large scar that had been recently stitched together. Blood caked in the middle. He hadn't shaved either, which gave his face a haggard, malevolent look. He kept thumbing a carnation head and wouldn't let the other pallbearers approach. Finally, he bent over and wrapped his mighty arms around the casket, and it looked as if he were about to lift the casket on his shoulder, all by himself.

I couldn't speak, when prompted, afraid that if I did, stones would fall out, crushing the flowers, that anything I said would be a lie and that Milka would somehow know it. When I finally walked up to the casket, everyone stepped back, including Milka's parents and Lopatin. I drew my fingers along the chintz-covered wood and was amazed at how petite the casket was, as though for a child. It was warm, too, from all the flowers or the sun, which had parted the clouds. Tears gushed down my cheeks, a salty torrent I attempted to hold back with my fists. I bit the skin so hard it spotted blood, but I kept biting, kept gnawing on my knuckles until my mother seized my hands and dragged me away.

For weeks after the funeral, I couldn't eat or sleep. I lay in my bedroom most days and nights, watching the net curtains puff up on my window and go limp like a piece of a shroud. I listened to the trees shivering with new leaves and dogs barking somewhere on the street and my parents discussing my pitiful state in the next room. Both Lopatin and Trifonov attempted to contact me, and Trifonov wrote me letters, which I tore up and threw in the bin unread. Once I heard him at the door, apologizing as my mother explained to him that it wasn't a good time—I wasn't ready for visitors. Out of my bedroom window, I watched him trudge along the curb, thin, stooping, hands in pockets. His old shirt fluttered in the wind, which seemed to be blowing right through him, through his fine hair and rickety limbs. I wanted to call out for him, but my throat shrivelled, my tongue a prisoner in my mouth. Tears dripped down my face and mixed with a puddle of cigarette ashes on the sill.

A month staggered by, but I still wouldn't see anyone, and I wouldn't leave the flat, not dressing or washing for days. I became pale and thin, a skeleton in a sack, a ghost hovering about the flat, lurking in corners or behind doors. Sounds hurt me, but silence did too. Sometimes it felt as though my ears crawled with spiders spinning labyrinths inside my head. I shook it and shook it and buried it under the pillows so as to muffle that incessant tedious rustling like raindrops hitting trees. My teachers showed compassion and overlooked my absence in school for those final weeks of the term. When I received my diploma in the mail, my grades were just as high as they'd been all year, prior to Milka's death.

My mother, who feared the worst, had used all of her vacation time staying home with me, but then arranged for an unpaid leave of absence. It was the only time she'd ever smoked. We even did it together, huddling on a bench in the yard or the balcony, smoking the days away. Cowering on a stool next to me, she'd rub my shoulder or comb my hair behind my ears, a gesture I found all too unbearable, but otherwise she was afraid to touch me, to scoop me in her arms or kiss my head like she used to. Occasionally, she and I would go to the movies, and instead of watching the film, I would catch her staring at me, her face contorted with fear. She'd grab my hand and wouldn't let go until the end of the movie, and I could feel her heart throbbing in my palm.

Urged by my father and grandmother, my mother had found a doctor, a psychologist, whose speciality was trauma. She hoped that he'd encourage me to talk, to let all the pain out, to free space for her to fill with love and food. She accompanied me to the sessions and waited outside the clinic. When I sat in the room, I could see her treading under the windows, smoking. The doctor was a middle-aged man in a pin-striped suit, whose manners were courtly yet subdued. He moved with elegant ease and had a soft, benign voice. "How do you feel?" he'd ask. "Do you want to tell me about your friend? Your most recent memory perhaps?" Occasionally, he permitted his voice to rise and his tone took on a desperate edge, which he would banish with a sweet smile. "Enough talking for one day. Let's do something creative." He asked me to compare coloured shapes and draw pictures and listen to tapes that were supposed to help me share and analyse my tragic experience. After each therapy session, I felt as though a train, a locomotive, had passed through my chest, leaving nothing but silence in its place, a void. But I still wouldn't talk about Milka's pregnancy or our fight. I was afraid to betray her, even in death. Once, following the therapist's advice, I attempted to compose a letter to Milka, in which I had to address my best friend as if she were alive, but I could never write anything past the first line, which I would repeat over and over until I filled the page: *Dear Milka, Dear Milka, Dear Milka, Dear Milka, Dear Milka, Dear Milka, Dear Milka, Dear Milka, Dear Milka, Dear Milka, Dear Milka, Dear Milka, Dear Milka, Dear Milka, Dear Milka, Dear Milka . . .*

A whole year passed, and spring arrived again, and I dropped the therapy sessions. Implored by my parents to pursue education, I passed the entrance exams and matriculated into the Institute of Foreign Languages, where for a while I became distracted by the turmoil of assignments and projects. I didn't know anyone, and no one knew me. I was like a small cloud pushed and shaded by others. My desire to learn or rather to bury myself in other people's work was commendable, and the professors supported and encouraged my zealous efforts. Never a model student at school, I grew more attentive and diligent while in college, defying fatigue and heartache, hoping that knowledge could outweigh the grief.

I spent hours in the local library and became acquainted with all seven floors of the building, the studying rooms and reading halls, the maze of bookcases and authors, whose ghostly steps echoed mine. I devoured the Greeks in their velvety covers the colour of an evening sea—Homer, Euripides, Sophocles; their immense epics made everything else a pale imitation. I read Chaucer, Milton, and Shakespeare, believing that they must've been tormented by truths and spirits to be able to conjure such worlds, to shrink all that pain into language. I held Dante's *The Divine Comedy* and thought that the poet had known love beyond death, beyond all that was mortal, inconstant, volatile, while Goethe's *Faust* convinced me that souls could travel between the worlds—like feelings or the wind.

My father didn't lose his job, as expected, and on weekends he and I drank at the kitchen table while my mother scraped dinner together. Our means were tight, but vodka was cheap and reeked of ethyl, and he and I snorted black bread as soon as we dumped it in our throats. We crunched pickles or sucked on thinly sliced lemon, which too had become scarce, along with oranges and other fruit, except for apples—we still had plenty from our orchard. By then, my grandmother had difficulty not only seeing but walking as well, so she never left her bed except to use the bathroom. Although soon even that would become a problem, and my father would construct a portable toilet out of a tin pail and an old plastic seat. My mother or I would help her sit on it, and she'd close her eyes, embarrassed we had to witness her emptying her bowels. But such was life, as my mother was in the habit of saying. "We

have no other choice but to live it." And then she would narrow her eyes at me. "Right?" she'd ask. And then again,
"Right?"

When night fell, sky to earth—starless, moonless,
shadowless—I could slink about the flat unnoticed. I could
open the kitchen balcony and climb on a stool, and then on
a narrow railing, where I continued to stand for an eternity,
barefoot, arms akimbo, the balance of my body so delicate it
would take one gentle stir of the wind, a raindrop or a flurry, to
tip me over.

Once, on a late autumn afternoon, when my parents weren't
home, I was dusting the bookcases in the living room, where
my grandmother rested on her bed. As I rearranged heavy dishevelled dictionaries and stacked-up issues of *New World*, she
caught my hand. She held it tight, just as she did when Milka
and I used to pull her out of the river and she kept sliding back,
down the steep muddy banks. Her hand was bloodless and
twisted like a root.

"What's wrong?" I asked. "Did I wake you? Do you need
to use the toilet?"

"No," she said. "But there's something I have to tell you."
She let go and leaned against the wall, a snowdrift of pillows
behind her back. Her face was parched and fissured with wrinkles. She stretched her arm forward, patting the bed until I sat
down.

Rain brewed outside; the sky frothed with clouds that resembled upside-down ships. The room grew darker, and I
fumbled for the switch on the bedside lamp, but my grand-

mother stopped me. The silver mass of her hair lay across her shoulder while her crooked fingers brushed through it, separating it into three equal parts and then weaving them together in a single braid.

"In Leningrad, during the Blockade," she began in her low threadbare voice, "we saw death every day, and every day became the last for our neighbours, friends, children. But we stayed busy. In the morning, some of us went to factories, others searched the city for crumbs of food, stepping over corpses like felled trees. In the evenings, we gathered in someone's flat, thirty, forty people, and shared what we could, what we'd been able to find. We made cakes out of silo mass and potato peels and boiled starch with sugar cubes. We ate snow and later our pets, and we breathed hard in our babies' faces to keep them from freezing to death. At night, to forget about cold and hunger, we read books out loud until we burned them for heat, and then we told stories, stories of our childhood and youth, good family times. We wanted others to know and tell the world after we died. Whoever was to survive was to tell all the stories, so our husbands, if they returned, and our children, if they lived, could remember us. We didn't lose hope, and we didn't lose faith, even when it seemed that we had no strength left to do anything, to open our eyes in the morning. Not once did any of us think of ending her life, of jumping from a balcony or a roof. If we did, Hitler would have won. Inconceivable. We had to live, if only to tell our stories.

"But of course, there's more to one's grief than others can imagine, because there's always more to a story than one is willing to tell. What I'm about to share with you, nobody in this family has ever heard. But I want you to know the truth because someone must carry it forward when I die."

"You aren't going to die," I said, touching her knee, so sharp and bony, even under the blanket. "Not soon, I mean."

"God gives, and God takes," she said and paused, her fingers now unbraiding what she'd just braided. "When the old die, the young feel no pity. But when the young die, the old are inconsolable. When my son died, there were five of us left in the flat, and the daily food ration for a grown-up was no bigger than a fist. There were no birds, dogs, cats, or even rats left in the city. I couldn't bury my son because it was so cold and also because I was so weak, barely placing one foot in front of the other. So I put him on the balcony, wrapped in a sheet. Your mother was three, getting weaker and weaker. She didn't even ask for food anymore but lay on her side under a blanket that was so heavy I kept thinking it would suffocate her. Every now and then I placed my cheek to her lips to make sure she was still breathing.

"One day she couldn't get up. I held her in my arms and kissed her face, her sunken cheeks and cold mouth, a mere thread of life still connecting each one of her breaths. That was when I knew: my daughter would live; she would survive the Blockade, even if I died. I asked one of the women to keep her warm while I took a knife and stepped out on the balcony and began to unwrap my son's body."

My grandmother's voice grew thin and taut, words catching in her throat.

"We all ate it," she said. "And we all survived."

PART TWO

21

I'd arrived in America as an exchange student in 1988, but got married and stayed. When we had first met—nineteen years ago—my husband worked for a construction company, doing mostly renovations: patching and painting, restoring old floors or kitchen cabinets, replacing carpets, laying tiles, installing new windows and countertops. He was what people called a handyman—he could repair anything that had been broken. We both wanted children, and at first we'd tried with all the fervency of newlyweds. We'd been full of hope and joked about it each time we'd failed. We changed sex positions and made love at all hours of the day and night; I stayed in bed for forty minutes afterwards, my buttocks raised, hips propped up on pillows. I took my temperature with a basal thermometer and drew charts of my menstrual cycles, highlighting the days of ovulation in red. We consulted several obstetrician-gynaecologists in the area, who did a sperm count on Mike and blew dye into my fallopian tubes to check for scar tissue or any blockage. Back in Russia, my mother had procured some ancient herbs she claimed would help with fertility. She sent them to us and urged me to brew and sip the concoction before bedtime. Nothing ensued. Years stormed by and slowed down, and eventually our efforts ceased.

We let things turn into a memory. Not a bitter one, just vague and distant, like the mountains on a snowy day. We knew they were there, although we couldn't see them.

Since then, I'd gone back to school and completed a PhD in comparative literature. My husband switched from renovating to building, mostly residential, but occasionally a restaurant or a factory. Well respected in the area, he continued to earn a good, honest living. He'd gained weight and lost some hair, the rest turning silver, glistening like fish scales under the sun. He was tall and brawny and resembled an ogre who could carry a house on his shoulders. He had big kind hands that he wrapped around me every night before we went to sleep. He nuzzled my hair and joked that it smelled like books. We were comfortable. We rarely argued or disagreed or had long passionate conversations, and sometimes I thought of us as two pet fish in our aquarium, navigating through tall, wavering weeds, or hibernating inside a plastic castle, or hiding under a rock, ostracized by the glass walls. We depended on each other and those walls.

Autumn was hunting season in Virginia, and when Mike returned from work one evening, I pointed out the window at the two skinned, gutted deer hanging from the swing in our neighbour's yard. The mulch and sand around the swing were dappled with blood, a puddle directly under the deer carcasses, and two dogs were lapping from it.

"My mother called," I said, and kept staring out the window. The sun hadn't quite set, the sky ablaze with colour, a scarf of red and mauve and deep purple.

"Oh, yeah? What did she say? Are they finally coming to visit?" He took his shirt off and threw it on the chair, then just as quickly picked it up, tossed it into the laundry basket—years of commitment to me and our tidy household.

"No. But she needs me to come over. They're being bullied by some crooks into selling their dacha. Since it's so close to Moscow, the land is a gold mine. The house isn't much, kind of dilapidated."

"So, what seems to be the problem?" Mike was in the shower now, and my words reached him through a curtain of water and soap.

"It's my parents' apple orchard. The contractors will cut it down for sure. And I think my parents can't bear the thought of it. They're old and sentimental, clinging to every scrap of their past. That country house, that little bit of land, and the orchard—it's all they have left. They feel at home there, while in Moscow they feel like refugees. They don't belong."

"Did they ever?" Mike's head appeared from behind the curtain. Suds in his hair and face, his eyes shut, his nose crinkled; a sweet, helpless giant puppy.

"Sure," I said, smiling at this naked creature in need of a rinse and a towel. "They come from a different time, a bygone era, but one that existed. It's still real to them. It had its drawbacks, but what time doesn't? They were so passionate once, so opinionated, fierce."

My husband ducked back behind the curtain, didn't reply.

"Mike?"

"Yes?"

"Why aren't you saying anything?"

"What do you want me to say?"

"Should I go?"

"It's up to you, Anya. What about your classes?"

"I can go during the Christmas break. Just for a few weeks."

In a foggy mirror, I saw the outline of my head, a mop of curly chestnut hair pinned in a bun. The rest of my features were smudged, indistinguishable.

"Do you want to come with me?" I asked.

"You know I can't. Too many projects. But I'll be all right."

"Will you?"

"Yes. But you won't go, so there's no point in discussing it any further."

"Why so sure?" I wiped the mirror with the back of my hand, but it fogged over again. I drew a face: broad and moon-like, two small eyes set far apart and slanted, pulpy lips. "Remember I told you about my best friend, who died at sixteen?" I asked, and erased the image. It was a blur now, a patch of fog and mist.

"Yes. Something tragic. You never found out what happened."

"Well, as it turns out, her former boyfriend, Lopatin, works for those crooks who want to buy my parents' dacha."

"Really? That *is* odd. You should definitely go," he said, and began to hum a kid's song, a bubble of words I couldn't make out.

Though perceptive and kind, Mike lacked sentimentality. He'd lost his mother at sixteen, the age when a teenager was supposed to be inundated with love, not grief. But who can know all the grief the other person has felt or lived through?

We aren't really allowed any intimate knowledge of someone's past, just a glimpse and speculation. An unfulfilled dream at best, a sorrowful secret at worst.

The truth was—I hadn't been home for ages, and my parents had never met Mike. First, I couldn't go because of all the paperwork involved with the change of my immigrant status. But after that, I was afraid, afraid to face the ghosts of my youth, the guilt I felt about Milka's death. As for my parents, they too had refused to cross the ocean. For years they took care of my grandmother and neither would travel without the other; then, after my grandmother died, they couldn't get a visa, and they were afraid to leave their flat and their dacha, the land to which they'd devoted their lives. Now they were getting old, so they were reluctant to take any trips, not to mention overseas. My mother kept telling me how everything had changed in Russia—music, clothes, food. Shops groaned with goods, but prices were rocket-high, so people couldn't afford much. Some threw their dogs out on the streets because they couldn't feed them, and there were all those strays scouring the city.

Since Vladimir Putin became president, he often spoke about the collapse of the Soviet Union as the greatest geopolitical disaster of the twentieth century. Many Russian people, including my parents, shared his opinion. KGB trained, he tried to fight corruption by implementing a series of educational and structural reforms; on the other hand, the oligarchy rose, and political murders doubled. He'd been in the office close to eight years, and there were rumours that he wanted to change the constitution so he could remain in power indefi-

nitely. My father said that Putin was the last Russian czar, and
my mother said that the last Russian czar, Nicholas II, had
been murdered by Bolsheviks and that Russia had always been
too large a country to be ruled successfully by one crazy mon-
arch. Sooner or later, people would distrust his ubiquitous
power and revolt.

Both my parents had retired and, until just recently, spent all
their summer and autumn months at the dacha, raising flowers
and vegetables, tending to the trees, canning and making apple
preserves. Last year, they said they had to cut down one apple
tree and replace it with another, sweeter variety. But I didn't
ask which tree or what kind exactly they had planted instead.

"I'm ready to eat, dear," Mike said, and I shuddered, the
weight of his damp hand on my shoulder. I patted his fingers,
which still smelled of soap. He was dressed in old flannels and
a Life Is Good T-shirt. The man on the T-shirt was climbing a
mountain, a backpack on his shoulders and a happy curly-
tailed dog at his booted feet. My husband had been the same
for the past nineteen years: bath, dinner, a little TV if there was
a game on.

"I'll set the table. The living room? In front of the TV?" he
asked.

"Any games tonight?"

"Maybe. But we can watch a movie, a foreign film? Something French and zesty."

"Why French?"

"They have beautiful women. Remember how many we
saw in Paris?"

"Not like in Rome," I said.

that there was so much shame in my country's history, personal shame and communal, and also grief. If it was a rock tied to our feet and we were thrown into a river, we'd all drown, quickly and soundlessly, pulled by the size and weight of our burdens.

A few days earlier, one of my students had asked why most Russian poets had either been murdered or committed suicide, why most Russian writers had been mentally or physically ill, or both: Gogol, Dostoevsky, Chekhov, Bulgakov. And why all Russian literature was fraught with pain and suffering—all the important characters died or death was looming, and there happened to be no retribution at the end. Did life mirror art? Or art life? Was it really all that hopeless? There had been a heated discussion in class, a crossfire of opinions, but in the end, I'd said, "Read Shakespeare, *Hamlet*—it's all in there—murder, death, endless misery. And we're all willing participants."

The garage door rolled open and closed, and I heard a shuffle of heavy feet on the steps. Mike was home earlier than usual because we had to visit his father.

"You getting ready?" Mike shouted from the kitchen.

"No. I forgot it's at five. Who eats that early anyway?"

"Most people do."

"Already in the shower," I said, dropping my robe on the floor.

I stood under a stream of hot water for a while, then Mike peeped behind the curtain and climbed in the tub. He took a piece of soap in his hands and began to lather my body, his fingers running slippery circles around my breasts.

"We'll be late," I said.

"God, I love these things," he murmured, eyes half-closed. His hand slipped between my legs. "If a man was asked to choose between pussy and eternal life, he'd still choose pussy. What good is life without pussy?"

He breathed heavy into my ear and pressed his naked body into mine. He was strong, taut, and fully erect, which I welcomed, the water sloshing against my thighs. Our lovemaking was unsurprising, mundane even, but also satiating. There was comfort in the familiar, security in the knowing. I was always amazed how bodies could convey that, how they could exchange information without words or much sound, how they could protect, nurture, and sustain, the bare tremble of someone's skin against your own. I closed my eyes and leaned into Mike, and he moaned softly, sinking deeper.

He ran his fingers up and down my back, his lips so close to my ear. "Let's try in vitro," he said. "We're still young."

"I'm almost forty," I said, swallowing water. "You're forty-eight."

"Yes, but we're healthy."

I didn't answer but reached for the towel and stepped out of the shower.

22

I'd finished packing two days ago but kept sneaking things into the suitcases: sanitizing wipes or ziplock bags or cortisone cream. I had no idea what they sold in Moscow apothecaries, and I could ask my mother only so many questions before she started assuring me that everything was possible in the new country they lived in, if one was willing to pay. You could die with dignity—the casket varieties, the beauty of the wood, the carvings, all were exquisite. My mother had begun talking about death not as about something terminal, the nonexistence, but something one had to live through, like another chapter in a book. You had to read it to get to the end. I was baffled by her calm optimism in the matter.

Mike's face was an autumn day—eyes clouded with thoughts, lips curled, folded at the corners like dry leaves. Sad as he might be, he tried not to show it, pressing harder on the gas pedal, in a hurry to get me to the airport. The question of in vitro had been raised and dropped like a river stone, sinking to the bottom of our hearts, leaving large, dark, overlapping circles. Or maybe it was only the separation anxiety, which had begun to settle in. In the past nineteen years, we'd never been apart, never in different cities, not to mention countries or continents.

The sky started spitting snow, and the flakes whirled in the air, landing on the windshield. I remembered the blizzard the day we got married in a small local church on a hill. It was the same church where Mike's parents had been wed and where Mike's father hadn't set foot since his wife's death. I remembered people driving up the hill in trucks and SUVs, the road sprinkled with sand. I got dressed in one of the rooms in the basement, Mike's sister, my only friend and bridesmaid, helping me to fit into the gown without disturbing my curls, which were stiff as wire. We'd sprayed them heavily before leaving the house. She'd clipped the veil to the back of my head and covered the pins with baby's breath, then held out her mother's ring, a chip of a turquoise stone in the centre. All the time she chanted, on and on, like a prayer, "Something old, something new, something borrowed, something blue." I didn't want to wear her mother's ring, because my grandmother had told me that trying on another woman's ring was like trying on her fate. But I didn't want to upset Mike's sister either, so I said, "How about I put it in my bra? That's where my grandmother hid her rings when she left the flat."

I lost the ring sometime after the wedding, when all the commotion started, when the guests opened the church doors and couldn't see anything beyond the two flowerpots filled with dry millet to be tossed at the newlyweds. The rest was smothered under snow: the roads, the cars, the pine trees that sprawled their shaggy paws around the building. Some guests brought potato chips from the church kitchen, crackers, cheese dip, and even apples. They were green and tart, but otherwise had no taste. Mike peeled one with a pocketknife. He cut the apple with his huge, bearlike hands, then placed a piece in my mouth before kissing me, tearing the veil off my hair.

A pianist, a thin ancient woman with a cloud of bluish curls, played "No Other Love," a sweet slow song originally performed by Jo Stafford, Mike's mother's favourite. A few people still remembered the words and tried to sing along, but I could see Mike's jaw tremble and so did his father's and sister's. When the woman finished playing, I walked up to her and asked, "Do you know any contemporary songs? 'We Are the Champions'?"

"No." She shook her head. "Sorry."

"What is it?" Mike asked.

"It's an old song my friends and I loved back in Russia. 'We Are the Champions' by Freddie Mercury."

"I know that song. Just heard it on the radio. I think he died."

"Oh my God. When?"

"Not long ago. I can get you the album. It's no problem."

"No," I said, sitting down on the altar steps. "I don't want it. I really don't."

I looked over at Mike, his eyes focussed on the road. He wore a chunky beige sweater and blue-jean overalls. He was a big man, but somehow, behind the wheel of his truck, he seemed slight and fragile. Or maybe the mountains were to blame. Flanking the road, they veered into clouds like pillars of black granite, their demeanour absolute. Who could contest their age and attainments? Their weight and stamina? The multi-tude of fissures that grooved their backs?

"I just read an interesting article in *The New Yorker*," I said.

"What about?"

"Kübler-Ross's famous book *On Grief and Grieving*, which is a follow-up to *On Death and Dying*."

"Don't know either one."

"Well, basically she claims that like the dying, the grieving undergo the same five stages: denial, anger, bargaining, de-pression, and acceptance. We see it in literature too. For ex-ample, we can assume Hamlet acted the way he acted because he was grieving his father's death."

"Makes sense. Although I don't remember exactly how he acted," Mike said.

"Well, some critics insist Hamlet had a strong sexual desire for his mother."

"Because he was angry or depressed?"

"Or both. But I think there's more to grief than just those stages. Some people never accept the loss because their whole identity is inextricable from that of the deceased. When Milka died, I didn't even want to go to the funeral. I didn't want to make it final. I was so messed up. I couldn't eat or sleep. I re-fused to talk about it either."

"I remember when our mother died, my sister and I, we were very confused. And my sister later decided not to have any children because she didn't want them to see her die and feel that same grief. In the months after the funeral, my sister talked to herself a lot. We didn't know if she was hallucinating or what."

"In some cultures, the dead aren't really gone, so you keep in conversation with them. Russians believe that after a person dies, her soul hangs around for nine days. Then it travels back and forth between heaven and earth for forty more days before leaving for good. However, if a person committed suicide or was murdered, then her soul never leaves but hovers among the living. Brings up the metaphysical questions about existence, yes? You think there's life after death?"

"No. This is it. This is all you get. My mother drank herself to death. So, did she kill herself? Or was she poisoned by people who produced the shit? Sometimes it's hard to know who to blame."

"That's true." I kept quiet for a moment, then said, "We should've been there by now."

"I took a different route. The roads are icy," Mike said, and squeezed my knee. "I'd love to go with you, but I need to finish that house."

"I know, and it's such a hassle to get a visa. Besides, four weeks isn't that long."

"Still, I'd like to meet your parents."

"Maybe I can persuade them to visit in the summer. But I really wish you could've met my grandmother. She was such a force."

"Just like my father," Mike said. "Seventy-eight and still as feisty as ever."

"That's for sure."

"After our last visit, he asked about you, said you seemed sad or upset."

"Did I?"

"He still isn't used to your Russian ways."

"Which are?" I turned to look at Mike, his shaved face, a Band-Aid right at the jawline, where he cut himself that morning. I suddenly became aware of his perfume, tangy, spicy, a mix of cloves and wintergreen.

"Well, you know, Northern people aren't as cheery. It's been proven. Where you grew up, there isn't enough sun, which affects people's behaviour."

"But there're more people, especially young people, committing suicide in America than in Russia."

"Good point. But what I mean is when they show Russians on TV, they don't smile much."

"Not much to smile about, but it isn't the sun, believe me."

Mike kept quiet, then said, "Why won't you try to have a baby? It isn't gonna happen unless we try."

"We already did, and nothing happened. Maybe we aren't meant to become parents."

"Or maybe we just need to try harder."

I didn't answer. Out the window, the mountains looked scorched black, a rugged spine in the dusky, mauve sky.

My flight to Moscow was delayed for five hours, and when I finally boarded the plane, I had an abominable headache and my chest was congested. During the flight, I drifted in and out of feverish sleep, not eating a thing but asking for hot tea, which they always brought in such minuscule cups. I emptied them in thirsty gulps and asked for more. An elderly Russian man in the neighbouring seat offered Tylenol, for which I was grateful, then covered me with his blanket. He woke me up for breakfast, but all I wanted was tea and more Tylenol.

My father was among the first people in the crowd of greeters, hugging me so tight I nearly collapsed from pressure and heat, melted like a snowball in his arms. I felt his wet cheek against my burning one, his tears cool and hot at the same time. He looked old but not so changed, still loud and hearty and a bit crude. I could almost imagine that those twenty years I'd lived in America hadn't passed but were about to happen. That instead of arriving, I was leaving, and that my father was crying not from being happy to see me, but from being sad to let me go.

As he drove us home, I struggled to stay awake. The landscape appeared barren and unremarkable, unchanged except for the massive billboards that contrasted with the birches, so many, slender and graceful, I almost cried when I first acknowledged them and pointed them out to my father.

"Sickly," he said. "Growing like that by the road, breathing all that shit. Now, near our dacha, they're as mighty as they come. Your arms won't close, that's how wide those trees are."

"At least that hasn't changed. That and the dirt on the roads." I closed my eyes and didn't breathe or hear another sound.

The next thing I saw was my mother's face, weary and wrinkled. She kept sweeping away my hair, trying to get a better look, her fingers meaty yet dry, but so soothing. She cried, and I did too before falling on a pile of blankets and pillows, which were like clouds, soft, puffy, carrying me through distances, through spells of dreams and wakefulness.

I opened my eyes from time to time as I was spoon-fed meat broths and raspberry tea with lemon rinds floating on the dark red surface. A cool, wet cloth was pressed to my face and neck, my feet were rubbed with greasy ointments that smelled like eucalyptus and mint, and a mustard plaster had been adhered to my chest. I wore my frayed high school pyjamas, a revelation when I finally woke up one afternoon, confronted by the crisp brilliance of a winter sun.

I called for my mother, but my voice was a scratch and a squeak. I forced myself first to sit up and then freed my legs from under the blanket, my feet stuffed in a pair of darned dog-wool socks.

"Awake. Finally," my mother said as I appeared in the kitchen. "Hungry? I fried chicken liver."

"I hate liver," I said.

"You used to love it. Ate platefuls."

"Not me, Milka. And she ate it because there was nothing else."

My mother stopped chopping carrots, knife in hand, and stared at me, her face stern and motionless.

"What?" I tried to preen the unruly mass of my hair like a dry haystack on my shoulders.

"We always had food. Always," my mother said. "You always had everything you needed."

"But not what I wanted."

"Nobody had what they wanted back then."

"They do now?"

"All you can afford. The choices are limitless."

"If you can't afford it, it stops being a choice. Know what I am saying?"

"Hello to you too."

"Sorry," I said, lifting the lid from a saucepan on the counter, the smell of fat yeasty dough bathing my face. "Pierogi," I said. "Oh, how I've missed them." My hand fished out a pocket of tender, egg-glazed dough. I bit it and chewed with applied force. Then again and again, until the entire pierog disappeared in my mouth, and I looked like a greedy famished hamster.

"Have some bouillon. It's on the stove," my mother said, and resumed chopping, and I saw how much she'd aged, how much snow was in her hair, how mottled and creased her skin. I walked up to her and wrapped my arms around her shoulders, mouthing through the dough and meat, "So good to be home."

"I'm glad," she said. Her hands scooped the carrots into a bowl. "It's been a long time. We didn't know if we'd ever see you again."

I chewed and swallowed. "America isn't that far. A ten-hour flight."

"You count in hours while we count in years—twenty."

"Nineteen and a half. And you could've visited. Or we could have met somewhere in Europe. Mike offered to pay for everything."

"Your father will never accept charity."

"It isn't charity. He's my husband. We share."

"If your grandmother were alive, she would've said, 'You share with no one but your children.'"

I didn't answer, and for a moment, we just eyed each other, not like a mother and a daughter who'd been apart for years, but like strangers who would never be close, no matter how much time we spent together. There'd always be that gap, that distance, which neither of us would cross. And not because we didn't want to, but because we didn't know how: there existed no bridge and no rope.

"I'm sorry I didn't come to her funeral. The timing was hard." How sad and shallow the words sounded; I regretted them.

Silence grew between us.

"Where's Papa?" I finally asked.

"At work," she answered; her hands were now skinning boiled potatoes. Thin brown shreds fell on the cutting board.

"I thought he retired." I picked up a potato and fingered the loose peel, then tore it off.

"He did. But he works for some co-op, sells wallets at the market."

I stalled, baffled by what she'd said. "He does what? Why? Do you need money? I've offered to help a thousand times."

"No, we don't need money. But your father can't sit still, you know how he is. Especially after he quit smoking."

"Mike is like that too, which reminds me—I need to call him."

"We already did."

"But you don't speak English."

"Our neighbour's daughter does. We asked her two days ago, as soon as you arrived."

"It's been two days already?"

"Yes. Nineteen years, six months, and two days." She raised her eyes at me, and they seemed so infinitely kind. I wondered if it was a mother's thing, to store kindness for her children, even when they disappointed.

"Thank you, but I still should at least email him. Do you have the Internet?"

"Yes, your father got everything working. He wrote down the instructions to hook up your laptop. They're on your desk."

"I still have a desk?"

"Of course. Haven't you noticed?" She was so tireless, my mother, still chopping the potatoes but already reaching for the eggs. "Making your favourite salad."

"*Olivie*? I fix it for Mike's dad and sister every Christmas, but I don't think mine is as good as yours." This solicited a smile from my mother. And for a moment she was young again, unharmed by years and our long-drawn-out separation.

"What meat do you use?" she asked.

"Boiled chicken or beef," I said.

"Wrong. You need sausages. The cheaper the better." She laughed, and I did too, a straw of happiness to which we both clung.

"I'm just going to check my email really quick and then help you chop. And then maybe we should go out. Get groceries?"

"We really don't need anything."

"But I'd still like to look. I have to exchange money too."

"You can pay with a credit card pretty much anywhere," she said, and cracked a boiled egg, began undressing it.

"What progress," I said. "Things have certainly changed." Pieces of shell landed on the table, and I brushed them inside my hand, then tossed them in the bin.

"Yes, they have. Not all for the best, I'm afraid."

"Meaning?"

"The collapse and dissolution of the Soviet Union. We can't even travel to the Baltic republics without obtaining a visa."

"That's ridiculous."

"And the attitude, the hatred—heartbreaking. The Russian language is prohibited. In Ukraine too."

"Are you serious?" I scooped the rest of the eggshell into the bin.

"Maybe the old country wasn't so bad. At least there was order."

"It was a prison, Mum. A dictatorship."

"Yes, but our land thrived—science, arts, agriculture. We lost it all. There's no pride anymore, no love either. We don't love our country, and we don't love one another. That's become impossible."

"It's so strange to hear this from you. I expect Dad to say such things, but not you."

"Your father takes it pretty hard."

"I'm sure. His patriotism is insane."

My mother raised her eyes and looked at me as she would at a stranger who'd barged into her flat uninvited. She allowed no excuse and no pity. I waited for her to say something else, and when she didn't, I brought out my hand and preened her hair, brushed it away from her face, as she'd done mine when I first arrived. My gesture baffled her. She placed her knife on the table and wiped her hands on a towel, then wrapped her arms around me. For a while, we just stood there, embraced by silence and the sound of the old wall clock reaching us from the living room.

23

The first ten days in Moscow had flitted by like birds. At one moment I could see their grey strained wings charting the sky, and the next, they'd already disappeared behind the clouds, leaving a ghostly breath in their wake. I called Mike late every night, and we chatted while he cooked and ate dinner, gossiping about his father or the neighbours. I had trouble adjusting to the time difference, but after the first week it began to feel as though I'd never left, that all those years in America had been a dream. Surrounded by my childhood trinkets, those memories that followed me from room to room, I felt my youth returning from the shadows.

Our flat had the same faded, fissured walls as before and a leak-stained ceiling in the bathroom my parents had once tried to patch and repaint. I doubted they'd done any redecorating while I was gone, maybe at the very beginning, but now everything looked just as shabby and run-down as when I left, although back then I didn't really see it that way. Our flat was modest and ordinary, like everyone else's, but it was also not communal, close to the metro, and in a relatively safe neighbourhood, thirty minutes away from the city centre. The flat was my dowry, as my mother had underscored while I was growing up. That and the dacha, with its apple orchard, which we would soon lose unless we could persuade the buyers not to buy.

In my bedroom too, things had remained just as they'd been two decades ago. My grandmother had stayed there for some time after I'd left, but when she died, my parents didn't have any other use for the room. Like many Soviet people, they never threw anything away—their past remained their present. An old wardrobe leaned in the corner, whose doors didn't shut completely because the floors were uneven and my parents had lost the key. The same curtains framed the window— sun-bleached flowers against a coppice-green background. Opposite the window was my school desk protected by the glass top, under which I remembered sliding photos of famous singers—Alla Pugacheva, Toto Cutugno, Viktor Tsoi—rare stamps and beloved poems, and even a lock of Milka's baby hair. Except for the latter, all the items were still there, although faded and switched places. The threadbare rug shifted and lumped underfoot as I walked to my bed table and touched the familiar knickknacks: a candlestick, a single-flower *gzel* vase, and my grandmother's amber brooch I'd forgotten to take to America. The stone was large and sunny and as pure as a tear. You could see minute bubbles of air trapped inside. Down below, on the bottom shelf, lay four odd-shaped pebbles from the beach in Yalta, the only reminder of my high school days. I picked up the pebbles one by one and rubbed them between my palms, the warmth of the late-spring night spilling through my chest; in my ears, the sound of the Black Sea, the splash and murmur of waves. I could almost taste salt between my lips, those fine grains of crushed shells.

Against the wall, my schoolbooks sagged on shelves. Fitted tightly among them, I spotted Bulgakov's *Heart of a Dog* and pulled it out, running my hand along the stained cover. It had separated from the rest of the book, exposing a ragged seam, where some of the pages had been torn out, leaving uneven edges, like poorly healed scars. After Milka's death, my mother was afraid that something terrible would happen to me too, so she'd disposed of all the things that could've reminded me of my best friend, including the *Cherry Orchard* tape and the Freddie Mercury poster. But there was no way for my mother to know about the book, how we'd rescued the novel from Lopatin's destructive hands.

All of a sudden, I had an urge to call my friends and ask them to go with me to the cemetery, to visit Milka's grave, to drink vodka and sniff black bread, to cry, to reminisce. My mother said that Lopatin had become a businessman, dealing in real estate—and in fact was involved with the offer on our dacha. But she provided no information about Trifonov, having lost touch with the family soon after I'd gotten married. I remembered the last night the four of us had been together at my parents' dacha: the fight, Lopatin smashing his fist into Trifonov's face, his body splayed on the ground in a puddle of blood and snow.

I sagged on the bed, pressing the book against my heart; the past like a mad, wounded dog baring its rotten teeth.

—

In the living room, the old clock struck every hour as it had for the past seventy years; the fragile porcelain cups with sculptured edges and yellow and pink roses still emitted that faint ringing sound when placed on saucers; the books—the complete editions of Pushkin, Lermontov, Gogol, Tolstoy, Chekhov, and others—occupied the same sagging shelves built onto the living room walls. The old Kalmyk rug still hung behind the sofa bed, where my mother now took her naps while watching TV. The colours on the rug had faded, but the lovely design, the curlicues of gold and emerald against the deep berry-red field, made me want to brush my hand up and down, to touch the coarse tufted wool. It seemed as though I touched time itself, and for a moment I forgot that my grandmother wasn't in her bed.

I said, "Sorry, I didn't mean to wake you up, Baba."

My mother, who'd begun looking more and more like my grandmother, with her mushroom-grey hair and her shrivelling skin, opened her eyes and asked, "What time is it? Ready to eat dinner?"

She turned on an old-fashioned lamp with a fringed shade, and it cast a shadow over her face. Squinting at the clock, she swung her legs off the bed, her feet in hand-knitted oversized socks. When at home, she still dressed in shaggy outfits, bulky sweaters patched at the elbows, frayed robes and slippers. She'd stopped caring about her appearance, disregarding fashion and makeup, her faded hair. She joked about it too, but she sounded sad in a way that made me think of creases in old aprons. She wasn't seventy yet, but her face seemed to harbour all the sorrows of her generation. The joy had been washed from her eyes; they were no longer blue but a dark, morose grey.

We moved to the kitchen, where my father had already sliced bread and *salo* and was cutting green onions, sitting at the table. In his navy sweatpants and tartan slippers, he looked like a character from a Soviet movie. He'd put on weight and grown a beard, all silver except for an islet of brown on one side. It resembled a birthmark or a hole on his cheek, and I almost expected to see food falling out and my mother reaching to catch it.

"If there is another coup, and I die, and my face is disfigured, you can still identify me by this patch." He laughed, rubbing his beard.

"No more coups. You're too old to protest." My mother smacked him with a towel, and he caught it, pulling her to him and wrapping his arm around her.

I grew uncomfortable, somewhat. "You took part in that putsch?" I asked, joining him at the table. "How come I didn't know?"

"There're many things you don't know. Living in America does that to people. They develop amnesia," he said.

"Isn't that why you sent me there? To forget?"

"I didn't send you there, and we had no idea you'd stay. It was your choice." He yawned to mask his rising anxiety, an inveterate habit the years hadn't dulled.

"But you supported my decision. You were happy," I said, not so much surprised by his words but annoyed.

"*You* were happy. And we were pleased that you'd found

someone, and that you stopped sounding like a zombie. You were excited, and so were we."

"What changed?"

"Nothing."

"Let's just not get upset over the things that happened long ago," my mother said, and unfolded a new linen tablecloth with cut-out snowflakes embroidered around the edges. It was too big for our kitchen table, but she kept adjusting the length on the sides and smoothing out the creases, her hands clean and dry, crisscrossed with veins.

"I'm sorry I haven't visited for such a long time," I said. "I thought you understood."

"We did, baby. We do," my mother said, nodding, but I could see her foot tapping on my father's. "We just missed you, that's all. We're glad you're here."

"Yes," he said, a tremble in his voice, an urge. "You're here, that's all that matters. Let's celebrate, shall we?" He got up and took from the freezer a bottle of vodka, unscrewed the cap, and poured three crystal shot glasses.

My mother raised her thinned brow in the same manner she'd done twenty years ago, hands on hips, a condemning silence in her eyes.

"Just one. I have to work tomorrow," he said, sitting back down.

"It's odd that you want to do that—to sell counterfeit goods at a flea market," I said.

"And if I sold real stuff?"

"It's not that. You're a space engineer. You—"

"Shhhh . . ." He leaned back and dumped the vodka in his mouth, which he wiped with the sleeve of his new sweater, a gift from Mike and me. Mike had suggested buying my father a fishing vest because I'd told him that he and I used to go to the river a lot, but the truth was, my father hadn't fished for years, since I'd left, so in the end I opted for a sweater. It was pure merino wool, dark navy with a small breast pocket. My father was shorter than Mike, but he was stout, full-chested, so I'd tried the sweater on Mike and ended up buying two.

"Let's eat, women," my father said. "What did you cook today?"

"Borscht," my mother said.

"Cabbage pie," I added.

"Love both. Bring them on."

And when my mother turned to face the stove, he quietly refilled his shot glass and just as quietly swallowed the vodka.

While my father rushed to the flea market every morning because the time before New Year's Eve was the busiest and he couldn't afford to lose customers, my mother and I cleaned, shopped, and roamed the city. I found myself both appeased and confronted by everything that I heard and saw: the grumbling sounds of stalled traffic, a thunder of Russian voices with their growling *r*'s and hardened *d*'s, the pandemonium of austere faces in buses and on the streets, the smell of cigarette smoke and exhaust, and then a sudden waft of sweet perfume like an apple blossom in the midst of winter.

With the twelve-day holiday approaching, the city stood lit and festive. Supermarkets spilled with food and liquor, their windows strewn with Christmas lights. Haberdasheries had become fancy boutiques, displaying silk lingerie, chic fur coats and elegant footwear, cashmere shawls, hats and scarves, berets and cloches stitched with beads, stones, and even feathers—like those *boyare* or royalty had worn. The prices were as high as the stars, so I didn't know how many Russians could afford to purchase any of those fine things, especially when the majority still considered a country house or a two-bedroom apartment in the city a lifetime achievement. And yet, someone must've been earning enough to support the sales and encourage all the industry and growth. New hotels and office buildings nosed the sky. They resembled spaceships, without doors or windows, just sheets and sheets of seamless liquid metal. Some buildings even had rooftop greenhouses, petite custom-made oases thriving behind glass.

"They're apartments, not flats," my mother said, pointing at two tall skinny towers. "For people whose chickens lay silver eggs."

"Not golden?"

"Those live facing the Kremlin and the Moskva River." She smiled, but her cold, stiff lips hardly parted.

When without my father, my mother and I ate out as much as we could. I insisted on trying new places and new dishes; I also wanted my mother to take a break from cooking. Since I'd left, nineteen years ago, Moscow had become a beehive of labour and scrumptious cuisine. Restaurants and cafés beckoned on every corner: Russian, Georgian, Armenian, Italian, French, German, and, at the most lucrative locations, McDonald's, Subway, KFC, and Pizza Hut. Somehow, here, in the hub of Russian culture, among proud ancient façades and churches that had been recently renovated and whose golden domes rose in the sky, the fast-food joints resembled artificial limbs or bionic parts that could never coalesce with the body, numb in their fake perfection. Unlike my mother, I refused to eat in such places, in America or Russia, where I continued to be spoiled by native delicacies, the tender long-forgotten tastes of my Soviet childhood.

Because there had been no snow yet, the city grew more anxious with each day. Trees and buildings, though swathed in garlands, remained grey like old bones. The air was thick; the land heavy, like a pregnant woman long past her due date. People nattered and griped on the streets and in supermarkets, and my mother swore that if it didn't snow by New Year's, she'd up and move to Siberia.

I had no idea why I called Milka's flat. Old habit, perhaps? Stubborn memory? Or was it because despite death, we keep searching for those we still love, keep reaching out to them—through time, and heartache, and loneliness? I hung up before anyone answered, then dialled again. I waited and waited, my heart pounding louder with each long, desolate ring. When a man finally picked up, I couldn't say a word. The room filled with the echo of my heart labouring somewhere outside of my body. The sound was dull yet persistent, reverberating through the silence of years.

"Hello?" the man said, his voice gruff. "Hello?" he repeated. "Who is this? Speak now or forever hold your peace." He laughed, a sharp, brazen laugh, which made me think of villains in horror movies. A flash of a smile. Crooked yellow teeth. There were also the hands: those fat hairy fingers, crumbs of dirt under the nails, the man's birthday tattooed right above his knuckles. The day and month on one hand, the year on the other.

I hung up and sat quietly, drew in shallow breaths.

"I'm going for a walk," I told my mother a few minutes

later, jerking my coat off the peg by the door. But she was busy in the kitchen, washing dishes, so she didn't say anything.

At the nearest kiosk, I bought a pack of Marlboros, a lighter, and mint gum to mask the smell. I didn't want my mother to notice and lecture me until dawn. I'd quit smoking years ago, but had been craving a cigarette since I arrived. As I scurried to the other side of the road, I noticed a woman with three small children crossing in the opposite direction. She was like a mother duck, steering her brood safely to the pavement. She might have been my age, although it was hard to tell underneath all the layers of clothing. I glimpsed her cautious eyes set too far apart, her slightly snub nose and red puffy lips she kept covering with her mittens. When we got closer, we both slowed for just a moment, long enough to know that we'd never met, that whatever familiarity we held for each other was misplaced. Still, I couldn't help but turn around and trace the woman's slim figure all the way down the alley, until she vanished behind a building.

The evening air was stiff, the ground splintered with ice. Dead grass clung to the bared roots of trees. No stars could be seen, but I knew they were there, burning holes through the universe. After the familiar fifteen-minute walk, I reached Milka's building. There was light in her bedroom, but the curtains were drawn. I smoked a cigarette, which tasted bitter, like a sip of silty water, then climbed the steps.

The door to Milka's flat had been replaced, and the new metal one reminded me of a mausoleum or a vault, where ghosts lived. I shivered and untied my scarf, my heart hammering under my coat. Suddenly I wished I'd told my parents where I was going, but I hadn't dared; my mother would have never allowed it. I could almost see her face, back in 1985, sad and terrified, a fluster of restless muscles.

I rang the bell, but was met with silence. No one rushed to the door, no sounds of footsteps or voices. Leaning against the wall, I lit another cigarette, but tossed it on the floor and crushed it under my boot when the door opened and the same gruff voice asked, "What do you want?"

The man in front of me was much shorter than I remembered. He was fat, bald, and resembled a wine barrel. Smelled like one too. He was dressed in a pair of dark blue jeans and a flannel shirt that hung loose, exposing his balloon of a belly and grey tufts of hair above the belt. He made no attempt to button the shirt or tuck it in.

"Anya? Anya Raneva?" the man asked. "How? Why?"

"Hello," I said. "I'm glad you recognized me."

"Of course! You hardly changed, just as pretty. What brings you here to these dark parts of the world?" He let out a chuckle, and I saw his crooked front teeth. They weren't yellow, but the gap was wider. "Come inside. So happy to see you."

For a moment, I thought I must be mistaken. I didn't know that man, although he somehow knew me. But then I spotted the tattoos on his swollen fingers, when he took my coat, and I was face-to-face with Milka's stepfather.

Smells encompassed me: liquor, smoke, and fried meat. Someone was in the bathroom; I heard water running.

"My girlfriend," he said. "My wife died years ago."

"I know."

"Do you want something to drink? Wine? I still make my

own. You girls used to steal it from me, remember?" He swaggered down the hallway, and I trailed after him, taking small soundless steps.

The kitchen had been recently refurbished, the old cabinets replaced with white shiny ones. Stainless-steel appliances. A collage of orange and brown tiles on the floor. A small modular sofa was fitted under the windows, and in front of it, an oversized table. I spotted dirty dishes in the sink, a lacy valance over the window, and a large wooden crucifix on the sill.

"Quite a difference since you saw it last, eh? We just finished renovating." He placed a box of candy, Vecherniy Zvon, in front of me. From the fridge, he produced a decanter of red wine, dark and thick like blood.

"I don't want any," I said.

"No?" He turned to look at me, surprised, scratching under his chin. "I have vodka too."

"None for me."

"You aren't pregnant, are you?" he asked as he poured himself a glass of wine. "Do you have children? You and Milka always said you didn't want any. I remember that. Where is it that you two wished to elope? Rome?"

"Paris."

"Right. Beautiful city. I went once with my girlfriend."

I watched him swallow the wine as though it were water, in loud gulps and without the slightest pause, and I regretted my visit. He talked about the past with a kind of casual nonchalance, dismissiveness even, as though the past didn't exist, had never existed. I wanted to ask him how he'd lived all those years; didn't he feel responsible at all? How could he stand in front of me—so brazen, so cocky? An old man without a trace of remorse.

"Pour me some of that disgusting wine of yours," I finally said.

"That's my girl. And it's a great wine, I swear." He set an empty glass on the table and filled it up. "Cheers!" he said, and passed it to me.

I drained the glass; the wine burned my throat, but I managed, allowing him to pour another. I shivered. My head swayed; my heart—a flogged animal racing through the steppes of my childhood.

Out the window, I imagined the lilac tree bursting with purple flowers, like minuscule crosses Milka and I used to pluck by the handful. We'd stuff our handkerchiefs and place them under our sheets, so everything smelled like spring, like dreams, like everything we wished to keep.

"So, how have you been?" he asked. "How's life in America? Rich and glorious?"

I didn't answer but walked up to him and stared into his drunken eyes. I saw Milka's pale terrified face reflected in the darkness of his pupils. I pinched his chin, hard, but his expression didn't change; it remained motionless, dumb. His breath sour.

"You molested my best friend," I said. "And you act like you don't even know it. Fucking arsehole. You probably killed her too."

"What are you talking about?" He threw me against the

table, and I lost my balance, falling backward on the sofa. The wine spilled on the cream upholstery, stained the cushions blood red.

"Milka died because of you," I said, rising.

"Strange, I remember it otherwise—she died because of you."

"No, she didn't."

"You were the last one to see her alive. I found your text-books on her desk."

"You're a liar. A motherfucking liar." I punched him in the chest, with as much force as I could summon, and he allowed me. I continued hitting everything in sight: his gut, his shoulders, and even his cheeks. My hands hurt as I slapped his face until he caught them, squeezing my wrists.

"That's what you did to her, didn't you?" he asked. "You beat her up. There were bruises. She couldn't do it to herself. You were the only one she trusted. Be thankful we didn't mention your name to the cops. We said she fell. And we didn't want anyone at school to know about the pregnancy. We spared you from questions and gossip."

I stared in his eyes—cold, without mercy. Tears surged up my throat.

"You disgust me," I said. "I hate that she's dead and you're alive. I hate that nasty look on your face, as though you've outsmarted the whole fucking world. I hate—"

He nearly dragged me to the door by my wrists. "Go back to America, to your spoiled, happy life. Eat burgers, smoke Marlboros, drink Coke. Forget about her. She was a filthy cunt. She fucked everything that moved. It isn't your fault or mine that we loved a whore. She's dead, dead. She killed herself. Took her mother's pills and washed them down with vodka. We couldn't save her. No one could."

He yanked my coat off the hook and threw it at me, but it landed on the floor. The room tilted, and his face was askance. That shallow derisive grin I longed to erase.

"Milka would've never killed herself," I said. "Never. She was daring, true, but she loved life more than anyone, including myself."

There was a pause between us, a lapse of time. The door to Milka's bedroom opened, and a girl of nine or ten emerged out of the darkness. She rubbed her eyes with one hand and hugged a bear with the other. She wore striped flannel pyjamas and had long golden hair that flowed down her shoulders like sunbeams.

"What's wrong, Daddy?" she asked. "Why are you yelling?"

"Everything is fine, baby. Go back to bed. We're just talking. Old friends."

"I'm scared," she said.

"The lady is leaving. No need to be scared."

Tears swelled in the girl's warm and trusting eyes. He kneeled in front of her and tucked her hair behind her ears. "Go to your room, baby. Your mama is taking a bath. She'll be right there, I promise."

The girl obeyed, though reluctantly.

I picked up my coat from the floor but accidentally dropped my scarf. He grabbed it and passed it back to me. I studied his face, old and weary, softened by wine and the girl's voice.

"It's not what you think," he said. "She's my girlfriend's

daughter, and we love her very much. My girlfriend doesn't know anything. Please, don't come back. Let's have our good memories and forget about the rest. What happened, happened. No point in hurting anyone else. Please."

"Tell me what happened to Milka."

"Why, after so many years? Why dig through the past?"

"If you don't, I'll tell everything to your girlfriend. In bloody details. All that I know."

He sighed and looked behind his shoulder. A tremor gripped his face, and he winced, stalling. "She bled to death," he finally said. "She took something, some herbs or pills, to induce labour. We had a late meeting at work, so when we came home that evening, she was still alive, although unconscious. Her mother didn't let me call the ambulance right away. She was afraid I'd end up in prison. She said she couldn't lose me too."

My hands and legs began to shake, my entire body, and I sank to my knees and vomited. It felt as though I'd swallowed my own heart, and I continued to retch, trying to spit it out.

25

Mike phoned on Christmas Day, when he came back from his father's house. As always, he sounded sincere when asking about my parents, their health, and the overall feeling of my visit. We talked about the country's changes, the lack of snow, and how things tasted and smelled after my prolonged absence.

"Like a dream," I told him. "You don't want it to end, and yet it must."

"Can you stay longer?" he asked.

"No. The semester starts on the twelfth."

"Did you get all the grading done in time? How's the Internet?"

"Fine. Grades submitted."

"Any good papers?"

"Yes, a few. One on *Bastard Out of Carolina*, the other on the gulag literature—Shalamov, Solzhenitsyn."

"Have I read them?"

"I don't think so. But in her paper, my student argued that the relationship between Stalin and the rest of the Russian people—their veneration of the great leader despite all the atrocities they'd witnessed—could be explained by Stockholm syndrome. Stalin held them hostage, and they feared him at first, but later they developed positive, and even loving, feelings toward their captor."

"Sounds strange, but not unreasonable. Do you think she's right?"

"Not really. But the more I think about it, the more it seems possible. Yet now, the longer I stay here, the less I agree. So many forces are at stake. So many conflicting feelings. It's hard to explain."

"Empires are like that—grand and evil at the same time. Hard to explain."

"How was your Christmas?" I asked.

"Fat. My sister cooked two pumpkin pies."

"Why two?"

"She sent one for you, as a welcome-home present. It's in the freezer."

"She's the best."

"We rode horses for hours. It was incredible, like when we were children and our mother was alive. We'd gallop by the window and wave, and she'd wave back."

"What did your father say?"

"'Put on your damn coats. It's wintertime. Stupid bastards.'"

I burst out laughing.

"Not funny. Sometimes he forgets his manners. I don't know how you put up with him."

"It's either him or my parents," I said.

"They can't be that bad."

"Well, no . . . but—"

"When are they coming to visit?"

"In the summer, maybe."

"I sent you some mountain pics to show them."

"I did. Beautiful."

There was a pause in our conversation we couldn't fill with words. I stood by the window and watched a few sparrows squat in a tree. Among them was one crow, but it flew higher and settled in the upper branches, hanging like a black rotten fruit among the naked limbs.

"I went to Milka's flat," I finally said.

"And?"

"Her stepfather still lives there. He has a new woman with a young daughter. They renovated, bought furniture. It's like my friend never lived there, never existed. He's such a filthy arsehole. I worry about the girl."

"Can you talk to someone?"

"Like who?"

"Your parents?"

"No. They don't know I went. They wouldn't approve. They don't even like to mention Milka's name."

"When my mother died, my father never said 'my wife' or 'your mother', he called her by her name. For him, it created some kind of an emotional boundary. Then my sister started doing the same thing, referring to our dead mother by her name. It was very weird. They still do it every once in a while, especially around the holidays."

"It's lonely without you," I said, after a slight pause.

"Come back home."

"I will. Soon."

As I laid down the receiver, I peered outside, at the grey

mass of clouds sulking over the city. I thought how things conceived for a good reason could become just as terrifying as things conceived in error and out of spite. And how, amidst all the chaos and the brutality of life, one tried to control a peculiar, alien, intimate world, while longing for the wind to waft away all memory, every residue and odour of the tragic past.

I attempted to contact Lopatin through his old number and talked to his mother. She said he was out of town, and when she asked who was calling, I hung up. I realized that perhaps he didn't want to discuss the dachas, was avoiding the confrontation. I debated about reaching out to Trifonov, but decided against it—he wouldn't have anything to do with Lopatin, and I didn't wish to get him involved or resurrect the old feelings for either of us. The truth was, I still missed him sometimes. Not in a sexual way, but as a human being for whom life meant knowledge and perpetual self-improvement. I missed his sermons, his moral righteousness, his selflessness, his naïve ambition and desire to save the world. I missed his literary and religious explorations, his hunger for learning, his veneration of Chekhov, his pride, his stubbornness, his inexorable spirit. I remembered how when we'd discussed *The Cherry Orchard* in class, he'd said that the orchard represented the old order; it had to be cut down, eradicated before we could move forward. As always, Lopatin had argued with him about the difference between Chekhov's times and ours, the serfdom abolished a century ago, but Trifonov had said, "Serfdom—yes; serfs—no. This country needs them. There always must be someone to exploit, abuse, starve, punish."

Back when I'd left for America, Trifonov visited my parents on occasion, borrowed books and drank tea, ate my mother's potato salad. He even dared to argue with my father about our country's atrocious past and murky future, my father's face changing from curiosity to bafflement to anger. My mother described their good-natured arguments to me in detail over the phone, but when I met Mike, she began to omit Trifonov's name from our conversations. Whether it was because she didn't wish to meddle in my new life, or because she no longer saw him, I couldn't know, and I preferred not to ask, leaving that part of me forever behind.

Two more days passed, and one morning I got up early, dressed, and tiptoed out of the flat. My parents were asleep, and I hoped to return before they woke up, surprising them with hot sugar-powdered *ponchiki*, as they'd done so many times when Milka and I were little. It made us feel like royal heirs living in Versailles, surrounded by faithful servants, gaudy furniture, and life-size portraits of kings and queens. But then the holes in our wool socks would remind us of our commonplace peasant existence, with black bread and boiled beetroot and canned sprats.

It was a sunless, frostbitten dawn, the air so white, as though sewn from snowflakes. Cars rumbled in the distance; a few people shivered under a glass wing of a bus stop. Most flats were dark caves, packed with sleeping bodies. A gaunt shaggy dog pawed dirt under a tree. The ground was hard and unyielding, and he could only scratch through some dead leaves. He wagged his tail and nosed the dirt, then dug some more.

The wind stabbed through my coat and sweater, numbed

my face. The lack of snow was disconcerting, the landscape grim, barren. It seemed as though nature wasn't hibernating but dying. On the street corner, I passed a few food kiosks, where you could buy anything from vodka to hot roasted chicken to condoms to candy. Farther down, I spotted playgrounds with their rusty swings and monkey bars, empty sandboxes, a half of a seesaw; large metal dumpsters heaped with rubbish, beer and vodka bottles, pools of cigarette butts. Paint hung in long, frayed strips, like bleached tongues, from balconies and windows of old buildings, walls marred with profanity.

Not without sadness, I walked through the neighbourhood where as a child I'd spent hours sculpting mud cakes or rolling snowmen, sliding down from ice hills on pieces of cardboard or torn linoleum tiles. Where I'd added colour to water and frozen it in plastic moulds, shaking them off the next day, a rainbow of ice figurines scattered in the snow. They sparkled like jewels before melting in the sun. I remembered how Milka and I and other neighbourhood children had gathered sticks and made fires and baked potatoes, eating them hot, half-raw or charred, unsalted, with skin on. We looked like chimney sweeps, with our sooty faces and hands.

Sometimes, we'd play the "death" game, and it was always Milka who pretended to be dead, lying on the ground or a bench, us threading fingers under her slim body, trying to lift it up. "*Panochka pomerla. Panochka pomerla.* Lady died. Lady died," we chanted, and waited for the soul to separate from the body and hover into the clouds. I remembered how we'd carry her, in mournful circles, around the yard, her hair swaying, her hands folded on her chest, a twig wedged between her fingers in place of a candle.

I remembered how weeks, months, after the funeral, I imagined that Milka hadn't died but had been recruited by the KGB and sent on a secret mission abroad because she could read and speak English better than anyone in our class. I imagined that she'd been an informant, but couldn't tell me. Perhaps she had to join a witness protection program, where they'd changed her name, her face, her fingerprints. The silk of her hair dyed red or black, braided or cropped short. She was made into a new person, reborn, living in France or Italy, eating pizza or confetti-coloured macarons. I imagined her roaming Paris, boating along the Seine, or exploring the ancient streets of Rome, the Pantheon and Colosseum, where for centuries gladiators fought man and beast.

Later, when Mike and I travelled to those places, I imagined finding Milka there as I browsed through gardens and markets, basilicas and art galleries, a labyrinth of museum rooms, the Vatican, where for the first and the last time I entered the Sistine Chapel Michelangelo nearly went blind painting. In the chapel, in a barnlike rectangle, I had stood surrounded by the portraits of popes and wall frescoes with biblical scenes, the nine stories of Genesis depicted on the immense ceiling and *The Last Judgment* behind the altar. I saw the image of Christ the Judge deciding the fate of the human race with a gesture of his arms, compelling the damned to hell and lifting up the saved to heaven. I saw the boatman Charon ferrying the sinners, and Saint Bartholomew holding the sheet of his own skin, the artist's self-portrait. I remembered how I trembled and then began to cry, weeping bitterly, for the beauty and horror captured before my eyes.

The memories swept through me like wind through the trees, carrying me all the way to Milka's block of flats. On the playground across the street, I sat on a bench, watching the entrance door and smoking one cigarette after another. It wasn't even eight in the morning, and I'd already smoked half a pack. I felt light-headed and my stomach growled, heart swinging, heavy like a pendulum. A few cars drove by, a man walked his dog. Not many people exited the building, and I'd almost abandoned the idea of meeting the woman who lived with Milka's stepfather, when I saw her daughter wobble outside. She looked like a head of cabbage, layers and layers of clothing. A lime-green schoolbag dangled from her shoulder, a monkey on its zipper. The girl's mother came out too, dressed in a brown sheepskin coat, a red beret, and a red scarf. She took the girl by her hand, and they both glanced right, then left, before crossing the road. They stopped for a second, and the mother leaned over to adjust her daughter's scarf, the girl lifting her face up, surrendering to the woman's gentle touch.

I tossed the cigarette on the ground, waited until they turned the corner, then followed.

As I had guessed, the girl attended my old school. A fancy shopping centre had been constructed on the field Milka and I had trekked across for years, bogging in mud and snow. Now the place crawled with tidy pavements along the rows of shopfronts. Approaching the familiar grounds, I could see that except for the colour—dusty blue—the school building hadn't changed: the same weathered double doors and sagging windowsills. The roof was still brown like tree trunks.

The woman waited for her daughter to climb the front steps, then pivoted on her toes to discover my cold, numb, troubled face.

"Hello," I said.

"Hello."

She was young, younger than me, and had an open affable expression, slightly haughty, but that could be because of her nose—small, straight, with a sharp tip and flaring nostrils. She wore very little makeup; her lips so small, a tight pale circle.

"I need to talk to you," I said, fingering out yet another cigarette. My hands shook, but I managed to light it.

"Why? What do you want?" she asked, and her voice, her manners—the way she cocked her head and squinted—made me think that she knew who I was.

"My name is Anya," I said. "Anya Raneva. I . . . I—"

"You came to our flat."

"Yes." I blew out the smoke, and she took a step sideways, shuffled through the leaves and muck.

"I don't have time. I'm late for work," she said, and suddenly I couldn't bear the very sight of her—the squeaky voice, the dismissive curl to her upper lip, the absurd rushing way she moved her hands, and even her red scarf that noosed her neck like a thick bloody rope.

"You must listen to me," I said, with more urgency, more challenge. "Leave that arsehole. He's dangerous."

She narrowed her eyes, examined my face for a tight uncomfortable moment.

"Are you married?" she asked.

"What difference does it make?"

"All the difference in the world. If you're after my boyfriend or his money, you can forget about it. He doesn't owe you anything."

"Is that what he told you? That's not why I came to your flat. His stepdaughter used to be my best friend."

"And you beat her up, and she died. You're unbelievable. The nerve you've got." She pushed me aside with her determined gloved hands.

"Milka died because of him," I said. "He raped her, and she got pregnant. He's a filthy lying arsehole."

The woman slung her bag across her shoulder and took a few steps toward me. "If you don't leave us alone, he'll go to the police and tell them you killed his stepdaughter. They'll be forced to investigate. You won't go back to America for a long, long time."

She turned around and began walking away, in the direction of the subway. Just as she was about to cross the road, I ran after her, ripping off her beret and throwing it in front of a passing car. The red wool resembled a skinned animal, flattened against the asphalt.

26

The owners of the dachas were scheduled to meet on 30 December. My mother had been convinced from the start that no matter what they said or did, in the end, the oligarchs would win. They were shameless thieves who'd been looting the country since 1985, buying up plants, factories, and oil refineries, as well as all the valuable real estate in the centre of Moscow. They cheated old people out of their flats, replaced bookshops and libraries with restaurants and hotels. Now they wanted poor people's land, their meagre orchards, so they could build a summer resort for the rich by turning hundreds of pitiful allotments into one posh, privately owned estate.

"Moscow is too small for them," she said, bitterly. "They must expand their spheres of influence, secure their kids' futures, in case their fathers die prematurely, which, according to the newspapers, has become routine."

My father, on the other hand, held a slightly more optimistic view. He insisted that if all the shareholders of the dacha cooperative stood united and refused to sell, the buyers wouldn't succeed. He'd spoken to some of the neighbours, and they'd pledged solidarity. Still, my mother remained unwavering in her doubt.

She said, "Those crooks will either cut down the price or cut our throats."

"But the orchard, Liuba—our youth, our dreams. It's Anya's inheritance," my father said.

"Anya lives in America," my mother said. "I doubt she'll ever come back."

"I might," I said, although I didn't sound convincing.

"If we're forced to sell, we need you to look over the papers, Anya, make sure everything is right, and we aren't being cheated. We don't want cash; we want them to transfer the money to your account in America. Do you have a separate account? Not with Mike?" my mother asked.

"Why do I need a separate account?"

"It's your money. We want you to own all of it, in case something happens. We hear stories how American men marry Russian women and then, if they have any property, those men force them to sell it and pocket all the money."

"Mike would never do that," I said. "We've been together for nineteen years. If he was going to rob me, don't you think he would've done it by now?"

"You can never be sure," my mother said. "That's what happened to our neighbour's daughter."

Her words baffled me. She'd always spoken of Mike with kindness and awe; a man who could build a bridge, a house, a factory—anything with his own hands—was worthy of admiration. But now, it seemed as though she'd changed her mind, or perhaps she'd doubted my decision to marry an American from the start, but had never said so. And later, she hadn't

dared to. Or maybe she'd been afraid that if she did say something to me over the phone, I'd never return, and there'd be
just the two of them for the rest of their lives, their aloneness
amplified by age and illness, bleak snowless winters.

"Mike is a good man. If you came to visit us once, just once,
you would've never said such hurtful things about him."

"Your mother worries too much," my father said. He cush-
ioned his words with a smile, reached to caress my shoulder.

"*You* are the one who blames America for all of the world's
sins," my mother snapped, then rose from the chair and lit the
stove. She sloshed water into the kettle and placed it on the
blue flame, turning it up a notch.

"Not all the sins, but many," my father said. "Just like they
blame us."

"Americans don't give a damn," I said. "It's the Russian
propaganda."

"Propaganda?" my father asked, all signs of friendliness
erased from his face. Sharp wrinkles cut across his cheeks and
forehead. He'd lost almost all his hair, except for a few stubborn patches like dying grass on the back of his head and above
his ears. "You think Russians are too stupid not to know it?" he
asked. "Just like anyone else, Americans aim to expand their
territories. They have already offered Ukraine and Georgia
to join NATO. Why? So they can build military bases there,
station troops. Again—to surround Russia, to weaken our
borders."

"Where do you get such information?" I asked. "I know
nothing of the kind."

"Liuba, our daughter is a stranger, a foreigner. She's turned into one of those dumb people who cannot find their own country on a world map."

My mother kept quiet, refused to interfere. She fussed with cups and a teapot, spooning loose black tea out of a box.

"Just stop," I said. "Stop saying those things about my husband and his country. Just because you hear something on TV doesn't mean it's true. All news is censored here, and it's all bullshit."

"You think it isn't censored in America? Six corporations control all of the mass media in the States. Six people. That's all."

"Six is better than one."

"It makes no difference; the only difference—not *what* is being reported but *how* it is being reported. Now, as Russians, we understand all too well what a shitty government we have, the things we had to survive because of it and more to come. But how much does your husband know about his country? Or yours, for that matter?"

"He knows a lot," I said, but perhaps too low for my father to hear.

"He knows shit. Just like the rest, he thinks we're bears here, snow up to our crotches, and that America saved the world from fascism. And it's not them but us who saved the world from the Nazi plague. Our boys, your grandfather, whose guts hung to his knees when they found him."

"This conversation is over. I'm not your little girl anymore. I didn't come here to be lectured. You know nothing about my husband or America. You've never been there." I got up, jerking the sweater off my shoulders. Tears surged up my throat, and I swallowed the air, the bitterness in it, sharp stinging needles.

"I don't *want* to go there. They did it to us, to your family, to your country. They broke us apart. They conspired to ruin Russia, and they succeeded," he shouted at my back.

"Russians are no better. They fucked up half of the world," I said, before taking refuge in my room. "You're just as brainwashed as those Russians who claim that this country needs a czar like Stalin or Putin. An iron fist to beat us into submission because we're serfs, always were, always will be. That's such bullshit. We're all people—we have no other purpose but to fucking survive."

The kettle whistled, and then my mother lifted it off the stove, muttering, "I've asked you not to start, not to yell at her." She attempted to keep her voice down, but our flat was a hollow box divided by cardboard walls—a mouse couldn't crawl unnoticed.

I didn't turn on the light but sat on the edge of the bed, in the near dark, my room crowded with shadows, so many of them, drawing me in—a tight, choking circle. The wind picked up outside; the trees thrashed against the windows. I felt achy and sick, and as though a hundred truths had suddenly bared their wounded hearts.

The next morning, when I woke up, my father had already gone to the flea market, and my mother was in the kitchen, dressed for the day in a brown tweed skirt and a blue mohair sweater, a deck of playing cards fanned out on the table. She held a few cards in her hands, adding one at a time to her fortune maze, her face pinched in thought. I could see she hadn't slept, her eyes red and sunken, cheeks caved in.

The kitchen smelled of blini, yeasty and buttery. A stack slouched on a plate by the stove. I peeled off a few, folded them, and placed them on a plate, plopping on sour cream, then apple jam. My mother was incorrigible that way—the need to cook outweighed any old umbrage or anger. As I joined her at the table, she fetched another card—a king of spades—and placed it over an ace of hearts.

"Hmm," she said, more to herself.

"What? What do you see there?"

"A man. A stranger. In our home."

"He's coming to take our land, I'm sure."

"It's not a joke. At that meeting," my mother said, "please pay close attention. And don't argue with your father, let him handle it."

"How about I don't go at all?"

She raised her eyes, her stare intent, heavy. She could never control her face; the past lived in it, the sorrow of years. "I'm sorry about yesterday," she said. "It was wrong of me to say those things about Mike. Please forgive me, and please go with us to the meeting. It's very important."

I touched her shoulder, which was sharp but also frail, and I was reminded that shoulders, too, were so many interwoven bones. Sometimes a parent could become a mountain in flatland; other times a mountain could be washed down to a mound of sand.

"I just hope you meet Mike someday," I said. "I think you'll like him."

She nodded, then asked, "How are the two of you?"

Even though we'd been apart for almost twenty years, my mother still knew me better than anyone else. She felt things, things that were invisible and inexplicable because they'd been reduced to instincts, genetic codes. We could just look into each other's eyes and feel pain or happiness or love.

"We're good, Mum. The trip has been hard, though. We haven't ever been apart this long or this far from each other."

"Are you still trying to conceive?"

I sighed. "I don't want to talk about it. Not now."

She didn't reply, cheeks flushed from heat or disappointment.

"Hey, do you remember how Dad used to bring home a tree every year on 31 December?" I asked, trying to change the subject. "It was so scrawny he'd go and get a pile of limbs and tie them to the sides to make it look fuller?"

"Yes. We had to rush and decorate it while cooking. But that's the only time you could find a cheap tree, right before New Year's."

"I remember he stood it up on an old trunk or a stool, and Grandma put wads of cotton around the base, like snow."

"Once, when you were little, you went to the balcony and scraped real snow into a bucket and started arranging it around the tree. You were so upset when it melted."

"Let's get a tree today," I offered.

"After the meeting. Or maybe you can find one tomorrow with your father. Too bad there's no snow, you could've dragged it back in your old sled."

"You kept it?"

"Of course. On the balcony. Under the kraut bucket."

"We have kraut?"

"Just made it. But it needs to frost to be perfect."

"That's what Grandma always said. Milka and I loved scraping the first frosted layer and putting it in our mouths. It was so crunchy, so sour."

"Old memories, the only real treasure." My mother smiled and gathered the cards off the table, slipping the deck in her pocket.

"I still think about her all the time. I still miss her, but it doesn't hurt as much."

"That's how it should be. How God intended it to be."

"No, Mum. If there was God, we wouldn't be having this conversation, because Milka would be alive. And her ex-boyfriend wouldn't be bullying my parents into selling the dacha. And I wouldn't have to come all this way to try and stop him."

My father met us at an old schoolhouse, which had been recently converted into an office building. The interior no longer resembled a school, with smooth blue walls and fancy crown mouldings. Massive chandeliers swung on chains; their many crystals touched and shivered as people opened and shut the entrance doors. The staircase had twisting wrought-iron posts and remarkably detailed bronze flowers. The steps gleamed, carved out of marble or granite, with a deep-red wool runner in the middle. It was impossible to imagine that once the place had been an old Soviet school, buzzing with children and smelling of reheated cafeteria food.

In the former gymnasium, which was now a conference hall, a crowd gathered: men and women mostly my parents' age; a few had come with their grown-up children. The Semionovs were there, Boris and his daughter Dasha, and also the Khodovs, Panteley and Aunt Charlotta. Both women were dressed in balding fur coats, and the men wore *dubleonkas*, sheepskin jackets shiny at the hems. Everyone had changed so, stooping under the weight of years and disappointments.

"How's America treating you?" Boris asked, leaning to hug me. "Are they still afraid of us? Still calling us Reds?"

"Do they still think it snows here all the time?" Dasha asked.

"Bears in Red Square?" Khodov teased.

They laughed, and I suddenly saw them young again, grilling meat and splashing vodka into the tin mugs, arguing about books and politics and our country's bloody past. I remembered Khodov playing his guitar in the evenings, the rest singing old war songs and making toasts to my grandmother. How strong and wise they'd seemed to me then, how fierce, the true ogres tethered to their land and history.

"Anya! Anya Raneva! A friend of my youth, my glory and shame, is that really you?" A tall man walked across the room, waving his large hands high above his head. He wore a long black trench coat of supple glossy leather, hair swept back, cigarette in mouth, not lit, hard lined face and shrewd eyes.

"Lopatin!" I almost screamed.

He pulled the cigarette out and swiped it under his nose before slipping it inside his pocket. "*Skol'ko let, skol'ko zim . . .* I can't believe it, Raneva. I thought I'd never see you again." He ensconced me in his arms, just as wide and powerful as before. He smelled of fine cologne and smoke.

"I'm visiting for a short while," I said, ducking out.

"How short?"

"Until the seventh."

"Our Christmas?"

"I have to be back at work."

"What do you do?"

"Teach."

"What?"

"Literature."

"Lovely. Married?"

"Yes."

"Kids?"

"No."

"Did your husband come with you?"

"No." I took a breath, eyeing his face. "And what about you? What do *you* do? Although I've been informed—real estate, right?"

"Right. Buy-and-sell. I own this building."

"So, you're what they call a New Russian?"

"Me? Naw. I'm an old Russian with new money." He laughed, and I could hear Lopatin's innate irony seeping through the snazzy clothes.

"Now I recognize you," I said, and felt the urge to step behind my parents, to seek refuge from Lopatin's appraising stare.

"You haven't changed that much either, except for the weight. You're half the size."

"Thank you."

"Not that you were ever fat. But living in America, I kind of expect you to be."

"Why? You've been?"

"No. I go by Yashka's words. Ruchnik, remember?"

"Kind of. You're still friends?"

"Partners."

"Who would've thought." I paused, threading my hair behind my ears, then pulling it free. "I need to find my parents."

"No, you don't."

"Excuse me?"

"They're right behind you."

I turned and saw my mother readjusting the collar of my father's shirt. He stood tall, shoulders taut, belly drawn in and belted. He resembled his former self, aged yet feisty.

"Liubov Andreevna, so glad to see you again. You haven't changed either, just as lovely." Lopatin took my mother's hand in his and bent low, kissed her red, chafed fingers. I could see that he'd begun to lose hair on the crown; the rest of his brown mane was frosted grey.

"Hello, Aleksey," my mother said.

"You remember my name. I'm touched," he said, assuming an infallibly straight posture. His smile was warm, if a bit lascivious.

"Yes. I even remember how I first saw you, at the school."

"My father was picking me up, and I was late, playing Fantiki, and he hit me in the face, almost broke my nose. My face was all bloody, and you took me to the bathroom and held a white, crisp handkerchief to my nose. I remember you wetting the handkerchief in the sink and wiping my blood and tears, saying it'd all heal before my wedding. And it did, although I never married." He guffawed, loud as a gander, letting my mother's hand slip through his.

"And your father? How's he?" my mother asked, baffled at Lopatin's merriment and also the abrasive intonations with which he expressed himself, the language that felt almost dangerous in his mouth.

"My father passed away a few years ago. He was an alcoholic. After the collapse of the Soviet Union, there was nothing to hold him back, no Communist Party, no job, my mother finally left him too. He died, as we say, among mice and cockroaches."

"How awful," my mother said.

"You shouldn't be bragging about it," my father added.

"Oh, I'm not. Just telling the truth." Lopatin bit his lower lip until it disappeared. "I think they're about to start. Shall we?" He allowed my parents to skirt a row of chairs, choosing the seats next to the Khodovs and the Semionovs, then dragged me up front by the sleeve. "If this goes well," he breathed into my face, "drinks afterwards. Need to catch up." He winked and squeezed my hand, hard, my fingers scrunched inside his fist.

At first, the meeting proceeded on friendly terms. Our former neighbour Firsov, a bald coughing man, attempted to serve as a mediator, explaining to my parents and others why it was a good thing to sell their dachas. To my surprise, money wasn't the main issue. He preached about honour and pride. He insisted that most dachas had been run-down because the people who owned them had insufficient means to maintain their property. As a result, the entire settlement was nothing but a huddle of shabby houses, deteriorating fences, and nearly dried orchards that produced fruit every other year, and even when they did, half of the crop was sour and the other half infested with disease. There wasn't even enough to make a decent jelly.

"I remember times—ten, fifteen years ago—when we dried the apples, marinated them, cooked jams and marmalades. We took the fruit to markets, the profit we made! Those were the good times. Our people knew the recipe."

"And where's that recipe now?" Semionov shouted from his seat.

"Long forgotten. No one left to remember." Firsov took a tissue and wiped his forehead, then proceeded. "What you're being offered is a chance to allow smart, prosperous businessmen to take care of your land. A new resort will rise by the river. It will be the most beautiful place outside of Moscow. You're offered to sell your lots, for which you'll be paid large sums of money you can invest or use toward the purchase of new land or a new country house. The buyers are wealthy, generous people who have every intention of pleasing the seller. As of now, the buyers are prepared to pay three times as much for the land as it's officially worth."

"Who's appraised the land?" Khodov asked. "It's too low to begin with."

"The land was appraised by two independent surveyors and in accordance with the state's law on real estate. Originally, none of you paid for the land, it was given to you to free-farm. But times have changed, and now you own the land, and we're asking you to sell it, to make money out of air, so to speak. It really is a deal of the twenty-first century."

I switched my eyes to Lopatin, who looked poised and serious, a twitch in his brow. His hands fumbled a cigarette, and it shed tobacco on his slick polished shoes. Otherwise, his face expressed no emotion, neither worry nor sadness.

"Friends, neighbours. I have something to share with you, something that perhaps is of no value to anyone but me. Yet, I feel that I must."

Both Lopatin and I turned around and watched my mother get up from her seat and walk toward a tall podium. She stood behind it, thin, stern, trembling, a confluence of grief and doubt on her face. It was just how she'd looked in the spring of 1985, when I'd lost my best friend and refused to eat or drink or leave my bedroom. She'd sit on the other side of my door and read novels and short stories to me, poetry and fairy tales, anything to counterweight the silence. But sometimes, she'd be silent too, though I could still feel her presence, her heavy breaths, on the other side of the wall.

My mother cleared her throat, coughed into her dry fidgeting hands, which were really my grandmother's hands—veins like roads running toward her exhausted heart.

"When I think about my youth," she began, "I don't think about the way I looked or felt or how there was very little in the world that upset me or didn't impress me. I was just as naïve as many of you. I believed in the future of my country and that I was contributing to it by doing my job and raising my family. When the nineties hit, we all understood that it wasn't enough, that the boat was rotten through. We were all sinking, no matter how fast or hard we paddled. Granted, some of us were better swimmers. They made it safe to the other side; a few drowned; the majority are still floundering, hoping to reach shore. It seems to me that the duty of a good swimmer is to rescue those who're about to drown. To build a boat and not to steal the last tree limb. Think about it. That land, that shabby house, that half-dead orchard, is my youth. It's forlorn, and it's poor, and it's imperfect, but it's mine. It holds all the memories that I cherish. It's the one and only thread that links my past to my present. Without that thread, I feel like I have no right to exist, that I've never existed. In this world, in this new country, a lot of us feel we have no purpose. We're sorry, useless, discarded people, but we aren't empty, aren't hollow like the new generation. We have values, and we have our past. Yes, it's heavy like a rock, and we can't rid ourselves of it. But it's also like our orchards, which, after a dark wet autumn and a cold snowy winter, burst into bloom. And we feel young again, full of hope, walking between the apple trees, down that long, curvy, moonlit path."

When my mother finished talking, it was very quiet in the room.

Lopatin burst with applause. "Liubov Andreevna, what a lovely speech. Just lovely." He leapt from his chair and rushed to my mother. His arm draped around her shoulder. Next to him, she resembled a frozen starling in the leafless limbs of an oak tree. "I've known this beautiful woman since I was a boy, and her kindness and gracious manners have made me fall in love with her. I love her as much as I love my own mother. It's true. Believe me, Liubov Andreevna."

"Such shit," my father said. "Cut the crap, start telling the truth."

"Indeed," others echoed.

Lopatin seemed undisturbed, his face impervious. "The truth? Such a short, powerful word, isn't it?" He took his hand off my mother's shoulder, and she fluttered back to her seat, not looking at me or anyone else.

"Who's this young man?" Aunt Charlotta asked, her voice low. "He sounds frightening, but women must adore him."

"My name is Aleksey Lopatin. As you might've guessed, I'm one of the buyers. So I'd like a few minutes of your time, please." Lopatin paused, unbuttoned his coat, and pushed a strand of loose hair away from his face. "All my great-grandparents and even grandparents," he continued, "were peasants, like yours. Or maybe not, maybe yours were never peasants, maybe your ancestors owned mine. Yours—landlords; mine—serfs. But it doesn't matter now, does it? We're all equal."

"The hell we are," my father said. "I don't care who your grandfather was, what I care is that you're forcing me to sell my land, the land that is drenched with my sweat, not yours. These hands"—my father rose—"these hands have been ploughing that land for decades, and now you want to chop them off together with the trees. I planted those apples, and you aren't cutting them down. The deal is off, there was no deal, never will be." My father sat down, and my mother rubbed his shoulder. Both Khodov and Semionov reached out to shake his hand.

"I understand your anger, Mr. Ranev. I do," said Lopatin. "But it's really in your best interest to sell. And to sell as soon as possible. The price is more than you could ever hope for. The Russian economy is extremely shaky. The ruble will crash any day now. You'll lose everything, including this offer. I'm really your friend, not foe. There're no gimmicks. It's a wonderful opportunity. Brave it, make up your mind for the sake of your wife's future, for your own sake. For Anya's."

"That's enough humiliation for one day, Lopatin," I said, jerking my bag off the chair. "We aren't selling. Period. Forget about it. No orchard, no land."

My parents and their friends stood up and walked toward the exit, a heap of coats and hats in their arms. Khodov's scarf dragged on the floor, and I stepped on it, causing him to trip and nearly fall. His face blushed as he regained his balance, supported by his wife.

"Anya, wait." Lopatin ran after us. "Wait, please." He caught my elbow, pivoted me, face-to-face. "Let's go somewhere we can talk. This is serious. If Yashka wants to buy, he'll buy—no stopping him."

"Fuck off, Lopatin. Are you trying to scare me? We aren't in high school anymore."

"Precisely my point. You aren't in America either. The game is different. Or maybe not, but this isn't 1985. You have no idea what this world is like, no fucking clue."

"Your world is of no interest to me, Lopatin. You, Ruchnik, and others have stolen enough from this country. Measly profiteers. If you could, you would've sold stars from the sky. When will you stop? When will you start caring about the rest? Have you no decency? No shame? No pride?"

He didn't answer, but gawked at me, wild-eyed. His face trembled, the scar puckered, and he scratched it again and again.

"I'm sorry," he finally said, his voice cold and slick, like the icy edge of the river. "I'm sorry I can't help you."

And then he bowed, a subservient nineteenth-century bow, unhurried and to the knees.

27

It was New Year's Eve. My father had tied a squatty pine to a stool, and my mother draped the bottom of the rickety trunk with a white sheet. I carried in two boxes of ornaments, dusty from sitting on top of the wardrobe for many years. Most were handblown glass balls, fragile and worn, glitter rubbed off; some were missing their decorative velvet ribbons; others, bows or sparkly beads. At the bottom of the second box, I found ornaments bought or made to commemorate a special occasion: a red bird with a golden beak and a few remaining feathers from 1968, the year I was born; a house, a primitive cabin my father had assembled from plywood in 1970, when they'd been offered the piece of land where they would build their dacha and plant the apple orchard. I spotted a replica of their first car purchased in 1975, the same autumn Milka and I had started school.

Gingerly, I picked up the ornaments one by one, held them in my hands, and then hung them on the tree. It amazed me how far away the past had gotten, yet how close it could be, at the touch of one's fingers. Memories raced through my heart, a welter of images. I saw Milka and myself as children, small, happy, chaste girls trudging across the snowfield, sharing a school desk, kissing at the discotheque, or sleeping in the same bed, the heat of my friend's body keeping me warm but also awake. I would lie next to her and try not to breathe, not to stir, except for my eyes isolating, studying, her childish face, which somehow looked displeased or strained, even in her sleep. I saw us spending summers at the dacha, spreading cow manure under the apple trees, our arms and legs covered with scratches and mosquito bites, hair plastered against our sunburned cheeks. I saw us grilling sausages on crooked sticks, stewing apples into jams, or taking baths in the backyard, staring at each other's naked bodies and then up at the night sky, where clouds like gauzy scarfs dragged across the moon. I saw us roaming birch and aspen groves, searching for mushrooms or wild strawberries, which we threaded on long straws, then pulled off with our lips. I saw us swimming in the river, racing to the other side and back, crossing the plank bridge, and crawling on our bellies to the old tent where a Gypsy woman was giving birth. I saw the black coils of her hair, and her face—weary, confused, angry—her eyes burning through me like hot coals. But then I remembered that breezy spring afternoon, the argument, the taste of vodka and blood in my mouth, my fists landing on Milka's chin, shoulders, chest; the swell of tears in her eyes and mine.

A moment froze, became an eternity. I continued to stand next to the holiday tree, unable to lift my arms, drawing in ragged breaths, my palms sweating, my heart thrashing against my ribcage. "I'm sorry," I whispered. "I'm sorry. I'm sorry. I'm sorry. I'm sorry. I'm sorry. I'm sorry. I'm sorry."

———

We finished our holiday preparations an hour before midnight. The tree stood fully decorated, and the table groaned with my mother's culinary masterpieces. While I'd been cleaning the flat, changing sheets, and doing laundry, she'd made mushroom-and-rice pierogi, eggs filled with chicken liver pâté, *olivie*, *shuba*, and *golubtzy*, cabbage leaves rolled with meat and spices. Together we stuffed the duck with our Antonovka apples, the few left from the summer. The cooked bird was a beautiful amber colour, the pale green apples spilling from its belly like chunks of jade.

In the living room, our old dining table exploded with dizzying smells. Both my father and I couldn't help but steal a pierog or a slice of salami, an olive from the cheese plate. My mother swatted a hand towel at us, shooed us away like pestering birds. Busy with cooking, she'd forgotten to take the curlers from her hair, and half-loosened strands brushed against her shoulders. One dangled over her eyes, and I reached to adjust it. She'd gained weight in the past weeks, mostly because I'd insisted on buying all the foods she claimed weren't healthy—lamb, sausages, smoked sturgeon, cheeses whose names she struggled to pronounce, all the delicious pastries.

"You spoil us," my mother said. "What will we do when you leave?"

"Eat as though I'm still here. I'll send you money every month."

"We have money," my father said. "That's not what she means."

"I know. But can you at least use the new pots and bedding that I bought?"

He grunted. "I'll save the sheets for when I'm dead, you can bury me in them."

"No one is dying anytime soon," my mother said, sliding the dishes on the table to fit more.

"We're all dying," my father said. "Living is dying."

He arranged champagne glasses in a semicircle and turned on the TV, but muted the sound. He was determined not to miss President Putin's New Year's address, his last before Medvedev took power, although my father commented that there wasn't much difference, that those two would just toss the office back and forth until one of them expired. He smirked, but then assumed a serious posture, adjusting the collar of his shirt. He'd dressed up for the holiday, wearing a pair of brown trousers my mother had ironed that morning and the wool sweater I'd brought from Virginia. He'd groomed his beard and looked more youthful than when I'd first seen him at the airport. Or maybe it seemed that way because in the weeks we'd been together, he'd grown familiar again. Our arguments had mellowed to disagreements, kept from boiling over by my mother's indefatigable gaze. Somewhere, deep down, the three of us knew that we'd never be what we'd once been—a father, a mother, a child. We were different people, burnished by years, distance, and grief. We were our own nesting dolls, a person inside a person, a family inside a family.

When the doorbell rang, my mother had just finished styling her hair and my father was talking about a blizzard ten years ago, which had nearly uprooted all the trees at the dacha. He sank a long, sharp knife into the duck while the ringing grew loud and persistent. My mother rose from her seat, but her new blue dress that we'd purchased together just yesterday caught under the chair leg, and she tripped and spilled the duck sauce, saved by my father at the last minute.

She pressed a wad of napkins against the stain, then rubbed it with salt.

"I'll get it," I said, shuffling in my slippers through the hallway. I was the least dressed-up, wearing a pair of dark blue jeans and a maroon silk blouse that flared at the hem and sleeves. My hair was a zoo, as my mother had pointed out, pinned but wild.

At the door stood a man in a Father Frost costume: a long red robe fringed with white fur, a matching dome-shaped hat. He had a fake cottony beard and moustache and wore a gilded tasselled rope for a belt. His shoes were black and shiny, with pointy toes, of the finest leather. A large cloth sack drooped over his shoulder.

"Ho, ho, ho," he said in an exaggerated gruff voice. "I brought a gift. I'd be happy to exchange it for a song or a poem."

"The word 'gift' doesn't imply exchange or refund, Lopatin. You should've called before paying such a late visit. It's almost midnight."

"It's New Year's."

"So?"

He pulled off his hat and beard; it had left marks on his cheeks, where the strings held it around his head. His hair was flattened at the top, making him look like a troubled puppy. "I need to talk to you," he said. His voice a bit raspy, a voice needing to settle, like that of a teenage boy.

"Not now."

"Yes. Now."

"It's New Year's, as you've dutifully noted. Don't you have somewhere glorious to be? Some hot party? Rich folks, naked girls?"

He curled his lips, then sucked air through his teeth. "I do. Absolutely. But that can wait; they aren't going anywhere, as opposed to you. It may be twenty more years before I see you again. If I live that long."

His grinning face, his eyes that seemed to plead as they pierced, all deepened my discomfort. "Why?" I asked. "Why do you need to see me? Because of the dachas?"

"Who's there?" my father shouted from the living room.

"A neighbour is asking for a cigarette," I lied.

"We don't smoke," my mother shouted back. "But we have duck. And it's getting cold."

"Duck," Lopatin repeated. "My favourite."

"Get out, Lopatin." I attempted to shut the door, but he inserted his foot.

"Look, we've known each other since grade school."

"You haven't changed."

"But I have. Maybe not for the best. But those years, I remember them." He paused, drew back his foot. "And I still remember Milka."

I held my breath when he uttered her name. He raised the sleeve of his robe, the coat, and then the smoky-blue sweater. I saw my best friend's name tattooed in purple.

For a while, we were both silent.

"It isn't going to be pretty," I said. "My parents hate you."

"I know. I'll try my best." He dragged the sack off his shoulder, untied it, and took out a bottle of Dom Pérignon. "The rest is for you." He passed me the sack; it felt weightless, empty. "Don't look now, but when I leave. Or better, on the plane."

"What is it?"

"Two things: one I bought, the other I stole." He winked and fitted on the beard and the hat, pulled it down. "I feel safer that way. Maybe they won't recognize me."

"Not a fucking chance," I said, placing the gift sack inside the coat closet.

At first the silence was so complete I could hear champagne bubbles rise to the surface of the bottle that my father had just uncorked. My mother finished cutting the duck, and it steamed at the centre of the table in a nest of apples. Lopatin complimented her looks and praised the sublime beauty of the table while my father turned up the TV volume, and the room filled with music, a medley of crooning Russian voices. The singers, all females, were dressed in white like Snow Maidens—fur coats, hats, gloves, and even boots—performing on a temporary stage, erected across from the History Museum in Red Square.

"When did they start doing that?" I asked. "Dance in Red Square?"

"A few years ago," Lopatin said, his Father Frost attire already piled on the floor. "Soon they'll make a nightclub out of the Mausoleum."

"Not a nightclub, but they should finally bury the guy," my mother said.

"I agree," Lopatin said. "We have a dead body at the heart of the country. How can this place ever get better, right? Someone has to stop the necrosis."

"Like who? New Russians?" My father smirked and dumped a shot of vodka in his mouth, reached for the black bread. He pressed it hard against his face.

"I'll have a drink too," Lopatin said.

"Of course you will. Anyone else?" My father picked up the bottle and poured three more shot glasses. "It's cheap, not like the fancy shit you brought," he said.

"Why do you say that?" my mother asked.

"Everything he has is fancy, starting with his underwear and ending with his car. Ask about his flat. How many buildings does he own? He probably owns ours too."

"No. No. I don't own it," Lopatin said, attempting to defend himself.

"Not yet," my father said. "Pretty soon, you'll own all of this country. Us too. I'll never surrender, Lopatin. I'll never be your damn serf."

"His name is Aleksey," my mother said.

"I don't care what his name is; he's in my flat, and I'll call him whatever I like. Why did you come? What do you want? My land? You aren't getting it. Nick your damn nose, as we Old Russians say."

"I don't want anything," Lopatin said, holding up his vodka. The scar on his cheek was redder, thicker somehow. "I just wanted to see Anya before she left. She's my first love, and people are allowed to reminisce."

"Shut up, Lopatin," I said. "Such a jerk. I wasn't your first love."

"How do you know? Just because I've never admitted it doesn't mean it isn't true. I fell in love with you in fifth grade."

"Stop bullshitting."

"Whatever the truth is, first love deserves a toast," my mother said, and raised her glass; her other hand patted the tablecloth, where her plate had slid off to the side. She sniffed the vodka, then set it back on the table. "I think I'll have wine instead." She reached for a bottle of Kindzmarauli, but Lopatin snatched it from her hands. "Allow me," he said, shaking a few drops into a spare glass. "I'm going to taste it first. Sometimes they counterfeit those Georgian wines. You won't die, but your stomach might revolt." He grinned and swallowed, smacked his lips. "Not the best year, but authentic. Safe to drink."

"Maybe I should have vodka instead. Or whatever you brought," my mother said.

"Champagne. Very fine. Save it for a better occasion." He paused, then added, "Do you know that Chekhov drank champagne right before he died? We learned it when we were sixteen, on that Crimea trip."

"What do you mean?" my mother asks.

"I mean his wife sent for a doctor—they were in Germany— but when the guy came, Chekhov ordered a bottle of champagne instead of drugs. He knew it was over." Lopatin exhaled. "To our first loves then." He lifted the vodka, and we all followed, but instead of clinking our glasses we just drank.

My mother sipped her wine, and both my father and Lopatin emptied their glasses in one desperate jerk. I tasted the vodka, cringed, and placed the glass back on the table.

"Horrible," I said. "How can you drink that shit?"

"Actually, it's pretty good vodka. Kremlevskaya. Distilled, not diluted," Lopatin joked, and rubbed his hands together.

"For once I agree with him," my father said. "Clean, smooth taste."

"If men don't agree on their vodka, all is lost," I said.

"True," Lopatin said.

"Why don't we eat," my mother said. "Maybe I should warm up the duck." She attempted to get up, but Lopatin caught her hands in his.

"The duck is fine. Please, don't worry. Women worry too much. We'll eat it. Cold, raw, burnt. We'll eat it all because you took time to cook it. Your hands, those hands"—he squeezed my mother's fingers—"they put in all that labour, hours and hours of labour—"

"Stop the spectacle, Lopatin. You're such a buffoon. Always were," I said, shaking my head. "Unbelievable."

He released my mother's hands, and she continued to smile absentmindedly.

"Shall I serve the duck?" he asked. "I didn't get to taste it the last time I was here, also on New Year's," he said, and she nodded, curled her hair behind her ears.

Nobody had eaten since early afternoon, so we plucked and tore and chewed and dabbed grease from our lips, but only for a short while because it was almost midnight, the year was nearing its end. Lopatin praised my mother after each dish; he sounded amicable and sincere, and my mother kept putting more food on his plate. She was blushing too from all the compliments my father pretended not to notice.

"You have a warm home," Lopatin added. "So many books. I admire people who find time to read, who enjoy it. I never did, especially novels—too long, heavy. I don't have the patience. But I learned to appreciate plays. Just a few days ago, I went to MXAT and watched *The Seagull*. So funny. Except for the ending, of course."

"Funny?" my father repeated. "There's nothing funny about that play. If you read"—my father crunched on a pickle—"all those long, heavy books, as you pointed out, perhaps then you wouldn't have mistaken a tragedy for a comedy or tried to swindle honest hardworking people out of their most precious possessions."

"You may be right," Lopatin said. "I don't have your degree, can't read or even write properly. My penmanship is embarrassing. But I'm not a swindler; I'm a businessman."

"It's five minutes to twelve," my mother said. "Hurry, pour the champagne."

When Putin began to speak, we lifted our crystal flutes. We were awaiting not so much his greetings, but the sound of the Kremlin clock, the *kuranty*, that counted the last seconds of the old year and welcomed the new. For whatever reason, it filled us with pride and comfort; we trusted that sound as we trusted our parents and grandparents, unconditionally.

The president's speech was generic, however, not much different from his predecessors', and yet he was neither numb nor formidable. Short, pallid, with nervous eyes and tight jaws, he resembled a frugal rodent, the Mouse King from *The Nut-cracker*.

"He'll be back," Lopatin said. "Like Khan Mamai, to collect duty from his servants."

"He wants the empire back," my father said.

"For sure," Lopatin said. "He commands, and he dares. If there's World War III, Russians will follow him. They'll die for him like they did for Stalin."

"Not a flattering comparison by far," I said. "I wouldn't be so sure."

The wall clock began to chime, and then the Kremlin clock caught up.

"Happy New Year!" Lopatin said, touching his glass to mine. It made a gentle vibrating sound.

"Happy New Year," I said, and drank my champagne until the glass was empty. The bubbles crawled up my nose, and I sneezed.

We ate some more, but our conversation didn't stick, like first snow, thin and scattered. The mood was tense, despite the delicious feast and all the liquor. Soon we began to feel the weight of the hour and the company. Lopatin thanked my parents for the dinner and for letting him stay and shouldered inside his coat, scooping the Father Frost costume off the floor.

"I bought it for my nephews," he said. "My sister's kids." He produced a weak smile, and for a moment he appeared humble, like a spring icicle, on the verge of melting.

"How is she?" I asked, walking him down the hallway.

"Divorced, but fine. They live in our old flat. I renovated it top-notch, all the luxuries."

"I have no doubt. Where do *you* live?"

"I rent. But I just bought a new flat. Two actually, turning them into one. In Taganka. Remember that old church we attended on Easter?"

"Yes."

"The *vysotka* right across. You can view the church from my balcony. They just renovated the entire thing. I gave money too. Many people did."

"Wow. That's so great."

"You want to see it? It's close, will only take us fifteen minutes, no traffic at this hour."

"It's one in the morning," I said, my back against the coat-rack.

"Come on, Raneva. When's the next time we'll meet? Remember how adventurous we used to be?" His words, his tone—a rush of warm air over my body. I felt the urge to lean into him, like a tree into the river, which saw its own reflection in the ruffled glassy surface.

I said, "Perhaps we should call Trifonov too. He's surely a fat academic by now."

Lopatin didn't answer. His face changed colour; even in the darkness of the hallway, I could see it switched from milky white to scarlet, suffused with blood.

"You don't know?" he asked.

"Know what?"

"Petya died."

"Oh my God, when?"

"Nineteen ninety-one."

"Asthma?"

Lopatin shook his head.

"No?"

"No. He was killed in the coup. Your parents came to the funeral. I had no idea they didn't tell you."

"Oh my God . . . That's . . . That's . . . ." Tears gathered in my throat. I kept biting my lips to stop myself from crying.

My parents emerged out of the living room.

"You were getting married in a few months. We didn't want to upset you," my mother said.

My father didn't say a word, but his silence confirmed his guilt, as well as his inability to contradict my mother at certain moments. They were like a two-headed dragon: when one head was incapacitated, the other took charge.

"I can't believe it," I said, swallowing. "Did you really think you could keep it a secret all your life?" My feet were already inside my boots; I jerked my coat from the wall hook. "You've accused me of abandoning you, of staying in America, but as it turns out, you didn't want me back."

"It isn't true," my father said.

"But it is." I found my scarf on one of the sleeves and wrapped it around my neck in several tight layers.

"We didn't want you to come back because it was too soon, we worried you might do something, something terrible," my mother said.

"Like what? Kill myself?"

No reply, shoulders tight, lips sealed in defence.

I stared at my father. "During the coup, whose side were you on? The Communists'?"

His eyes flared with anger and then regret. It seemed as

though he'd travelled a long way and finally arrived at his ultimate destination, which promised neither peace nor glory, but shame and bewilderment. He turned around and trudged down the hallway, slammed the living room door.

"That's what I thought!" I yelled. "That's exactly what I thought."

Lopatin exited the flat first. "I'm sorry," he said, half to me, half to my mother. "It's my fault."

"It isn't your fault," I said. "None of it is your fault. You aren't to blame that Petya died, or that my parents didn't tell me. All they worry about is their land, the orchard that you're about to take away from them."

"Please don't say that," my mother said. "You know it isn't true."

I jerked my head, facing her. "All those years, you talked to me, but you didn't. You didn't tell me the things that mattered."

"It was very hard. So many times I wanted to tell you, but I couldn't bring myself to put the words together. Somehow, it seemed pointless, but also wrong. We're sorry."

I shut the door and stood still for a moment, then followed Lopatin into the darkness.

28

In Lopatin's shiny Mercedes, I smoked several cigarettes in a row. He did too. The car was running, but it was still cold, the windshield foggy. Lopatin turned on the wipers but, after a few sweeps, cut them off. The interior was all black and the windows tinted, so it seemed as though we were in a tomb, buried alive.

"Were you there?" I asked. "When Petya died?"

"No." Lopatin blew out a long stream of smoke. "But someone recorded it and put it on the Internet. We can still probably find it, if you want."

"I don't."

Lopatin crushed the cigarette into the ashtray. "You know what he had in his hands when he stood in front of that tank?"

I switched my eyes from the dark windshield to Lopatin's face. "The Bible?"

"*The Cherry Orchard*. He was quoting from it too, trying to lead the crowd. Can you believe the fuck? He was about to be killed, and he still wouldn't part with the damn book. He didn't care. Stupid fucking Savior."

"Saints and revolutionaries are alike not because they serve God or humanity, but because they're willing to die for both."

I took a long drag and rolled down the window, flipping the butt into the trees.

From somewhere came laughter, snippets of a song; a group of young people, two men and two women, staggered by. They had no hats or gloves; their coats flapped at their knees. They hugged, passing a cigarette from mouth to mouth, exchanging kisses. Then the street was deserted again.

"Drive," I said, shutting the window.

"Where? My new flat?"

"The dacha."

He lit another cigarette. "It's supposed to snow in the morning. This car doesn't do well in shitty weather, despite the size." He backed out, swerved around the corner, and pulled onto the road.

"Maybe we should get something to drink," I said.

"Look behind you. In the back seat. There's cognac, caviar, candy, and other shit I bought for my sister."

"Won't they be worried?"

"No. I called earlier. Somehow I knew I wouldn't see them tonight." He cracked a smile, and the car lurched forward, and the rest was suddenly behind—the street, the flat, my parents' sad, tormented faces.

Even at this hour, the city seethed with life as we passed one district after another, crowds of tipsy, laughing people. The buildings burst with lights; giant ornaments hung under the roofs in place of real icicles. We saw people dancing on balconies, champagne and cigarettes in hands. A few running from building to building, door to door, hugging salad bowls or cake platters. Women wore high heels and tight, shimmery dresses, while men were dressed in slim, fitted suits or jeans and sweaters. They didn't really walk but drifted in groups, happy and tireless as though sipping all that energy straight from the air or the earth. In their holiday glee, their drunken amusement, they didn't differ from Americans or anyone else, and yet, even from a distance, I'd always know that they were Russian. I'd know it in America, or France, or Italy, anywhere Mike and I had travelled. He used to point out Russians in museums or restaurants, even if he couldn't hear them speak. He'd say, "Their faces are always sad, yet lovely, especially the women's. Like on ancient Russian icons."

I remembered when we had first met, while I was still in college, we used to take off in the middle of an afternoon to nearby towns and browse through antique malls, touching other people's belongings: a grandfather clock, a wardrobe, a rocking chair. Mirrors in which we found imperfections, hairline cracks and dark, faded spots. I tried on old, dusty hats and joked, "If it isn't at least three hundred years old, it can't be called an antique." And Mike, leaning on an eagle-headed cane, would say, "We aren't even four hundred years old. Our genetic memory is much shorter than yours."

I suddenly imagined Mike in a dark, empty, undecorated house, eating reheated pizza and watching football, a single beer half-empty. To save energy, he'd be staying downstairs while I was away, in the guest bedroom, not bothering to change sheets or draw curtains. "Why? It's dark when I go to sleep, and it's still dark when I get up," he'd say, smiling that broad, heartfelt smile. He'd rub his sleepy, unshaved face with his large paws and preen his hair, a spiky tuft at the back of his head, which made him look all too innocent, turned a bear into a cub. It was still the old year back in America and would remain so for the next six hours. It amazed me how time could never be captured, slowed down or sped up, but how you could go back and forth between the years in a single day.

I glanced at Lopatin, who'd sprawled behind the wheel, which he barely touched with the tips of his fingers. His rigid shaved face bore no resemblance to that of the boy I once knew. His chin touched his fuzzy sweater, and every now and then he pulled it down his neck, stretching the collar. His jawline was a sharp bone, separating his face from the rest. He hadn't gained much weight, but his muscle mass had increased, and his shoulders seemed to have hardened as though acquiring a carapace, a shell. There was no lightness to his body, but layers of scaled, ossified rock.

He reached between the seats, pulled out a CD, and inserted it into the player. "Copied it from the tape. You'll remember."

The moment stalled, and Trifonov's voice ruptured the silence: *"Madame Lopakhina!"*

Startled, I jumped in my seat, and then Milka's voice said: *"The Eternal Student! Thrown out of university twice already!"*

I heard my own voice, so distant and unnatural, saying: *"What are you getting so cross about, Varya? He's teasing you about Lopakhin, so what? If you want—go ahead and marry Lopakhin, he's a decent, interesting man. And if you don't want to—then don't; nobody's forcing you, my darling."*

My skin prickled with goosebumps, my heart a cold petrified lump. "Stop it," I said, reaching for the player, but Lopatin intercepted my hand and pressed the Eject button.

"I thought you'd love it. I put mine, Milka's, and Trifonov's tapes on the CD. Do you still have yours?"

"No. My mother threw out everything after Milka's death." My hands shook as I tried to pinch out another cigarette.

"When did you get Milka's tape?" I asked.

"After her mother died, I bought all of Milka's things from her stepfather. All that was left."

I struggled not to say anything I'd regret, but the words fell out of my mouth like broken teeth. "It's his fault Milka died. He molested her since she was a child, then she got pregnant. It was too late to get an abortion, and her mother wanted to send her to Siberia to stay with her grandparents. She worried about Milka stealing her man. So Milka tried to get rid of the baby. I buried it at the dacha, under one of the apple trees."

Lopatin floored the brakes, my face almost hitting the dashboard. The cigarette fell on the floor.

"Are you crazy?" I screamed. My mouth was dry, my breathing came in shallow spurts.

"Sorry," he said, his voice suddenly hoarse, robbed of vowels. "Is it true? Are you sure?"

"Yes, it's true." I picked up the burning cigarette.

"That's why the cops came to my place. They asked if I saw Milka the day before she died and whether we'd gotten into a fight. But I'd been with my parents. Besides, I hadn't seen Milka since Easter."

"I know." I took a long drag from my cigarette, then rolled down the window and tossed out the butt.

Lopatin rubbed his chin, hard, his fingers clenching his jaw.

"Let's listen to Tsoi," he finally said. From the space between the seats, he took out another CD. "We used to love him, remember?"

"Yes, the voice of our generation. Didn't he die in a car wreck?"

"In 1990. Trifonov died a year after."

"Everyone died."

"I'm still here. You are too."

Back on the road, Lopatin steered the car with an almost eerie calm. We didn't talk, listening to the old songs, "Blood Type", "Cuckoo", "A Star Named the Sun", Tsoi's thick, throaty voice pulsing through the silence.

"Do you think Russians carry some profound, detrimental sadness?" I asked.

"Depends on what kind of Russians."

"I mean in general, Russian people who survived all the terror: the Revolution, the wars, Stalinist repressions. Perestroika."

"Survived? Most are still going through shit. It's never really over. Even for those who left." He paused, then asked, "How do you like this new place? Your native city?"

"Like I have no legs. I can't really find my footing. It's familiar and foreign at the same time. An odd feeling."

"Pretty soon the whole world will feel like that. The same people own shit here and in Europe, America too. Our fuckers even buy your football teams. They'll keep doing that until their dicks are nipped." He laughed, his laughter gruff, roofless.

"But you're one of them."

"Not exactly. I respect the law, and I pay taxes. I love this land."

"Of course you do," I said, and stared out the window, at the hazy outline of trees, tangles of maples, birches, and pines.

On the outskirts of the city, the landscape thickened with shadows, changed to dark and empty and undreamed. It wasn't much different than what it was in 1985, except maybe for giant billboards and a roadside restaurant, whose posh exterior was somewhat alarming amidst harrowed fields. The road became bumpy and deserted, carrying us farther and farther away as we sped along the interminable hills and forests, coppices where, as children, we'd wandered in chest-high grass. A few cars passed us in both directions, their headlights like torches, swirling bull's-eyes of light. But after they were gone, all sank into darkness, the sky completing our solitude, not a star visible, not a planet.

"Is your dacha insured?" Lopatin asked, a kind of edginess to his voice.

"I guess. Why?"

"I can send someone to set it on fire. Your parents will collect insurance, and then they'll still sell the place to Yashka. They'll double their money."

"Are you serious?" I shook my head and reached for another cigarette; he passed me the lighter.

"If they refuse to sell, someone will burn the place anyway and make it look like an accident. But they may die in the fire. Yashka always gets what he wants."

"And you do too," I said, swallowing smoke.

"Not always. I don't have an American passport. I can't hide across the ocean. I have responsibilities—my mother, my sister, her kids. If something happens to me, who'll take care of them?" He slowed down before swerving off. "I think we cross here." He pulled in front of the train tracks, looked right and left, then drove through. The car rumbled across the tracks; jars and bottles rattled on the back seat.

"What exactly do you have in that box?" I asked.

"Sprats. Black bread. Pickles." He flashed a crooked smile. "All the good Russian food. No hamburgers, sorry."

"I don't eat hamburgers," I said.

"I bet your husband does."

"Yes."

"Like all dumb, lazy Americans."

"Fuck off."

"Don't get pissed. Russians are dumb and lazy too. I love that."

"You're such a jerk, Lopatin. Such a fucking jerk."

"If you had to describe your husband in three words, other than dumb and lazy, what would you say?"

"None of your business."

"Come on, I'm joking. Or is he too fat for words? In a good way."

"Kind. Honest. Non-drinker."

"That's what I thought—wouldn't last a week in this post-socialist hell."

"Such shit. You don't know everything," I said.

"No, I don't. So how did you two meet?"

"What difference does it make?"

"I want to know how a wild thing like you could've married a sweet American boy like him."

"He was my college roommate's brother. He could fix things. He'd come to our room and hang pictures or paint walls or replace a broken chair leg. I started spending holidays with his family, and the rest sort of fell into place."

"Is he a good fuck?"

"Shut up, Lopatin."

"All right, but sounds like a Hollywood movie. I have to find some drawbacks to make me feel better."

"He has plenty, and we do fight, like anyone else."

"I don't fight. I kill." Lopatin laughed, a nonchalant, almost kind laugh, and for a moment it felt as though nothing separated us, neither the years nor the deaths.

Except for a few lampposts, the dachas stood dark and desolate. Slowly, we drove past the Khodovs', a squat brown cabin assembled from pine logs. I glimpsed their upturned table, where Aunt Charlotta had performed card tricks and told our fortunes. Next was the Semionovs' place, a slanted-looking house with faded scalloped trim and the spacious yard where, in the summer, field flowers—buttercups, goldilocks, Ivan-da-Marya—grew wild in tall grass. After that came Garev's two-storey brick construction with a roofed veranda and a sagging clothesline tied between two trees.

"By the end of August, all this land will be Yashka's," Lopatin said. "His fucking cherry orchard. Cherries are the new apples."

"Cherries don't grow well here," I said.

"Yashka will make them."

I didn't answer but got out of the car.

My parents' dacha hadn't changed, the same blue sunken house, the toolshed, and the rough, crooked trunks of apple trees that looked like old people starved of love. The fence had been patched in places, the rotten boards replaced. Lopatin set the box of food on the ground and lifted me up, helped me climb over, then passed the box. He pulled himself up and swung his feet. He was just as strong as in his teenage years, although not as swift. When he jumped, it took him a few seconds to regain his balance.

"Let's hope the keys are still in the same spot," I said, and he nodded, walking behind me.

Roof shingles lay scattered on the ground. A wooden barrel in which my mother had collected rainwater for her garden had been turned upside down, the bottom like a sieve, riddled with holes. Even from a distance, I could see that my parents hadn't replaced the tree where I'd buried Milka's baby. On the contrary, it had grown taller and wider, weaving its generous limbs with the others. I pointed the tree out to Lopatin, and he stared at it for a long minute, sucking air through his teeth.

The night had gotten colder, and my skin prickled; my hands turned to icicles as I pried the padlock open with the old key. The house wasn't much warmer, but in the kitchen we discovered a bucket of chopped wood next to a metal stove my parents must've put in after I'd left. Lopatin volunteered to build a fire while I lit a candle and unpacked the box. The kitchen smelled of autumn, of old coats and dried mushrooms that hung in long threads against the walls. And also herbs—

chamomile, calendula, mint, marjoram, Saint-John's-wort—my mother had gathered over the summer to use in teas and balms, healing potions. The bouquets were pinched upside down on a rope extended between the windows.

"God, I haven't been here since that damn night," Lopatin said, squatting, poking at the fire, which barely kindled. He picked up an old paper from the stack on the floor, examined it, then crumpled the sheet and fed it to the stove.

"What happened back then? You never returned to school," I said, passing him a bottle of cognac.

"I got pulled over that night. The cops took me home. My father was so mad he yanked out his belt and hit me as hard as he could, didn't even wait until they left. This scar is from the buckle." Lopatin patted his cheek. "He did pay them off to avoid jail time, but he also broke my ribs. I was in such bad shape I couldn't go back to school. And then Milka died. Summer came. I was on the streets, buying shit, selling shit, counterfeiting shit." He unscrewed the cap, rose, and poured the cognac into the old tin mugs. His shadow stretched across the floor, tall and unwavering.

"You never finished school?" I asked.

"Nope." He touched his mug to mine, his face a wreckage of pride and shame. "But I don't regret it, I really don't."

We both swallowed the cognac, and he poured more. There was a can of sprats on the table, which I hadn't opened, and Lopatin snapped the metal tab. "Gotta have them," he said. "My favourite food."

The wood hissed and crackled, and before long, the entire room was a hell pit, smoke and fumes; my eyes burned, and I rubbed them with my fingers. Lopatin fanned at the stove, then shut the hole.

"Almost forgot," he said, reaching inside his trousers. He produced a small yellowed envelope. "From Yashka."

"What is it?" I tore the envelope and found a thin notebook page folded in half and addressed to President Reagan. "Our letter? No way."

"Yes. Yashka didn't risk taking it with him in 1985. So, just recently, as we looked at some old photos and shit, he stumbled on your letter. I offered to buy it, but he just gave it to me, said it didn't belong to him anyway."

Quickly I read the letter, then folded it back inside the envelope and laid it on the table.

"Remember Samantha Smith?" I asked.

"The child ambassador?"

"Yes. Milka and I wrote this letter the summer Samantha visited our country. We were so inspired."

"Didn't she die in a plane crash?"

"In 1985. A few months after Milka. So awful."

I drank more cognac. It flowed down my throat, pooled into a hollow space somewhere below my ribs. It tasted like poison, a fatal concoction.

"It's my fault Milka died," I said, my voice echoing through the walls. My lips trembled. "We had a fight the day before. I hit her. I hit her very hard. She wanted me to beat the baby out of her. I should've told the cops."

The candle wiggled, and shadows lumbered on the walls. So many of them, like memories without voices. Tears ran down my chin, and I began to cry, weeping uncontrollably.

"Fuck that. Fuck, fuck, fuck that," Lopatin said, lumbering across the room. He patted my hair, closed his arms around me. His chest expanded, all muscle and flesh. "Don't cry," he said. "Don't you fucking cry now. We know whose fault it is, and he'll pay. I swear."

"We're cowards, Lopatin."

"Fuck no. We aren't cowards. We're survivors, the fucking champions—of the whole goddamned world. Remember?"

He scooped me in his arms and lifted me high in the air, pranced around the table. *We are the champions,* his voice rattled. *We are the champions . . .* He carried me outside and stared into my face, bent close, so close I could smell cognac and cigarettes on his lips, a hint of sprats. *And we'll keep on fighting till the end . . .* His mouth brushed against mine, a strong, fierce gesture. I could see in his eyes something resembling terror but also desire. My body was a silence, a prey in his arms. I couldn't resist or claw my way out or extend my hands, bring myself to touch his face, which was both dear and frightening, and a world away.

For a moment, the past was reduced to a trace, the heart's shout to a murmur.

"They stole our lives, Lopatin," I said, whispering into his lips. "No one cares about us, and in another fifty years, no one will know we existed. Generation Perestroika."

"That's not true. We did exist. We do now," he said, and kissed me, first gently, then harder, the longing, the years pouring into my mouth, the taste of booze and smoke and sprats.

My head reeled, and my stomach swelled up to my throat.

"I'm going to be sick," I said, freeing myself from his arms and nearly collapsing on the ground.

"What's wrong?" he asked. "What did I do wrong?"

I crawled under the apple trees. It'd started snowing, a cluster of flurries like petals shaken from the black sky. Amazed, I tried to catch them with my mouth, but they melted as soon as they landed on my lips.

Lopatin fetched the tin mugs filled with cognac, the sprats and black bread. He dragged an old blanket out of the house and then scooted onto the ground next to me, spreading the blanket over our knees.

"I wonder who'll be next," he said, and raised his mug.

"What do you mean?"

"I mean who'll die first—you or me?"

I shifted my head and eyed Lopatin's face, close and distant, as though under a magnifying glass. Each line, each hair, all the doubts pricking his tired skin. I shivered and turned away.

"I have to tell you something," he said. "I bet Trifonov a hundred dollars that he wouldn't go to that protest."

"Shut up. I don't want to know."

"But I want to tell." He took a swig of cognac and dipped a heel of black bread into the sprats. "After you left, we sort of became friends again. He was always calling, inviting himself in. During the day, he studied at Moscow State, but in the evenings, he hung out with us. At the time, I did small stuff—managed a few food kiosks, counterfeited jeans. Trifonov didn't want any part of it, but he didn't mind being around us, lecturing the guys on occasion. Quoting, fucking always quoting. New shit every week. No one ever took him seriously, and he refused to partake in our 'foetid' business. But the more I think about it, the more I realize that he was just waiting, waiting for that one chance, one perfect moment to prove himself a hero."

Lopatin paused, took a mouthful, then swallowed. "I paid for the funeral," he said. "I still give money to his mother, help her out as much as I can. She makes dinner, and we drink vodka, and I listen to her talk about Trifonov as though he hadn't died but is about to return from some long damn pilgrimage."

He refilled our glasses. I tried to protest, placing my hand over the mug, but my strength was waning. My tongue grew thick and hot. I felt Lopatin's breath on my cheek and my ear, which tickled, and I rubbed it against his shoulder. But otherwise, we were both in outer space, fumbling, floating, no gravity, no fulcrum, but bursts of white shimmery dust.

No amount of truth could change us, of course, but the little that we knew felt like everything.

In the morning, I woke up in my old bed, fully dressed, under a heap of ragged blankets Lopatin must have found in my grandmother's trunk and piled over me. He snored heavily on the couch that stood in place of Milka's bed. He was also in his clothes and one shoe, his hands folded on his chest, close to his heart. Out the windows, I could see snow spread on the ground—a virgin radiant pelt. The trees stood limb-heavy and silver, stooping, as though under a sudden weight of blossoms.

With as little noise as possible, I crawled out of bed and tiptoed to the kitchen. Every cell in my body seemed present and aching. I drank icy water out of the canister, splashing some on my face. I took a cigarette from a Marlboro pack, but as soon as I brought it to my mouth, I felt nauseated, craving hot tea or coffee, but not cigarettes or the food that had been left on the table: the torn bread, the cheese, the caviar, the empty can of sprats Lopatin must've gobbled after I fell asleep. I found my coat, pulled on my boots, and stepped out onto the porch.

The sunlight was so bright it scalded my eyes. All was white, breathless. I gathered fistfuls of snow and pressed them to my face, rubbing until it hurt. I studied my wet hands. They were really my mother's hands before hers became my grandmother's: veins crisscrossing like roads, long and lonely. In a few hours, Lopatin would drive me home, and I'd have to face my parents. I was no longer angry at them, though still deeply saddened, because I knew they, too, had lived a life of disremembering, of unlearning everything they'd been taught, a maelstrom of experiences turned to snow, then to water. I also knew that sometimes *not* to say things could be harder than to say them, and that revealing the truth couldn't have rescued me or them from pain.

For a moment, I stood still and listened to the silence, the inaudible sounds the earth emitted on a chilly winter morning. I remembered my grandmother saying how the earth could make invisible the deepest wounds, hide the thickest scars, and that suffering made us human, moved us from sorrow to hope. Even though the past could never be rectified, it could be revisited; memories lay down with us, stitched together like old quilts.

"The desirable place is always elsewhere," she'd once said, when Milka and I were children and dreamed about other countries, other lives. "But you must never forget your home."

I remembered how we'd laughed at her back then, looking into her eyes, the colour of the earth, in a nest of creases like sunbeams spreading down her cheeks. Wisdom lived in her ancient face, and wonder, and warm summer nights, with riots of storms and a chorus of crickets, whose tiny chirping bodies we'd gathered in glass jars for luck. I remembered how we'd run headlong through the orchard, through a spray of leaves and hard verdant fruit, knee-deep in the grass, pushing, jumping, shouting at the universe—at the trees, and the sky, and the almighty God.

Carefully, I stepped off the porch and into the snow, my feet sinking in the fluffy carpet. The sun rose high, and there was no wind. I stretched my arms and tipped my head upward, inhaling a chestful of cold air, again and again. I knew I'd always miss this place, just as I missed my childhood and my friends—the past, hovering like clouds at the tips of the trees.

I trudged to the toolshed and unlocked the door and entered the dark mustiness, where among the building supplies and garden tools, forlorn trinkets and years' worth of paint, I found an axe with a burnt wooden handle, which looked identical to the one my friends and I had used in the spring of 1985. I paused, thinking how guileless we'd been back then, how innocent, how heartbreakingly unaware. And desperate too. Desperate to grow up and break away from our parents, our past, our country we deemed an abominable monster that had unhinged its jaw and threatened to devour us whole. We really believed we could do that, could shed our old skin and grow a new one, beautiful, glossy, befitting the rest of the world.

I called out my friends' names—Milka, Petya; Putova, Trifonov—first in a bare whisper and then louder, yelling at the top of my lungs. I ran into the orchard and swung the axe sideways, hitting the closest apple tree. Snow fell off the branches and exploded into shimmers, chips of wood flew, and it felt as though I were cutting through my own flesh, the pain and loneliness of years.

When the tree was about to topple, Lopatin rushed out of the house and caught my hand. He forced me to drop the axe, and it sank in the snow, but after a moment's hesitation, he bent down and picked it up.

"Stay back," he said. "Stay the fuck back."

He lifted the axe high above his head; the blade caught the sun, glinting. In one decisive movement, Lopatin brought down his arms and hit the tree, and it crashed on the ground in a cloud of white dust.

29

Before my return to America, Lopatin drove me to three cemeteries. First, we visited my grandmother's grave, following my mother's exact directions drawn on a box of matches. At the bottom of the pink granite tombstone, I placed one of the tin mugs I'd brought from the dacha. Lopatin splashed some vodka into it, and I topped the mug with a piece of black bread, watching snow spread over the bread like a thick sugary glaze. All was white and peaceful, the soft-edged quietness of gravestones and the sky, a blank infinite stretch of crystallized air we could taste on our lips. Lopatin took a few swigs of vodka to keep warm, then offered me the liquor, but I refused. I remembered how my grandmother had caught Milka and me drinking one night at the dacha when we were teenagers. In our frayed pyjamas, we sat on the bench in the yard, passing the bottle back and forth. My grandmother couldn't see what was in the bottle, but she could smell it. She poured the liquor in the grass and hid the bottle under the porch, and the next day she didn't say a word to my parents but made us pick gooseberries until our fingers bled raw from thorns.

At the second cemetery, it took us a while to find Trifonov's grave. Lopatin had never been there in winter, and the ceme-

tery resembled one giant snowdrift with tombstones like frozen bodies sticking out of the ground. Lopatin had ordered and
paid for both Milka's and Trifonov's monuments. He tried to
be original because he could afford it, and also because he
wanted to survive time by giving shape to his memories, his
love and grief. So, for Trifonov, he'd made a sailboat of white-
and-grey marble; around the base, carved into the stone, were
the lines from Lermontov's poem "The Sail": *But he, rebellious, seeks a tempest, / As if the tempests give a rest.*

Just then I remembered how Trifonov had said when we
were driving to the dacha that whoever died last among us had
to find the rest in heaven.

And Lopatin had said, "Fuck that. I've had enough of you
here. And what if I'm the last to go and I end up in hell?"

"I hate how there're only two options—hell or heaven," I
had said. "Nothing in between."

"The earth," Milka had said. "It's the only place the four of
us can be together. The only place for both sinners and saints."
As always, she'd laughed, her vulgar crushing laugh. And then
we all did, just as loud and just as vulgar, the way life felt at the
moment—a dark, hurtling car on a dark, empty road among
trees, shadows, fields.

On the way to Trifonov's cemetery, Lopatin and I had
bought five red carnations, but when we laid them on the
grave, Lopatin remembered that the number of flowers should
be even, so he bent down and plucked one carnation from the
snow, tearing off the long stem and thrusting the head through
the lapel of his fancy black coat. He tossed the stem away, patted the flower with his hand, then leaned forward and drew his

fingers along the granite sail. There was something so gentle in his face, so humble. Dreams still lived in it, and teenage curiosity, a touch of boyish hunger, but also rain and snow and fallen leaves, amidst which a tuft of grass was trying to push through.

It was late afternoon when we arrived at the third cemetery. The snow had stopped, but the clouds lingered low. A shroud of thin whitish air enveloped trees and tombstones and our shoulders as we walked among the graves, pulling our feet in and out of the snow. Even from afar, Lopatin showed me Milka's burial place capped with a black marble sculpture in the shape of an open book. "Can't close it or put it away, can you?" he asked. Before I could reply, he scraped the snow from both sides of the book with his bare hands, then brushed the rest of the sculpture with his coat sleeve. When he stepped back, I could see Milka's name and the dates etched in gold on one side, the other left blank. Sensing that I wanted to be alone, Lopatin offered to wait in the car, leaving me standing ankle-deep in snow.

At first, the silence was terrifying. I couldn't hear or see anything but the black stone, like the remains of a burnt body laid to rest on the snow. When I leaned forward and stared inside the book, I caught the reflection of my own face inside the wet marble, divided in half by a thick groove. I touched my hands to both sides of the sculpture and felt its cold, smooth surface, like that of a river glazed with a thin, sheer layer of ice. The longer I kept my hands on the stone, the warmer it became, and the less frightened I was. Out of my pocket, I took Milka's favourite chocolate, Slava. Peeling off the wrap and the foil, I laid the chocolate directly on the grave, pressing it gently

into the snow. I shook out two cigarettes, lit them, and placed
one between the book's halves, the other in my mouth. As I
inhaled, I remembered how in some cultures, mourners burned
small lumps of coal or frankincense on graves; the smoke was
to tell the soul that it had visitors. If the deceased recognized
you, she'd acknowledge your presence in some way.

I finished my cigarette and buried the butt in the snow. The
cemetery was quiet, no wind, no animals, no strange signs, except for Milka's cigarette still smouldering, stubbornly, a thin
coil of smoke in the air. I stood peering into the trees, their
solidified whiteness. All around, three-bar crosses resembled
startled frozen birds. A cluster of rowanberries burned orange
on a bush. Once, a long time ago, my mother had warned Milka
and me about tasting any wild berries without first asking her.
She'd told us a tale of the misbehaving children who ate wolf-
berries and turned into birds. When their parents came looking
for them in the forest, the birds flew low, circling around, but
the parents didn't recognize their children and left them in the
woods. We'd been too scared back then to ask my mother:
what happened to the children? Did they survive? Did they
grow up? Live to be old, trading their soft iridescent feathers
for grey armour? Could they still recognize each other,
stranded up in the sky? Or did they die of loneliness? Of hunger? Of guilt? Of grief?

I shivered and pulled up my scarf. The air was getting
colder. The light grew dense, dull, a thickening membrane of
ice crystals. Shadows lurked in the trees.

A fist of snow fell on my head, dusting my nose, and I
looked up, at the sway of branches. Perhaps a bird had switched

trees or maybe a squirrel, but I couldn't see it. The flurries continued to land on my face, the tiniest jewels of water. I didn't wipe them but kept staring up at the trees, at their fluffy white peaks and a triangle of blue sky like a swatch of silk caught between the limbs. Slowly, I squatted at the foot of the grave and, with my ungloved finger, scribbled *Anya + Milka* on the bed of snow.

30

I had been back in Virginia for a few months when Milka's stepfather disappeared from his flat; the place had been ransacked and set on fire. Neither his girlfriend nor the neighbours could provide any helpful information to the police.

Sometime later, my parents came to visit. Just like their neighbours, they'd ended up selling their dacha. They used some of the money to renovate their home. The rest they'd transferred to our account in the States. From Lopatin, they brought me the old tapes, and I started listening to them when no one was around, or when it stormed outside, my friends' voices echoing through my heart and the mountains, which looked so sad, diminished, stooping under the weight of trees and clouds, awash in rain.

Bit by bit, despite the language barrier, my parents grew to know and appreciate my husband. Mike was polite, candid, and hardworking, and he never interrupted if we were speaking Russian. He cared about what my parents ate and how they slept, but when he asked them questions, they raised their eyes at me, the impression of utter helplessness on their faces. They resembled children who'd suddenly encountered a new game. But unlike children, they lacked spontaneity and insouciance, disturbed by everything that surrounded them. Soon my mother took charge of the kitchen, cooking five-course meals every day while my father searched for things to fix. There weren't many, of course, and after the radiator covers had been repainted and the windows tightened and washed, my father and Mike decided to plant an orchard—since we had all that land, just lying there.

My mother and I sat on the couch, studying a farmer's catalogue. I translated the pages as she helped pick out the tree varieties: Yellow Transparent, Liberty, Freedom, Virginia Beauty, Victoria Limbertwig, and Granny Smith. She took into consideration the ripening time, pollination, climate, and resistance to diseases. She worried about summer heat and winter blizzards, as well as apple scab, rust, and fire blight, which was capable of destroying an entire orchard in one growing season. We chose to plant three-year-old semi-dwarfs because they were easier to manage and could produce fruit earlier than standard-size trees. We also discovered that apple cultivars were usually grafted onto different rootstocks, most of which originally had come from Russia.

Out of the kitchen window, while brewing iced tea my parents would never learn to love, I watched the three of them space the trees across the field, measuring the entire orchard first, and then the distance between each tree, then staking the exact spot, my mother guarding it until the men finished planting and moved on to the next one. They didn't talk, and yet they had no problem communicating, following some peculiar fragile order. Mike dug, my father lowered a tree into a hole, and my mother sprinkled fertilizer and patted the dirt in place.

In the evening, as soon as the sun set, leaving a tinge of pink in the sky, we all took plastic jugs and carried water to the trees. They drank greedily, and we kept refilling the jugs, and the land kept soaking it all in.

My parents had never once reproached me or Lopatin for cutting down their entire orchard with my father's chain saw we'd found in the toolshed that New Year's Day. In the spring after their visit, Lopatin was killed, stabbed in the chest in his new apartment. They called me right away and then attended the funeral, where my father was one of the pallbearers. He said there was no viewing, but the casket was so heavy it took eight men to lift it. All the time he was carrying it, he wondered whether they'd dressed the body in metal armour or whether a dead man weighed as much as his sins.

I didn't answer but walked outside, where the apple trees trembled in the wind, new leaves quarrelling in my ears. For a moment, there was nothing but that sound, like a live wall, earth to sky. Behind the orchard, the mountains stood, stone warriors in green hauberks. I thought that if I could go to them, could touch their hardened chests, I would feel their hearts beating.

It was then that I remembered the gift bag Lopatin had left in my flat that night, on New Year's Eve.

"Where is it?" I asked my mother, who'd taken the phone from my father.

"In the closet here, with your other stuff. I completely forgot about it," she said.

"What's in there? Can you tell me what's in there?"

"Yes," she paused, and I heard her over the line, fidgeting with the bag. "An old tape. I can't read the writing. It's all scratched, but something 'champions'."

I drew a breath. "What else?" I asked, the words rolling off my tongue like tears, thick, salty.

"Two scribbled pages, nearly faded," my mother said, puzzled.

"What pages?"

"I don't know. Looks like a play."

I pondered a moment, then said. "It *is* a play. *The Cherry Orchard*."

Sometimes, late in the afternoon, clouds hang over the mountains like doubts, casting spells of silence. They linger for a while, then lift and veer elsewhere, and then the sun breaks through, unbidden, just before it sets. The sky bleeds with colour like a wounded heart. It amazes me how age moves in, how it arrives one day and stays, and how the past grows, thickens with distance. How with years we think we've finally discovered what has eluded us until now. Everything seems larger and clearer than it ever was, as if simply by passing, time has righted itself.

Russian people are fatalists; we believe that our future is preordained, irreversible. But then, we also believe in miracles, one grand sweep of imagination. Perhaps it's what allows us to survive and to endure. And maybe it isn't that at all, maybe it's our enormous pride, the aggrandized vanity, which we carry to the grave, and the rest is just weather, wind and rain, spurts of blinding snow.

—

Another year drifts by. More knowing, more wisdom, settles into our marrow; our bones begin to ache at night. Occasionally, in colder months, Mike builds fires, and we pile blankets on the bed and listen to the laborious sound the logs make as they die, extinguish themselves, to keep us alive. And then we make love, warming our bodies with touch and breath, kisses so soft and cautious at first, then harder, more insistent. Afterwards, we lie quiet for a while, trembling, like startled teenagers, in a cocoon of shadows. They wrestle, clamour on the walls and the ceiling—those beautiful slanted patches of light and darkness.

Author's Note

As a younger reader, I was always drawn to stories that dealt with loss. The loss wasn't always physical—that of a relative or a dear friend—it could also be the loss of love, dreams, innocence, one's identity. After I'd read such a story, something in the room would change forever, and I would no longer recognize or accept its habitual order. I would be overwhelmed by emotion, walking in it for days and days as though in a storm cloud. Later, when I started crafting my own stories, I became aware of how difficult it was to evoke powerful emotions without being excessively sentimental or maudlin, to render loss—something you couldn't see or touch—and make it palpable.

Memory is a silent, treacherous place. It reminds me of an old well—the deeper you slide, the darker it gets, the more profound is the silence. You keep thinking: Is that how it really happened or how I remember it happened? Or how I *imagine* it happened? Yet, as a fiction writer, I have learned to deal not so much with events, but with the consequences of those events. It isn't enough to have an experience: to understand what it means, all the possible implications and outcomes, may take months or even years. Actual events can provide raw material for a writer, spark an idea, but a fictional story is like an apple tree—it sprouts roots, matures, and ripens over time.

Growing up in Moscow, I had a friend, a skinny dark-haired girl who lived nearby. We climbed trees together, built fires in the yard, fed pigeons and stray dogs, rolled snowmen and made ice jewellery, slid down hills on pieces of cardboard, folded paper boats and watched them sail in puddles of rain. I remember that my mother always tried to fatten the girl up—she was that tiny, that fragile, but with a loud, raucous, almost abrasive laugh. She was pert and petulant, and very smart. She read obsessively and could play chess much better than me. She always won. The girl's mother had married her stepfather when my friend was three; her biological father had long abandoned the family. We never discussed that, nor did my friend ever complain about her parents. At fifteen, she came to our flat after school almost every day. She did homework in the kitchen, staying late, hinting that she had forgotten her keys or that her parents had invited guests and it was hard to concentrate. She ate like a grown man, everything my mother placed in front of her, but she never gained any weight. She also filched her stepfather's cigarettes, so when she visited, our hallway smelled of smoke, where she'd left her coat and her book bag with a rubber monkey on the zipper. One day my friend disappeared. Her family too. They didn't say a word to anyone, and when I tried to call her or ring the doorbell of her flat, I was met with silence. Later, various rumours reached us. Some neighbours said that the girl had died from an illegal abortion and the mother had fled the city; the stepfather had been arrested for rape. Others insisted that both the stepfather and the mother had been jailed and that the pregnant girl had moved to Siberia to live with her grandparents until her baby was born. There were also those who believed that she had poisoned her parents and then killed herself.

I have never been able to find out the truth. Instead, I made up a story to preserve a memory of our childhood friendship. The story was called "Champions of the World" and published in *The Southern Review* in 2011. (It is now included in my debut collection, *What Isn't Remembered*, the winner of the 2020 Prairie Schooner Raz-Shumaker Book Prize in Fiction.) It took me years to develop the original story line, which had only two main characters—Anya and Milka—into a full-length novel. The idea to loosely base the novel on Chekhov's play came to me one summer when I visited Russia and watched *The Cherry Orchard* at Moscow Art Theatre, where the play had first been staged a century ago. The similarities between Chekhov's play and my story were disconcerting. Just like Chekhov's characters, mine, too, seemed to have been trapped in the country's historic past, the never-ending poverty, the class struggle, and the abuse of power. And many arguments and conversations Chekhov's characters held onstage sounded heartbreakingly familiar, reminiscent of those my friends and I had in 1987, right after we graduated. When I left the theatre that evening, I knew that I wanted to write a novel about four young people who would lose their country and one another, and also to explore a personal tragedy instigated by a collective nightmare, the political chaos and utter lawlessness my generation had endured and that continues to haunt Russians today.

The narrative of loss is tragic by definition. It carries sadness, disillusionment, loneliness, abandonment. The loss of a country is hard to describe and even harder to bear. It equals the loss of a parent, or a lifelong spouse, or a childhood friend. It can feel like an earthquake when the ground buckles and splits open, and each step separates you even farther from those on the other side: your peers, your teachers, your neighbours, your family. One day you find yourself alone, standing on top of the tallest mountain, where all the sound has fallen away. It is extremely cold; your feet are numb, your arms, your whole body. Snow is all around you, a white frozen sheet. It hurts your eyes, but you keep staring, keep hoping to find remnants of life you once knew and cherished. You want something, anything you can bring home and keep, call your own. But the snow is unyielding, and it is too deep, and the mountain is too high; the sun tickles its slopes but never penetrates, never melts the layers of permafrost.

Most Russian people I know are disheartened pessimists who carry the weight of time and history on their shoulders, accepting a change of power or a regime as they do a change of seasons, those winter blizzards one has to survive, to live through, to be able to get to spring. But then, most Russians, including my mother, are incurable romantics, who are capable of glimpsing a sliver of beauty in a pile of ashes, of dreaming the unthinkable and believing that they have been put here, on this earth, to fulfil some divine purpose, to seek a higher truth. We say there can never be an ex-motherland, and perhaps it is true—one can only have one biological mother—but there can be an ex-country, just as there can be orphaned children whose parents are still alive, but who have abandoned them, not knowing how to love them, how to care for them, or who preferred drugs, alcohol, and crime, the cold recklessness of the streets to the warm safety of a home.

This is how my friends and I felt back in 1987 in the Soviet Union—like bastards who had suddenly stumbled upon the shameful truth of their conception and birth. Our past was bloody, paved with bones and teeth, all those millions of innocent people tortured and sacrificed on the altar of Communism; and our present was terrifying and empty: we no longer could distinguish truths from lies and didn't have the vaguest idea how long it would take to revise and reclaim our history. Just like Milka, Anya, Petya, and Aleksey in *Between Dog and Wolf*, so did we dream about a brighter, happier future, the new democratic world we would scrape together and erect on the debris of the old one. We were hungry, defiant teenagers on the cusp of spring and yet another revolution, our country's demise and rebirth. We were fearless, too, flooded with hope and optimism, a desire to travel, to experience other cultures, to compare them to our cripple of a motherland. But at the same time, we wanted so desperately, and perhaps fecklessly, for our country to get off her knees, to be able to walk again, to restore her pride and vigour and creativity.

In a single decade, my generation lived under Brezhnev, Andropov, Chernenko, Gorbachev, and Yeltsin. We witnessed the collapse of the Soviet empire, the August Coup of 1991 and the October Coup of 1993, the storming of the Ostankino television centre. We saw tanks rumble down the Moskva River quay and surround the White House. We protested, kept all-night vigils, helped build barricades. We listened to Tsoi's songs and shouted, " 'Changes! Our hearts demand changes!' " We drank, we smoked, we ate herring and hot dogs day in and day out. We argued viciously—with our teachers, with our parents and grandparents, with our neighbours, with one another—until our throats hurt, and our tongues swelled, and our lips couldn't form another word.

I lost two of my friends within two years—one was killed,

shot by a sniper, during the second coup; the other was stabbed to death in his newly bought apartment. It was November of 1995, and I had already moved to America to start a family. A week before I left, though, I remember visiting him in his dingy one-bedroom flat, where he'd grown up. A large poster of Freddie Mercury, our favourite singer, hung on the kitchen wall. My friend put on a Queen tape, and we sat at the shaky plastic table and drank vodka and munched on pickles and black bread and listened to "We Are the Champions" over and over again. And then my friend asked, "What do you think it really means—'champions of the world'?" And I answered, "It means that certain people can survive anywhere and under any circumstances. They can conquer the world."

"Not this arsehole," he said, laughing, pointing at his chest. "I don't want to conquer anything or anyone. I just want to live."

Twenty-six years have passed since that day. My generation, my classmates, we have grown staid, grey, somewhat wise. We have made homes in different cities, different countries, different continents. We rarely see each other or reminisce. But every once in a while, when it snows here, in Virginia, and it seems as though the sky has descended upon the earth like heaven upon hell and the mountains are all that is left to separate the two, I put on the old Queen tape and think of my friends, those who have survived and those who perished during perestroika. I think of the country that we lost and the one that replaced it, and I find myself running down the Moscow streets again, tearing through fires and barricades, clouds and clouds of black smoke. I'm running after my youth, after my country, after my friends, after the life we didn't get to live . . .

Acknowledgments

There are people on this earth whose kindness, wisdom, and fortitude have shaped me as a writer and a human being and without whom this book wouldn't have been possible.

Thank you:

Jackie Ko—my dream agent—for answering my initial email, for taking a chance, for falling in love with my work, for being patient, considerate, confident, dutiful, calm.

Andra Miller—my fearless editor—for her brilliant vision, her optimism, her professional ethics, the blossoming orchards of her work.

Luke Epplin—my production editor—for his sharp eye and astute editorial skills, for paying such close attention to the written word.

Everyone at Ballantine Books and Penguin Random House—for bringing this novel to life, for publishing immigrant authors, and for continuing to endow the world with diverse, multicultural literature.

Anton Pavlovich Chekhov—the literary godfather to millions of writers—for his love of humanity and our motherland, which he extolled and pitied, cut open and healed, with his unfathomable prose. (Excerpts from *The Cherry Orchard* in the novel are my own translation.)

Jeanne M. Leiby—the late fiction editor of *The Southern Review*—for reading and accepting my story "Champions of the World", which lies at the heart of this book.

The fiction editors at *Gulf Coast: A Journal of Literature and Fine Arts* and *Bayou Magazine*—for publishing, in slightly different form, several chapters/excerpts from my novel.

The teachers at Moscow special English school #55 and the professors at Moscow State Linguistic University—for making me fall in love with the English language and literature, for forcing me to memorize all the irregular verbs and idiomatic expressions, for being stern yet passionate, brutal yet nurturing.

Tim Poland and Donald Secreast—my first creative-writing professors at Radford University—for empowering me with knowledge and hope, for deciphering my early work, for their guidance, their honesty, their obsession with literature and storytelling.

The professors at the Jackson Center for Creative Writing at Hollins University—for accepting me into their MFA program, for awarding me a teaching fellowship, for not squashing my dreams.

Moira Baker—my stoic mentor and friend—for her wit, courage, and integrity; for believing that I had a story to tell and that I could tell it well; for introducing me to the literature of Virginia Woolf and Toni Morrison.

Toni Morrison—the Goddess of American Literature—for her immortal genius, her humanity, her gift of drawing writers into her orbit and never letting them go.

Christine Sneed, Cristina García, Christine Schutt, Jennifer Cody Epstein, Richard Bausch, Steve Yarbrough, and Ed

Falco—writers, educators, friends—for being so generous, so encouraging, so supportive, so prolific; for sharing my fictional dream.

Amy Hanson—my writing companion—for reading this novel in all its versions, for being a lighter side to my darker one, for the New Yorker Hotel and dreams of Paris.

Tanya Nadtochiy—my lifelong crony—for decades of talking, listening, believing, advising, for knowing me better than I know myself, and for always being there, on the other side of the world.

Masha Baukina—my childhood buddy—for letting us pick up where we have left off yesterday, last week, last month, last year.

Galya Suradze—my food and health bible—for her daily messages and delicious recipes; for her strength, which somehow becomes mine; and for cognac at dawn on her balcony.

Stipe Ostović—my first cousin—for reading my stories, for having something to say, for his sense of humour and gentle, lingering laugh.

Lena Ivanova—my would-be sister—for how caring she is, how generous, how supportive, how strong, how lovely, how familiar.

Elena Efimova—my late godmother—for her unwavering faith, her unrelenting humour, her character, her knowledge, her ingenuity and soulfulness.

Ludmila Makrova—a theatre aficionado—for those astounding plays she urged me to see in Moscow, for our late-night tea-drinking ceremonies, for never ever giving up.

The Solovjevs—my next-door neighbours—for being my

extended family, for sharing food and thought, for knowing how to feed an army with a fistful of buckwheat.

The Morozovs, the Kromins, the Plekhanovs, the Gold-shteyns, Leonid Mukhaev, Galina Vorotynova, Lesya Paisley, Svetlana Miller, Lena Boeva, Lena Hourihane, Tatiana Early, Irina Akimova, Vera Tolpina—my Russian-speaking community—for making me feel at home away from home; for our loud celebrations, dusk to dawn; for the life we have shared and the memories we have made.

Matthew Lansburgh, Julia Lichtblau, Liz Zemska, Sujata Shekar, Raul Palma, Brenda Peynado, Andrea Jurjević—my Sewanee pals—for all those days and nights we spent talking politics, literature, writing; for coming into my life and staying.

The Matushes—my first American contact—for inviting me to this country, for showing me how to concoct power drinks, for attending my wedding despite the blizzard, for Louis Armstrong's "What a Wonderful World".

The Phillipses and the Newberrys—my extended family—for welcoming me to their homes, for the holiday gatherings, for being who they are.

The Dodsons—my Virginia neighbours—for taking my writing seriously, for coming to my parties and inviting me to theirs, for feeding my husband when I can't.

The Taylors—my adopted parents—for always finding time to answer a call, to drop by, to lend a hand; for treating me like a daughter when I first came to Virginia and was homesick; for teaching me how to be an American.

The Gorchevs, Feodor and Klava—my late grandparents—

for winning the war, for surviving after, for those birthday feasts and summer months at the dacha, for my first apple orchard.

Randy Newberry—my beloved husband—for stealing my heart; for marrying me without understanding half of what I was saying; for the moon that was "on" that night; for his love, support, and dedication; for reading everything I write; for always putting the family's needs before his own; for being the kind of man I would marry again and again; for our son, life's greatest gift.

Albert Newberry—my only child—for growing up so restless, so creative, possessed by artistic hunger; for setting goals and for pursuing them; for loving me early in the morning and late at night and all the hours in between; for making me mad, proud, teary, overbearing, and overprotective; for all the teas, films, and music he has brought into my life, all the beauty.

Albina Ivanova—my inexhaustible mother—for raising me alone, for making me read, for spending her last money on books; for teaching me all that I know about life and how not to die from loneliness or a broken heart; for her insurmountable strength and spirit; for believing in miracles and that life is worth living, even under the direst of circumstances; for her ability to find the best in all people; for being my Mary Poppins, for saying: "There's a whole world at your feet."

Transforming a manuscript into the book
you hold in your hands is a group project.

Kristina would like to thank everyone who helped
to publish *Between Dog and Wolf* in the UK.

THE INDIGO PRESS TEAM
Susie Nicklin
Phoebe Barker
Honor Scott
Michelle O'Neill

JACKET DESIGN
Luke Bird

EDITORIAL PRODUCTION
Tetragon
Robert Sharman

I

THE
INDIGO
PRESS

The Indigo Press is an independent publisher of contemporary fiction and non-fiction, based in London. Guided by a spirit of internationalism, feminism and social justice, we publish books to make readers see the world afresh, question their behaviour and beliefs, and imagine a better future.

Browse our books and sign up to our newsletter for special offers and discounts:

theindigopress.com

Follow *The Indigo Press* on social media for the latest news, events and more:

🗙 @PressIndigoThe
📷 @TheIndigoPress
🅕 @TheIndigoPress
▶ The Indigo Press
♪ @theindigopress